The Saxville Sweethearts Series Book 2

WANTING *you*

J.J. Hart

To those who are independent, strong,
ambitious, and maybe a bit sarcastic...
your soulmate is out there.
You'll find each other!

A NOTE TO THE READER

Dear Reader,

Trigger and content warnings are important and although this book is filled with love, there are some topics that might be triggering to some.

This book contains stalking and past stalking with manipulation, emotional trauma (off page), explicit language, and sexual content.

Please consider these before continuing.

If you decide to continue to read, I hope you enjoy Dane and Kendall's story!

Xoxo

J.J.

WANTING YOU PLAYLIST

Falling – Trevor Daniels
Everything – Lifehouse
Love on The Brain – Rihana
Can't Get You Off My Mind – Lenny Kravitz
Always Remember Us This Way – Lady Gaga
Make You Feel My Love – Adele
My Sacrifice – Creed
If I Ain't Got You – Alicia Keys
With Arms Wide Open – Creed
Just Breathe – Pearl Jam
I'll Make Love To You – Boyz II Men
Marry Me – Train
Kryptonite – 3 Doors Down

ONE

Kendall

I'm not usually this distracted, but the man sitting in the back corner of the bar keeps sneaking glances at me. He's with a group of guys, all of them in suits. I can't help looking back and forth between my friends and his magnetic eyes, searching mine. I try to stay in the conversation at our table, but it's futile with his broad shoulders filling out his suit and his short beard distracting me.

"We have the best seat in the house tonight," says Faith, as she bangs on the table, just enough to tear my attention away from the man in the corner, snapping me back into their conversation.

"It is. Are we doing a round of shots?" I ask.

In unison, they all cheer, "Yeah."

We start every girls' night with tequila shots, and tonight is no different. We switched our night out to Friday since the restaurant, Buena Vista, began hosting a DJ and dancing on the first Friday of every month. From our high-top table, we wave down our waitress. She has been here since the restaurant opened, and we love her—and we tip well.

"Your usual, ladies?"

Addison answers, "Yes, thank you."

I love hanging out with my best friends—Faith, Addison, and Lane. We've been friends since college, and then moved in together here in Faith's hometown of Saxville. After a couple of years, one by one, we all bought our own homes. We still talk frequently, but these face-to-face moments allow us to catch up on the details that aren't always easy to share in a text.

I'm half listening to the conversation when my eyes meet his again. It's hard to rip them away. He has a face I could never forget. Carmel eyes, with dark lashes and eyebrows. His features are prominent, with a chiseled jawline, a beard that's short and professionally shaped—one that I could run my fingers along. He's dressed in a tailored suit. I can tell by the breadth of his shoulders that it's not a pick-it-off-the-rack kind of suit.

Pulling myself back into the conversation, I attempt to catch up, listening to Faith talk about something going on at her office. My work life is like Faith's, who is a therapist. As a stylist and salon owner, I don't have the degrees and licenses to counsel people, but once they are in my salon chair, the floodgates open, and they share all their secrets with me.

As for a personal life, there's really no time for a significant other while I'm building my empire. Men can be soul-sucking. After what happened with Jake, my ex, a couple of years ago, I have no interest in starting something new. He was manipulative, and it took far too long to realize he was controlling and struggling with mental health issues. But I was too blinded by love to see the red flags. Now, I look back and shake my head for not leaving him sooner. I'm in no hurry to rush into a man's arms after all that. Well, except maybe this broadly built guy in the corner. I could be in his arms for a night and have no regrets. If he's as good in bed as he looks, then I'd consider it.

"Kendall, how's Saxy and all the plans for the spa expansion?" Faith asked.

"It's doing well. We finally have some great stylists who are fully booked for at least six weeks. The spa expansion is coming along. We should be ready for the grand opening in the next few weeks, once all the necessary permits have been signed off. Then all that's left is hiring some more people. We have massage therapists lined up and are ready to book clients once we set a date."

I'm ecstatic about the spa opening. I've been dreaming about this day for three years. The spa complements my upscale salon. The new sign will go up over the next few weeks—Saxy Salon & Spa.

"Well, we'll be the first to see the new, finished space and schedule appointments," Lane says.

"You will be VIP guests," I assure them. They are my ride or die. I wouldn't have it any other way.

"Glad we're your VIPs," Addison says as she flings her hair dramatically.

The prickling at the back of my neck tells me the man across the bar is still staring at me, and I can't help but be hyperaware of his presence.

"Completely off topic...don't look. Don't move a muscle. There's a guy over in the corner who keeps glancing over at me." I don't move my head, but move my eyes. "Not all at once, but if you want to take a peek, he's the one in the corner booth closest to the bathroom hall."

Of course, they don't listen; they whip their heads around all at once. I'm pretty sure they gave themselves whiplash.

"Wow! He's big! And very stylish. Right up your alley," Faith says, with her mouth wide open.

"Uh-huh. How old do you think he is?" I ask as I fan myself. The way he's looking at me is going to leave a wet spot on this seat. The heat radiating from my core is uncomfortable. I haven't had a man look at me like he wanted to ravage me in a very long time.

Ugh, not since Jake. Not my finest life decision. He was a huge mistake.

"Early thirties..." Addison says as she raises her eyebrows. "You good?"

"Yeah, I think I'll go to the bathroom."

Sliding gingerly off my stool, I head straight for the group of guys in the corner, needing to walk right by them to get to the restroom.

Throwing my fiery red hair over my shoulders, I walk with my head high through the bar area. My sandals click on the dark tile flooring as I strut between the crowded tables. It's a hot summer day, and my olive skin is a deep bronze from all the sun I've had so far this season. I'm wearing a cute sundress that accentuates my booty and fabulous boobs. It's a white boho floral lace style that dips down and has ties in the front and an open back. The dress slightly puffs out for added dimension. In short, it works for me.

One foot in front of the other, I sway past his table, slowing ever so slightly, and catch a glimpse of him as I turn the corner to the bathroom. His eyes were tracking me from the moment I stood until I rounded the corner. I'm on fire, as the mirror reflects my pink-tinted cheeks, and I wonder what it is about this guy that's making my body temperature rise. I could use a cold shower. Every nerve ending is firing on my skin, and my nipples are tight, which you can clearly see through this white dress.

After washing my hands, I dab the paper towel along my face. I need a few minutes to collect myself before walking back out there. My friends will see his reaction when I head back to the table. Let's see what they say.

The door opens, and someone walks in. I grab the door and head out as they pass. As I'm walking back to the table, phone in hand, it hits my thigh just right and goes flying. I freeze for a couple of seconds, watching my phone slide across the floor right to the table in the corner. Sucking in a breath, I watch as it lands right beside the handsome, broad-shouldered stranger. Of course, it lands right there within his reach. Before my brain and body connect the dots, he picks up my phone and holds it close so I have to walk right up to him.

"Thank you." My hand reaches out, thinking he will just give it to me. But to my surprise, he holds it to his chest with a devious smirk on his face—a face that is even more handsome up close. His eyes are a dark caramel brown with eyelashes a girl would die for. They're hypnotizing. With that jawline and neatly trimmed beard, I can barely resist touching him.

"Hey there, you dropped your phone. It doesn't look to be damaged. Good thing you have a hard case on it," he says, making a show of inspecting it, then stands up.

Holy shit. My head slowly tips upward to maintain eye contact. My throat goes dry as I try to swallow. I wave and barely croak out, "It's me! Hi, I'm the problem, me. I do this almost every time I walk with the damn thing in my hand."

"Are you staying for a while...maybe dancing?" he asks, rubbing his jaw as he drags his gaze up and then down my body, lingering a little too long on my breasts.

Moving closer to me, it feels like he is breathing down my neck; definitely in my personal space, and I'm not complaining. I can smell him—coconuts and palm trees. The scent. The closeness. The question. It all has my body zinging.

Stumbling on my words, I say, "Yeah...we are. It's our first time here on a Friday. You?"

"We'll be here. I'll find you later...on the dance floor." His confidence radiates from him. With his large, sexy body taking up so much space in front of me, his eyes roam my body and meet my eyes with such intensity that it makes me want to melt into a puddle.

"Okay, guess I'll see you later then." I almost walked away without my phone.

"Oh, here. You might need this." He hands back my phone. As our hands glide over each other, sparks fly and my breath hitches. I'm taken aback by the sharp force that courses through my body with just a second of connection. He winks and turns on his heel, takes a few steps, and sits back at the table with his friends.

I'm left standing there, clenching the phone to my chest. Just trying to catch my breath. Once he sits down, those eyes are back on me, and my body wants to stay. I resist the urge to carry on the conversation. Playing it cool. I relax my arms at my sides, slowly turn, and sashay back to my friends. I'm trying not to run back to the table to dish the tea. It takes forever to reach the table. I can see their faces, a mix of shock and curiosity. Popping myself up on the stool, I open my mouth to talk, but my friends beat me to the punch.

"What just happened?" Faith asks, then covers her mouth in shock.

"He wanted to know if I was going to be around later...dancing," I say, as I bite on my lower lip, imagining his broad body up against mine. His strong arms holding me, and his hands roaming my body.

"When he stood up, we all were like, '*What kind of man looks like that?*' He towers over you. That suit, though, is definitely custom because his body is not average by any means," Lane says, throwing air quotes around 'average,' and leans further in. "Did you get a good look at him?" She winks.

"Of course I did." With a huge smile spreading over my face. "And damn, he's a fine male specimen making my lady parts hot and tingly."

The table erupts in ohs. They crack me up.

"Alright, alright...what are we eating tonight? We're going to need some calories if we're dancing." I wiggle my eyebrows.

"Yeah, we do." Addison moves in her seat. "We haven't been out dancing in a while. Tonight's going to be fun."

The waitress comes back over and takes down our order, which consists mainly of appetizers and a couple of full meals to split. It's like we can't decide on what to eat, so we order and share everything. Thankfully, none of us are picky eaters.

The next hour is filled with our catch-up session and filling our faces with a ton of food and drinks, not to the point of being stuffed, but just enough to soak up the alcohol. I guess we're deep in conversation because I didn't even see the DJ setting up on the other side of the room. I can still feel the guy's eyes on me the whole time. I do my best to avert my gaze as much as possible; every time our eyes meet, it feels hotter in this room. Keeping my attention on my friends has allowed me to be present in our conversation, and deep down, I know that once the lights dim and the music gets louder, I'll be on the dance floor. When music plays, I have no self-control; I'm dancing.

"It's almost time." I swing my head around to watch as people swarm into the room. They heard the music and are now ready to have a good time. I don't blame them.

I'm surprised by the number of what appear to be couples. It will be fun to watch—will the guys dance or just hang out at the bar and watch? Only time will tell.

And within a few minutes, the lights dim, and the music is loud. The tab we have going will continue once we give up our table, but I'll probably only have one more, cutting myself off early to keep a clear head on the dance floor. I know I need it.

As the first one jumping off the stool, I stand with a hand on my hip, waiting for at least one of my friends to join me. "Come on...someone, anyone? There's plenty of people dancing. We'll just blend in." I know they love to dance, but they need a little warming up.

Addison and Faith slowly slide off their stools, while Lane shrugs her shoulders and takes another sip of her drink. "I'll be out in ten minutes." She points at her glass. "I need to finish this first, and then I'll join you."

I point to Lane. "You have ten minutes and then I'm coming to get you." Then I swing to grab both Faith and Addison's hands and drag them onto the dance floor.

Addison yells at the top of her lungs, "I'm hitting up the bathroom. Be right back."

I shake my head, knowing even if I scream, with her back toward me as she walks away, she won't hear me.

Faith moves her hips like we're back in college. I mouth '*Yeah.*' She practically goes down to the floor and comes back up. I love watching her relax and have fun.

It feels like forever, but the next thing I know, Addison is back with Lane in tow. All four of us dance our hearts out song after song. Our hair is wet from sweat, and I pull them with me to the bathroom. "We need a breather." I'm not sure any of them even heard it, but as I turn to walk to the ladies' room, there he is, eyes on me. I blow him a kiss. Why not? And scurry to the bathroom with my friends.

"Oh. My. God. I'm having so much fun. We have to do this again," I say as I dab a paper towel around my face and on the back of my neck.

Addison fluffs her hair. "Geez, yeah, we haven't had this much fun on a girls' night in a long time. I'm glad it's Friday...no work tomorrow."

I whip back. "Lucky! I have to work, but I rearranged my clients so I don't have to be at the salon until ten o'clock."

We all wipe down and decide to head back out for a bit longer.

Strutting out of the bathroom, I know he'll be watching, so my hips sway a bit more than necessary. The girls are following me back to the dance floor. It feels like there are way more people now than when we went to the ladies' room. Nothing stops us from squeezing our way through the crowd to the middle of the floor. As usual, there are way more women than men, but we don't care. It's all about the fun.

My hands are over my head, my hips moving, and when I turn my head, I notice someone is really close. I feel their presence. It's the guy from the corner...right behind me. Not touching, but just inches from me, I'm already sweating. Still, the heat and electricity that shoot through my body—it's sensual. Making me hyperaware of every move I make as he moves even closer.

I turn around, and our eyes connect. We dance in sync like we know each other's rhythm. He doesn't touch me; it feels like he's waiting for me. So I move my hands to his shoulders, and that's his invitation; his eyes light up. Within a second, his hand rests on my hip, searing through the fabric of my dress.

The music fades into the background, and it's just us on the dance floor. My hands slide from his shoulder to his biceps. Holy hell, I realize now that he took off his suit jacket, rolled up his sleeves, and unbuttoned a couple of buttons. I can't help but squeeze his biceps. The smell of coconuts and palm trees radiates from him. It invades my nostrils, and I can tell I'll smell him for days.

With a smile on his face, he winks at me. He knew exactly what I was doing.

He leans down to my ear. "Want to get a drink?"

I nod and hold up a finger. Turning to my girlfriends, I say, "I'm going to grab a drink. I'll be back." The music blasts through the speakers; I'm not sure if they heard all of that, but they smile back at me.

When I walk a few steps back to him, his hand is on the small of my back, guiding me through the crowd to the other side of the restaurant. There's a full-size bar with dark wood surrounding the center where the bartenders are hard at work pouring drinks. The music slowly fades, and I start to hear the chatter of the people at the bar. It's muted compared to the dance floor.

"What can I get you?" he asks, leaning down so I can hear him better.

I laugh. "Right now, just some water. I never did get your name."

"Dane. And yours?"

Pondering for a split second whether to go with a new name, I opt for my real one, "Kendall."

"It's nice to officially meet you. How's your phone?"

"You too. No damage, thankfully."

We slide onto a couple of stools at the bar. My leg grazes his, and we both stare at each other. He felt the jolt too.

The bartender breaks the tension that's building. He puts down a couple of napkins and hands us the bar menu. "Can I start you guys out with a drink?"

"Water would be great to start," I say, wiping sweat away nonchalantly.

He glances over at me and smirks. "I'll do the same."

I look up, and there's a large mirror behind the liquor shelving. I'm completely disheveled—my hair is flat, my cheeks are red, and my dress is sticking to me. Wonderful.

My attention moves to Dane as I see he's pulling his hand back up. I can only assume he was adjusting that impressive bulge I got an up-close and personal glance at on the dancefloor. Otherwise, he looks put together, but I guess that's the difference between men and women when dancing. We move way more than the guys do. Hence, the pouring sweat that's dripping between my breasts.

I wonder if he'd notice if I swiped down my cleavage with a bar napkin. I grab the napkin and dab along my face and chest. When I look over at Dane, his eyes are on me. Well, my hand that's holding the napkin. His eyes tracking every movement. There's no way he wouldn't see me swipe my cleavage. Yet, it might be fun to watch.

TWO

Dane

I've spent all night watching every move she makes. She's hot, sweating, and flushed, and all I can think of is other ways to get her looking like that, only with much less clothing. When she snagged that napkin and swiped down between those perky tits, I would have gladly taken care of that for her. But my eyes never leave her, even when the bartender comes back with our waters.

"Can I get you two any food?"

Kendall says, "No, I'm good right now. Thank you."

"I'll take an order of the crab cakes," I say, but never look away from her, and she doesn't either. My eyes flare with heat as she swipes the napkin down her cleavage, quickly and with some teasing flair. I can't help myself. I'd happily undress her, cool her off, and then heat her up again. The smirk I flash her is downright seductive. Her breath hitches, and I watch her squirm a bit in her seat. The woman is all fire.

"What's that smirk for?" She sends me an arched eyebrow.

I rub my jawline with my finger and thumb, dragging them slowly across my beard, drawing her eye to the deliberate movement. She shifts again in her seat and slings her arm over the back of the chair. Challenging me, she holds her chin in her fist. My eyes can't break away from staring at those lush, plump pink lips. I know exactly where she can put them, too.

"I'm enjoying your company," I smirk and give a quick wink.

"Ah-huh, sure." She nods, her eyes sparking with interest, takes a sip of her water, and places it back on the bar. "I think I might need something stronger."

Tearing my eyes away from this fiery redhead with piercing green eyes, I wave to the bartender. "I'll take a Crown and Coke. And she'll have..."

"Patron silver on the rocks, lime, and salt, please." The order falls off her tongue as if she's said it before; she's a woman who knows what she wants and takes it. I like it.

The bartender makes our drinks in front of us. Once he places them on the bar, I pick up my drink and say, "To a night of fun, drinks, and good company."

Her thousand-watt smile spreads across her face. "I'll toast to that." Glasses clink, and we both take a swig.

She places her glass on the bar. "So, Dane, what do you do for a living?"

Lingering a little longer over my glass, I put it down and lean in. "I'm a defense attorney."

"I don't think I was ready for that answer." She stares at me as if there's something to figure out.

"Then tell me, what did you think I did?" I lean in closer to her.

She hums, "Banker."

"Was it the suit?" I ask, chuckling. I've been called a lot of things, but a banker hasn't been one of them. There's a first for everything.

"It's a vibe you have going on," she says, as her finger circles in the air around my face.

I lean over and place my hand close to hers. I can feel the heat of it as it rests on the bar. Her breathing is shallow, pupils dilated, and, fuck me, my cock is twitching to be released from these slacks. Under heated eyes, I watch as she shifts in her seat again. Oh yeah, she's done for.

Just as I reach my hand down to touch her thigh, we both jump at her name being called from behind us. I swing my head in that direction and see what looks like her girlfriends waving our way.

"Kendall..."

She gets up from the stool, but I stop her with my hand on her elbow, just enough to get her attention, but not enough to actually restrain her if she really wants to get away. "Don't leave me now." Giving her the smirk that always ropes the women in, but it's like she's immune to it.

"Well, my girlfriends are here so..."

"Can we at least continue this later?" I hear my voice shake, and it's pathetic.

What the fuck?

I rarely care when a woman walks away. They're a dime a dozen, and the next one is right around the corner. But then I realize...My eyes haven't left her this whole time. My attention has been focused only on her. And that never happens.

"Maybe."

"At least finish your drink." I'm begging now. Who am I?

She gently picks up her drink, licks the remaining salt off the rim, pulls the rest of the tequila into her mouth, and swallows. Watching her long, slender neck and that wavy red hair as she swings around again, facing me, has me captivated.

"Thank you for the drink, Dane."

Fuck, the way she says my name...

Sliding her my room key, I whisper in her ear. "Room 222."

She looks down at the room key and back up at me. I'm waiting for her to throw it in my face. It was a colossal risk with this one—so fiery.

"Is this what you offer all the ladies you buy a drink?" Kendall flicks her wrist at me, shaking the keycard in the air between us.

I chuckle. Calling me out like that? It sends blood shooting south. But I own up to it; I have nothing to hide. It's who I am. "Not all of them... I walk away from the crazy ones most days."

"I could certainly be crazy; I hide it well," she says as she flips her hair.

"I'll take my chances." I brush my fingers lightly down her arm, and goosebumps spread like wildfire, which is precisely how my fingertips feel—on fire like they seared her skin.

"I warned you...and I'll think about this." Holding up the room key again, the hope of seeing her later seeps into my chest. And just like that, she gently moves through my arm and walks over to her friends.

Left staring at her, and when she doesn't turn around to look back, I move to face the bar and order another drink—this time a double. Who knows if I'll see her again? And the minute I say it to myself, my shoulders tense. Fighting the urge to glance back at her, I take a long pull of my drink and stare up at the game on the large-screen TV.

THREE

Kendall

"Are you going to use that room key?" Faith asks with concern on her face.

"It could be fun. He could be a lot of fun. I know his type, so I'm not planning on riding off into the sunset with him."

"I think you're nuts to even consider it," Lane says, shaking her head in disbelief.

"I'm attracted to him, so why not? A one-night stand makes it easier to walk away once it's done. No attachments; expectations are simple. And it's been a while."

"It's your call," Faith says, as she holds my forearm for a few extra seconds.

"Yeah." I think about how he touched me, goosebumps erupted all over my body, and it felt like a fire ignited in my core. I want to feel that again—with him, tonight.

Addison stares at me and asks, "Where did you go?"

I shrug, not wanting to share how I feel because it's a moot point. He's a one-night and done kind of guy. All I know is he'll make me feel amazing. "I think I'm ready for a no-strings-attached night with someone I'm attracted to. The past few weeks and months have been pretty stressful. And..."

"You can't leave us hanging," says Addison as she leans in further.

"I haven't felt attracted to anyone in a while, so I'm going to use the room key."

Faith hugs me and whispers, "Be safe. We're here if you need us."

"You need to check in with us. I don't want to be worrying or calling the cops because you haven't updated us," Addison scolds, jabbing her finger in the air a few times. She's serious about this.

All eyes are on Dane, still sitting at the bar, and he hasn't turned around once. Is that a good sign or is he regretting giving me the key?

As we all watch, Dane slides off the chair and takes out his wallet. We are all staring at him, watching his every move, or is that just me? Those pants hug his ass and thighs, and there's no denying how strong he is.

He turns, making eye contact with me, and gives me that smirk I want to slap off his face. He pauses for a few seconds, then winks. Cocky. My eyes drag down to his rolled sleeves and take a good look at those forearms before meeting his eyes again. My body temperature skyrockets, while my heart beats faster, adrenaline coursing through my body. The rush of one night with him fills me—just like he will soon. I almost blow him a kiss or give him a wave, just to push back, but I refrain. Let him stew on whether or not I see him soon. So, I give him a small, tentative smile to keep him on his toes.

He turns on his heels and walks away.

"Okay, I'll text the group," I say, not moving yet. I don't want to seem too anxious. I'll give him time to make his way to the hotel room.

"We'll be here for another hour." Lane shifts her shoulder to nudge me.

"I mean, he seems like he wouldn't mind extra company," I whisper to them with eyebrows raised high.

"Maybe, but did you see how he was looking only at you? That says a lot. And you know we aren't into that stuff in real life, only in books," Faith says.

I give the girls an eager grin and a group hug. "It's time. Talk later."

I find the elevator, step in, and push the button for the second floor. I'm clenching my legs together to tame the throbbing. This should be a fantastic night.

The elevator arrives on his floor, and the doors slowly open. I step into the hallway, and the sign in front of me says, 'Room 222 to the right.' It's all the way down the hallway.

He definitely does this all the time. It's the only logical explanation. Who else has the balls to hand over their room key to a random woman? I could be crazy; he's taking his chances—or am I? Well, I guess I'm risking it. But I'm always prepared. I have protection in my purse, just in case. And I always carry mace too, but I have a feeling I won't need to use it.

Not bothering to knock, I use the key and open the door. I don't hear anyone, but I step inside the room and all I can smell is him—coconut and palm trees. The door slams shut behind me. It's an enormous suite, and the lighting is dim. Just enough light to see the modern living room with a sleek, large-screen TV, curved grey plush couch, coffee table, and an armchair in the corner.

I scan the room and spot him, like a king sitting on his throne, in the corner chair. All I see is him rubbing his jaw as he stares at me, a glass of dark liquid hanging from his other hand. He took off his shirt but left his slacks on. Holy shit, he's barefoot, and I can't help it; I bite my bottom lip.

The moment he stands up, the room feels smaller with him in it. And the next thing I know, he's stalking over to me like he wants to own me.

He's inches away from my face before I can fully process the movement. Threading his fingers in my hair, gripping the back of my head, he takes a minute and stares into my eyes—into my soul. Then, wraps the other arm around my waist, tugging me close. The heat in my core is like a stoked fire; my legs are already wobbly.

"I wasn't sure if you were going to make it. You didn't give me an answer." He glides his lips over my cheek, and I melt further into him.

"I needed to decide whether I was going to take a risk on a stranger or go home." His mouth is so close to my ear, I can feel his breath skate across my skin. My nipples pebble at the closeness, the attraction humming between us.

"You are gorgeous, and I can't resist you any longer," he says in a gruff voice that tips me over the edge—my mouth dry and my body buzzing. A moan escapes me at his admission and his touch. I'm holding on by a thread.

I don't know the last time a man had this effect on me. I'm not complaining. I thought my sex drive was gone because of what happened with my ex, Jake. Nope. I don't need to be thinking about that dirtbag right now. All my nerve endings are lit on fire, and goosebumps all over my skin the minute he touches me. He runs his thumb over my lips. I can't help but close my eyes and revel in his touch.

The air is charged with desire; my breath hitches as his thumb swipes across my lip one last time. As if he were reading my mind, he leans in and our lips meet for the first time. I needed the right person to bring me back to life, and Dane is doing just that, as fireworks explode throughout my body.

His kiss is all-consuming. Every inch of my body is exploding. We explore each other's mouths as he nudges my lips open with his tongue to slip inside, tongues dancing in a rhythm that keeps my mouth busy for what feels like hours. Our kiss feels natural—comfortable, perfect. I pull him closer, wanting all of him. Deepening the kiss, my arms wrap around his waist, one leg entwining with his.

"I'm in charge here. Is that okay with you?" he says, his gravelly voice in my ear.

Submitting to him feels easy, like I'd crawl to him on my hands and knees if he asked me to. "Yes, I'm all yours tonight," I say as I clear my throat.

In one smooth motion, he grabs my ass and yanks me up. I wrap my legs around his waist as he walks down the small hallway and into the bedroom. The lights are dim here, just enough to see each other.

He's just staring at me now. I wonder what he's thinking. He dips his head into my neck and kisses me. I squirm, which evokes a throaty chuckle from him. That sound makes me want him inside me even more.

His arms move up my back, and I slide down his body. My hands land on his shoulders, and I can't resist sliding them down his arms, stopping at his firm biceps. I linger a little longer there before sliding down to his forearms. If it weren't already a sauna in here, that does it for me: muscles that my fingertips can sink into and trace his tattoos. I could spend hours tracing and exploring them, but he doesn't give me enough time to really look as he kisses my shoulder.

"You taste so sweet. I can't wait to bury my face in your pussy." Taking the hem of my dress in his hands, he takes it off over my head.

He gives me a slight tap on the shoulder, so I tilt back, landing and sitting on the bed. His eyes go wide, and then, as if his pupils couldn't be any bigger, they take over his irises when he sees I don't have a bra on. He's on his knees, putting his thumbs through my g-string and slowly gliding them down my legs before I can take my next breath. When he reaches my ankles, I lift my legs, and he yanks the scrap of fabric off.

"Slide back onto the bed," he says as he unbuttons his pants, and they fall to the floor. All I see is his thick cock glistening with precum. He rubs his thumb over the tip and wipes it in a circle. Holy hell, that's fucking hot.

I do what I'm told and move up the bed. As I do, I leave nothing to the imagination as I casually open my legs and my hand goes down my stomach, ready to tease him. But he grabs my hand.

"I'll be the one touching you tonight."

He takes both of my knees in the palms of his hands and opens them even further. His fingers gently glide up my thighs. The throbbing in my clit is intense, longing for him to touch me with his fingers, his tongue. I just need to relieve the ache.

Dane's body comes up along my side as his hand touches my stomach, searing my skin. His fingers slide down, and he runs two fingers through my slit. He all but purrs, "You are so goddamn wet."

My hands grip the sheets as my back arches into him. I whimper. "Dane."

"I like my name on your lips," he says and pepper kisses down my neck.

I'm hyperaware of his cock pressed up against me. My hand wanders down to grip his length, velvety, thick, and hard as steel. Pulling my hand up with a fairly tight grip, he groans in my ear. Using my thumb, I swipe over his tip, precum dripping out. "I want my mouth on this." I grip him a little tighter.

He doesn't answer me with words, but thrusts his hips against me. And plunges his fingers inside me. The feel of his fingers has me tilting my hips for him. The smell of sex surrounding us and the sound of my slickness have my body wanting more of him. He curls his fingers, and I lose myself in his touch. I grind my hips against his fingers, my orgasm building.

Sliding his thumb over my clit, circling it, teasing it, has me begging. "Dane, please...faster."

That's what I needed to push me over the edge. I clamp around his fingers, toes curling, eyes rolling back. He continues finger-fucking me, slower, riding out my orgasm.

Stars, lots of stars...

My body goes limp, and he pulls his fingers out of me. Feeling the loss immediately.

"You're even more gorgeous when you come."

All I can do is giggle and say, "Yeah."

For a few seconds, I can't open my eyes until I feel his breath on my cheek and his lips drag over to my lips. A shiver runs down my spine, and I smile, running my fingers through his hair. Our lips meet tentatively at first, like maybe he doesn't do this often. I open for him, and he slides his tongue over mine, a rhythm that turns feverish. Heat blasts through my body with every swipe of his tongue.

His thumb grazes just under my breast, and my back arches into his touch. His fingers lightly scratch over until he pulls on my nipple a few times. I moan into his mouth. He moves to pinching, and I break away.

Throwing my head back, moaning, I cry, "Yes, don't stop."

He continues to play with my nipples, not leaving one unattended for too long. When I finally tilt my head forward, I'm staring into those caramel eyes with lashes to die for, half-lidded, staring back at me. His fingers that were just inside of me reach his mouth, and he licks every drop of my arousal, never breaking my gaze.

"I want the smell of you all over my face."

"Yeah, kiss me first." I move my hands to his face and tug him down to my lips. It's like I'm addicted to him. Shoving my tongue into his mouth, he grunts at the invasion but meets me thrust for lick. The taste of myself, the way he kisses me, causes a shiver to run through me.

My body has never reacted to a man like this. Perhaps he's had more experience than other men I've been with, or maybe he simply enjoys pleasing women. It usually takes a lot more warming up for me to have an orgasm. Tonight, it happened in record time, and I don't mind one bit.

My body continues to respond to him, aching, throbbing, and sending shivers all over. I want, no, I *need* more of him. His cock twitches on my stomach. Leaning slightly away, he stares at me, like I hold the answer to all his questions, but he says nothing. He moves down my body ever so slowly, kissing, swirling his tongue on my skin, and dragging his nails over me. I squirm underneath him—so much stimulation.

When he reaches my thighs, he kisses them, caring for them. And then I feel his tongue move along my pelvic bone to my clit, and my entire body constricts. Swiping down to my entrance, his tongue moves in and out of me, and I reach down and grab ahold of his head—feeling the movement that I can't seem to get enough of. Pleasure soars through my body, making my toes curl.

Our eyes meet, and the fire inside them tips me over the edge. My eyes roll, hips arch for more friction, and I ride the wave of ecstasy as he spears me with his tongue and uses the pad of his thumb to give me just enough pressure on my clit. My orgasm crashes down on me as I hold his head tighter, grinding my pussy into his face like I've lost all control. As I settle, my grip loosens, my hands fall from his head, and my body sinks into the bed.

FOUR

Dane

This woman is demanding, yet still allows me to dominate her. This rhythm we have differs from all other one-night stands I've had. Others have been too forceful or too meek and lie there like a limp noodle. No, thank you. Kendall—she's someone I might just want to do this with again.

What the fuck is wrong with me? Who cares? It's one night.

The scent of her watermelon-scented hair, mingling with our sweat, spurs me on as it lingers in the air. I break away to grab a condom out of the nightstand drawer. She watches me roll it onto my cock, and I hear her swallow hard. I slide myself against her entrance as I tease her, just barely putting the tip in and taking it back out. She gasps.

"Fuck me," she moans out, staring straight into my eyes.

She is falling apart under my touch, my cock, my lips. I want my name on her lips again with every thrust of my hips—every orgasm. Her glazed-over, half-hooded eyes tell me she is completely satiated.

"Dane, Dane."

Hearing her sends heat rushing to my cock, already hard as steel simply from the feeling of her.

"Don't worry, I'm going to fuck you, and you'll be begging me for more."

My thumb rubs and presses into her clit, making her go crazy, thrashing on the bed. She is close again, and I stop.

Her head pops up like I've offended her. "Why?"

"Just to see your reaction," I chuckle.

She squints her eyes at me and says, "You think you're funny."

Oh, she is sassy, too. It makes me want to spank her ass, but I don't respond. All I need to do is push my cock further into her, and she melts back down onto the bed. When I'm all the way inside her tight pussy, she gasps.

I suck in a breath, her warmth surrounding my cock, stealing my breath. "You were made for me, just perfect."

"You knocked the breath out of me."

"You have no idea what you got yourself into, Kendall. You're mine. For tonight at least."

Just tonight.

I grab the pillow while still inside her, and tuck it under her hips to deepen the pleasure for both of us. My eyes go to hers to check in; I don't want it to hurt.

"You okay with this?" Not moving at all until she gives me the green light.

Through her ragged breath and moaning, she says, "Yes, just go easy at first so I can get used to it."

My body shifts slightly into a position that will allow me to ease her into this. With a few pumps, she's begging me. "Dane, I'm ready. Please, harder, faster."

If she keeps talking to me like that, it won't take long for me to come. Her moaning is sensual as fuck. I want her to scream with pleasure. Pumping my cock into her pussy at a punishing pace, the moaning turns to panting...

"Is that as hard as you can go?" she taunts through a panting breath.

She is sassy as fuck. "That fucking mouth. If my cock wasn't buried inside of you, you'd be choking on it."

I thrust harder into her pussy as she clenches hard around me. The sound of my balls slapping against her echoes in the room, this angle hitting her in the right spot as she pants with pleasure. Her hands squeeze my biceps, and her legs wrap tighter around my waist, and that keeps me going.

I whisper in her ear. "Is that better?"

Her hands move up to my face, and she pulls me down to her mouth. Our lips crash into each other. I didn't think my cock could get any harder, but kissing her makes me lose all control, and I pound harder into her, my cock almost painfully hard.

She whimpers, "Yes...More."

And then, all I feel are her walls contracting around my cock, and I can't hold out any longer. My balls tighten, and cum erupts, filling her with my heat. Her nails rake down my arms, and her legs wrap like a vice around my body. My release seems to trigger her own, and her climax rattles through her, the feeling intense.

Collapsing on top of her for a split second and then pulling out, I take care of the condom and trash it under the nightstand basket. When I roll over, I take her with me. Facing each other, she places her hand on my face and gazes at me, deep into my soul, as if she sees inside of me. All she does is smile and brush her fingers along my beard.

Silence takes over as we savor the peaceful moment. After a few minutes, I crawl out of bed and head to the bathroom. Looking over my shoulder, I smile back at her. All I see is her red hair scattered all around her. She looks like a goddess.

I clean myself off and grab a warm facecloth for her. Walking out of the bathroom, my stomach drops as I glimpse what could be. She's lying in bed waiting for me to come back, gorgeous, and we just had the best sex in...forever. I think I want to get to know her better, as a person, a strong woman I wouldn't mind having by my side. But there's something more tethering me to her. This powerful pull to her is unmistakable.

I approach the bed where she is lying and gently clean her before tossing the cloth back toward the basket. She glances up at me with a slow smile, and she tilts her head, as if she is trying to figure me out. Like I'm a puzzle and she wants to put it together. Her eyes jump between mine, searching.

"That was amazing," she all but purrs.

"You were amazing. Would you like a T-shirt?"

"Umm..."

Oh, shit, did I just inadvertently invite her to stay the night? What is wrong with me?

Hesitating before I stand up, there are no overnights; it's the rule. But she's someone who sets my body on fire, and the sex? The best ever. I could see breaking the rules...just for tonight, just for her.

I stroll over to the dresser, grab a t-shirt from the drawer, and bring it over to her. "Here, you can sleep in this." Tugging on her to sit up, I slide the shirt over her head, then kiss her ever so softly.

She seems antsy. "Is this a typical night for you? Offering a t-shirt."

A deep laugh comes out. "Definitely not a typical night. And I thought you'd be more comfortable in one of my shirts."

She sits up and takes it off. "I like sleeping naked." Dragging her eyes over my body, lingering on my half-mast cock, I shake it for her.

I hop onto the bed, jostling her, and my eyes are wide, watching her tits bounce. I lay down and cozy up to her with my arm outstretched. "Come here."

"I wouldn't have pinned you as the cuddling type," she mumbles and rests her head on my chest. I wrap my arm around her, tucking her into me. Her warmth, the comfort of her touch, and her body pressing against mine have my chest tightening.

"Yeah, I surprise myself," I say with a self-deprecating chuckle.

"I don't mind this one bit, but do you really do this with all the ladies?"

Groaning, I mumble. "Never."

"Never!?" She shakes her head, hums, and turns her body to face me.

Right now, I'd give anything to know what she's thinking. As she shifts into her spot next to me, she scrapes her nails over my chest. "Geez, don't make me feel special; I might get attached."

I've learned over the years that women tend to become attached too quickly. Keeping things very casual—no sleepovers, no second times—keeps things simple. Sex, no attachments, no why didn't you text me...zero expectations.

With Kendall, the plan was the same when I spotted her earlier. But when we sat at the bar, things shifted. I didn't pay much attention to the shift at the time. The me of earlier today saw her as a woman who could walk out this door and never look back. While I'm lying here now, hoping she won't.

So maybe her getting attached wouldn't be the worst thing to happen—having her in my arms, my bed.

I chuckle. "You're one of a kind, Kendall."

Her lips meet my chest, but she doesn't stop there. Teeth drag over my skin, and my cock is rock hard again.

"That I am."

"Sexy. Gorgeous. Sassy. What am I missing?"

"Confident. Successful. Magnetic." She leans her head up, looking at me with a smirk.

I kiss her forehead. "My favorite thing is how sassy you are. Keep it up..."

"Or what?"

I slap her ass and then grab her. "Your sassy mouth is going to get you into trouble."

"Typical of me," she says as her head rests on my chest.

I trail my fingers along her arm and back up. Leaning my head a little further into the pillow, she feels right in my arms. Her entire body relaxes, and I realize she has fallen asleep. My eyes feel heavy, and then it's lights out.

———

The sun is peeking through the curtains, just enough to cast a ray of sunshine on the wall near the bed. We slept tangled together all night. Kissing the top of her head, I slink out of bed and into the main room, intending to order breakfast for us.

Are you out of your mind? First you gave her a T-shirt to stay the night, and now breakfast?

I want more time with her and to get to know her. I guess there's a first for everything. I'm keeping her here for as long as possible. The hotel phone sits on the side table. I pick it up and dial room service.

"Morning, room service. What would you like to order?"

"I'd like to order the ultimate breakfast for two, please?"

"Give us fifteen minutes and we will be up, Mr. Walsh."

"Thank you."

I hang up the phone, head to the bedroom to grab my grey sweatpants and a crisp white t-shirt, all the while watching her sleep. The view is different this morning as the sun tries to creep in between the curtains. She is peaceful, and her red hair is a drastic contrast against the white pillow and sheets. Her beautiful face keeps me staring.

I crawl onto the bed and lie next to her, draping my arm over her body. She moves ever so slightly. I kiss under her ear, pulling a moan from her. She turns her head; I see those green eyes flutter open and stare back at me. Heat bursts in my chest as I lean in to kiss her, feel her; she meets me with a searing kiss. My lips move with hers...

A knock on the door interrupts the moment.

I hop out of bed and over my shoulder, I say, "I'll be right back."

Room service is at the door with a cart full of silver plate covers. He wheels it inside for me. I thank the guy, give him a tip, and bring the cart further. Walking back into the room, I see she's out of bed and wearing the dress from last night.

My stomach is in a knot, and my heart drops to the floor.

Is this disappointment that's rippling through my body?

In an effort to keep her here a little longer. I stalk over to her, cup her face in my hands. "You're leaving already?"

Her mouth opens and then closes. Maybe struggling to make a decision, but then she says, "I really should get home and shower. I have to be at the salon to meet my contractor. We have a big meeting on Monday with the town's building inspector."

"That's fine, but you still need to eat. Come on, grab at least a couple of bites with me."

I'm begging for a little more time with her. But maybe it's for the best if she leaves, because I'm not even sure what I'm doing at this point. Having breakfast with my one-night stand, who also slept over, and I want to get to know her better? Who even am I right now?

With resolve written all over her face, she says, "Okay, fifteen minutes, then I really need to go."

She gives me that smirk again, the one that makes my dick twitch in my pants. Trying not to adjust myself right in front of her, but there's no use, I quickly do it. She eyes my crotch and giggles.

I tug myself over my sweatpants. "Yeah, giggle again and this will be so far down your throat you won't know what to do with it."

She licks her lips and stares. "I don't think I'd mind that at all." And then she fucking wiggles her eyebrows at me.

Self-control around her is nearly nonexistent. But I pull her close and let her feel what she's walking away from this morning.

"It's impressive." She kisses me on the cheek.

I want to throw her on the bed, but she needs to be somewhere. Breaking away, I take her hand and lead her to the table where the room service cart sits.

"I didn't know what you would like, so there's a variety."

I pour her coffee and then mine, watching to see how she likes it. A little sugar and cream, noted.

"Tell me more about this meeting with the building inspector," I prompt, trying desperately to distract my other head from taking over the conversation.

"Ugh, I own a salon down on Main Street, and we are expanding to accommodate a spa. The town's making it difficult, to say the least. I'm meeting with the building inspector for the last inspection—fingers crossed." She double-crosses her fingers and puts on a fake smile to go with them.

Curious, as this town is full of political bullshit, they don't know their ass from their elbow half the time. It's probably because she is a woman, those chauvinistic assholes. They use their power to push people like her around, and I'm not okay with that. With my jaw ticking, I rub my beard as I shift from one foot to the other. I should probably sit down. I yank the chair out a bit too roughly and sit down.

She eyes me, searching for something. "You good?"

"Yeah, yeah, go on."

"My contractor is helping me with all of it, but it really seems like there's always something that comes up on the report. It's frustrating. When I first opened my salon, the process was easier. This time around. It's like they keep finding things wrong. I wonder if it's because I'm a woman. The minute I had my contractor there, things went smoother, but it still took forever to get the sign-offs."

"The town is notorious for this. It's good that your contractor could handle it for you, as unfortunate as it is that it's even necessary. Will he be there with you on Monday?"

Her face angles down as she looks at her fruit. "Yeah, thankfully."

"That's good. When are you expecting to open?"

"We're hoping to invite our current customers and friends to our soft opening in five weeks. All I need is a couple more sign-offs, and we will be able to have our grand opening."

"Is Roland the inspector you're dealing with?"

She looks at me with an arched brow. "Yeah, why?"

I wince at his name. "I know him. I've had a few run-ins with him and with the town in general. Anything I can do to help you out?"

She stares at me with wide eyes. "You don't even know me, and you want to help me."

I lean over the table so she can feel my presence. "That's true, I don't know you very well, but what I do know is...I'd like to." All my rules are out the fucking window.

She stops mid-bite of her cinnamon roll, one eyebrow arched. "Dane..." She finishes her last bite and sips her coffee.

I watch her intently. Thinking about those thick, dark pink lips wrapped around my cock. Shaking myself out of the dirty thoughts, I say, "Kendall..."

"Dane...you don't seem like the type."

Dragging my hand over her arm, I say, "Apparently, I am with you."

"Come on. One-night stands are your thing." A sly smirk crosses her face. "Tell me I'm wrong."

"Okay, okay. You got me there. They usually are. You're someone I don't want to have just a one-night stand with, though."

"I used the key for something casual. I'm not sure I'm ready for anything more than that." I hear what she's saying, but I see it flash in her eyes, something I can't quite make out.

"My nights are usually just casual. But last night, Kendall was unforgettable."

She eyes me with suspicion. "Do you say that to all the ladies you take back to your room?"

She makes me laugh, but she isn't wrong. That's my usual M.O.

Ignoring her rhetorical question, I stand up and grab her hand to stop her from leaving just yet. Slinking my arm around her waist, I tug her against me. Her emerald green eyes glow back at me as she bites her bottom lip. I lean in and rub my thumb over it. My hand moves to the back of her head as I kiss her. Soft, luscious lips press against mine, and I can't help but slip my tongue into her mouth. The warmth and taste of her sends all my blood to my cock. I'm sure she can feel that against her stomach. Smiling as I kiss her, I instantly miss the feeling of her pressed against me when she pulls away.

Man, pull it together.

"I hope your meeting goes well. And if I wanted to see you again, how would I find you?"

She laughs. "You're serious?"

"Dead serious."

Hesitating a bit, she digs into her bag and hands me her business card. "I won't be offended if you don't call."

I wave her card in front of her. "You'll be hearing from me."

"Have a great day, Dane."

The only thing that comes out of my mouth is a lame, "You too, Kendall."

She walks out the door, not even looking back, and the door closes behind her. I'm left standing there holding her card and wondering why I let her walk out the door.

FIVE

Kendall

I can't believe how quickly this day went by. I'm already pulling into my driveway, and it's not surprising my friends are already here—most likely to get the scoop on last night. I texted them all this morning with a very brief update.

When I walk through the front door, I hear them chatting in the kitchen. I drop my bag on the floor, put the keys into the bowl, and slip off my shoes. When my feet pad their way to the kitchen, there's a charcuterie board sprawled out on the island—cheese, grapes, strawberries, nuts, meats. I'm starving. The last thing I ate was at the hotel with Dane, and a smile crosses my face at the memory.

"Hey, you finally made it home. We made sure to have provisions and drinks ready." Faith holds up her margarita. "Want one?"

"Of course. I thought I'd be out of there a little earlier, but when you're the owner..."

"Totally get it." Faith shakes her head. "It always falls on you. But we wouldn't have it any other way."

I shake my head and grab my margarita to propose a toast. "To big dreams." And our glasses click together with Addison and Lane, too.

We all take a long sip and set our drinks down on the island. I thought for sure I'd be bombarded with all the questions about Dane when I walked through the door, but they're tame tonight. I pick up some grapes and pop them into my mouth. Then, I make myself a prosciutto and cheese sandwich on a couple of crackers, and within a couple of bites, it's gone. We all continue to eat off the board.

Addison snags a fig and starts eating it as she leans further into me. "Is it time for you to tell us what happened with...Dane?"

At first, I was shocked that she knew his name, but then I remembered I had mentioned it in my text message this morning.

"Yes, do tell, do tell." Faith rests her elbows on the island and folds her hands together, waiting for the juicy details of my night.

I've been waiting all day to share. "I have to admit, it was hard to leave this morning. I tried to play it off as casual, but I'm not sure I pulled it off as well as I think I did."

I dive right in, starting with the moment I stepped into the hotel room, how he asked me to stay the night, the morning with breakfast, and how he knows the building inspector.

"Wait, you gave him your business card after telling him it was casual?" Lane shakes her head.

"I hate to admit it, but I wouldn't mind seeing him again, but I have my doubts that's really what he wants. We didn't get too much into it. It sounds like he has been a one-night stand kind of guy for a while. I can't deny the electricity bouncing around inside of me with every touch, every look, and it's like fireworks when we kiss." I shrug my shoulders, knowing this is different from anyone else before.

All three of them stare at me with their heads tilted. Silence. All I hear is the hum of the refrigerator.

Breaking the silence, Lane says, "Are you feeling okay? You haven't talked about a guy, never mind fireworks, in...forever."

I stare down at my drink. She has a point. Bringing my face back up to them with a small smile, I say, "I know."

"What are you going to do now?" asks Faith, pressing her hand to mine.

"Honestly, at this point, I need to make it through this final inspection. All my attention will be on that and then the grand opening. I don't have time to figure out how I'm feeling, and I'm not sure I really want to. If that makes sense."

"I get that. And like you said, maybe it's not even what he really wants and was talking out of his ass this morning." Faith moves back and takes a sip of her drink. "You might not even see him again, and then it's a moot point."

My heart drops to my stomach at the thought of him just forgetting about me. I ignore it and continue to pick at the charcuterie board. "Yeah, you're probably right." The dread that rolls through my body has me questioning everything about the last twenty-four hours.

SIX

Dane

This woman has a hold on me. She's all I thought about the rest of the weekend. And now I'm heading to the Town Hall to give Roland a push to close out her permits. He shouldn't be giving her a hard time, and it will be remedied this morning.

I swipe my suit jacket off the passenger seat and hop out of my car, throw my suit jacket on, and march through the doors. Once I'm at the building department, I walk in and look for Roland.

"Ah, Walsh. What brings you to this side of town?" he asks, his tone deceptively warm.

"Roland...I heard through the grapevine you've been holding up some permits," I say casually.

"What are you talking about?" Roland dramatically waves his hands in the air.

"There's a salon on Main Street that's expanding. Ring a bell?"

He freezes for a second and looks sheepish. *Caught ya, asshole.* This guy is constantly overstepping.

"Ah, yeah. I have a meeting with her this morning."

"You'll approve everything, as there's no reason to delay this small business opening any further, correct?" Heat is rolling up my neck, and I'm getting fired up. It's one thing to do your job, but it's a whole other ballgame when you decide to make it harder for others to get permits.

"Of course not," Roland stutters, clearly thrown by my involvement.

"It's nice to know you'll do the right thing, Roland."

What a fucking schmuck. My good deed is done; off to the office.

That guy practically shit his pants. Experience should've taught him better than to delay permits. We had to file against the town a couple of years ago, and that seemed to wake them up. Yet, they didn't fire this guy. I suspect he knows someone higher up, and that's how he keeps his job. Hopefully, my visit will not only help Kendall, but I'm sure there are other small business owners he is trying to bend over the barrel. Not on my watch.

I get into my car and look at myself in the rear-view mirror. This woman has me doing things for her, and she doesn't even realize it. Grabbing my wallet out of my pocket, I hold out her business card. I stare at it for a few seconds and flick the edge. It's then that I decide to program her name and number into my phone. Trying to decide if I should text her or not, I slap it against the steering wheel a couple of times.

I can't resist sending her a text.

Dane:

You'll be all set for your meeting with the building inspector.

I don't wait for her to text back; instead, I drive to my office. Traffic is light this morning, which gets me there faster than expected.

Once I'm in the office, I'm bombarded by Logan, tearing me a new one. His dark brown eyes squint at me—does he need glasses or is he really annoyed? I settle on annoyed.

"Dane? You were supposed to be here an hour ago." He's running his fingers through his dirty blond hair and down his neck. Stress. He is definitely losing his mind with this case. His family probably hasn't seen him much this week.

"Have you been home for more than a couple of hours?" I ask, avoiding his interrogation.

"No. We need to get this case in order, or we'll lose."

"You need to go home. And I ran an errand this morning. We have..."

He interrupts me. "An errand?"

"I detoured to the town hall," I say, attempting to shrug it off.

"Why?" He stops what he is doing to watch my every move.

"It was my good deed for the day."

He drums his fingers on the table with his mouth open. Finally, he says, "If we weren't so buried with this case, I'd interrogate you. But for now, this conversation is on hold until we go grab lunch or a beer."

Off the hook easily, thankfully. I can't wait to hear what he has to say about the Kendall situation.

Logan, my brother, is five years younger than I am and is married to the most amazing woman. They have a two-year-old daughter. He lets things bother him, and they burrow into his skin too easily. We are partners in our father's law firm. Dad was supposed to retire, but hasn't yet. I don't think he'll know what to do with himself if he retires, so he meddles in the cases and the day-to-day business of the firm. Logan and I could run this firm without him, and hope to, sooner rather than later.

"Let's determine our next steps regarding the Finney case," says Logan.

"Your head needs to be in the game."

"It's in. Let's get to work."

As my phone vibrates with a notification, I swipe it off the table before Logan can look.

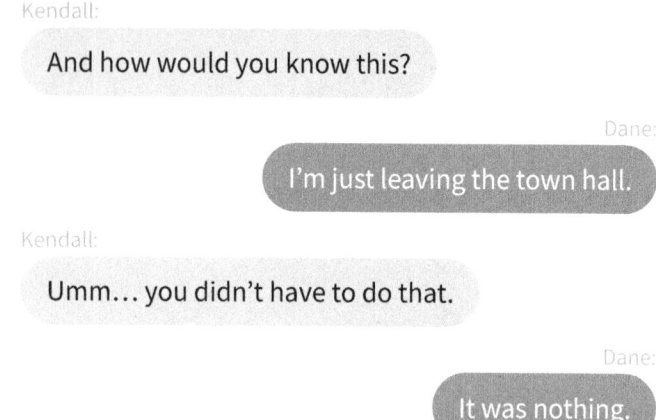

Kendall:
And how would you know this?

Dane:
I'm just leaving the town hall.

Kendall:
Umm… you didn't have to do that.

Dane:
It was nothing.

A huge smile crosses my face as I shake my head. I know I didn't have to do it, but I felt compelled to take care of it for her. She shouldn't have to deal with that mess.

Logan interrupts me. "Hey, enough with smiling at your phone. We have work to do."

Files and boxes litter our conference room table, and information on this case fills the whiteboard. Being a defense attorney has its luxuries, and at other times, it's a lot of pieces we are trying to fit together. And then at any moment, everything falls into place… most of the time.

This case has us working through the afternoon. We talk about almost nothing else. Eventually, we look at each other and decide it's time for lunch. Time is of the essence here, so we ask our executive assistant, Rylee, to order lunch and dinner for us. We'll be working another late night on this case. There are so many boxes to sift through.

"This is fucking bullshit," I complain, talking to no one in particular.

But Logan answers, "Stating the obvious." He shakes his head.

It feels like we just gave Rylee our order, and she's already walking through the conference door with lunch and, as if on cue, my stomach growls pretty loudly. We take a brief break to eat and refresh our brains. Although it's hard to completely shut it off.

"What were you doing at the town hall?" Logan asks as he takes a bite of his sandwich.

"I heard Roland was giving a small-business owner the runaround with permits."

"That guy! Is he ever going to learn?" He shakes his head.

"He seemed sheepish when I showed up. I'm guessing he's up to his old shit again. I put him in his place. He'll make it right today."

The Italian sandwich makes my mouth water with the smell of dressing, deli meat, and veggies. A huge bite straight into my mouth just as Logan asks me, "What business was he dragging his feet on this time?"

I say through a mouth full of food, "Just a salon expansion on Main Street."

"That's very specific. Which one?"

Which one? I didn't even realize there was more than one.

"Some woman I met named Kendall."

He snaps his head to me with wide eyes. "Kendall, huh? How did you meet her?" He looks me up and down, trying to decipher whether he should continue. "You going to share more about her?"

"Nope, let's finish our lunch and get back to work."

"You're being evasive. Something is up with you. You're resisting now, but I'll break you soon."

I ignore him and finish my sandwich. After hours of concentrating on the case, my mind wanders to the fiery redhead with penetrating eyes that can see right through me. She is gorgeous, independent, and sassy as fuck. All the other women I've slept with always ask for my number right away. She didn't even hint at it.

One night is my motto. It keeps my personal life transactional, just the way I like it. Why does it always come back to fucking Maggie? She crushed me.

But now, transactional won't do. I want more because I've never met anyone like Kendall. I'm hooked and still trying to figure her out. Yeah, she's skeptical, and for good reason—look at my life. All one-night stands, no attachments. And then she walks through my door, and I'm practically begging her to stay longer. What is wrong with me?

"Hey, where did you go? It's like you aren't even listening," Logan says, waving his hands in front of my face. I must have been really out there.

"Yeah, I'm right here."

Work is a priority for me, and that's what I need to focus on right now. Clearing the Kendall cobwebs out of my head, I dive back into the case files. My head needs to be in the game with this case, not with the fiery redhead.

"I think we need to attack this from a different angle." Logan stands up and writes on the whiteboard. He drones on, essentially repeating everything I said earlier today. He continues talking, and I let him believe the fresh approach was entirely his own idea.

"Logan, that's brilliant. Who do we need to talk to?"

Brilliant, probably borderline genius, and he is quick on his feet. He does well in this dog-eat-dog world. Me, I'm here to work and do my best to defend people. Innocent until proven guilty. I listen to my gut with clients and can smell a lie from a mile away. We make a good team.

My phone is ringing, but I can't find it. Moving files until I find my phone, I catch it just before it goes to voicemail. "Gram calling," I say to Logan.

I look at my brother and shrug my shoulders. There are only a few reasons for her to call right now.

Answering the phone, "Gram, is everything okay?"

"Oh, you know. I'm doing well. When is our next lunch date?"

She never just calls. There's something up her sleeve, and right now, I don't have time to figure it out. I click speakerphone and bring up my calendar to see when I have her scheduled for lunch.

"Okay, you are on my schedule for dinner this Friday. Does that still work for you, or do you need to reschedule?"

"This Friday, yes, that's perfect. It's on my calendar. See you then."

Gram keeps her cards close to her chest until you are face-to-face with her. The entire world could burn to the ground, and she'd wait until you were in front of her to tell you. I'm going to forget about it for now.

"Okay, I love you, Gram, and we'll talk then."

She hangs up in the middle of me talking. Something is bothering her. If I had more time in my schedule, I would reschedule our lunch for tomorrow. But we have too much to do.

Logan and I look at each other, and I say, "That was weird."

"Well, keep me in the loop. I'm sure she will tell you all about it on Friday. If she needs anything, I'm here too. I know she doesn't like bothering me because I have a family, but I always have time for her."

"I will. I'm going to the gym to blow off some steam and clear my head. I'll be back later."

"You're all over the place today. Come back with a fresh outlook because we're going to need it."

"Head home too, I'm sure Theresa would like that," I say, encouraging him to take a break.

When I'm all fired up, the gym allows me to work it out and reduce stress.

Logan points his finger at me. "And don't get caught up between some chick's legs. We've got work to do. Be back by seven."

"See you later." I ignore his last comment and walk out the door.

SEVEN
Kendall

J ust as I pick up my phone, a text comes in from Dane. I wasn't
expecting to hear from him at all, even though I gave him my card.
My gut pushed me to do it. Not knowing what the hell I was doing, I
handed it over. Feeling conflicted, does he really want to get to know
me, or is this part of his routine?

And then to just talk with the town's building inspector and say,
"I'll be all set", I don't know what his angle is. I'm conflicted. The
whole thing gets under my skin. His assuming I needed help is pre-
sumptuous and a big overstep in my eyes. Yet, if all goes well today,
it's him I need to thank. And I sigh hard, thinking about this entire
situation I've gotten into over the past few days.

All I want to do is finish planning for my grand opening and build
this business to support local workers and the community. I look
around as I drive to the salon and realize that I've been in deep thought.
I don't even remember driving all this way. The salon is up ahead.

Thankfully, Blake, my general contractor, will be there with me.
As a woman business owner, I find it difficult to deal with the town,
especially this building inspector. I'm close to filing a complaint with
the town manager's office. But since Dane stuck his neck out, maybe
I don't even have to worry about it.

I cross my fingers and hope that this meeting goes as planned and we
get the final sign-offs. Then we'll have time to finalize the soft opening
celebration with my closest friends and loyal clients the night before.

Hopefully, we will start getting reviews that will catapult us in the local market. Being the only spa in a thirty-mile radius, it far exceeds the local competition.

As I'm parking and swing my legs out of my SUV, Blake strolls out of the back entrance of the building. Looking good as usual, his dirty blond hair is in disarray in that ruggedly handsome way of his. He's been working a lot of hours to finish everything for this morning's inspection. An early morning for him starts at 6:30 a.m., so I'm guessing he's been here since earlier than that today. I admire his dedication to his work and to this project. He knows how much this means to me. Approaching him, he glances over at me with his baby blue eyes.

"How was your weekend?" asks Blake.

My mind instantly goes to Friday night and how Miss Take-A-Risk met Dane in his hotel room. I don't regret a second of it, but now that's all I'm focused on. My core heats and my thighs rub together almost involuntarily.

I need to change the subject quickly to distract myself. "It was great. We had a girls' night. How was your daughter's game?"

"It was a close one, but they won."

"She must have been excited."

Blake is a single dad to his eight-year-old daughter, Olivia. She is his entire world and the only thing he talks about. I admire his work ethic and his commitment to his company and daughter. You don't see that often enough.

"The entire team was cheering, and we went out for ice cream to celebrate."

"That's awesome. Are you ready for this meeting?"

"The real question is...are you ready for this meeting?" He turns slightly so I can walk by, and he follows through the back door. The meeting is in less than an hour, and the first stop is coffee.

"Can we take ten minutes and review everything? I'll feel better if we can make sure there are no holes in our paperwork, the requirements, and the requests from them," I say, and then make coffee.

"Of course, let me go grab the plans and folder."

We've been diligent throughout the project. Now, all our files are in pristine condition. The work is done and documented from start to finish, along with any necessary inspections along the way.

"Kendall, I double-checked everything," he says as he opens the job folder and pulls out the plans. "We should be good."

The next hour passes in the blink of an eye. Roland comes in the front door with his clipboard in hand. Blake and I share a brief look. Since throat punching this guy is not an option, I decide to be overly friendly and shake his hand. It can't hurt.

"Good morning, how are you?" I ask as pleasantly as possible.

Something is different about him this time around—he's smiling. Even Blake glances at me with a smirk on his face and slightly shrugs his shoulders. At least we are on the same page. The last time he was here, he pointed out things that didn't even pertain to the permits.

"Morning. Let's get this done quickly for you." He's flipping through his checklist and doesn't even bother to look up at us. "Okay, do you have the paperwork that we requested for this meeting?"

Blake shuffles through his folder, grabs a few pieces of paper, and hands them to Roland. "Here you go; that should be everything."

Roland reads the pages, and after a few minutes of silence, he says, "This all looks to be in order."

Almost everything that Blake handed over, we've given to him before.

"I'm sorry. What's changed since the last time we met?"

Roland stares at me with curiosity. "You didn't send down your attorney to take care of things with my office?"

"What? I have no idea what you're talking about."

"You're telling me you don't know Attorney Dane Walsh."

The realization flashes across my face. What did he say to this guy? I have so many questions.

Do I even admit to knowing Dane?

Yes, he was my one-night stand who decided to come and rescue me from the building inspector.

None of this is settling well with me.

"To answer your question...no, I didn't send my attorney."

I'm not even sure he believes me, but he says, "Okay, well, let's keep the inspection moving along. There are a few things that I need to check."

The entire process takes about thirty minutes. I haven't seen this guy check things off his list this fast—ever.

"All the work looks great, and I'm signing off on my part right now. The office admin will have everything for you early next week to pick up."

"That's wonderful news," I say, smiling.

Roland leaves, and Blake looks at me and says, "That went smoothly. I have no idea how. You must have a fairy godmother."

"Apparently, this attorney is in fact my fairy godmother," I say with an arched eyebrow and a slight shake of my head. I don't know how to explain it all.

"Okay, well, you should find that attorney and thank him. We just got the final sign-offs for your permits. Now you can finish planning your openings."

I'm thankful he didn't ask any further questions about the attorney. I really don't want to get into it right now. "Yeah, I can't wait."

Rummaging through my bag, I dig out my to-do list and review it again to see what's left. My friends will be excited about this update. I promised them the VIP experience during the soft opening, so I text them the good news, which has me smiling widely and bouncing on my heels.

"Congratulations, Kendall. This place is going to bring a lot of business to the town." Blake touches my shoulder and squeezes. He's the nicest guy and deserves someone special. I wish one of my friends would give him a chance. I can matchmake with the best of them, but that will have to wait until I have more space on my plate.

"Thank you, and yes, it really will. Come on, let's go grab a coffee and breakfast at Saxville Coffee House."

"Raincheck for later this week?" I regretfully ask to pass.

"Okay, I'm keeping you to that. I'm going to work on the shelving now while I'm here."

"Excellent. I'll be in my office if you need me."

He turns and heads back to the storage closet. My heels click on the floor and echo off the walls of the hallway to my office.

Stepping inside, I shut the door. I slip off my shoes and slide onto my couch before digging into the pile of work on my desk.

Should I text Dane? Call him? I don't know.

The mixed feelings swirl through my body. I'll have my final permit next week, thanks to him. Still, he assumed it was okay to step into my situation without fully understanding what was going on. He could have made it worse. Frankly, if he wanted to help, why didn't he say something?

I flip my phone around in my hands as I think through how best to address this with him. I went from thinking I'll never see this guy again to where we are now.

I shake my head.

The best way to address this will be to send a text. I have other pressing items on my list that need my full attention.

> I appreciate what you did. Thank you. The permits will be ready next week. I wish you had asked me first before assuming I needed or wanted your help.

Staring at my phone, I'm waiting for a quick response, which doesn't come. I push myself off the couch and toss my phone onto the desk.

The next hour is spent in my office, tying up all the loose ends for both opening celebrations. After completing almost my entire list, I realized that most items were confirmations, which made it easy to check off. Taking one more look through the list, I'm all caught up for today.

The countdown to the soft opening begins.

With excitement rolling through my body, a huge smile crosses my face. It's almost here, and I can't help but feel my heart drop into my stomach. I remind myself that this is everything I've wanted for so long.

Stretching my arms over my head and wiggling my body, I place my hands on the arm of the chair to crack my back. I can't wait for the massage therapists to be right down the hall. Until then, I rub my temples a few times and stand up. Snagging my phone off the desk, I take a quick look at it.

I scrunch up my nose, seeing that I missed the text Dane sent over thirty minutes ago. When I'm in the zone working, I block everything else out—unless you are right in front of me.

Dane:

It wasn't meant to step on your toes or even ignore you altogether. Noted to ask you next time.

I stare at my phone. His text indicates there could be a next time. I really don't have time to read into what he's saying. This week will keep me busy enough; I don't need to worry about him. I mean, we probably won't see each other again anyway.

EIGHT

Dane

M y alarm blares loudly from my nightstand. It takes me a few seconds to recognize it and shut it off. This week has been brutal.

What day is it?

Shit! It's already Friday.

I'm dressed to hit the gym first thing this morning. I'm feeling off kilter—unfocused. Kendall pops into my thoughts more than I'd like to admit. Multiple times a day...all week, especially after her last text a few days ago. She seemed pissed about me butting into her business. And I'm over here thinking I did a good thing. I guess I see her point, but I'd still do it all over again. She wouldn't have the permits if I hadn't stepped in.

I need to stay focused on this caseload. It needs to be my number one priority; instead, Kendall's face and body show up in my thoughts on repeat. I try to shake them off, but she's ingrained in my mind.

My bag is packed, and I'll shower at the gym before heading to the office. It will be another late night working on the case. The gym isn't busy at this time of day, which works well for me. In and out, ready for the day. I'm on autopilot through my workout, and next thing I know, I'm pulling up and parking in front of the coffeehouse.

My head leans back on the headrest as I close my eyes and rub the center of my forehead. This woman has a hold on me. I can't stop thinking about her. Her legs. Her sassy and sarcastic mouth. Bringing my head back down and blowing out a sigh, I open my door and head inside the Saxville Coffee House.

I'm hitting it up at a good time; it doesn't look too busy as I peek in through the storefront windows. I walk in and all I can smell is coffee, bacon, and some sort of muffin. After that workout, I could eat a few breakfast sandwiches. Music pumps through the speakers, and all I can see are dark wood floors, tables, and chairs, with a few booths inviting me in further. All the way to the counter, where they display dozens of muffin tops, cinnamon rolls, homemade Pop-Tarts, and what look like cake pops. The menu above is all written on a blackboard in chalk. There are so many choices, but I stick with my usual. They do have the best pistachio-flavored coffee; it's smooth, and I like it black with a couple of sugars.

I take a few seconds to glance around to see if I know anyone. Okay, maybe a specific someone. She would stand out with her fiery red hair. She isn't here, and I swallow hard. My shoulders slump just slightly. Her salon is right down the street. The odds of her being here seem high, but I'm out on a limb.

Who am I right now?

I order my coffee, and I almost ask for a mug to stay a little longer. Just in case Kendall walks through the door.

"Dane, right?" asks the barista. I come here often.

"Yes," I answer, and she writes my name on the cup.

She's cute enough. Maybe I can fuck someone else and get Kendall out of my head. My cock drives the ship, and he has no reaction—not even an inkling. Nothing.

I order a turkey bacon breakfast sandwich on a croissant to go, but decide to sit for a bit at a table that has a straight line of sight to the door. You never know; it might be my lucky day.

My phone chimes, and I look at the screen. It's Logan, wondering when I'll be in the office. I let him know I'll be there within the hour.

The office is only a twenty-minute ride from here, but I leave a buffer, just in case.

The coffeehouse bell dings, and I lift my head as the door opens. A flash of red hair spikes my heart rate, and my chest is heavy. Just as I lift myself up off the chair, I see a guy behind her holding the door. I sit back down and observe.

Wait, are they together?

She doesn't seem like a woman who would cheat on her boyfriend, since I don't see a ring on either of their fingers. But I guess Maggie didn't seem like that kind of woman either—and she cheated.

Observing like a hawk as they interact, I watch from my corner. She is sporting a bright pink skirt that falls a couple of inches above her knees, paired with a white button-down top. My eyes roam down her long, strong legs to those studded heels. Her red hair is flowing around her. It reminds me of that night when her hair spilled all over my pillows. The mere thought of her like that sends a jolt straight to my dick, and the damn thing twitches, making me have to adjust myself. Guess he isn't dormant. He just didn't want the barista, but Kendall? He's all in.

Tracking her through to the counter, I listen to what she orders and file it for future reference. Medium iced mocha with almond milk. I'm so lost watching her that the barista has to say my name louder the second time. Oh shit! It still isn't busy here, and Kendall turns around just as I stand up and walk over to the counter. Our eyes meet, and she smiles, looking happy to see me even after her stern text the other day.

"Dane, what are you doing here?"

To see you, I want to say. The coffeehouse is a couple of blocks away from her salon. I'm here on purpose. And she knows it.

"Just grabbing the best pistachio coffee in town."

"You live in town?"

"I do," I say, nodding.

Her eyes widen and flicker with surprise. She steps forward but then hesitates for a split second before she wraps her arms around me. "Thank you so much for what you did with the building inspector. I have everything we need to host our opening celebrations in a few weeks."

She's stiff and a little awkward against me, but once I hug her back, she melts into my embrace. Feeling her body against mine, the smell of her watermelon hair, and she ever so slightly rubs the back of my neck with her thumb. It sends shivers down my spine. An unfamiliar sensation, but this woman has an effect on me like no other.

As she loosens her hold, I tighten my arms briefly and then let her go slowly. I stare back into her eyes. "You're very welcome, and you deserve to open without that douchebag, Roland, holding you up." Then I remember we aren't here alone. "Who's your friend?" I can't help myself; I need to know.

She turns to the guy standing next to her and says, "This is Blake, my contractor."

I offer my hand. "Attorney Dane Walsh."

"Nice to meet you...Dane."

We both squeeze a little tighter than we normally would. I wonder what his deal is. Wonder if anything is going on between the two of them.

And why would that matter?

Because you have it bad for this woman, that's why it matters. Shaking that thought away. "You too."

He glances over at Kendall and back at me. "So you're her fairy godmother. Not sure what you said to Roland, but it worked. I've worked with him before, but that rapport went nowhere with this job."

"I've had a few run-ins with him. He needed a reminder of how to treat a lady and how this town works."

Kendall takes a slight step between us that doesn't go unnoticed. "I owe you, Dane. And maybe you can swing by the grand opening."

"You don't owe me. I was helping a fellow business owner, and I'd love to be there. When is it?"

"Four weeks from tomorrow," she says with a smile on her face and her eyes twinkling back at me.

"I look forward to it."

Interrupted by the barista calling her name, I stand there as they collect their drinks and to-go bags. They must not be staying, which makes me smirk. To hide my excitement, I take a sip of my coffee.

"Dane, nice to see you here. Enjoy your coffee. We need to head back to the salon and work on a few design elements for the spa," she says with a soft smile.

"You too. I'll see you at the grand opening then." Taking her hand in mine, a warmth spreads through my body. Her touch has this effect on me. Not wanting to release her, I rub my thumb over the top of her hand. Not making it obvious because this Blake dude is watching us intensely.

Finally releasing her hand, I direct them to the door.

"Have a great day." As I wave to them, getting into my Ferrari, the look on Blake's face makes me laugh. Yup, man, I've got this on lock.

"You too." They say in unison as she walks to her car, which of course is parked in front of me.

After running into her, I decide to text her.

Dane:

> Not gonna lie…that black-on-black Maserati suits you and your fiery red hair. Bold. A little intimidating. Definitely turns heads.

Kendall:

Corporate life was good for one thing…my car. And you're too funny. I was just thinking that your Ferrari screams, "Look at me," and somehow, it works.

Dane:

So you're saying we're a dangerously sexy…power couple

Kendall:

That…or we both have excellent taste and zero patience for the ordinary.

Dane:

Yeah, both. Makes me wonder what else we have in common.

Kendall:

Besides mutual caffeine dependency and top-tier sarcasm? Not sure.

Dane:

Let's find out. Dinner?

I see the three dots indicating she is typing, but then they're gone. It happens again and then is gone once again. I start the engine and decide to drive to the office. Maybe, just maybe, she'll change her mind.

Kendall:

Tempting. But I've got a lot on my plate right now—with the spa opening and life being… life. So… maybe.

Dane:

Is that a maybe-maybe or a don't-hold-your-breath maybe?

Kendall:

Let's just say… I'm not not thinking about it.

Dane:

That's enough to work with. I'll be patient… for like, a day.

Kendall:

Impressive restraint.

Dane:

You haven't seen anything yet.

NINE

Kendall

I spent last weekend and all this week hyper-focused on getting everything in order for the grand opening. There has been very little time outside of the salon and spa. Early this week, I picked up the final permits.

I'm surprised I heard from Dane only once this week. After our interaction at the coffeehouse, I thought I'd hear from him sooner. This morning, he sent over a text.

Dane:

> Any chance you can make a little time to have dinner with me this weekend?

I'm on the fence about having dinner with him, and the list for the opening events doesn't seem to shrink, even though I'm checking things off.

A text message is the right thing to do to let him know. What do I even say?

Kendall:

> Thanks for the invite, but I'm buried in spa opening prep this weekend. And you don't exactly strike me as the type who waits around when a woman says no.

Dane:

Guilty. I don't wait around…unless it's for something I really, really want. And right now, that's you. I'll keep asking with heart eyes until you say yes.

Kendall:

Flirty and flattery noted. Still sus

Dane:

Of me or your own interest?

Kendall:

Let's go with both.

Dane:

Fair enough. To be clear, is this a polite brush-off or…a potential raincheck?

Kendall:

Potential raincheck. I haven't decided if dinner with a known one-night-stand guy is a brilliant move or a terrible lapse in judgment.

Dane:

Then let me surprise you. I promise not to seduce you over appetizers.

Kendall:

You're a real charmer ;)

Dane:

What about next weekend?

Kendall:

We'll see. Ask me again next Friday.

Dane:

> I'm setting my alarm to text you next Friday.

The rest of the day and weekend were spent finalizing the details with Blake for the spa. The few built-ins and a couple of minor things. I won't be seeing clients until after next week. I'm thankful for the stylists who work here; they are always willing to help. My girlfriends came to me on Sunday for lunch; otherwise, we wouldn't have seen each other. I don't think I would have eaten if they hadn't shown up.

Then, during the week, there were more items to finish. Blake worked on the accent wall in the meditation room. Then he did all the walls in the Himalayan salt cave, along with the floors and built-in benches. We selected all the zero-gravity chairs that are in one area of the room. Along the wall, a row of leather chaise loungers is situated. Outside the room, there are built-in storage areas where guests can leave their shoes and grab a blanket.

Blake did all the flooring throughout in a deep chestnut, including all the massage rooms. We decorated each room with bookshelves, essential oils, diffusers, and plants. The more the spa vision comes to life, the more excited I get. All the details are coming into focus as each room is finished for the opening celebrations.

Standing in the salon, I scan the space, and I can hardly believe it's been three years since the salon opened, and now the grand opening for the spa is just a couple of weeks away. My dreams are coming true. I didn't think this would be possible for at least another two years, but business is exceptional, and the demand for a spa was too strong not to pursue it now.

One of my stylists comes up to me and says, "This is going to be an amazing grand opening."

"Yes, it is," I say with a bright smile.

My next client walks through the door. "How's your day, Ms. Jane?" She was one of my very first clients and has appointments every two weeks. Many of our current clients are referrals she has given to the salon. Our number one cheerleader.

"I'm doing well. Your grand opening is hastily approaching. Everything all set?"

"It's going to be a day to remember. Food, drinks, ten-minute chair massages, and tours of the spa. I think you'll love the Himalayan salt cave."

"That all sounds like what this town needs. You're really making a difference in this community."

"Thank you. It's home, and supporting the economy is a bonus to the services we provide. Will you be coming out for the soft opening? We would love for you to be here."

"I wouldn't miss it for the world. Do you need any help around here? I have a grandson who would be more than happy to do whatever you need." She pats me on the arm.

I cover her hand with mine. "Oh, that's really kind of you. I have some furniture arriving today, so yes, I could probably use the help."

"Okay, you have my number. Call me when it arrives, and I'll make sure he's here. You two should go out for dinner sometime." She smirks at me with her eyes lighting up.

Nothing like adding a little blind date action into the conversation. She's the sweetest, so how do I let her down easy?

"That is so kind of you to think of me. But I'm not in a place to date right now. The spa has me working a lot these days."

"You two would get along really well. He says the same thing, and you can talk about how to have a better work/life balance."

I laugh really hard. This woman is spunky.

"Better work/life balance. Your grandson sounds intriguing."

"Well, if that's what you're thinking, maybe once the grand opening happens, you'll have more time for something other than work." She laughs and nods, as if the matter is settled.

We discuss what's going on in her world, beyond her grandson. She's busy with her girlfriends, and her social life is way better than mine will ever be. She was widowed a few years back and finally found her people. It's nice to see she's doing so well. I'm excited that she'll be joining us for the grand opening as a very loyal customer of a woman-owned business.

A few hours after Jane leaves, I finish up my workday, lock up, and clean the salon.

Dane:

> It's Friday. Any chance I can steal you on Sunday?

Kendall:

> Depends…what's in it for me?

Dane:

> Me, obviously. We'll have a great time, and I'm looking forward to hearing about the grand opening plans. Just say yes.

I have so many reservations about this, but I'm trying to give it a chance. He has been so persistent, but not to the point of being overbearing, like texting me every day.

Since my girlfriends said I'll never know unless I try to see what he's all about, I feel like I should give him a chance. I don't want to end up in his bed again, though. If I'm doing this, I want an actual date. Don't get me wrong, the time with him a few weeks ago was the best night of my life—he's like a magnet that I'm drawn to.

Kendall:

> Okay, yes. I hope I don't regret this.

Kendall:

Pick me up at 5.

I send him my address and close my eyes, thinking either this is the stupidest idea I've ever had, or it's going to be a ton of fun.

The music is pumping through the salon speakers, and I'm dancing around as I sweep. Being able to let my hair down and be free to dance opens something inside of me. I remember when my grandparents used to dance in the kitchen. They'd always invite me to dance with them. Their love was unmatched. The way they took care of each other. Until I was a young adult, I'd witnessed them dancing all the time.

My heart aches realizing my life is fulfilled in so many ways, but I'm missing out on sharing it with someone special—someone who knows me and loves me all the same.

Although my girlfriends are my lifeline and support me no matter what, it makes me think about how lonely I feel at moments like this. Maybe it's because Jane came in today, and I love listening to her.

She was widowed and never stopped talking about the life she and Richard had had for over forty years. That's a long time to be with someone. All the trials and tribulations they withstood over those years. Jane tells me love picks you. I've asked her what she means by that, and all she says is love picked her and Richard—soulmates. If I were guaranteed a love like theirs, I'd go for it. Love isn't ready to pick me. My eyes prickle, but I brush them off.

Jake, the one guy I thought picked me, was a nightmare. He lied and manipulated me at every turn, and what pisses me off the most is that I was blind to it. Until Faith took me aside and had a frank conversation with me. He was adamant that I spend all my time with him, which left no room for my friends. Especially since I had just opened the salon and was working there a lot. I remember one night; I was at the salon late:

It's late, and I need to text Jake. Otherwise, who knows what will happen? The last time I was late, he was questioning me about where I was and who I was with, even though I had told him all of that a few hours before when we spoke. He said I didn't call. I told him that my client was running late and had just arrived. He calls my phone, and I hesitate to answer, but I do anyway. He asks twenty questions again, and he says I'm not really at the salon. I say I'm at the salon, and my client walked in and is sitting in my chair. I need to let him go. He was still yelling into the phone about how I do this all the time, and we never have time together. Once I hang up, it hits me hard that he just isn't the same person as when we first met. I need to break up with him.

My client is finally done; it's still light out. The sun is just about to set. I walk over to the front door to lock up, and I see him sitting in his car that's parked on the side of the road.

Has he been there the entire time, watching me? I've been so busy I didn't notice. This isn't normal behavior. The conversation with Fatih reminded me he's a manipulative, gaslighting, and negative person. I guess we're adding stalker to the list.

This whole situation is creeping me out, so I call Faith.

"He's here."

"Jake? What do you mean? Do you need me to call the police?"

"I'm not even sure what to do. He's sitting in his car that's parked on the street right before the salon. I've been running late all day. I called and texted him about it and even said I'd text him when I was done."

"Okay, are all the doors locked up?"

"Yes."

She is freaking me out, and now I'm freaking myself out. I double-checked the back door, and it's locked too. Never have I been afraid to be here when the salon closes, but tonight, I'm scared. He's like a loose cannon ready to blow. There have been so many other incidents that have driven him out of control. I'm afraid this will bring everything to a head, and frankly, I can't take it anymore. I need to get out of this relationship. It isn't healthy, and I shouldn't be feeling afraid of my boyfriend. For the last couple of days, he's seemed more unhinged than I've ever seen him. I've asked what's wrong, but he says nothing. Nothing, my ass.

"Then I'm going to call the police and meet you over there. This is it, Kendall. You're going to need to end things with him."

"I know; he's totally lost it."

"I want you to take a few seconds to think about this. Do you feel safe?"

"No, but he won't do anything. Well, I don't think he will."

"As your best friend, we aren't taking any chances on this one."

Worry takes over, and I decide that I'm barricading myself in one of the back rooms that has a lock and things I can put up against the wall. Staying on the phone with Faith, she connects us to the local police department and tells them what is going on. She requests that they not come screaming into the area with their sirens and lights, but more like a wellness check. We stay on the call with dispatch until the police arrive. Faith is in her car, but she's waiting until the police approach the situation first. She hangs back a couple of streets over, ready to move when they arrive.

The cops confirm it's him in the car, creeping. A part of me was hoping I was wrong, and it wasn't him. He tells the police he was concerned because it was so late, and I wasn't picking up his calls or responding to his text messages. That is a complete lie. I answered his text messages. I told him I couldn't talk because I was finishing my client's hair. But he incessantly called, so finally I excused myself to answer him.

Thankfully, Faith is with me. Jake eyes us both, and it feels like he is going to lose it. But I know him; he won't do it in front of anyone, especially the police. The chill down my spine and the nausea that is rolling up my throat tell me everything I need to know.

Someone knocks on the door. I jump back and scream. Dropping the broom on the floor and clenching my chest, I look at the door. It's just my girlfriends. They are here to help put the finishing touches on the spa. And I may have promised them some champagne.

"Why are you screaming?" Faith says.

"I locked up, and the whole Jake situation popped into my head." I rolled my eyes at how I had let him into my life so easily and had no clue who he really was.

"He was a manipulative asshole. You haven't heard from him, right?" Faith asks skeptically.

"No, nothing like that." I wave my hand. "I don't want to dwell on him anymore."

"Understandable." Faith hugs me. "So, tell me something good that happened today. You've been on a streak."

"Well...Dane texted and asked to take me on a date again."

"And you said..." Addison leans in. "Yes?"

"I said yes, but not until Sunday. I have way too many loose ends to wrap up going into the weekend."

"You finally said yes. That guy must really want to take you to dinner." Lane drops into the seat by the window.

I tell them about the text messages, and they want to see for themselves, so I pass my phone around.

As the heat radiates through my body, I cross my legs, thinking about him.

"Listen, I'm not even sure I made the right decision in saying yes to dinner. I don't have time for a guy."

"I don't know; you light up when you talk about him. It's been a while since you talked about a guy like this, really any guy." Faith chuckles and stares, waiting for me to say something.

And I break instantly. "There was an instant attraction to him, and a night that I'll never forget. It took everything I had last week to say no to him for dinner. I was ready to drop everything and have dinner. But the spa took priority. He consumes me with this magnetic pull to him, like I'm tethered to him. Text messaging...it's fun."

"We can see how much fun you two were having." Addison wiggles her eyebrows dramatically at me.

"Hence, the reason I can't say no, but I have a ton of stuff to accomplish here, or I'll have to cancel."

They all yell at once. "No."

"No, you will not." Addison wags her finger at me. "No matter what, you made the decision. Now you follow through and have some fun."

"Then I'll need all of your help to whip this place into shape."

They all nod yes as I pour champagne, and we raise our glasses. "Let's focus on getting this spa ready." We clink glasses.

TEN

Dane

My gram won't let me forget that we have dinner plans tonight. I promised her, so there's no going back on my word. Stepping out of the courtroom, I head to meet her. She gives me perspective and always has some insight that I haven't thought about. Right now, I need some.

Gram drives herself everywhere, which I am grateful for because she's meeting me at the restaurant down the street. It's less than a five-minute walk. A few blocks away, I turn into the restaurant and find my Gram sitting at one of the tables by the large, almost floor-to-ceiling windows.

With a warm grin, I say, "Gram, glad we can do dinner again." And hug her tight. She pats me on my back.

I slide into the chair across from her.

"I'm sure you've had a long day in court, so I love that you still want to have dinner with your Gram."

"I wouldn't miss it for the world."

"Well, I really enjoy our dinners." She leans over the table and grabs my face. "You look exhausted. Have you been sleeping?"

"Not that much. This is a big case for us."

"Well, dear, even though they say you can sleep when you're dead. If you haven't lived, then what's all this worth anyway...I want you to think about that."

"I know, Gram, I will." I rub the back of my neck and say, "What's going on in your world?"

"Nothing much; the girls and I are heading to the casino next week to play bingo."

"Do you think any of you will be lucky enough to win?"

"We usually have pretty good luck when we go. I'll let you know." She takes a sip of her water and then says, "Let's talk about you. How's your love life? Dating anyone."

The love life talk again. She's been good about not bringing it up every time we get together, but I'm not getting out of it tonight.

"Same as usual, Gram. I don't have time for a love life. My schedule is ridiculous; no woman would stick around. You know that."

"Maggie wasn't for you. It doesn't mean there isn't someone out there who will be perfect for you. I know a woman who might just keep you on your toes. That's what you need—someone who can match your ambition, your intensity, and your big heart. It's in there, you know. I see it. You may think it's buried too far down there, but it isn't." She taps me on the heart.

It's coming...she's about to try to set me up again. The last three ended up being complete disasters. Take them on a date, bring them back to the hotel room, and then they want to get married. Not for me. Yes, I'm at that age where women want to find someone to settle down and have babies. I don't think I'm that kind of guy.

But Kendall might be the exception, and I'm looking forward to our date. I stick to the line in the sand and tell her, "No setups."

"Do you remember what happened with the last few dates you set me up on? They didn't end well."

"Dane, I know it's hard for you to trust for good reason. Not every woman is Maggie. She didn't know a good thing when it was standing right in front of her. And your buddy, Bill..." Gram shakes her head. "Well, shame on him. It's time to heal from that relationship;

otherwise, you will continue down the path you are on and end up alone and lonely."

"Gram, I am not lonely. I'm alone, and I love it that way."

She gives me one of her looks, eyebrow raised and a smile on her face. I can't get anything past her. She knows me too well. I'd never admit it out loud, but I am lonely sometimes. It felt good the night I was with Kendall, then at breakfast the next morning, and during the brief time we spent together at the coffeehouse. The best part of the past few weeks has been the text messages. She is so fucking sassy. I can't wait to take her out to dinner. Maybe, just maybe, I'll show her a side of me she's been missing.

"Will you at least think about the woman I'd like to set you up with?"

"I'll think about it. But I'm swamped."

"Your grandfather told you that you could do whatever you put your mind to. That's not just for work, my dear. It's for all the things in your life. What you make a priority grows, and your grandfather and I knew that."

"You guys had a special kind of love." My head bows down and back up to meet my Gram's eyes.

If I could find the love that my grandparents had, I'd be more than willing to prioritize my love life. After seeing my parents' failed relationship, I can't stop thinking that I'll end up being just like my dad. Our mom cheated on him for years, and he allowed it to happen. I think that's why, when Maggie cheated on me with my best friend a few years ago, it wiped love out of my vocabulary. I don't want to go through that again.

All I ever want is to scratch the sex-itch and move on. I'm honest and upfront about my intentions with them. Still, I use my masculinity and cock to persuade them to sleep with me. It's not typical for a woman to pass up all of this.

Gram interrupted my inner monologue. "We were, and in time, love will find you too. You have to be open to it, though."

Kendall crosses my mind, and our dinner on Sunday comes to mind. The smile on my face right now is not from what Gram said, but from the woman with the fiery red hair.

ELEVEN

Kendall

After our champagne and toast, the girls and I unpacked almost all the supplies and organized them. They left a few minutes ago, and I only have one more box left.

My mind wanders to Dane again because I can't seem to help myself. I wonder where he will take me for dinner. Interrupted by the doorbell, the camera reveals that it's the furniture delivery. I practically jump for joy, running to the door. The delivery guy brings in all the boxes and furniture. The excitement is radiating from me as I clap my hands and rub the plush, dark grey fabric of the new couch that will be placed in the lounge, where customers can gather after receiving their services.

Once he leaves, I close the door, take a seat on the couch, wiggle my bottom, lean back, and say, "This is comfortable." Trying another position, I flip off my shoes and lie down on it. Oh yes, this thing is comfortable.

Popping up off the couch, I need to call Jane and see if her grandson can come sometime tomorrow, or at least within the next couple of days.

After searching for my phone and finding it on the shelf near the supplies, I call her.

"Hello."

"Hi Jane, it's Kendall. How are you?"

"I'm doing well, my dear, just having dinner with my grandson. Is everything okay?"

"Oh, yes, it is. But that's perfect, Jane. My furniture was delivered a few minutes ago, and I was hoping your grandson had some time tomorrow to help move things."

"Absolutely, what time works best for you?"

"First thing in the morning, probably seven? I'll already be here, just send him along. I really appreciate this, thank you, Jane."

"Have a good night, and I'll see you soon."

"You too."

Just as I hang up the phone, the doorbell rings. A quick peek at the camera—it's Blake.

"Hey, you don't have your key?"

Blake shakes his head. "I do, but I didn't want to just barge in."

"Well, I can appreciate that. Thank you."

He looks freshly showered, and does he have hair gel in his hair? I gave him a thank-you basket last week with his final payment, which included a special hair gel as a gift. Not the stuff that makes your hair all stiff, but it gives his hair a softer look. I like it.

"You've been such a great customer. Let me take you to dinner. No arguments this time. Right now."

"That's kind of last-minute."

"Well, you've been working so hard and never taking a break for yourself. So, for tonight, you can have dinner with me."

He is not wrong. I've been working a lot and not taking time for myself. Isn't that ironic? Since I'm opening up a spa for self-care and self-love, I should practice what I preach. I've said no to him a few times, so I feel obligated to say yes. I was about to finish up and head home for the night.

"You look ready, and I look like I just mopped up off the floor."

"You always look beautiful."

I feel my cheeks getting a little red. "Thank you. Okay, but I can't stay out too long. I need to rest tonight. Let me see if I have a change of clothes in the office."

Blake stays rooted in place as I walk down the hall to my office. I check the back of my door and, as I suspected, I have a sundress hanging up.

I yell to him, "I'll be out in a couple of minutes."

"Okay." But he continues talking, "I can't wait for the grand opening."

As I get dressed, I think about how great the opening will be. Blake's attendance at the grand opening is part of the community support I've added to the event. We have selected ten local businesses to showcase during the event. It will be an event people won't want to miss.

I stroll out of my office in an emerald green sundress and silver flip-flops. My hair still looks great even though I worked all day.

"I'm excited for you to be there. The spa is a superior project to showcase. Hopefully, your schedule will fill up from the showcase."

"Wow! You clean up nicely. That would be great for business. I appreciate you thinking that through; it's a great idea. So, want me to drive?"

"Why don't we take separate cars, then I can drive straight home after dinner. It's been a long week, and I have a lot more to do this weekend."

"Okay, I'll meet you at the restaurant."

"Did we decide?"

"On the Waterfront work for you?"

"Yes, love it there."

Double-checking that all the lights are shut off and doors are locked, I finally feel ready to walk away for the night. We walk to our cars and head to the restaurant. I'm looking forward to a good night's sleep, but thankful for some dinner first.

The restaurant is just a few minutes away, and there's plenty of parking available. I slip into a spot and walk into the restaurant.

Blake is already there to greet me as I walk in. The hostess asks us if we have reservations, and of course, he had called earlier to make reservations. She guides us through the front of the restaurant, where people are dining inside. Her shoes are clicking on the hardwood floors as we enter the covered deck area overlooking the lake. We have premier seating tucked in the corner with a beautiful view.

We sit down, menus handed to us, and we give our drink order.

"A great way to celebrate—dinner with a view. It's nice to be out and have adult time."

"You're a great dad and deserve some adult time."

"We are here to celebrate you and all your accomplishments. This was a rewarding project to work on. The grand opening will be a success. You had a vision." He raises his water glass to me and then takes a few gulps.

"You were the one who brought all my visions to life on this project. I'll give you glowing recommendations to everyone I know."

Blake leans back in his chair, looking out at the water, and says, "Looking forward to your referrals. Oh, actually, my next project is at your friend's house, Lane."

"She hired you. Why hasn't she told me?" I strum my fingers on the table, trying to remember if she told me, but I've forgotten with all the craziness of the past few weeks.

"We just finalized the kitchen renovation contract today, so maybe she was waiting until it was a done deal."

"Lane is one of my best friends. You two will work well together. I can't wait to see what you do with her kitchen. It needs a complete makeover that she has been talking about for a couple of years now."

"That's what she was telling me. It'll be a fun project. She has it all sketched out, so I'm working with her to finalize the design. I'm sure she'll share it with you."

"I'm sure she will."

We order our food and chat about his daughter, Olivia. Before our food is brought out, I excuse myself to use the ladies' room. As I finish up, I look in the mirror while I wash my hands. Drying them off, I leave the ladies' room and almost walk into someone.

"Oh, sorry about that...Always in a hurry."

As I look up, my mouth drops open. Biting my bottom lip, I stare up at Dane. An intense electrical shock moves through my body as he touches my arm. I'm not even sure how it's possible to be body-shaken to the core, but I've felt nothing like this in my entire life.

Why does he make me feel this way?

He steps closer to me with a smile so big it reaches his eyes.

"You have a lot going on. Are you having dinner with someone?" he asks.

"Yes..." I hesitate. "I'm here with my contractor, the one you met at the coffeehouse."

His smile fades from his face and turns serious. What is that all about?

"Having a nice dinner?"

"I am. Blake and I are celebrating the completion of the spa. I'm waiting for a couple of things, and we will be ready for our grand opening. Oh, you're coming, right? It's in two weeks—soft opening Friday and then the grand opening Saturday."

"I will absolutely be there."

Watching his facial expression change when I mention Blake's name, I search for answers in his eyes. He gives away nothing.

"Blake, huh?"

"Just friends. He's my contractor."

As he stands in front of me, staring, he steps a little closer. It's enough for me to glance up at him. Prickles run down my back, and heat sets into my body. I want to run my fingers over his beard and down his neck.

When I think he might kiss me, he leans down to my ear. I feel his breath on my neck as he says, "I'll see you Sunday." And kisses right under my ear. The moment he lifts his mouth off of me, my hand rushes to my neck, savoring it, as heat pulses through me.

He turns on his heel and walks back to the dining area. Leaving me wondering what the hell just happened?

TWELVE
Dane

I yank my chair from the table and sit. My chest is tight, my heart is beating faster than when I work out, and the adrenaline coursing through my veins is magnifying all of it. With Kendall's red hair flowing around her face, that green dress that brings out her eyes—she's mesmerizing. And all I wanted to do was grab her by the neck and kiss her on those luscious, pink lips of hers that are stained red.

There's no reason for what I'm feeling. I barely know her, but she's here with Blake. She says they are friends. I left her with a little something to carry her through the dinner, thinking about me while she's having dinner with him.

Gram stares at him and finally says, "You look upset."

"It's nothing."

I'm not telling Gram. She always encourages me to open up and express my feelings. Nobody's got time for that. Kendall says they're just friends, but that doesn't stop me from being upset. I can't even explain why. When I touched her, there were sparks under my fingers, and I didn't want to walk away. The need to be around her is like nothing I've ever felt—to be in her presence, to protect her, care for her. My entire body felt electrified. Every nerve ending was hyperaware of her. I didn't want to break the connection. Standing there with her, it was like nothing else mattered.

"Well, honey, that sure doesn't look like nothing. You flung yourself in that chair like it up and insulted you."

"Gram, just a lot on my mind."

She knows something isn't right with me. Let's see if she pushes any further. There are times when she lets things go, but I'm not sure if this is one of them. Usually, when I'm resistant to talking, she has a way of coaxing it out of me. I really don't want to get into this here. I want to leave and blow off some steam at the gym.

"Okay, let's talk about it."

Guess she's pushing it. Thinking fast on my feet, I start a conversation that has nothing to do with Kendall.

"Father is up to his old tricks. Logan and I wonder when he'll retire. Then we realize he'll die in his office before he retires."

"Work has always been where your dad excelled."

"A couple more years, Logan and I will take it over, and then we will be able to make decisions about the firm."

"You and Logan have done well for yourselves. It's nice to see you boys working together."

"It's great working with him."

Gram has always been there for me. I'm a different person around her, which is interesting, because I'm not opening up to her about Kendall. Maybe it's because I have no idea what I'm feeling. It's foreign to me. I've never caught feelings before with a one-night stand. It's deeper this time, from the minute I laid eyes on her.

Off topic, I blurt out, "Gram, sometimes I don't know what I'm feeling, and it ends up coming out as anger."

"That's alright. When you can finally sort through and delve deeper into yourself, that's why Gram is here. So, what has you so angry? I know you better than that. You can't hide from me. You left the table fine and came back angry and upset."

"The thing is, I really don't know. It's confusing," I say, massaging my neck to release some of the tension.

"So what happened between then and now? I haven't seen you this worked up since 'you know who.'" She leans in and rubs my arm.

"You can say her name...Maggie." I shake my head, thinking about that horrible relationship. It was good at the beginning, but it all went to hell when she slept with my best friend. It's an image that haunts me. I thought she was the one. Now, when I look back, I wanted her to be the one, but in reality, she was not the kind of woman I wanted on my arm. The future for me doesn't include a woman, or so I thought. I swore them off to concentrate on the firm and winning cases, as the top defense attorney in the city. Work is easy for me, but relationships not so much.

Shaking my head, I continue. "Okay, so I met a woman." Her eyes light up like a Christmas tree. "Gram, don't get excited, it was casual." Without getting too detailed, I keep it simple. She doesn't need to know I prefer one-night stands over trying to make anything work out by dating. Dating is overrated in my book. Or that's what I thought until Kendall said no to me last week. When she said yes today, I was about ready to celebrate with a party. She brings out something in me—life, happiness, hope.

"Go on." She gestures with her hands.

"I've never met anyone like her. From the moment I saw her, all I have done is think about her. Seeing her. Talking to her."

"And the problem is..."

"She's different. When I'm around her or think about her, I smile. It's hard to describe it to you."

"Ah, now I see." She says it like I dropped a truth bomb, and all is coming together for her.

"I saw her when I came out of the bathroom, but she's here with another guy. She says they are just friends."

"Why would you question her? Do you think she would lie to you?"

"No? Maybe? I don't know."

My head is hurting. I don't think she'd lie to me, but trust is earned, not given freely. I've been burned before, and it's part of who I am. The one time I gave it freely, it bit me in the ass—thanks to Maggie.

"Oh dear, you're in a real pickle."

"Gram, it's hard to trust, but with her, I don't want to question it. She seems sincere. But maybe I shouldn't be doing this."

Now talking with Gram about this, I think I'm making a mistake by asking Kendall on a date. I'm way better at one-night stands. I work a lot. Most women won't tolerate that kind of schedule.

"Ah, well, that's where you're wrong. This could be good for you, and you'll never know unless you decide to give it a shot."

"Ugh, I don't know. Kendall is independent, successful, and gorgeous. What can I offer her? Long workdays and canceled plans."

Gram's face lights up, and a broad smile spreads across her face. I can see all of her teeth.

"So her name is Kendall, huh? Okay, well, why don't you go home and think about how you're feeling right now, as she's having dinner with that other guy? Then grow some balls and get over yourself."

Gram never holds back and tells me like it is. I wouldn't want it any other way.

"Gram!" I laugh. "Why don't we get you home?"

"Pushing me home so soon. Was it something I said? Anyway, we can talk in the morning when you come to pick me up at 6:30."

"What are you talking about?"

I rarely forget things, so this is coming out of left field.

"Oh, you're going to help one of my friends move some furniture. Now, before you argue with me about how busy you are, it won't take too long."

I can't say no to Gram. I'll be moving furniture tomorrow morning.

"Alright, don't you want to meet me there?"

"No, it's better if you come to pick me up."

Once I pick up Gram the next morning, she becomes the GPS. The directions point to the downtown area. When we pull up to the curb, we're outside the Saxy Salon, Kendall's salon.

"Why don't you drop me off here, park, and I'll wait for you in the salon?"

"This salon?"

Does Gram know Kendall? Kendall will be surprised to see me. Just as surprised as I am dropping Gram off here.

"Yes, dear, this salon."

"Ah, okay."

"See you in a couple of minutes." Grams closes the car door and walks to the salon.

After parking the car, I use the walkway through the two brick buildings that leads me out onto Main Street. Pausing with my hand on the door handle, I take a deep breath and step into the salon. Immediately captivated by the vibe and the layout. It's not at all what I imagined or expected. Chandeliers hang from the ceiling, and stylish booths are set up with chairs. The reception desk is made of dark wood and features Kendall's logo. The bright red stands out—just like her.

When Kendall finally notices who walked in the door, her face falls, and her mouth opens. Yup, she's caught off guard and surprised to see me.

Rubbing the back of my neck, I need to say something, so I mutter, "Good morning."

"Good Morning...Dane. Can I help you with something?"

"Oh, dear...this is my grandson. The one I've been telling you about. How do you know his name?" she asks as her lips tug into a smile.

Gram gives that smirk as if she has something to hide. Did she know who I was talking about last night and decide it would be a good idea to bring me here today? Honestly, she's been trying to set me up with a couple of women for a while now. But she never mentioned any names. I'm thinking Kendall was at the top of her list.

Kendall tries to speak, but instead, she stumbles over her words. To help ease the discomfort of this conversation, I jump in.

"We've met before."

I'm not mentioning the date with Kendall tomorrow to Gram. I don't want to disappoint her if it doesn't work out. Although I'd be disappointed too.

"Yes, we have." Kendall is finally able to speak as the shock wears off.

Clasping her hands together, Gram says, "Oh, isn't this wonderful?"

I'm not sure if 'wonderful' is the right word to describe this situation, but I'm going with it.

From what I know of Kendall, this place is a reflection of her. Elegant, gorgeous, fiery. It's all wrapped up in the decor of this place. I'm really impressed and excited to see the spa she's been talking about. It will make this place even more exceptional.

I continued to look around the salon. "My gram told me you need help moving furniture. Want to show me the way?"

Gram finds a seat, pulls out her book, and says, "You two can move furniture, and I'll finish my book."

"Well then, right this way." Kendall gestures to the back.

The short hallway leads to the recently renovated space. I have to give it to the guy, Blake...his craftsmanship shows in his work. The tall ceilings in this old brick building, with everything exposed, give a modern feel. It's relaxing back here with the light green walls and paintings. It smells like citrus, and I make a mental note to schedule a massage appointment. I'm long overdue, especially with the stress of our most recent case. Usually, I hit up the one near the office, but I'd rather support her local business.

"If I didn't say it enough before, I want to thank you and make sure you know how much I appreciate what you did to help with the town."

"You're welcome again. It was nothing. You talked about this place with such passion; it was hard not to do something for you. Did you design this yourself?"

"Yes, with the help from Blake. He really brought my vision to life."

I walk a bit closer to her. She bites down on her bottom lip, and I swipe my thumb over it.

As if no one else is around, I stoop to meet her lips with mine. She is my kryptonite, and the need to kiss her is overwhelming. I slide my hand into her hair, moving her closer. My tongue slides on the seam of her lips; she opens for me, and our tongues are in sync. Within seconds, blood rushes to my cock, and I'm rock hard. I know she can feel it, and the roughness of our kiss turns ravenous with teeth clashing, and my hands slide under her dress to touch just under her tits. I don't even care that the dress rides all the way up. Neither does she, since she doesn't move to pull it back down.

I've been dreaming of a moment like this. When I saw her at the coffeehouse, I wanted to hold her longer. Now it's quiet here. The electrical shocks that are ricocheting between us only intensify the longer our lips are joined.

I can't stop. She tastes and feels too good for me to step away. There's a couch nearby I'd like to throw her down and fuck the shit out of her, but I shake that out of my thoughts, for now. Instead, I move my lips down to the crook of her neck and kiss her.

She moans and then whispers in my ear. "We really should move this furniture before your gram comes searching for us."

Moving my lips to her ear, I whisper, "That's probably a good idea."

Not wanting to move, I hold her for a few more seconds. Letting her go means I'll crave her again. When I have her in my arms, I feel alive, which is probably why I'm drawn to her with such fury. She fits in my arms, on my lips, in my bed. Taking in the scent of her shampoo, which smells like watermelon, I'll never forget it from the first time we met.

I finally step away from her. It's painful not to be close to her, to touch her. The ache in my body, in my chest. I rub the back of my neck and then run my hand down my shirt to smooth it out. My erection pushes against my zipper. Adjusting myself ever so quickly, I try to do it on the sly. But she notices; she always notices. And this morning, she can stare all she wants.

"Okay, let me know what needs to get moved."

She collects herself by fluffing her hair and smoothing down her dress. "Um, first, I want to say that I really enjoyed that." Staring into my eyes, I want to grab her again.

"I'd be lying if I said I didn't enjoy it, too. Could we reschedule our date for tonight?"

"Dane, I can't tonight, but you have me considering canceling. I really don't know what it is about you that makes me lose all sense of control." She pauses and bites her lip again. That kills me. Her green eyes shine back at me as she tilts her head and says, "To be clear, I'm not just a booty call. This is an actual date."

Thinking about what my next move will be, because although I love to be deep inside of her, there's more to this. I enjoy talking to her. She's someone I could share things with, and her personality is fiery and upbeat—just the way I like her. She keeps me on my toes. It's hard not to smile and be happy when I'm around her. Or just thinking about her.

"To be really clear, it's a date, date. Dinner, wining and dining...only the best for you."

Her lips form the widest smile, which reaches her gorgeous emerald eyes. It's hard not to stare into them and lose myself in what she's saying.

I haven't been on an actual date in a couple of years. But it seemed like a good idea, and now it seems like an even better idea, as I stand in front of her. Captivated by her beauty.

"I'm ready to be wined and dined. And you've just gone up a few notches because you're Jane's grandson. I love that woman, and she's been talking about you since she stepped foot in this salon three years ago."

Gram talks about me to Kendall? That's interesting information. I was unaware of how close they were. I never put two and two together until now.

With my eyebrow raised and a slight smirk on my face, I ask, "She has?"

"I'm her stylist, so of course, she talks to me about everything. I love the stories she shares with me about her husband, your grandfather. It seems like your grandparents were soulmates, and it's a privilege to hear her talk about their love while I do her hair."

I'm not sure why this shocks me.

"She has some great stories."

I look over at the couch as she says, "Thank you for your help. That couch needs to go to the relaxation room, which is down the hall. I can help you."

"That would be great." Any extra time with her, I'll take.

Once we move the couch to the room, I plant a quick kiss on her cheek, so she doesn't forget how I feel on her lips and her body. Lingering my hand on her face, I glide my thumb across her bottom lip.

THIRTEEN
Kendall

H e leans down and kisses me. Heat erupts like a volcano, and I slide my hands around his neck to have something to hold on to, as I melt into his body. His muscular arms hold me up, tugging me closer. Feeling his erection on my stomach, I open my lips ever so slightly, and it's an invitation for his tongue to slide in.

If we were here alone, I suspect we'd be on that couch or up against the wall. The thought of him slamming me against the wall gives me tingles and throbbing between my legs. With our lips together, it's like nothing I've ever felt. And I'm still wondering how we ended up here.

The kiss slows, and Dane pulls away first, staring into my eyes. He says, "My grandparents were soulmates. I wish I were that lucky." He takes his hand and gently touches my cheek, and slides it down my neck.

My breath hitches, and I swallow hard. How did we end up having this conversation again?

"From what she says, it has nothing to do with luck. Love finds you." I can't help but stare into his caramel eyes while butterflies threaten to take flight in my belly. My body needs to calm down. I can't get too invested in him. Reminding myself it's just dinner, and who knows if he'll even want to do it again. The newness might wear off. It's hard not to doubt his intentions.

He shakes his head and shrugs. "That's what she says."

I place my hand on his chest, and he draws me into his body. An intimate hug, as our arms wrap around each other in a way that makes my eyes close and my head rest on his chest. Breathing in him—coconut and palm trees—it tickles my nose yet relaxes my body. When his arms loosen around my body, I squeeze a little tighter. I'm not ready for him to let me go.

He nestles his face close to my ear and kisses me. "I'll hold you as long as you need me to."

My heart skips a beat, and my eyes jump open. His sultry voice sends shivers down my spine, and then he uses his fingers to stroke my back. I mold even further into his body. We stay there, soaking up the moment.

He slowly releases my body, and his hands linger on my hips. "What else can I do for you?"

I can think of all kinds of dirty things he can do for me, but I realize quickly that he was talking about the furniture. A smirk spreads across my face. "Oh, um..."

Dane looks at me and chuckles. I wonder if he has any inkling of what I was thinking about. He glides his thumb over my cheek. Closing my eyes and feeling him on my skin, I slowly open them.

I lead him down the hall. "Come this way and I'll show you where the rest of the furniture is."

He takes in what needs to be moved and says, "Let's get this done." His authoritative voice slides under my skin, and the hair on my arms stands on end. Holy shit. This guy is embedding himself into me one small gesture at a time, and that voice, oof, it's seeping into my body, drenching my panties.

Still questioning if this is a good idea—getting involved with him. Realizing I'm digging myself deeper.

After I explain where things need to go, I say, "Thank you so much for helping. I really appreciate it."

As Dane takes care of moving items for me, I head back to the salon area. Walking straight over to Jane, I say, "Thank you again for bringing your grandson to help me. Opening day will be spectacular. I look forward to showing you everything that's been completed. It's coming together perfectly thanks to Dane helping with the furniture this morning. It's a dream come true."

"Oh dear. You're very welcome. Dane is a sweetheart...once you get to know him."

What does she mean by that?

I take a minute and then mutter, "Yeah, he seems it."

"Exactly, you get him." She looks at me with loving eyes and a smirk.

"Acts of service are my love language; this means more to me than he will ever know. He's one of the good ones." I believe every word I'm saying to Jane. Yet, I have reservations, but I'm not giving it attention at the moment.

"I've been telling everyone. You're a local celebrity, Kendall."

"Ah, you're so sweet."

Dane swaggers out from the back looking handsome as hell. Oh man, if no one were here, we'd be all over each other. A part of me is thankful Jane is here. The other part is ready to get back into bed with him. I'm so conflicted. I've been waiting my entire life to feel a connection like this, but it's hard to think he'll change his whole life for me. No more one-night stands and settle down. I shake the thoughts and focus on this moment.

"Dane, thank you again." Reaching for his arm, my hand lands on his bicep. Feeling his strength under my hand is heavenly.

"If you need anything else, be sure to reach out. You have my number." Then he whispers, "See you tomorrow."

Squirming under his grandmother's watch, I feel her staring at us. It's like she knows what we were doing in the back. Is it written all over our faces? She can't possibly know, but she's picking up on something between us because I feel it too—the magnetic charge between us.

I move closer to Jane and place my hand on her shoulder. "Thank you for everything. You've been such a big supporter of the salon. See you for the soft opening."

Jane pulls me into a hug. "I wouldn't miss it for the world."

We let go of each other, and I look over to Dane, who is staring at me with eyes full of love and admiration. No, not for me, but I'm sure it's for his Gram. He really loves her. Bringing her here and helping me with the furniture warms my heart.

Walking them to the door and saying our goodbyes, I linger, then turn around to start my day and move about the salon, making sure everything is perfect for our clients. As I prepare my products, Sally, our receptionist, walks in the door.

I say, "Good morning."

"Good morning." Sally looks at me with an arched brow. "So who was that man who walked out this door with Jane?"

"You don't miss much, do you?" I shake my head at her.

She puts her coffee down on the counter and turns to me. "Give me all the details because I can tell by that smile on your face...you have something to tell me."

"You know how Jane has been trying to set me up with her grandson." I give her a pointed look. "Maybe I would have said yes if I had seen a picture of him. He has a look to him, huh?"

Sally settles into her chair behind the reception desk and says, "He needs to take you on a date." She is fanning herself.

"Well, Jane doesn't know, but he already asked me on a date."

I wasn't about to tell her the one-night stand story. That is for another day, at this point. When you think you have life figured out, you are thrown for a loop.

Deciding it's time to cut the Dane talk, I say, "He seems great, and I'm looking forward to our date. But I don't see it leading anywhere too serious; he just doesn't strike me as the settling down kind."

"I mean, it might just be a fun night." She winks at me and laughs.

"Alright, enough about that; let's finalize these details for the openings."

My phone vibrates, and I glance down to see Dane's text.

Dane:

> Seeing you this morning is the highlight of my day. If I had known, I'd have brought you a coffee.

FOURTEEN
Dane

After I drop Gram off at her house, I hit up my home gym, trying to burn off some of this restless energy. Kendall has me on edge, my mind racing. When I was close to her, it felt like my whole body was vibrating. Touching her, kissing her—it felt instinctual.

As I work out, my phone vibrates. It's a text from her, and I don't think this smile is leaving my face anytime soon.

Kendall:

> Coffee would have been fabulous. But really, thank you for moving all that furniture.

Seeing her this morning has me on a high. Working out helps me think through things for work, but today it's not work that floods my mind—just her.

I keep my workout to thirty minutes and am still sweating profusely. I'll probably head into the office today. Weekends are workdays for me. So, I make my way to the kitchen first to fill up my water bottle and head straight to my shower. There's a mountain of work waiting at the office, and Logan can't handle it all alone. I'm surprised he hasn't texted me to see when I'll be in. Usually, I'm already at the office by now on a Saturday.

Once I'm in the shower, I can't shake off this inner reckoning. Maggie crushed my heart and my soul. I've been living under the impression that I shouldn't date anyone, that it would save me the heartache. One-night stands solved that problem until Kendall. I have no idea what I'm doing, but what I do know—she might be worth it.

The water from multiple showerheads pummels my body. I had the shower custom-built, and I can control the temperature and pressure. It's luxurious, especially after a workout when my muscles need some heat and massaging. As I step out of the shower, I reach for my towel and dry off my body.

My feet sound softly against the hardwood floor of my enormous room, each step measured and purposeful. In the spacious walk-in closet, roughly the size of a small bedroom, there are custom-built shelves and drawers. Deciding to head into the office casually, I grab a pair of dark jeans, a crisp white button-down shirt, and slide them on. A last glance in the mirror reveals a face that has seen too many sleepless nights, prompting me to run my fingers through my slightly disheveled hair.

Scanning the room for my phone, I spot it sitting on my bed. The urge to text Kendall about our date is overwhelming. Even though I just texted her an hour ago, I can't hold back and just do it.

Dane:

I can't get you off my mind… dress up tomorrow. I'm taking you somewhere special.

Kendall:

It was like a sauna in here earlier ;) Okay! Is it a secret?

Dane:

Yes!

Kendall:

Secret, huh?! Can I guess?

I could hear a pin drop when I walked into the office. On the long table, my brother, Logan, sits with his head cradled in his hands, frustration seeping into the air. The case we're working on has proven to be a relentless storm of complications. The sun blasts through the wall of windows, illuminating the huge glass-topped conference table. With over a dozen chairs around the table, it's hard to think that this is our second home these days.

I pause at the doorway, silently bracing myself, and then stride in, closing the door firmly behind me. "What now?" I ask, my tone half-ironic and laced with exasperation.

Logan lowers his hands to his face, mumbling between strained breaths, "This case is going to be the death of me." His voice is heavy with despair as he gestures vaguely toward a corner where the clutter of a dozen boxes looms ominously.

My jaw is tight. "No shit! Another endless cascade of problems?"

With a frustrated sigh, Logan explains, "The prosecutor's office dropped off all those damn files after you left last night." He points toward a mountain of evidence-filled boxes, as if they were ready to engulf us entirely.

I rub my temples. "Alright, let's recruit a couple of interns for this. We need to move through these quickly." I stride purposefully over to the pile, methodically shifting boxes onto the conference table, each thud echoing our shared exasperation.

The two of us quickly sift through the first stacks, sorting them into piles of obviously irrelevant documents and a separate stack we plan to catalog. Amid the controlled chaos, Logan can't help but tease, arching an eyebrow as he jabs, "Why are you so late this morning,

Dane? Another late-night rendezvous with the flavor of the night?" His tone is teasing, yet laced with genuine curiosity.

I shoot back with a curt, "Fuck off," all while rifling through yet another box. "Gram had me doing chores early this morning. I can't ever say no to her," I add with a dismissive shake of my head.

Logan chuckles, shaking his head as if recalling an old, inescapable charm. "Nobody can say no to Gram."

I offer a wry smile as I continue pulling out files. "Yeah, I ended up moving furniture for a downtown business owner."

"You need to give me more than that vague answer. This is the second time. Give me the details on her," Logan probes with a hint of amusement.

Desperate to steer the conversation back to our ever-demanding case files, I avert my gaze from Logan and focus on the documents spread before us. "Oh, just the hair salon that Gram goes to," I say vaguely, hoping to keep it light, and he'll be satisfied with that information.

Logan's eyes widen with curiosity as he leans in slightly. "Are you talking about Kendall's salon? Wait, she's the one you went downtown for, too?" His tone betrays genuine interest as he contemplates the unexpected twist in our morning chatter.

"Eh, yeah, how do you know her?"

"I've had to drop Gram off there a few times over the years. The fiery redhead. I'm sure you noticed." He winks at me knowingly.

I rub the back of my neck. "Yeah, I noticed." Feeling thankful Logan wasn't there at Buena Vista's the night I met Kendall. The night she crept into my subconscious. Not knowing what I was getting myself into. Shaking off the feeling, I look up to see my brother staring at me. "What?"

He searches for something, anything to give him a clue. Looking at me with his skeptical eyes, "So..."

Shit. He knows me too well. As I try not to give away too much, I say, "Yes, she seems nice enough." I keep myself moving and distracted from this conversation. "These files are chock-full of irrelevant paperwork. It's going to take us hours to rifle through all this crap to find the one or two pieces of paper they fucking buried in here."

Logan stands up and moves to the boxes that sit on the table. He riffles through the pile of irrelevant paperwork to confirm it's not worth keeping. "Yeah, I don't know how an intern is going to help. We might need to pull Kai in for this. He's detail-oriented, and we had him on this case earlier. Let's get him in here."

While Logan takes care of the pile, I pick up the conference room phone and slam my index finger onto the keys for Kai's number. It rings three times before he picks up. "Kai, can you come to the 5th-floor conference room within the hour?"

Without hesitation, he says, "Be right there."

"Before Kai arrives, is there something going on between you...and Kendall?" His eyes are soft, and I'm wondering what he's thinking.

"Nah, she's just another really hot chick I wouldn't mind fucking," I say with as much conviction as I can muster.

"Cool, cool," he says before moving on to the next pile.

Kai doesn't live far from the office, so it was no surprise he'd show up quickly. The minute he walks in, we debrief him. The rest of the morning was spent sorting through the boxes. Kai finds an important piece of paperwork—a document that the prosecutor definitely tried to hide in these boxes. It could be our smoking gun. Dragging the whiteboard over to connect the dots of the day in question, we comb through the day minute by minute. We mark down the holes in the prosecutor's timeline, and this document proves our guy wasn't where the prosecutor says he was. Finally, we catch a break.

It's well past lunchtime, and I hear Kai's stomach growl. "Let's take a break."

"I'm hitting up the corner diner; want something?" Kai offers.

"I'll take a Reuben," I say.

"Make that two," Logan pipes in from behind the pile of boxes on the floor. He looks determined to find something.

The minute I stop focusing on this case, my thoughts are like a movie in my mind. With my hands on her face, our tongues play like we can't keep our hands off each other. And then the memory again of her fiery red hair fanned on my pillow, like that first night we met.

Needing a break from looking at this paperwork, I snag my phone from the table and decide to write Kendall back. Leaning back in my chair, tipping it onto the back two legs, I text her.

Dane:

You can ask three questions, and I'll even give you a hint. We need to take a ferry.

I watch to see if she reads it and responds, but after five minutes, I put my phone back on the table.

"Bro, hey! I've been talking to you, and you're somewhere else." Logan looks at me with concern.

I really don't want to confide in him, but he'll figure it out.

"You can't say anything to anyone. Seriously, I'm confiding in you," I respond, staring daggers his way, letting him know I'm fucking serious.

"Guy, I'm definitely busting your balls, but I always have your back. You know that," he says as he strides over to the table. "What's up with you, and who are you texting?"

"Kendall..."

"Oh, shit!" He doesn't say another word as he leans in closer to me, waiting for the words to come out of my mouth.

It takes a few extra beats before I'm able to even open my mouth, but finally, "I slept with her a few weeks ago and...well, I can't stop thinking about her. She's stuck in my head."

"Did you catch...feelings?" He looks at me, confused, with furrowed brows and a teasing tone.

I take a deep breath, trying to find the right words to share with him without sounding like I'm already pussy-whipped. I dive headfirst into the story about her, all of it from the one-night stand to the visit to the building department, the coffeehouse, the texting, and I end with this morning's furniture moving. He's shocked and can't speak a word. Speechless. That hardly ever happens with Logan.

"I don't fucking know."

"What's all this talk about a girl?" asks Dad. Of all the fucking timing, he walks in on *this* conversation.

"Nah, just another random girl." Logan jumps in to brush off the conversation as no big deal.

"Well, you know, son, we have standards in this family."

Here we fucking go. If I have to hear him on his soapbox about how we can only date certain types of women—ones who come from powerful families, with money and political influence. I might walk out the door. I have to hear his speech a few times a year ever since I broke up with Maggie. Logan is lucky. He got off scot-free when he married his high school sweetheart. He'll try to hold me to that standard, but he allowed Logan to marry someone who didn't meet all the criteria. Let him try that shit with me.

"Dad, you tell me all the time. I hear you," I say, not making eye contact.

"Well, a lot is riding on your image, son," he says sternly with his finger pecking at the air.

He can say whatever the fuck he wants. I'll marry—well, if I ever do—who I want. For love. Not for status, not for his bullshit inheritance clause or anything else.

Lean casually in my chair with my arms overhead and say, "Isn't it time to move on from that ideology, Dad?"

"You have responsibilities to this family," he snaps, his face turning red.

"Okay, okay. Logan and I need to focus our attention back on this case. Is there anything else?" Being dismissed is not something you do to Edward Walsh, but he has no choice with both of his sons sitting at the table. He lets out a deep sigh and leaves the conference room.

Logan looks at me with sympathy. "Man, you're under a microscope."

"Yeah, I know! I haven't had to worry about it, and who knows, maybe this thing with Kendall won't even amount to anything serious."

I lift myself off the chair and say, "I need some fresh air. I'll be back in a few. Let me know when Kai gets back." Picking up my phone, I walk out the door.

FIFTEEN

Kendall

With back-to-back clients, the day flew by, and I took periodic peeks at my phone. I don't want to get my hopes up with Dane, but it's tough when we are exchanging text messages that have me replaying our time this morning. His lips on mine. His hands on my body. And my heart beats faster.

Finally, everyone is gone for the day, and I can text Dane back.

Kendall:

Hmmm…I do like a good surprise, and now I can ask questions :)

Dane:

You caught me taking a break from the case. What's your first question? Only one at a time.

Kendall:

That was a good hint. How long will we be on the ferry?

I waited a couple of minutes, hoping for a quick response that didn't come. As I sweep up the last of the hair, everyone else is cleaning up their stations. Taking my apron off and hanging it up, I switch out of my work shoes for a comfy pair of slip-ons. I grab my purse and say goodbye to everyone.

Heading quickly to my car in the back, I slide into the driver's seat—enjoying the feel of the expensive leather on my skin. With hope, I glance at my phone to see if Dane messaged back. Nothing yet. Taking a deep breath, I start my car and pull out onto Main Street.

It takes me only ten minutes before I'm pulling into Lane's driveway. I jump out of the car and power-walk to the side door. Time spent with friends is always therapeutic. Even more so when one of your best friends is a therapist.

I knock and walk in, saying, "Hey, I'm here."

Lane comes around the corner and gives me a big hug. "What's going on? I didn't think you were going to make it tonight."

"I was running a bit behind at the salon." I throw myself into one of her kitchen chairs. Looking around dramatically as I say, "So...I heard you might be doing some updating around here."

"And where might you have heard that?" she asks, taking a seat at the table across from me, eyeing me with suspicion.

"It just so happens that I went out to dinner with Blake last night."

She interrupts me with an arched eyebrow. "And you had dinner with him because..."

"You know he's been asking me for a while, and I said yes." I give her a pointed look. "But, I heard from him that you are updating your kitchen. When were you going to tell me, tell your friends?"

"It's not that big of a deal, Kendall." She averts her eyes.

I'm not buying it. She was keeping this close to her chest. I'm more than a little interested in what she's thinking about Blake and this kitchen renovation.

"So when are you meeting with him?" I prod, knowing full well, they met this afternoon.

She hesitates and fidgets in her seat, but then says, "He came over this afternoon."

"Oh, this afternoon, huh?" Lane hasn't said a word to us. She must have known I'd find out.

They would be such a cute couple. I'd like to see them together. An idea pops into my head. I can make that happen during the soft opening. Lane will be there, and so will Blake. I'm always looking for ways to set up my friends as their personal matchmaker. I live vicariously through them, since I haven't been interested in dating. Well, not until this week, when I couldn't seem to say no to Dane.

I glance at my phone again to see that he has finally responded.

Dane:

> I knew you were smart AND gorgeous! One hour and fifteen minutes...

I'm giddy and glance up to see Lane staring back at me. My smile doesn't go unnoticed.

She pipes up and makes a circle in the air with her finger. "What's all that for, and who's texting you?"

Phew. I'm saved by Faith and Addison, who barge through the side door with bags of groceries in their arms.

"What is all this?" Lane says as she helps them with the bags. Setting the bags on the counter, one of them falls, and the groceries spill out.

"We're going all out with our ice cream sundaes tonight," Faith says as she removes bottles of toppings from the bag. Then I see four containers of ice cream that are pulled out as well.

Lane nudges me. "You're not getting out of this."

Faith and Addison look over at us, waiting for any more comments. Then, Addison moves closer to us and squints her eyes. "What's going on?"

My mind races through images of this morning with Dane, and the electricity that was between us. It was hard to ignore. There's no way I'm getting out of sharing with them. And we share everything, so...

"Okay, you're never going to believe who showed up at the salon this morning with my client Jane." I shrug and shake my head.

"I love Jane. She's such an amazing older woman—full of wisdom," says Lane.

"Remember that guy from Buena Vista—Dane. Also, the one who took care of the permits..."

Everyone is nodding as they stare back at me on the edge of their seats.

"What?!" they all yell in unison.

"Yup! I couldn't believe my eyes when he came strolling in the door this morning. I think he was just as shocked as I was. He's Jane's grandson, you know, the one she's been trying to set me up with forever?"

With Faith's hands still to her mouth, just as she's dragging them away, she says, "More details...how did he end up at your salon? This sounds juicy."

I fill them in from the minute he walked into the salon to the moment he walked out.

"Holy shit." Addison blows out her words. "That's unreal."

"You have no idea." Thoughts of his hands and mouth roaming all over my body—touching and kissing me this morning.

Faith nudges my shoulder. "What are you thinking?"

"I just..." I take a quick breath. "He's been really nice and has been pursuing me with text messages all week...I said yes to a date tomorrow," I say, letting that hang in the air as they process.

Addison stumbles over her words. "I... wait...you are going on a date?" As she says date, the other two chime in with 'tomorrow'.

My friends are the best. It's been over ten years, and we know how to entice each other for information.

"You can't just drop a bomb like that and let it linger," Addison fires out.

"You're in deep, aren't you?" my wonderful therapist friend, Faith, asks.

The words hit me like a brick, and my arms cross over the table as my head bangs down on my forearms. "I think so, but I don't want to get my hopes up."

I lift my head slightly and take a peek at their faces—full of warmth and a bit of concern.

Faith rubs my forearm. "Tell us more."

"He's been so attentive. His actions have shown a side of him I didn't expect after that one-night stand. It feels different. I feel different. The sparks that fly when we are close—it's jolting." I lean back in my chair and shrug. "I'm excited for this date. The text messages keep me tethered to him, and my belly does somersaults every time I read them."

Lane slides in closer. "You went through a lot with Jake, and I'm sure it's hard to even contemplate a relationship with a guy, especially someone who makes you feel gooey inside. I haven't heard of sparks flying with any other guys. There haven't been that many, anyway."

"I don't want to fall into a trap either. Jake sucked me in with manipulation that was dressed in charm and attention. It took so long for me to twist out of his grip. I'm trying to look at the positive and see where it goes. I'll admit it's hard."

"Then you see where it goes, have your eyes wide open," Lane says as she lifts herself from the chair.

We all finally decide on our sundaes and sit back at the kitchen table. The clinking of spoons on the bowls rings like a symphony of goodness as we all dig into our ice cream.

With ice cream still in my mouth, I ramble on about Dane. "His grandmother says he's a sweetheart, but don't all grandmothers think that?"

"Yeah, but it's a nice insider look into how she views him—maybe she knows the real guy under all those one-night stands," Lane pipes in.

"I guess you're right...I invited him to the grand opening."

Addison taps on the table. "If he shows up to the grand opening with everyone there, I think he earns some points for that. He's not trying to keep it a secret."

"Here's the thing." I rub my temples and sigh. "He whispered to me when he left the salon so his Gram couldn't hear that we were going on a date. What do you think that's all about? It has me reeling a bit. I can't figure out why he wouldn't just tell her."

"There could be many reasons. Something to talk about on your date. I understand why you would think there's something wrong with that. It's odd, but don't forget he just asked you minutes prior," says Faith.

"It gives me pause to think he wouldn't want his Gram to know. Maybe he doesn't want anyone to know. That gives me Jake vibes," I say, and an icy chill runs through me with the thought of Jake.

Jake was so controlling of everything that I did, the people I saw, and he manipulated me in a way that I didn't even give a second thought—until it was too late. Not falling into a trap like that again is really important for my mental health and overall well-being. It's taken me a while to work through some of the madness and all the confusion it brought along with it.

"You've grown since that whole situation. It's time to take a risk and see where it goes tomorrow. I'm so proud of you for saying yes to a date with Dane. That took courage, Kendall. You are a strong woman, and you deserve to be happy."

I stand up and give Faith a hug first. "Thank you for that. It's exactly what I needed. I guess I'll find out tomorrow and make the next decision."

"Oh, you need to ask another question. It's kind of a fun way to find out, guess, or eventually be surprised," says Addison.

"Well, I know the only ferry that is that long goes to Long Island, unless you guys have a different guess?"

Lane shifts in her seat. "That's correct, so..." She digs out her phone. "Let's look at what's around there when you get off the ferry."

"Oh, oh, ask him how far from the ferry port the secret location is." Faith smiles brightly at all of us.

"Yes, that's a good one."

Kendall:

How far is the secret location from the port?

Holding my phone, it vibrates immediately after sending.

Dane:

What are you up to?

Kendall:

Playing detective with my friends, trying to figure out your secret date location. What are you doing?

Dane:

Walking through the garage door after working all day.

Kendall:

Damn! I thought I was the only one who worked late on a Saturday.

Dane:

Guess we have some things in common.

Kendall:

Yeah, we do… so what's the answer to my question?

Dane:

Oh yes… I was trying not to answer your question.

I glance up from my phone, and three pairs of eyes are staring back at me.

"Oh, we are just chatting about work stuff."

They nod their heads. Faith says, "Well, has he answered your next question?"

"Not yet."

> I'm getting in my hot tub. It's been a long day. You are more than welcome to join me...

I giggle to myself while an audience watches me.

"You can't keep it all to yourself." Addison leaves her seat to read over my shoulder. I share everything, so it doesn't matter.

She's hitting my shoulder as she says, "He's inviting you over to soak in his hot tub. Um...you're going right?"

My head swings so fast I think it might fly off my neck. "Are you crazy?"

"Apparently, I am, since I would absolutely run to my car and drive to his house with an invitation like that." Addison smiles at me.

"You're a bad influence on me."

Her head tilts back, and she belly laughs so loud it echoes through the living room. She can't stop herself.

Faith says, "You know you're usually a bad influence on all of us, right?"

I grin because she's right. "I can't just go over there. A date is a good next step, not ending up in his hot tub where we won't be able to keep our hands off each other."

Lane stands up from her seat and leans her body against mine. "You're no fun." She says it in a voice that sounds familiar—mine. It's my favorite line to my friends. I'm usually the one taking risks and going after what I want. But this...the intense electricity in my body when he touches me—it's different from what I've ever felt with anyone else.

Interrupted by my phone.

> Are you considering my invitation to come over?

> Not tonight…but I may not be able to resist if you invite me tomorrow.

The heat rises up my neck, and my cheeks are on fire.

Addison leans over, trying to read my text messages. "Share."

I do. And I'm wishing the date were tonight instead.

All our bowls are empty; one by one, we get up, rinse, and put them into the dishwasher. Lane walks toward the living room. With our feet scuffing along her hardwood floors, we follow her, and I plop myself down.

I glance at Lane, trying to take the pressure off the text messages and tomorrow night's date. "What's it like now that school is out?"

"This past week, I was outside in my chair reading. I've also taken a few walks."

"Nice way to relax and decompress from the school year," says Faith.

"Anything else you have?" I air quote, "going on."

"Yes…Kendall, I do." Lane side-eyes me.

I jump in and say, "And…"

"Oh my, you are relentless."

"I know."

"Blake came over this afternoon to discuss my kitchen renovation. I've been talking about this for a while, and when Kendall spoke so highly of him, I reached out."

"Oh..." Faith says as she moves her elbows onto her thighs and leans into Lane.

We are all anxious for Lane to continue, but we know better. Silence is the killer for her.

"He's just renovating my kitchen. What are all these looks for?" She points at each of us.

"Hot contractor to the rescue," I say with a smirk.

"OMG, yes, he looks hot as hell in those jeans that fit perfectly around his ass and hug his thighs. And I may be looking forward to my air conditioning breaking so he has to take his shirt off," she giggles at herself.

"I knew it! You find him attractive."

She shakes her head. "Who wouldn't? But that's not why he's here. New subject. You've been busy preparing for the openings. Once it's all over, we need to finalize our girls' trip for this winter."

"Fine. We'll let it go for now, but we want weekly updates of your kitchen renovation." I wiggle my eyebrows dramatically. "Well, my focus this week is getting everything situated, so leading up to the openings, there are only final touches that need to happen...I'm also hoping for less stress." I'm on the edge of my seat. The energy rolling through my body for the opening is contagious. "Oh, and I was interviewed by a couple of newspapers after sending in the press release a few weeks ago. Those will run the week of the grand opening."

"I can't wait to be there for the soft opening. Are you still having mini-sessions for all the spa services?" Faith asks.

"Not all of them, but we will have chair massages, and the Himalayan salt rooms will all be open for ten-minute mini-sessions. Then we'll have our local artisan store items for sale, along with unlimited time in the relaxation/meditation rooms. The soft opening will help me market the spa with some testimonials and professional pictures of the space and event."

My energy is buzzing from all the excitement that will lead up to the big day. I decided one day this was what I wanted to do, and it's all coming to fruition.

"That all sounds perfect, Kendall," Addison says, leaning forward. "What can we help with?"

"Right now, it's all under control. But if you want to come an hour earlier, just in case. You know there are always those last-minute things I'll need help with."

I probably have a few hours of decorating and cleaning to do. Thankfully, I love doing it. Well, not so much the cleaning, which is why I have a company coming in on Thursday night to do a deep cleaning of the entire salon and spa. There was a lot of dust from the construction, and this will clean up any lingering dust.

Faith looks around the room at everyone to confirm and says, "We can all be there ready to help with whatever you need."

I stand and give my friends a hug. "Thank you! I'm so fortunate to have you guys in my life. The ice cream and girl time were just what I needed tonight, but I'm exhausted."

SIXTEEN

Dane

The jets beat on my back muscles as I roll my neck, trying to stretch out the knots. Snagging my phone off the nearby table, I reread Kendall's text. I sure as hell am going to invite her back here after our date. The thoughts running through my mind with her in the hot tub next to me. It's making my dick hard. I shake it off and respond to her.

Dane:

Then you have an open invite… anytime. You, me, the hot tub, and no need for a bathing suit.

Kendall:

If I don't, then neither do you ;)

This woman—she's feisty, sassy, and she will be all mine. Tomorrow night, I will treat her like the strong, independent woman that she is.

I'm starting to sweat way too much. Time to hop out and shower. Drying myself off, I hang up the towel on the hook by the hot tub and make my way inside. As I step into the bathroom with the cool floor on my feet, I stare at my reflection in the mirror. It reminds me I haven't been sleeping well. I undress and slip into the cold spray of the shower, cooling off my body.

Once I'm done in the bathroom, I pull the covers down on my bed and slide in. It doesn't take me long, and my eyes are so heavy I crash into a deep sleep.

In my dream, I see Kendall's face, her smile, her lightness. She's like an angel twirling in a white dress. The sun is beaming down on her like a spotlight. I'm in awe of her beauty and her fiery red hair flying in the air all around her. I feel a smile spread across my face as I watch her. Then our eyes meet, the excitement and heaviness in my chest, and all I want to do is hold her in my arms. She never breaks eye contact as she moves her body toward me. Her smile never leaves her face. When she finally stands in front of me, I reach up, cup her face, and caress her cheek with my thumb. She leans into my touch. Those emerald green eyes hypnotize me, like I can't look away from her if I wanted to. She has a hold on me. My entire body is electrified, sparks firing as I gently press my lips to hers.

Then there's a ringing noise that has my head spinning as I look for the source.

Turning ever so slightly back to Kendall, she's gone. Vanished. *Where did she go?*

The ringing is getting louder and louder. Just as I try to move, I realize I'm in bed. The sheets are tangled around my legs.

Once I untangle myself from the sheets, I sit up and run my hand over my face. I glare over at my nightstand, where my phone is lit while the alarm keeps ringing. Reaching over, I slam the stop button to shut the alarm off. I groan. A few more hours of sleep wouldn't hurt, but the day must begin, so I throw my legs over the edge and lift myself off the bed.

First things first—coffee. My mug is full, and the sun is shining, which means I'm sitting out on the deck to drink my coffee. Dropping myself in the chair, I kick my feet onto the ottoman. With my phone in my hand, I find the text messages with Kendall. Rereading them, a smile takes over my face. She isn't even here; just thinking about her makes me smile. I haven't smiled like this in a very long time.

Dane:

> Good morning, Gorgeous! I've been thinking...what if we start our date a little earlier? Noon work for you?

Not thinking she'll respond immediately, I'm about to exit the message, and I see three dots.

Kendall:

> Noon? You're bold. You didn't even answer my question from last night. Dodging me already?

Dane:

> If I tell you, it will ruin the surprise. And you strike me as the type who loves to be teased. So... you sure you want to ruin the fun?

Kendall:

> Fun is my middle name. Don't tempt me with a good time. I love surprises.

Dane:

> Then be ready at noon. And Kendall...wear something that'll make it really hard for me to be a gentleman.

I can absolutely do that :)

Noon can't come soon enough for me. My palms are sweaty, and I keep wiping them on my shorts. It's like I don't know how to act. I've been on plenty of dates—well, maybe not dates. Casual hookups are usually my thing. This woman makes me nervous, which is laughable considering I can go toe-to-toe with some pitbull defense attorneys and not flinch. This woman, though, has my blood flowing in all the places, including my dick. No questions asked, but now? Now I'm standing here, and it's still an hour before I pick her up. Fuck it. I'm picking her up now.

Swiping my keys off the ring, I stalk out to my car and jump in. On the way to pick her up, I think about spending time with her, getting to know her, and soaking up her sass. I'm feeling like a teenager on my first date with a girl. I shake my head at myself. I already know she's someone special, and I can't deny the instant attraction we had; now, it's intensified. I want to touch every part of that gorgeous body, but first... our official date.

I turn into her driveway. Running my hand over my hair and down to my beard, it's go time. I didn't bother texting her. She said she likes surprises, so this is one of them.

As my foot hits the bottom step, she opens the door. "What are you doing here?"

"Surprise!" I say with a bright smile.

Kendall is shaking her head. All I see is her red, fiery hair swaying in the air around her, like a goddess. She is wearing shorts and a tank top, with no bra—definitely no bra.

Keep your eyes up.

"You can't show up unannounced an hour early to pick up a girl!" Crossing her arms over her chest and staring at me with daggers, she doesn't move.

With my eyes glued to hers, one foot in front of the other, I move toward her. She stands her ground. Lifting my hand, I brush a stray piece of hair back behind her ear. "You look gorgeous in anything...or nothing." A sly grin passes over my face as I drag the back of my fingers over her cheek.

She closes her eyes, and I lean in to kiss her cheek. When she opens her eyes and feels me on her cheek, she chuckles. "Is this your way of distracting me?"

"Is it working?" My other hand holds her face, and I kiss her cheek one more time before saying, "You can take as long as you need to get ready."

"You're ridiculous."

"I won't argue with that."

Grabbing my hand, she leads me inside with no hesitation. Her confidence is radiating, and it's attracting me to her with extreme force. We take a quick right and end up in the living room. She tries to swing me around to sit on the couch, but I'm too strong. I end up sliding my hands over her arms and tugging her to me.

Gazing into her eyes, I move closer to her ear and whisper, "Go get ready. I want to take you out and show you the time of your life."

She squeezes my biceps. "Okay, then give me fifteen minutes. I'll be ready."

"I'll be waiting."

Off she goes, swaying those sweet curves across the room. I stand up and look around her living room. Pictures of Kendall with a group of friends, which appear to span time, possibly starting in college. Her hair stands out in each of the photos, and then her smile captivates me. As I start at one end and make my way to the other, she becomes even more gorgeous with age.

I hear her shoes clicking on the hardwood floor. Turning around, I watch her walk into the room. Stunning. She takes my breath away;

my feet automatically meet hers. "You are gorgeous." Sliding my hands through her hair, my thumbs linger near her cheeks. Her eyes close as I caress her cheeks in a circular motion, and she lays her hands over mine. Touching her. The heat from her hands sends fire through my arms, and like a wildfire, it spreads through my body.

Resisting her is impossible. I'm drawn to her every time she is in the same room as me; I just can't keep my hands off of her. Or my lips.

With her eyes still closed, I dip down and glide my lips along her skin. So close to her lips, they move. She wants it too. Dragging my tongue over her bottom lip, she lets out a gasp. "Dane."

"Kendall, I can't keep my hands off you."

Opening her eyes, she stares deep into me. "I thought you came over early to start our date."

"You're right." I rub the back of my neck and then scratch my beard. Picking her up and bringing her to bed would be the perfect way to spend the time before heading to the ferry, but she's right; there's more to today than having sex. Although we could start with it if she wanted. But it seems like she wants something more.

I slide my hands down her arms. "We could..."

SEVENTEEN
Kendall

"We could, but we aren't going to." I raise my eyebrow.

Although I wouldn't mind... I want more than another night with him. The feelings that roll through me when I'm around him—I know I can't do casual with him. Is that all he wants, to be casual? I thought this was a date, an actual date to get to know each other better. Maybe start something with him, but my life is too busy with work and my friends to get involved with someone who is a one-night guy.

"Hey," Dane says as he tips my chin with his fingers. "Where's that smile that I love?"

I try to fake it, but I've never been good at that.

"You're terrible at faking it." He winks at me. "I know when it's real. You can't fool me."

I laugh and shake my head. "What are we doing today?"

"It's a surprise. Come on."

He lingers close to me for another few seconds. He touches my arm one more time, leaving a wake of fire on my skin. Then, he moves his hands down to mine, clasps them, and tugs me to him.

"Today will be a day we remember as one of the best dates ever."

"You're pretty confident."

He stands up a little taller. "Yeah, I am."

Twisting and dropping one of my hands, he interlaces the other with mine. He guides me outside to his car and opens the door for me to slide in. I watch him stalk around the car, flexing his arms as they move through the air.

Is it hot in this car?

He sits in the driver's seat and looks over at me. "Ready?"

"Do I have a choice?"

"Sweetheart, you always have a choice with me."

With my hand raised to my heart, it melts with his voice. Then I realize he called me 'sweetheart.' Oh, that's probably just a reflex, but I'm hopeful it's not.

I feel the blush on my cheeks as he reaches over and gently moves his fingers over my cheek. The feeling sends warmth ripping through my body and down to my core. Every nerve ending is firing one after the other. I want him to touch me forever; I like how his touch makes me feel.

He turns over the engine, and we drive, listening to his playlist. My kind of music: all 90s and 2000s. There was one point where we were both singing along. Me into my imaginary microphone, and him shouting at the top of his lungs. Carefree. Fun. Memorable moments.

"Are we almost there?"

He brings his hand over to touch and squeezes my leg. "Almost."

He leaves his hand on my thigh. With slight hesitation, I lay my hand on top of his. His eyes meet mine, and neither of us can help but smile—at each other, at the heat radiating from where we are touching.

I break eye contact to look out the windshield, and in front of us are the beach and the ocean. "I didn't bring my bathing suit."

"We can walk on the beach if you want, but I have other plans."

I'm giddy, but keeping it in is hard. I love surprises. I love the beach. No doubt he's going to hit this date out of the park, but I'll keep that to myself for now. Don't want it to boost his ego too much. I giggle to myself.

"What's so funny over there?" He shakes my leg a bit as he parks near the entrance to the beach.

"We have VIP parking?" I ask, shocked.

"Only for the best."

He jumps out of the car, runs around to my door, and opens it up. He stoops down with one hand outstretched; I take it, and he lifts me to my feet. Our fingers intertwine as we walk on the sidewalk for a few minutes. The salty sea air invades my nose. While I sneak a peek into each store we walk by, there are a couple of gift shops where you can buy sweatshirts and T-shirts, boogie boards, and sand toys. Then there's a jewelry store with a window display of aquamarine pieces—rings, necklaces. A consignment shop with racks on the sidewalk of bright colored shirts and dresses. I'm tempted to lead him into the store, but I'll wait for the walk back.

He stops abruptly at a restaurant called *Nick's On the Boardwalk*, opens the door, and guides me inside. It's nothing like I expected. Dane seems like an over-the-top kind of guy, but this restaurant is far from it. I'm not disappointed; actually, I'm pleasantly surprised. There are lobster traps and a large net with fake lobsters hanging from the ceiling. My eyes need to adjust to the dark wood floors and dim lighting.

The hostess says, "Table for two?"

"Yes, can we grab a seat on the patio?"

"Of course, right this way."

She leads us through the dark and somewhat dingy dining room. If they turned the lights up a bit, it might not be that bad. The sun is blinding the moment we step onto the patio, music vibrating through the speakers, and people talking and laughing fill the air. And the most perfect high-top seat by the railing overlooks the beach and ocean. Ships passing by, a cool breeze on my face, and over on the left is the boardwalk.

"Here are your menus, and your waitress will be over shortly."

"Dane, this is surprisingly breathtaking. You had me there for a minute. The inside was a bit dark and dingy."

Dane laughs and scratches his beard. "I wondered what you were thinking. Though you didn't leave too much to the imagination with the scowl that was on your face."

"I did not." Slapping him on his arm, yet feeling slightly embarrassed that I probably had a face on. It happens. I try to keep it locked up, but it occasionally escapes.

His eyes squint at me while still scratching his beard. "If you say so. Let's order some drinks."

Since it's only a little after noon, I have a margarita. The waitress comes over, and he gestures for me to order first. Then, he says, "I'll have an IPA; you choose."

"Okay, I'll be back with your drinks and a round of water."

The vibe is laid back, with everyone wearing beachwear and sandals or flip-flops. It's my kind of place.

We both open up the menu and browse it. The lobster roll is calling my name. I close the menu and gaze out onto the beach. People watching at its finest. Kids playing in the sand, people walking around, some alone, some in groups, and others holding hands. It's a mix of everyone doing their thing.

"Let's play a game."

He looks at me with his head tilted. "A game?"

"Yeah, people watching is fun; add another layer and we have out-of-this-world fun."

"You had me at fun. What's this game all about?"

I move closer to him and whisper, "You pick out a couple and tell their story." I nod my head to a couple of tables over. "She's his boss. He was her intern. They've been hiding it for a year. She's about to tell him she's pregnant."

He gasps and presses his hand to his heart in horror. "She's pregnant? You went there." Laughing, he adds, "and he's about to tell her he applied for a job in Florida."

"See? You've got the hang of it already. Okay, it's your turn to pick a couple."

Swiveling his head around, he searches for the right couple, and then I see it too. A couple close to the boardwalk. They look like a hot mess; tension roils between the two as they talk face-to-face.

"She's a yoga instructor, and he wanted to get close to her, so he signed up for one-on-one classes. Now, they are stuck in the are we dating or are we just getting sweaty together phase. She wants more, but he's emotionally stunted from his last relationship."

I can't help but burst out laughing. "Kind of reminds me of someone I know."

"Bold, very bold. I'm more selectively...open."

"Such a lawyer answer." Shaking my head at him, I lean back in my chair.

The waitress is at our table with our drinks. I mouth to him, '*saved by the bell*'.

"Thank you," he says politely.

We order. Surprisingly, he ordered fish and chips. I wouldn't have pegged him as a fried fish guy. I shrug. Once she leaves, I say, "Alright, my turn." Scanning the unsuspecting couple, there they are: the woman, dressed in a crop top and shirt; she tosses her beach-wavy hair as he talks to her. Biting her bottom lip, she leans in further to him. He looks like a preppy boy, wearing blue board shorts with a crisp, collared white polo.

"She likes him...a lot. They met while in college, and now that they've graduated, they're seeing if they work off campus. He's not sure if she's it for him. See how his body language is reserved, and hers is engaging?"

"Interesting observation. Want to know what I see?"

I nod my head and mumble, "Yes."

"We'll stick with their meeting in college. You think she is totally into him, but I see she's overcompensating for something. Her body is practically on the other side of the table. He's questioning why she is over the top while out in public."

"Skeptical much?"

"I call it like I see it. Something is up with those two. One of them is going to break it off tonight."

"Don't you dare send bad juju to that couple!"

He rubs the back of his neck. "I'm not sending bad juju." His tone sounds apologetic, so I'll let it go, but there's more to this story. And I'm going to find out what.

"What would people say if they saw us?" I ask, my chin in my hands, looking at him with dreamy eyes.

"They'd say you're hooked, can't get enough of me, and we're going home together."

"Arrogant, yet you sugarcoat it with confidence." I shake my head.

We are interrupted by the waitress placing our lunch in front of us. The oversized lobster roll stuffed with chunks of lobster that I can't resist picking up and taking a huge bite.

Dane stares at me with a smirk on his face.

Covering my mouth as I chew, asking, "What?" while shrugging.

"Nothing...it's nice to see you are comfortable enough with me to shove it in your mouth like that," he laughs and continues to look at me with wide eyes.

Did he really just say that? I laugh and practically choke on my food. Coughing, I grab my water to clear it out and give him a wicked grin. "Careful, Dane...you keep talking about me shoving things in my mouth, and I'm gonna start wondering if you're offering dessert before we even finish dinner."

After I finish swallowing and taking a sip of my margarita, I clear my throat. "I love a good lobster roll, and this one might be the best I've had in a long time."

He picks up his fork and dives into his fish and chips. "I could watch you eat all day, moaning with each bite."

"I do not moan while I eat." I roll my eyes.

"Um, yes, you definitely do. Go ahead, take another bite." He shoves a massive bite of fish into his mouth.

I tip my glass ever so slightly and run my tongue along the salted rim. Taking my eyes from the glass and slowly looking up through my lashes at him, he just about choked on his food, coughing.

I slam my glass down. "Oh my, are you okay?" I mean it, but there's a tinge of sarcasm in there. I knew he was watching, waiting for me to take another bite and 'moan.' In all fairness, I moan a bit when I eat good food, and this is so good. What else am I supposed to do? Stay quiet?

He grabs his water and swigs it a few times. He finally stopped coughing. "Okay, I take it back. I could watch you eat and drink all day," he says while throwing me a wink for good measure.

EIGHTEEN

Dane

Time has flown by with Kendall. I can't believe we've had such a good time. Laughing, playing a dating game—not my typical date trick, but with her, it was fun. I love watching her eat and drink. The pleasurable noises that come from her mouth make my dick jerk.

Refocusing on the mission of the best date she's ever had, once we finish eating, I pull her up from her chair. I want to walk on the beach with her, but it's busy this afternoon, so I decide to take her back to the shops. She lingered outside the consignment shop earlier, so we head that way.

Opening the door for her to step out onto the sidewalk, I glance at her to see a smile on her face. I slide my hand into hers, and we walk down the street. The heat radiating between us is scorching. "Ready?"

"Do I have a choice?"

"You always have a choice."

With her other hand, she swipes her hair back off her shoulder. Gorgeous. This stunning woman has me hooked.

I stop abruptly, turn, and guide her into the consignment shop. "I saw you eyeing this place when we walked to the restaurant."

"Very observant." She glances up at me as if I had just brought her into a candy shop.

Browsing the clothing, gifts, and shoes, I've never seen someone shop with purpose. The items Kendall has resting on her arm will all look drop-dead gorgeous on her, especially those dresses she just grabbed.

"Will there be a fashion show?" I gesture to her armful of clothes.

"You can't take me into a consignment shop without one." She laughs, and my whole body feels it. I shake my head. Shopping isn't my thing, but with her, I'd spend the day watching her do it. It's fascinating.

I don't have a clue how long we've been in the shop, but we are finally leaving with two large paper-handled bags full of clothes. The fashion show will be forever seared in my memory.

Deep down, I'm hoping she accepts my invitation for another date. We aren't even done, and I want to spend more time with her. She makes me feel free and light. Focusing all of my attention on her, it's refreshing to have someone to share time with and have fun. We've had a lot of fun so far, and we also have dinner plans. I can't wait to surprise her again.

We walk to the car and drop all the bags in the trunk. Once I shut the trunk, I see her staring out onto the open ocean, as sailboats and tankers line the horizon.

"Let's take a walk on the beach." She whips her head around and throws her arms around my neck. I wrap my arms around her waist, and for a moment, we are gazing into each other's eyes. A wildfire roars through my body. She fits with me.

As her grip loosens, I snag her closer. She isn't going anywhere. I dip down and slowly kiss her lips. Gently, I slide my tongue over the seam; she opens for me. The most perfect kiss in the middle of a parking lot overlooking the ocean. Not exactly romantic. It doesn't matter because she is in my arms and on my lips. I never want to let her go.

There's only so much of her I can take before my dick decides to share his presence. She giggles into my mouth. I pull away just enough to say. "Something funny?"

Her eyes glance south and back to me. "We should take that walk and cool off."

Yup, I'll need to adjust myself as we walk down to the water. Being discreet isn't my thing, so I flip her around and pull her back into me. "Like how that feels?"

She just shakes her head at me. As we walk, I adjust myself while she's turned away from me, and I take her hand in mine. It feels right. When we reach the sand, we both kick off our shoes and hold them in our other hands.

The sand is warm under our feet, and the breeze picks up Kendall's fiery red hair and whips it in her face. She lets go of my hand and ties her hair up into a messy bun on the top of her head. Wisps of red are still falling out. I feel a smile spread over my face.

The sand kicks up behind us, and the sun beats down on our skin. Getting closer to the water, we dip our toes in. It's chilly. We continue walking along the shoreline on the packed sand. Silence consumes us as we take in the beauty of the waves splashing onto your legs and the salt drying on them.

It's not that I have nothing to say; it's that I'm enjoying this time with her. Talking isn't necessary. It doesn't even feel awkward. It just is. People watching on the beach is interesting. You have families with little kids, couples, teenagers, and the gamut of others playing football, making sandcastles, and swimming—the waves and breeze dull the screaming and chaos of the beach.

I look at my watch and say, "You ready to go back? It's almost time for another surprise."

"Yeah, I'm ready. The beach, well, the ocean, brings a certain calmness to my body." The peace written all over her face is different than earlier. I'm happy we had extra time to shop and walk on the beach. It was exactly what she needed. And me? I want to see that peaceful face more often. Mental note for another time.

Once we are back in the car, I plug in our next destination—the Port Jeff Ferry. It's a quick fifteen-minute ride.

"You have me curious." She clasps her hands together, and a big smile takes over her entire face.

"It's going to be a good night."

I try to keep my excitement level down. Kendall is going to die when she sees where we are heading. I want to capture her reaction with my camera.

———

We walk off the ferry and down the dock, past boats tied and swaying in the water as we pass by. She keeps glancing over at me. I bet she's trying to figure out what we are doing.

In just a few minutes, we arrive at Danford's. The white colonial-style building stands tall, right on the marina. As we arrive, all we can see are blue umbrellas on the patio. Once we're closer, tables are scattered over it, umbrellas blocking the sun.

"Danford's? I've always wanted to come here, but I haven't made it over yet. I have clients who talk about this place all the time. The food is supposed to be top-notch."

"Yes, the food is, and I wanted to show you something else."

"OMG, you're not showing me a hotel room, are you?" She looks at me with suspicion.

I place my hand on her back and rub it slightly as I guide her to the front door. "Not today. Unless you want to? I'll reserve a suite in a heartbeat."

She slaps my shoulder and says, "Okay, well that sounds entic-ing...maybe another time? So what do you want to show me?"

We walk through the door. "You'll see." Continuing to walk through the lobby, we are greeted by gleaming hardwood floors, chan-deliers, and furniture that matches the decor. The ceilings in the very center soar several feet high.

"This is amazing. I've seen pictures of this place, and it's so much better in person than online," she says as her head swivels on her shoulders.

I lead her down the hallway straight to the spa. Her eyes are wide when she sees the sign. "I thought it would be fun to see the spa here, so I coordinated with the manager for the VIP tour. And if you'd like to have a service or two, we can do that. Then we have reservations on the patio of the Chophouse."

"I'm happy you didn't answer my question. This is the best surprise and very thoughtful of you. Thank you." She wraps her arms around my neck and hugs me. Encircling my arms around her waist, I pick her up ever so slightly and kiss her neck.

"You're welcome. I thought that with your grand opening coming up, there might be something here that inspires you. Though your spa is just as gorgeous as you are." I flash her my biggest smile.

The manager comes around the corner. "Hi, Dane, thanks for com-ing out to see us."

She holds out her hand to Kendall. "I'm Heather, you must be Kendall. I've heard a lot about you. All good things. Tell me about your salon and the new spa."

The two of them discuss spa-related things as they walk. I linger behind them, listening to the excitement in their voices. They are fin-ishing each other's sentences while walking through the reception area to the treatment rooms. The sage walls, with nature paintings lining the hallway, and beige flooring complete the calming look. Doors line the hallway, most of them closed. At the end, there's one door open with the light off.

"Let me show you a treatment room that is used for facial treatments, massage, and energy work." Heather flips on the switch. The room is illuminated in a dim, yellow-colored light. A chair and a table dominate the center. The smell of lemon, lavender, and something else I don't know lingers, but it isn't too bad.

"This room is relaxing. I love the design and layout." Kendall is in awe as her eyes jump around the room. "These chandeliers really make the room stand out... subtle luxury. I might have to put that on my list of upgrades for my treatment rooms. They add such an elegant touch. We have recessed lighting that dims, but this elevates the experience."

Leaving the treatment rooms, we walk through a glass door, with a relaxation room on one side, a pool on the other, and the locker rooms beyond. The ladies go one way and I go the other. The locker rooms feature hot tubs, showers, sinks, and counters, as well as wooden lockers to store your items during treatment. There is a relaxation room with cucumber water and snacks as well. It reminds me of Kendall's waiting room. Her grand opening will be spectacular.

"Heather, thank you for the tour and inspiration for my small town spa." Kendall shakes Heather's hand. Her bright smile lights up everyone around her.

"Yes, thank you for your time, and hopefully we'll be back to enjoy these amenities soon." I look over at Kendall—her hair flowing over her shoulders. She's a sight to be seen. I place my hand on the small of her back and bring her to the restaurant for our dinner date.

Walking through the lobby straight to the Chophouse entrance, the hostess asks if we have reservations.

"Yes, it's under Dane Walsh."

The hostess looks down at her screen and says, "Yes, right this way to the patio."

As we walk through the few tables in the dining room, we reach the wall of French doors.

"Dane, Dane!" I hear a woman's voice behind me yelling my name. It's familiar, but I can't place it. I turn my head to lock eyes with the blonde.

NINETEEN
Kendall

Who knows Dane here? I'm staring at a tall blonde woman wearing a red dress that hugs every curve of her body. My eyes drag down her long legs and straight to her red sparkling heels.

"Dane, how are you?" The blonde wraps her arms around him and pecks his cheeks.

He steps back away from her. His face looks contorted and confused. "It's been a while, Shawna. What are you doing here?"

"Just passing through. What are the odds of our running into each other? How have you been?"

Dane interrupts her. "This is Kendall." He holds me a little tighter around my waist as he pulls me to his side even more. Something is off with him, but I can't pinpoint what—old friend, girlfriend, someone he dated, one-night stand...

"Nice to meet you." She holds out her hand to shake. I do it out of courtesy and plaster a fake smile on my face.

"It was great seeing you, but we have a reservation." Dane turns us and walks back to the hostess, as she holds the door open.

I can't help but glance over my shoulder to see a scowl on her face. One day, I'll hear about that story, but right now, I'm good with forgetting all about her and having the best date ever, just like Dane promised.

The hostess leads us to the corner table. I'm not complaining; it's the best seat on the patio.

He slides the chair out for me to sit, and I do. When he pulls his chair out, he flops into it, elbows on the table, and his hands on his face.

"You good?" I ask, curious to hear about Shawna, but not willing to push the issue.

"Ugh, that was weird as shit."

I nod, letting him process and decide if he'll say anything more. I lean forward and touch his forearm, offering him a small measure of comfort.

"She's an ex-girlfriend from college; our parents know each other. They wanted us to get married, but she wasn't the one for me. I haven't seen her in years."

"No need to say anymore. This is our night, and you promised that this would be the best date ever." I squeeze his arm. He slips his hands down his face, and our eyes meet.

With a slight smile on my face, I wink at him. Just enough to see his shoulders relax and a breath escape him.

"And it will be." He reaches down and rubs my arm. Smiling at me, he continues. "We have the best seat in the house, and I have the best, most gorgeous woman sitting across from me. I couldn't ask for anything more."

I'm melting in my seat. He's tracing circles with his thumb on my arm, and goosebumps erupt from my arm down to my legs. His smirk is a bit arrogant, and the tilt of his head makes me say, "What?" As heat creeps up my neck to my cheeks, I shake my head at him.

"Nothing. Nothing." He shakes his head and glances down at my arm.

He's so observant; his attention sends tingles through my palms. I'm feeling things even more intensely than ever before. With him, it always feels different; his eyes gaze into mine, and I'm done for.

The waitress approaches our table to take our order, which separates us. With a sigh, we reluctantly release each other. The menu was full of dishes that piqued my interest, so I opted for the fillet and lobster tail. My mouth was watering as I placed my order. Dane orders oysters for an appetizer and the NY strip—medium.

"Thank you for arranging the spa tour. It's reassuring that I've created a relaxing and calm space for clients."

"You deserve the best. Your grand opening will be the talk of the town. I know it. How's the planning going?"

"I'm ready. We will be cleaning, adding final touches, and some decorations over the next week or so, but other than that, I think we are ready. Although I'm a bit nervous."

He leans in and says, "I'll be there, so you don't have to be nervous. And my Gram will be there too. She will help you host." We both laugh; Jane knows almost everyone in town.

"You know, now that you mention your Gram, why didn't you tell her we were going on a date?"

He massages the back of his neck and then says, "I think she has been trying to set us up for a while now. She's my everything, and with my recent track record, I didn't want her hopes up and be disappointed."

"Ah, okay. I thought you were keeping me a secret, and that brought up a lot of baggage. So thank you for explaining that to me."

He stands up, walks to me, holds my hand, and lifts me to my feet before kissing me with hungry lips. "Sweetheart, I don't want to keep you a secret. I want everyone to know that you're mine—when the time is right. So far, this date is beyond expectations, and I might be confident in saying this isn't the last one."

I melt in his arms as he says all of this to me. "Yeah, I don't see this being the only date for us."

Twirling me around and dipping me, he kisses my neck. "I can't wait to see where this goes."

A laugh escapes me. "You're over the top... but I like it."

He slides the chair out and gestures for me to sit. "Get used to it. I have more where all this comes from."

Our dinner comes out, and we eat. With every bite, Dane stares at me. I'm trying my damndest not to moan, but this lobster is too good not to. The wild look in his eyes doesn't go unnoticed.

"There's still time to change your mind about the hotel room," he says with one eyebrow arched at me and a sly grin to match his tone.

"Dane, it's not happening," I say with as much conviction as I can because I want nothing more than to be wrapped in his arms tonight. But...I need to know that's not the only reason he is treating me like he worships me.

He groans. "It was worth a shot."

I'm surprised he doesn't try to convince me. He's being playful, but also respectful of my wishes not to. My body sinks further into the chair. Maybe he's turned over a new leaf, and this is something he wants to pursue for real.

"I'll give it to you for trying," I smirk and flutter my eyelashes at him.

"He can't look at me like that and expect me not to keep trying."

"Stop it. You're being dramatic."

"Me?" He points to himself. "That look was dramatic, and I wouldn't mind seeing those eyes staring back at me with your feet by your ears."

I gasp and let out a laugh so loud that the party next to us stares. "Well, maybe one day your dream will come true," I tease.

"I'm persistent." I watch him adjust himself. Fanning myself is not an option; I don't want to send him mixed messages.

"Oh, I know firsthand how persistent you are." We wouldn't be here if he weren't.

"Alright, sweetheart, the ferry will be here soon. Ready to take a walk."

I never imagined having a date like this with him. Clearly, he is focused only on me. It's endearing, and my body fills with the warmth of his hand on my lower back as we walk back to the dock.

Once we are on the ferry, the sun is setting, with bursts of orange and hints of pink. He holds me while my hand rests on his thigh, and my head on his shoulder. The ride back went by faster this time around.

Walking to the car, he says. "I can bring you home, or the invitation is still open for a dip in the hot tub."

I stare at him, contemplating his invitation. "This has been one of the best dates I've ever been on."

"Me too, sweetheart." He runs his hands through my hair.

"I'll need a rain check on the hot tub invitation." I want a bit more time with him before we end up in bed together...or, in this case, in a hot tub together. I would have zero willpower if we were alone, close to each other, naked. Just the thought has me squeezing my legs.

Those caramel eyes flash with desire and care. "Okay, maybe after the next date."

"Maybe."

TWENTY
Kendall

I can't stop thinking about our date. It was perfect. I don't know how Dane will outdo himself after this one. He suggested another date for this upcoming weekend, but I asked to move it to after the openings. He looked a bit disappointed, and so was I. I'll enjoy myself more once all of this comes to a close. I want to enjoy it, not stress about anything else.

The weekend passed with more preparation for the salon and spa opening. I finally got in a good CrossFit workout, thankfully. I've been pushing it off for a couple of weeks, as exhaustion has taken over every day, but this week I'm getting back to my normal schedule—workouts, work, and sleep.

When Tuesday morning shows up, I'm up feeling refreshed. I even woke up just before my alarm. Since I had a few extra minutes, I made a pit stop at the coffeehouse. Approaching the door, someone comes and opens it, and there Dane is, standing on the other side.

"Finally decided to join me for coffee?" He holds the door as I walk inside.

Quick to the punch, I look around. He can't possibly be talking to me. "I'm sorry, did I miss the invite?"

He chuckles and places his hand on the small of my back as we walk to the counter. We arrived at a good time, with no line. Dane steps in front of me and orders my coffee and then his.

I squint my eyes at him. "How do you know my coffee order?"

"I know things. And when you think I'm not paying attention, I am."

"Okay, Mr. Cryptic, tell me."

He scratches his jaw and hums, but gives me nothing.

Giving his arm a little squeeze, like I mean it. "Come on, spill."

"Just this once, I'll let you into my secret...The first time we met here, I listened to your coffee order."

My head tilts, examining him, and it seems legit. "But that was weeks ago."

He taps his temple. "There's a plethora of knowledge up here, including all the things you love."

"Oh, big head." I can't help but giggle at the word that just came out of my mouth.

He doesn't miss a beat. "You would know."

We grab our orders and walk outside. There's a pause. Do we kiss? Do we wave? I wave tentatively, and he comes in and kisses my cheek. Dragging his lips to my ear, he whispers, "I hope you have a productive day." He kisses my neck, right below my ear, and pulls away.

My body is firing on all cylinders, and I want to wrap my arms and legs around him. Yes, right here on the sidewalk. Briefly imagining him leaning me up against his car and taking me on Main Street. Nodding to myself, I say, "Ah...you, too."

He takes my hand and leads me to my car. Opening the driver's side door for me, I look at him with curious eyes, wondering what it is about me that has him doing things for me...like taking me on a date, meeting me for coffee, opening the door... "Thank you."

Once I'm in my car, I watch him hop into his and drive away. Still sitting in my car, I text the group chat about our coffee rendezvous.

The rest of the week is the same. On Friday, he asks one more time if I'm possibly free for dinner over the weekend. I politely decline, knowing I'll be at the salon and spa tomorrow. I hope to complete everything that needs to be done tomorrow and avoid getting caught up all day on Sunday. I'd really like to invite my girlfriends over for a pool day and relax.

Thankfully, Saturday went as planned, so Sunday was a day of relaxation. I slept in until eleven o'clock—not sure the last time that happened. My girlfriends came over, and we floated in the pool, grazing on snacks and sipping margaritas. It was a perfect day. I might have been thinking about Dane all afternoon, but we didn't really talk much about him. They asked a few questions after the text last week. I think we all needed a down day.

Grand opening week starts off just like last week, where Dane is already at the coffeehouse waiting for me. It's like he arrives just in time to open the door for me, orders my coffee because he heard once and memorized it, and then walks me to my car. A part of me believes there's something between us, even though I was telling myself he isn't one to make a commitment, enjoying his one-night stand life.

Dane buys me coffee all week. We exchange just enough conversation to keep the connection going, respecting the fact that this week is one of the biggest weeks in my life. I like that about him.

On Friday, the soft opening day, he even asks if there's anything he can do. I told him he should come tonight. I want to share this moment with him, so I suggested he come and hang out with his Gram. I'm trying not to make too big a deal—but for me it kind of is.

This is surreal. I remember opening Saxy Salon almost three years ago, after deciding I didn't want to stay at my corporate job one more day. It was sucking the life right out of my soul.

The ribbon-cutting ceremony for the salon feels like yesterday. I've accomplished so much in a short period of time, and now the final touches for our soft opening are all in place. The staff is here making sure everything is ready to go. We open the doors in less than two hours. My friends should roll in anytime now.

I check my phone.

Dane:

I'll see you soon.

I'm all giddy knowing he'll be on his way shortly to celebrate with me. I feel seen. I feel supported. And definitely not a secret.

It's still a blur, even with the newspaper articles that came out yesterday. Some of my clients were texting me pictures of the press release and the picture of me in front of the storefront. It brought tears to my eyes, knowing I had built something everyone wants to be a part of.

Refreshments are set up on a long table, accompanied by goodie bags filled with swag. Today is reserved for the VIPs invited privately to the soft launch, and everyone will have a chance to receive two services before the night is over.

In the main room, we have high-top tables for people to stand at and eat their hors d'oeuvres. People will be roaming and taking tours of the salon and spa areas. We have a couple of our yoga teachers who will offer restorative yoga in the large studio. Four seated massage chairs line the back wall, allowing the tours to flow smoothly through the spa.

I hear the front doorbell ring and stroll over to the salon area to open the door.

"Oh, my. Kendall, this is completely transformed into an entertainment space. Great work," Lane says and hugs me.

"Thank you! You have no idea how excited and nervous I am right now. I'm happy you guys are here to support me tonight."

Addison is awe-struck as she glances around. "Yeah, this is amazing. Do you still need our help?"

"I think we're almost ready for everyone. Let me go check to see if the massage chairs are open and ready. You both can start there. I hope I won't need your help later in the event, but at least you can enjoy the perks of the spa."

I walk over to the studio, and everyone is ready. Lane and Addison spend their time getting chair massages.

By the time I'm back in the front with Sally, there are already people walking through the door. It's time to entertain our best customers and favorite people.

The evening continues with a revolving door of people coming and going. This is exactly how I envisioned the soft opening. People with smiles on their faces, raving about the space and services. When they leave Saxy's, they will rave about it, which will bring in the customer base needed to keep this place busy.

A big smile crosses my face. I'm proud to be the owner of this slice of heaven for the community. When my eyes scan to the door, I end up staring into the caramel brown eyes I've been missing all day. There's no mistaking them. One look at Dane and prickles spread into my hands and throughout my body. Our eyes lock for a second too long, as Jane jabs him with her elbow.

"Ow." His head whips to his grandmother.

She doesn't say a word, but a huge smile says everything. Yep, he was caught staring at me. There's no denying it.

He is dressed in dark grey chinos that fit his body perfectly, paired with a light blue button-down shirt that has a couple of buttons undone at the collar and the sleeves rolled up. Those damn forearms. I don't know what his workout routine is, but holy hell, the corded muscles in his forearms just might make me drool all over this floor. I casually wipe my mouth just in case.

When I finally stop gawking, I approach them with a bright smile on my face. "Jane, thank you so much for coming."

She steps forward and gives me a hug. "This place looks like the Ritz. You outdid yourself."

"There's an entire team behind me that brought my vision to reality." I turn to Dane, and he steps closer to me. Jane stares at both of us and smiles. I wonder if he has told her about our date yet.

He wraps his arms around me, picks me up, and twirls me around. "You look gorgeous, and everything looks perfect."

I enjoy his over-the-top attention on me, expecting nothing less from him.

"Thank you for being here and all your support this week." Wrapping my arms around him, I kiss him on the neck.

"I haven't even done much." He places me on my feet. Staring at me for a few more seconds, we are lost in the moment.

Jane clears her throat. He gives me a kiss on the cheek, and we release each other. If she didn't know, she knows now from how he just greeted me. It warms my heart that he had no reservations about public displays of affection here in front of everyone.

"I'm happy to bring Gram tonight so she can enjoy the spa services you have on the menu. She was telling me all about them on the car ride here."

"I hope you'll take advantage of some services tonight, too," I say with a bright smile.

Out of the corner of my eye, I see someone walk by on the sidewalk in front of the store window. I turn slightly to see who it is. A lump forms in my throat, and my chest constricts, shock coursing through my body.

Is that Jake?

The man has a baseball cap pulled low on their face. It's enough to obscure his face from being fully seen. He has a full beard, but I can't make out much more of his facial features. Although I can't make out his facial features, my entire body is shaking.

"Kendall, are you feeling alright?" Jane asks with concern as she turns to see what I'm looking at.

I look back through the shop window. The man is dressed in a large black t-shirt, loose jeans, and what appear to be well-worn work boots, shuffling his feet as he walks across the street. The unmistakable walk, with his hands tucked in his pockets, stirs something unsettlingly familiar within me. My face drains of color, and unease washes over me.

"I thought maybe I knew the person walking by."

Dane steps closer to me with his eyebrows furrowed. I see his hands clench at his sides. "Do you need me to introduce myself?"

"I...Umm...no, no. Everything's fine!" I stammer over my words, still staring out the window.

He is still across the street, walking, never turning back. Shaking off the angst in my body and thoughts, I tell myself I have a restraining order. He wouldn't come back. But I can't even sell myself on that thought.

This soft opening is important to me, so I smooth down my dress and put a smile on my face. I say, "Really, everything is fine."

Their faces tell me everything; they aren't buying it. I'm thankful they let it go.

"Okay, well, you let me know if there's anything I can do," Dane says as he stares deep into my eyes, searching for a morsel of something to go on. I give him nothing. The last thing I need is for this man to get involved in my messy past.

My award-winning smile is plastered on, and I gesture for them to move through the space. "We appreciate the two of you coming out. Please have a beverage, or enjoy our wonderful charcuterie spread. Help yourself, and when you're all set, you can head to the back. We have the studio open for relaxation and chair massages, the Himalayan salt rooms, and a tour of the space."

Jane glances at the spread and says, "This spread looks lovely."

I place my hand on her shoulder and say, "You are my biggest supporter. Nothing but the best for you."

Dane looks over with a smirk on his face and doesn't say a word. His eyes say everything. The love he has for his grandmother is truly off the charts. They really do have a special relationship.

I leave them at the refreshment table to greet other guests as they arrive. So many of my clients are showing up and supporting this spa; it warms my heart. Even other businesses on Main Street are stopping by to see how the renovations turned out. I haven't seen Blake yet, but I'm sure he's on his way. He'll probably get a ton of business just from being here tonight.

Out of the corner of my eye, I see Faith strolling in late. She's going to be late for her own funeral.

"Hey! You made it," I say as I sling my arm around her shoulders.

"Just got caught up at the office. I wouldn't miss this for anything."

"I know! The girls are in the back, either doing chair massages or in the salt room," I say, guiding her toward the back.

She needs some pampering after working all the hours at her therapy practice. I hope she takes advantage of all the services tonight. As we approach the back, Lane and Addison are hanging out in the waiting room, where there are more snacks, and they're sipping on cucumber-infused water. I suspect they already had their chair massages because their shoulders aren't hitting their ears anymore.

"How is it so far?"

"That chair massage was life-changing, and I already booked an appointment with her," Lane says as she slumps her body.

Addison nods, finishes chewing her snack, and says, "Oh my God! It was the best I've had. You did a great job hiring, Kendall. I booked too. Great idea to have the appointments ready to be scheduled. It makes it an easy *yes* for people to book their next one."

The next couple of hires will be estheticians because people have been asking about it. I just haven't found the right people. But I know they're out there. I have to be patient and find the right team members. Salon and spa culture matters, and that's why we don't have significant turnover at Saxy.

"We also have our schedule for the next couple of months all set up for appointments and all the yoga classes too."

"Well, it was smart!" Addison says.

"I'm going to leave you guys to it. Show Faith where those massage chairs are. She needs it," I say, squeezing her shoulders.

I turn and walk back to the front of the salon. As I walk through the doorway, I see Blake on the sidewalk. He finally made it. I can't wait to see Lane's reaction when she sees him.

"I'm excited you are here. There have been a few people asking who did the beautiful spa renovation. Of course, I gave them your card and said you'd be here in a bit. One of them has already left. The other two are around. I'll introduce you."

"As always, thank you for your praise. It was all your vision; don't forget to mention that to everyone," Blake says as he waves his hand in my direction.

He's a good guy. I'd love to see him and Lane together. But who knows? He won't mix business with pleasure. So, I might just have to wait until after the kitchen reno to get my matchmaking hands on those two.

"You made it come to life. Are you here for some services? You could use at least a chair massage. But if you want to grab a refreshment first, then I can introduce you to a few people before you head down to the studio."

"I'm probably not going to get a massage, but I'll grab a drink. Be right back."

I should introduce him to Jane. She knows everyone and would be a great person to be connected to in this town. As my eyes scan the salon, I see that man again across the street staring straight into the salon.

What the hell?

My friends will be here to help me close up, but this guy is giving me the creeps. If it is Jake, I might lose it.

TWENTY-ONE
Kendall

I yelp, and my hand goes to my mouth as someone touches my shoulder. It's just Dane.

"What has you so jumpy?" he asks.

I twist myself to face him with my back toward the door and say, "Don't look yet. The guy from earlier is across the street. Black t-shirt and jeans with a baseball cap low on his face. Can you see him?"

His eyes move ever so slowly to the left of me as he glances out the front window. "Yes, I haven't seen him around before tonight. Do you know him?"

"I might...know him."

"You've got to give me more than that." Dane stares at me, waiting for me to say more.

I think for a minute about how to even say the words, but finally I say, "I think it's my ex, who I have a restraining order against."

With eyes wide and anger settling into them, he says, "Alright! Well, you aren't staying here alone tonight when this event wraps up. I'll bring Gram home shortly and come back to help you close up."

A part of me wants to scoff and say it's no big deal, but with Jake...it's a big deal.

"My girlfriends are here, so I'm good," I say with as much confidence as I can muster.

"Yeah, that's not happening. I'll be here, and there's no argument on this one."

"What's not happening?" I hear another man's voice, a familiar one—Blake.

I slowly turn my head in his direction and then back to Dane, who is giving him a pointed look.

"Everything okay? You look pale," Blake says.

I skirt around the questions a bit and say, "Yeah, it's nothing." Looking at Dane, "You met my contractor, Blake, a few weeks ago at the coffeehouse."

Dane hesitates for a second before reaching out his hand to shake Blake's. Then Dane plasters on a smile and says, "Yeah, nice to see you again. Your work is top-notch, and I can tell you pay attention to the details. My Gram has a couple of projects at her house that need to be finished. Do you have any openings in your schedule this fall?"

"Thank you! It was all Kendall's vision back there, and she's a dream client...Yes, I have time this fall. Here's my card; give me a call," Blake says as he digs out his card and hands it to Dane.

"Great. I'll be calling you." He takes the card and pops it into his back pocket.

Blake looks at me and says, "What's going on?"

These men aren't going to let it go, so I suck it up and tell Blake, too. I haven't even finished my sentence when Dane stalks over to the front door and flings it open, with me rushing behind him. When I finally catch up with him, I grab his arm.

He stares down at my hand and then at me. Placing his hand over mine, the heat that rolls through my body is like an inferno. His eyes burrow into me, and he says, "I'll take care of this and you."

A part of me wants to kick and scream and tell him no, but something holds me back. His tone settles me—resigned to the fact he's going to take care of this.

I slowly release his arm and whisper, "Okay..."

"Go back inside and entertain your guests. I'll be right back."

I'm lost in his eyes, and his voice calms me. One quick look across the street, and the man I think is Jake moves away from the salon. With Dane's massive strides, he is catching up to him. I decide to listen and head back inside, as Dane had asked me to.

The bell on the door rings as I enter the salon. Blake comes over to me and says, "I didn't realize he would be here tonight."

Quick on my feet, I reply, "He is the grandson of my first-ever salon client, Jane." I didn't know what else to say. We're dating. He buys me coffee every morning. But we really haven't talked about what we are.

His face relaxes. "Ah."

In the back of my mind, I'm reeling about that guy who looked all too familiar, and if it is Jake. What the hell?! This is not what I need in my life right now.

I stroll along, talking with everyone as I head to the spa and see who is back there. Guests gather around the refreshments, looking very relaxed. It's all very exciting that all these people came out for the soft opening. I can't imagine what the grand opening will look like tomorrow.

Jane is sitting on one of the comfortable chairs in the spa waiting area. I walk over and sit down next to her. "How are you enjoying yourself?"

"Tonight has been lovely. I am really honored to be here. And it's nice to see you and Dane enjoying each other's company," she says with a smirk on her face.

That smirk. I smile back at her. "Yeah."

Am I really surprised that he would do this, even though he doesn't know the whole story? It didn't stop him from walking across that street like he owned it. The way he touches my hand and looks at me with those caramel eyes. I was practically a puddle on the ground. There's no denying the heat that pools in my core when I'm around him or even thinking about him.

"Have you seen Dane? He said he was going to get some food, but I haven't seen him come back," Jane says.

I take a deep breath and say, "Yes, I saw him. He was getting some fresh air. I'm sure he'll be back shortly. Oh, he also has my contractor, Blake's card. Dane said you have a couple of projects that you want finished this fall."

She raises an eyebrow and hums. Then she says, "Huh, that's interesting. I don't recall any projects that need finishing. I'll have to ask him when he gets back."

That's weird. Why would he say that to Blake?

As if I willed his presence, he stalks through the door. Searching around the room until our eyes lock, he comes straight for us with a bit less intensity. He sits down next to us.

"Hi Gram, sorry I had to take care of something real quick."

Jane places her hand on his and says, "It's fine, dear, I was just chatting with Kendall. So...what projects at the house need finishing?"

The smile on Dane's face fades, and he glances over at me, trying to read my expression. I'm holding in a laugh, and it just might escape. He moves his gaze to his grandmother and says as he stumbles over his words, "I...um...well, I thought the den needed that bookshelf installed you wanted."

I can tell Jane is holding it together. She's too kind and lets him off the hook. "Oh yes, that's right! I wanted to do that in the den, but haven't gotten to it."

Jane stands and turns back, and eyes both of us. "You two have a good time. I'm going to mingle."

And with that, she walks away from us. Dane stands up, and I think he is leaving, but he only moves closer to me. He leans in, and his breath skates over my cheek; he's so close. The hair on my arms stands on end. If he comes any closer, I might combust.

He whispers, "Can we talk somewhere private?"

"Okay," I say, and we walk to my office down the hall. I unlock and open the door. We both walk in, and Dane closes the door behind him.

I turn around on my heels, and he is so close to me. My body desperately wants him. When he reaches up and slides his hands to hold my face, I'm done for. Panties soaked. Will power disintegrating. Eyes close at his touch. Feeling him, the warmth of his hand on my face. He exudes power when he walks into a room, but when he stands in front of me, he's powerful, yet gentle and caring. It's such a contrast.

"Want to tell me about this guy?" His voice is gravelly, deep, and commanding.

It's like he has a spell on me, and I want to pour my heart out to him. "Did you talk to him?"

"You could say that." Not breaking eye contact with me, he continues to brush the pads of his thumbs on my cheeks.

What did he do?

"Dane..." I say as I close my eyes. Hoping he didn't do anything stupid. If it is Jake, I don't want to be the cause of bringing a psycho into his life.

"Kendall, please tell me." The softness of his voice leading me to cover his hand with mine.

TWENTY-TWO

Dane

S he hasn't spoken about this guy, Jake, before, but I'm guessing he was a fucking asshole to her. I'm trying to temper my anger because I wanted to rip that guy's throat out. The overwhelming need to protect this woman is all-consuming. My body zings with energy, but I need to keep it tamed. At any other time, Kendall is confident in herself, standing tall, and she doesn't let anything get under her skin. I can see her. She's scared of him. I want to know why. Then I'll figure out what to do next.

"Please..." I lean in closer. "Tell me."

With tears collecting in her eyes, she nods. I'm staying quiet so she can gather herself and tell me everything. I gaze into her emerald green eyes, with flashes of hurt and anger playing through them. She releases my hand, and with one last swipe of my thumbs, it takes away the tear that escaped. I remove my hands from her face. Guiding her to sit on the sofa, I never let go of her hand.

She takes a deep breath and says, "I think it's my ex-boyfriend, Jake. But I don't know why he'd be coming around. I have a restraining order against him, and I haven't seen him in a couple of years."

The rage of heat engulfs me as I listen to her talk about this douchebag, Jake. I keep my mouth shut and grip her hand tightly, rubbing my thumb over the top of her hand to encourage her to continue.

"We broke up; well, I broke up with him. He thought we were meant to be together forever, but it just wasn't working out for me. His mental health was declining, and he started stalking me. It only got worse when we officially broke up. He would wait outside the salon in his car to watch me until I left. At first, I chalked it up to his being devastated about the breakup, but then it got worse. He would leave threatening notes on my car and progress to harassing me on my cell phone and coming to the salon."

Her head hangs low, and she stares at our hands like they can finish the story. With another deep breath and a shake of her head, she continues to say, "It was scary. He was unhinged, and I couldn't take the risk of being at the salon alone. I reported him every time, and finally, one of the police officers suggested that I get a restraining order. There was enough to get one. So I did. I haven't seen him since. I don't even know if it was Jake."

I brush her fiery red hair off her face and skate my fingers over her cheek. She is gorgeous. I don't want to see this look on her face ever again. Ever again. I'm going to take care of this for her. Never again will this fucker, Jake, make this woman feel scared.

"Well...I persuaded him to hand over his wallet."

She interrupts me and says, "Oh, you didn't! He's a nutcase!"

"I'm a pretty good negotiator, sweetheart." I pause for a second. "Kendall, it was Jake Cross."

She jumps off the couch and paces the small office. I watch her process as she mumbles to herself and shakes her hands. "Dane, this is crazy! I should call the police."

I stand up and stalk over to her. I'll make sure Jake does nothing like this again.

"Kendall...I'll take care of it. You won't have to worry about Jake again. I promise. I'll need some time, but he won't be a problem for you anymore. And I don't want you alone here...ever." I may have shifted my tone to one of authority, and that didn't go over well.

"I appreciate your need to take care of this for me, but..."

"I want you to be safe. Jake—he's definitely unhinged." I move closer. Dancing with this fiery beauty is challenging, and it puts a smile on my face.

She wags her finger at me and says, "Don't you smile at me like that!"

I step close enough to her, inches away from her face. Not touching her, I stand there staring at her, waiting for what's coming out of that mouth, those lips. Leaning in a bit more, her breath hitches.

Holding her face, I say in a low voice, "I'm doing this. Whether you want me to or not. Hate me, point fingers, kick, scream—none of it will work. When I set my mind to something, I get shit done." I dip down and gently place my lips on hers. Sparks fly between us as our lips move in perfect synchronicity. It takes everything in me not to slide my tongue through the seam of her lips.

I'm about to pull away when she reaches up with both her arms and wraps them around my neck—rubbing the back of my head. Blood shoots down my body and straight to my cock. It's ready for her. Always ready, just for her. Her tongue pokes my lips, and I suck on it before we continue a kiss that feels like we've been kissing forever.

It's probably not the time to tell her I threatened Jake and told him I was her fiancé. I don't know what possessed me to say such an outlandish thing. I'm not sure how she will react.

She looks at me with eyes filled with concern and something else. "Please be careful. He may seem like a dumbass, but he is a snake."

"I've handled worse, sweetheart."

She runs her hands over my biceps and says, "Just be careful."

"I will." And I dive into her lips. The energy pulsing between us is too much for me to handle. I lose all control when I'm around her. She slips her hands onto the back of my neck and tugs me deeper. Letting go of her face, I move my hands to her lower back and that tight ass. I snag her closer, allowing her to feel what she does to me. Every. Single. Time. Sliding her tongue to my lips, she coaxes me to open for her. Anything for her.

There's a knock at the door that snaps us both out of this perfect moment.

"Kendall, are you in there?" a woman's voice asks.

"Yeah, one sec."

She brushes my arm ever so gently; it's like fire on her fingertips. I gaze at her with one last look before she moves to open the door.

"Faith, hey, are you guys done with all your services?"

That's my cue to find Gram and get her home so I can be with her again. "Kendall, I'll be back." And I walk out the door.

TWENTY-THREE
Kendall

My heart is beating out of my chest, and I'm surprised Faith has said nothing about my rosy cheeks. He ignites something deep inside of me. It's as if we are magnets, and whenever we see each other, we are drawn closer. And I can't believe he went after Jake.

Faith wiggles her eyebrows at me and whispers, "What were you two doing in here?"

Her eyes are searching for evidence. And just as I was going to answer, Addison and Lane pile into my too-small office.

"So, this place is amazing, and I can't wait for tomorrow's grand opening. You're going to be booked solid in no time," Addison says as she looks around the office.

Faith shakes her head and closes the door. "Wait, wait...we need the details."

"What details?" Addison's eyes jump from my face to Faith's, trying to figure out what's going on.

"Kendall and Dane were in here alone with the door shut." She is not dramatically wiggling her eyebrows. I shake my head at her.

"First off, yes, we were in my office, but not for the reason you're thinking. I was going to wait until after everyone left, but I saw Jake." I pause, waiting for their reactions.

And they don't disappoint. Gasps and jaws on the floor—sort of what I expected. They know all the details of the mess I was in following what happened with Jake. It was scary, and some days I feared for my life. Things have been going well over the past couple of years. I haven't seen or heard from him at all.

"You've got to be kidding me," says Faith, gasping and covering her mouth.

"Yeah, Dane was telling me he confronted the man I suspected was Jake, and he confirmed it was him. He was dressed in baggy clothes and wore a hat. He knew exactly what he was doing."

"He did what?!" Addison says.

I can't believe Dane did it, but a part of me is happy he did. "I know, right! He said he'd take care of it. I really don't know what that means, but he also said I shouldn't be alone. He's dropping off his gram and coming back. But can you guys stay until we wrap up?"

In unison, they say, "Yes."

Relief washes over me knowing they will be here with me. I don't think he'd try anything after Dane talked to him, but I'm not taking any chances. I thought I would argue with him on this, but in the end, I know he's right. I need to be safe.

"I don't need this in my life right now. Unfortunately, when life gives you lemons..."

"You throw them at people," Lane giggles.

"Let's get back out there and wrap tonight up with a bow." Addison grabs my arm and pulls me out of my office, back to mingling with people, although there aren't many people left.

I walk down the hall to the studio and salt rooms to see if anyone is milling around. It looks like everyone is out of the salt rooms, so I close the doors. I check out the yoga studio first and find the instructor cleaning up. All the mats are put away, and she is tidying up the space. The massage chairs are being folded up as well.

Well, that's a wrap. "How did it go tonight?"

The yoga instructor, Mandi, says, "It went really well. Eleven people signed up for the upcoming month and will probably renew for the full year. They want to check it out."

"Amazing news! I'll let you finish up," I say as I turn to talk with the massage therapists.

"Did it go well? My girlfriends said it was to die for and already booked full-hour appointments."

"We are mostly booked out for the next three weeks."

This news reiterates how much this town needed a spa. I'm bouncing on my toes with so much excitement. What a success, and I can't wait for tomorrow's grand opening. It's going to blow tonight out of the water.

"Well, ladies, we will see you tomorrow. Thank you."

Once everyone is gone, I know it's just me and my girlfriends. They are milling around, chatting, and cleaning up the salon.

"Thanks for cleaning up. Let me lock up the front door and head home for a good night's sleep. I'm wiped."

"No problem. Yes, thankfully, it's Friday. We will be back to help tomorrow. What time?"

I'm walking to the door, and over my shoulder, I say, "Probably nine-ish; the grand opening event starts at one o'clock. That should be plenty of time. There won't be much to set up, just the food and swag bags."

I turn my head to lock the door, and I scream. Dane's at the door. As I open it, I say, "You just scared the shit out of me."

He steps in and gives me one of his hundred-watt smiles. He then winks at me and says, "I'm here to take you home."

Now all I can hear are my friends in the background giggling and whispering among themselves. I glare over and give them a pointed look.

All at once, my friends give me a hug, and Faith says, "We gotta go. Looks like this guy has it all handled for you."

And they walk out the door. Once the door shuts, Dane locks it up tight.

"What else can I do to help you clean up?"

I shake my head and say, "Dane, you really don't need to do this."

He stalks over to me, inches from my face. With eyes smoldering, he says, "Yes, I do." And his lips crash into mine. His hands roam my body like a man starved. I melt into him, and my grip on his back is tight. I can't help myself. I slide my hands down his back and, finding the hem of his shirt, I graze my fingernails up his back. That creates a flood of heat between us, a fire that I have never felt before. Holy fucking shit! It's like bringing two small flames together and pouring gasoline on them.

I dig my nails into his back one more time, and he moans in my mouth. My panties are soaked, and if he dares to touch me, I'll come in seconds. Whatever this is between us, I like it—a lot.

I loosen my grip on his back and move my lips just slightly back. I say, "We can't do this here. Let's get things closed up, and you can take me home."

He gently kisses me and, without another word, he looks around and shuts off the salon lights. I'm just standing there, dumbfounded and not moving. He intertwines his fingers with mine as we head to the spa section in the back. He guides me along the hallway and shuts off the remaining lights, never letting go of me. I'm in such a daze that I allow him to do it.

All the lights are off, and everything is cleaned up. We walk into my office, and Dane goes over to grab my purse. We walk out the door to the back parking lot. He brings me to his royal blue Ferrari and opens the door. It has black leather-detailed seats. I love his car, and this color is jaw-dropping.

We drive until he pulls into my driveway. I glance over at him. "Want to park in the garage?"

"That would be a good idea."

I take my phone out of my bag and open up the app. The garage door opens, and he pulls the car in. We sit there for a minute, in silence. The only thing I can hear is our breathing, which sounds like it's in rhythm.

He slowly opens the door and lifts himself out. I go to open my door, but then he is right there to open it. He extends his hand for me to take, so I do. As I stand up, he snakes his arm around my waist and pulls me up against him. His cock is hard, and I can't help but think of the one night we had together—entwined with each other, under the bedsheets. It was a night to remember.

The door closes, and he leads me inside my home, gently tugging me closer.

I feel his warm breath on my neck as he whispers, "I want all of you."

All I want is him, and it's a bonus that he's a distraction from the Jake situation.

TWENTY-FOUR
Dane

Her body is tight against mine. I haven't wanted someone like this in a long time. I feel her soft skin as I caress her neck. The low moan close to my ear has my cock saluting and twitching to be inside her. But my heart is telling me to take it slow with her tonight. The thoughts ravaging through my mind only intensify this need for her.

She lifts herself closer to my ear and says, "Isn't that why we are here?"

That sassy mouth. I move my lips, light as a feather, over her cheek, kissing her as my lips are so close to hers. The kiss is passionate. She slides her tongue into my mouth. The rhythm. The tangling of tongues. This kiss shoots electricity through my chest, like it's going to explode.

Her hands slide up my shirt, touching me. The crackling power behind them has me aching. I pick her up and set her down on the counter. We continue to kiss, and I can't stop myself. I cup my hands on her face.

I pull back so I can look into her emerald green eyes, piercing through my heart, and say, "You are gorgeous." I see her, all of her. She's strong, independent, and successful, but I see the need in her eyes and feel it in her body when I touch her. Taking my fingers through her hair, I say, "I'll give you not just what you want...but everything you didn't know you needed."

She leans into my hand and closes her eyes. When she opens them again, there's the fire of desire deep in her soul. I'm ready to stoke it.

Humming in my ear, it gives me permission to grab her ass and pick her up off the counter. She wraps those sexy, strong legs around my waist. "Where to, sweetheart?"

She points to the front of the house. "That way, up the stairs and to the right."

This woman has me wrapped around her finger. I'd burn the entire world down to keep her safe and give her whatever she wants.

I step over the threshold of her bedroom, and my feet hit the plush carpet with her still wrapped around me. Her cheek touches mine, and her arms are around my neck. The room is dark, so I slowly allow my eyes to adjust to it.

She says, "Alexa, turn on the bedroom."

And magically, the dim light turns on, highlighting her face and fiery hair. Her bedroom features artwork on the walls, bright flowers on her comforter and pillows—lots of pillows—and everything looks neat and tidy. I want to stay with her just like this—wrapped around me. But I also want her naked spread on this king-size bed. There's plenty of room for what I plan to do with her. Opting to strip down all our clothes, I tap her ass. She knows exactly what it means, so she places her feet on the floor.

Holding her hips, I say, "I want to hold you in my arms, but we have a problem."

She stares at me with her head tilted. "A problem?"

"We have way too many clothes on."

A laugh escapes her. "That's a big problem."

I make quick work of ripping all of her clothes off; I take her bra and panties off, too. I want to see all of her. I want to take my hands and move them over all of her skin. The feeling of a live wire under my touch.

Once she is naked, I pick her up and lay her on the bed. Then, in seconds, everything is off, and my cock is dripping with precum. I grab it and slide my hand a few times to ease the pulsing.

What I least expect is for her to jump to her knees and say, "No, that's my job."

"You have no idea." I push her back onto the bed and hover over her. I take my cock and rub her entrance with it.

"Are you teasing me?" she asks with all seriousness.

"No, sweetheart. I'm just warming you up." I move to my side, and she naturally moves with me. We face each other in this intimate moment, and I slide my hand to the small of her back and bring her against me, and I prop my elbow on the bed.

Who the fuck am I right now?

She gazes at me with half-closed eyes. I know she is ready for me. If I reach down and slide my fingers through her, I'm confident she's soaking for me. This woman brings her hand to my jaw and rubs my beard with her fingertips. Like my cock couldn't get any harder, but it fucking does.

Fuck!

I want nothing more than to bury myself in her, but after tonight, I know I need to give her everything she deserves and more.

We lay there for a few minutes, saying nothing with words. We didn't need to; all was said with our eyes. Savoring our bodies tangled with each other, both of us ready to meld together as one.

With my arms holding her, I bring her closer. She sighs and nudges me onto my back. Slinging her leg over me, I can feel the heat from her pussy on my thigh. Her head rests on my chest as she traces her fingers along my pecs. The sparks flying off them make my heart feel like it will burst out of my chest. I close my eyes and tighten my arms around her.

We lay there in complete silence for minutes, holding each other like we're the last two people in the world. We work. We belong together. It's as if our bodies fit each other. Never in my life have I felt like this.

Is this what Gram has been talking about all these years? When you know, you'll know.

There's no way I can go back. Let's be real for a moment. I knew that the morning after spending the night with her, I was done for. Then, our date a couple of weekends ago sealed it for me. And now I know...she's mine.

With one more squeeze of her ass, I'm diving headfirst into what feels like mine.

In one quick motion, she twists her body onto me. The heat of her pussy radiates onto my balls. Oh, she thinks she's in charge. Well, it's time to show her who's in control tonight.

Grabbing her hips, I flip myself onto her.

"You'll have your chance to ride me, sweetheart, once I've made you come at least twice. I take care of what's mine."

"Oh, so that's how this works."

"Follow my lead and you'll want to do it all over again—begging me for more." I cover her mouth with my hand and say, "You ready for that, sweetheart?"

She nods her head yes. I remove my hand, and she says, "Yes."

I never imagined her being so willing to go along with what I say. She is so independent and outspoken. I would have expected her to dominate in the bedroom since she does in her own life. But she's allowing me to dominate her body. This revelation turns me on even more than I already am. And I can't wait any longer, so I lean back on my heels and kiss her stomach down to her pelvic bone. I slide my tongue over her clit as she pushes into my face. I keep going and flick my tongue. She's moving against my face in a circular motion. Needing the pressure, she grabs my head tight.

My fingers find her soaking, pistoning two fingers into her pussy, her arousal coating my fingers. I move my mouth down to her pussy and take a long lick, lapping her up. She keeps moving her hips, and her hands are tighter on my head as she fucks my face. I can feel her orgasm building—as she speeds up her hip motion, her pussy tightening. Her back arches, and her nails dig into my scalp.

I pull my face up to her clit, flattening my tongue. Flicking and sucking, as I slide three fingers back inside her pussy. I curl my fingers to hit that sweet spot and suck her clit into my mouth simultaneously. She explodes instantly, my name on her lips has my dick leaking all over her sheets.

"Dane, fuck. Oh my god," she cries, her hips bucking faster, nails digging harder into my scalp, and her thighs clenching me. She practically levitates off the bed. I hold her hips as she finally comes down from her orgasm. Her grip on my head loosens, and her legs fall to each side of me.

I slink up to her mouth and kiss her. She darts her tongue practically down my throat, tasting every drop of herself. My cock can't wait to be inside her.

My cock is like a heat-seeking missile and finds her entrance. "Condom?"

"No, I'm on birth control and negative. Please...I need you inside of me."

My hips move ever so slightly as I glide into her. She's tight, and it feels like her pussy is sucking my dick inside of her.

Lifting my head an inch, I say, "You feel like you were made for me—only me. I want you like this every night."

TWENTY-FIVE
Kendall

"Every. Single. Night." I moan into the space between our mouths.

"Mine," his gravelly voice vibrates through me.

He pistons in and out, his cock bottoming out and hitting all the right places. When he breathes on me, it scorches a path over every inch of my body. I can't help myself and move my hips, so he slides in even further. He fills me, but it feels more than that, more than it was last time.

The sensation of him inside of me, stretching me, has my clit throbbing—begging for attention. Shaking me out of my thoughts, he grabs my throat with his massive hand and holds it with a gentle squeeze. I automatically lift my head, and the rush of pleasure rolls through me. My legs wrap tightly around his waist.

"So you like that, do you, sweetheart?" he asks, yet it sounds rhetorical.

I can't speak, so I nod a quick yes. Rocking his hips, all I can hear is the slapping of skin echoing through the room. My body, my skin, is hypersensitive to his touch, his kisses, his cock, his grunting. Hearing him grunt as he fucks me sends shivers through my entire body.

The deliberate movement of his hips, slow and steady, as he continues to hit the spot, sends my body into a frenzy. He promised multiples. I'm holding him to that. His grip around my neck tightens, and I'm done. I can't hold out anymore; I shatter around him.

"Fuck me!" I push out as my eyes roll back, and I'm grasping his arms. He continues to move, drawing out my orgasm. He slides his hand from my throat to my clit, and stars appear behind my eyes. My head pushes against all the pillows. And my body sinks into the mattress as I come down from my climax.

Holy shit! What has he done to me?

"I will fuck you, sweetheart. Whatever you want, I will give you."

My legs slide off his back. He's still inside me, and I open my eyes. Gazing back at me are those caramel eyes, want and desire blazing deep inside of him.

"That's what I want now," I say firmly.

He grabs my thighs, pushing them back, until my knees are up by my chin. His powerful arms take my ankles up straight before he slams into me. I moan so loudly it sounds like it's echoing throughout the room. This position is euphoric, as he has my ass off the bed, continuing to fuck me like I've never been before. I hold his head, willing him to keep going.

Hitting the spot that has me begging him, "Fuck me harder." I am so close to climaxing again, every muscle is tightening, and I clench down on his cock so hard that he groans. He must be close, too.

"You were made for my cock," he groans again, louder, deeper this time. That's all it takes for me to plummet into my own orgasm. He continues to pump in and out of me with a force that feels like I'm floating off the bed. My hands squeeze his head as I ride it out.

Holy shit!

And just as I'm coming down from such a high, he lets himself go. Releasing himself inside of me, I feel him jerking his hips and groaning. I can't help myself; it's hot as hell, so I clench down a little harder to get every drop of cum out of him—the magic of coming together.

"Wow," I say, catching my breath. That was powerful—a powerful connection, and I loved every minute. Bound by some sort of inner need. I realize that I'm in trouble. I can't walk away without thinking about him with every breath that I take.

My legs gently fall to either side of him while he is still inside of me. I stare, still holding his head. How am I in this so deep, so quickly? And now what?

Of course, he leans down, brushing my hair from my face. His fingers glide along my cheek, and whole-body goosebumps appear on my skin. They don't go unnoticed by him. With the pad of his thumb, he swipes my bottom lip.

"You are the most gorgeous and amazing woman I've ever met. I'm not even sure how we ended up here. What I do know is I'm never letting you go. You're mine."

If any other man dared to talk to me like that, I'd clock 'em. Coming from Dane, I want to kiss him...I just pull his head closer to mine and put my lips on his. The mix of emotions swirling inside of me, the thoughts that consume me, is overwhelming. And yet, I live in the moment, this moment with him. This passionate kiss between us—it's hot, it's something, it's everything.

He lifts himself off and out of me. With his arm, he repositions me to my side. We are staring at each other as he runs his nails ever so slightly down my back. Waves of tingles follow in their wake. The sensation is overpowering, and I arch my back. Not realizing my boobs are pressed against his sweaty chest, he groans.

He brings his hands up to my face and says, "After tomorrow's grand opening, I want to take you out to celebrate...you and all your accomplishments."

"I'll probably be exhausted."

"Then why don't you let me pamper you tomorrow night, and we can go out another night?"

He is persistent, and I'm catching on that I won't be left alone tomorrow night. I'm not even mad about it. I actually don't mind spending time with him, since the last couple of weeks have been moments in time at the coffeehouse. It wasn't enough. I realize now that I like having him around. I like the way my body feels up against his, the way we talk to each other, and the way he makes me feel—protected, cared for.

"Geez, you are very persuasive." I pause and then say, "I'd really like that."

"Okay, then that's the plan. Get ready for me to pamper you."

He moves onto his back and pulls me closer to him. With my head resting on his chest, my eyes are heavy.

———

Sitting straight up in bed, I thought I had slept too late. But when I look around the room, the sun is just shining in through the windows. My heart is beating out of my chest. I lie back down and put my hand on my chest to settle my heart. Then I realize Dane is not in bed next to me.

Where the hell did he go?

I take a deep breath and sit up on the bed. I'm naked. I grab Dane's t-shirt, my pair of panties, and throw them on. I open my bedroom door and walk out into the hallway. My nose picks up the smell of coffee. Making my way down the stairs, I head straight for the kitchen. I don't remember setting the coffee, so my heart hopes Dane is in the kitchen. For a split second, I feel my heart fall to the floor, an emptiness, to think that he just left without saying goodbye, without a note, without a kiss. My expression is one of sadness, with eyes cast down, as I step into the kitchen and scan the room. Dane is nowhere to be found, and I feel a prickling in my eyes.

Thinking back to last night, I recall how he owned me and protected me. I put creamer in my coffee and take a sip. Staring out the kitchen window at the backyard, it looks peaceful. I decide to sit on the patio and watch the sunrise. As soon as my foot hits the patio, Dane says, "Good morning, sweetheart."

My heart flutters, and the widest smile crosses my face. This man surprises me in all the good ways. And he didn't leave without saying goodbye. My body relaxes.

He stands up and comes over to me, scanning my expression. "Did you think I left you?"

"I may or may not have thought that," I say with heat rising up my neck to my cheeks.

His hand reaches up and caresses my head, moving to my neck. He tugs me closer. "I wouldn't leave without saying goodbye."

I haven't had a guy at my house since, well, Jake. What happened yesterday at the salon comes flooding into my thoughts. I don't want to deal with him, and I hope that the chat Dane had with him makes it clear he can disappear back into the hole he crawled out of.

"I knew that, but then questioned it when you weren't in bed." I try to lower my head, but he doesn't let me. With his fingers on my chin, he tilts my head up, and I have no other choice but to look up at him.

"Look at me." His voice is serious, and his eyes are full of adoration as they soften. "I'm here for you."

It makes me pause. Over the past few weeks, he's been leaving clues for me, showing up every time I needed him. How did he even know? And every time, he was showing me the real him. The one that takes care of people—and that includes me. In a way, I never could have imagined after that first night. I'm seeing him in a different light and realizing I misjudged him. Now, I find myself looking closer at him and wanting time to see where this all goes from here.

TWENTY-SIX

Dane

I see trust in her eyes. She trusts me. Not that I don't want her to trust me, because I do. It's different seeing it in her eyes. It makes me want to continue showing her the real me, not the one-night stand guy. The one I keep locked away for so many reasons, but with her, I'm myself. I don't have to hide.

"Thank you." She wraps her arms around my waist and holds my back, like I'm the one who needs to be held up. But it's her I want to hold up.

"What time do you need to be back at the salon?" I hold her face and kiss her cheek.

She looks at her Apple Watch and says, "In about an hour."

"Then let's get ready and head out of here. We can stop at the coffeehouse first." My hand slides to the back of her head, while the other one wraps around her—hand splayed, holding her up.

"Sounds like a good plan."

We shower separately. Otherwise, I wouldn't be able to resist her naked curves—her tits, that ass. She hops in first, so I have time to grab my overnight bag from my car. Yes, I have a bag in my car. When I brought Gram home last night, I stopped by my house to pack quickly. I knew I wasn't letting her out of my sight after talking with her ex, Jake.

I hear her shut off the water and wait patiently for her to come out of the bathroom before heading in. She opens the door and strolls out in a towel. Water glistens on her skin. Those long legs that were wrapped around me just hours ago. And then it hit my nose, her watermelon shampoo. Linger a few extra seconds, taking her in. I walk by her and wipe my lips over hers.

Oh, fuck me!

I quickly walk into the bathroom, shut the door, and take a shower.

Once I finish getting dressed, I head downstairs to find Kendall. "You ready?"

She sits with her fiery red hair all done up and a beautiful emerald green dress that matches her eyes. "Yes, thank you."

I slide my hand into hers and walk to the garage. Opening the door, I gesture for her to sit, and I close it behind her. I'm feeling high on life, and she's the reason. We drive with soft music playing. I reach over and take her hand into mine. Glancing over, I catch her gaze for a few seconds before I have to turn back to the road. We stop for coffee on the way, and the salon is up ahead. I pull into the parking lot and park next to her car.

"You ready for today?"

"It feels like I've been waiting for this day for so long, and it's finally here. I know it's going to be a huge success. I'm giddy inside, but playing it cool on the outside." She laughs, her head tipping back. The sparkle in her eyes, filled with anticipation for today, makes my heart squeeze, knowing I'm here with her today to celebrate this huge milestone and accomplishment.

I lean over, hold her face, and kiss her. "Today is going to be everything and more. I promise."

We both hop out of the car and walk toward the back door. Out of the corner of my eye, I see what looks like a piece of paper under her windshield wiper. Kids must have been out early with the Main Street advertising.

I stalk over to her car to grab the advertisement off her windshield. When I grab it, I realize that this isn't an advertisement. It's a hand-written note. I don't want Kendall to freak out, so I fold it up quickly and pocket it.

We walk together into the back of the salon hand in hand. She is full on prepping for the grand opening. I excuse myself to the bathroom. I'm not saying a word to her until after the grand opening. The last thing she needs to worry about is this asshole.

I take the paper out of my pocket, unfold it, and read it:

I know you still love me. When you looked at me today, I could feel how much. I wanted to come in, hug and kiss you, but you looked really busy. I don't know why you sent that man after me because I didn't do anything wrong.

How could you leave with him? You love me, not him. You want to marry me, not himI'm going to make you see I love you more than the guy you shacked up with.

I'll see you tomorrow, my sweet love.

This guy has some brass balls writing this note, leaving it on Kendall's car, and saying he'll be back today. He has another fucking thing coming. I'll bury him if he even thinks about showing his face today—or any other time, for that matter. He should be locked up, not harassing Kendall.

I storm out of the bathroom to find her. I can't tell her about this note, not yet. But that means I need to be by her side or within a short distance of her every minute of the day, today. She might get suspicious, but I'll play it off.

"What can I do to help during your event?" This is my in. I'm going to help.

"That's kind of you, but you don't have to do anything. We have a team on all this. I appreciate your offer."

That backfired. New approach.

"Okay, then I'll mill around and take you home after. Is that still the plan?"

She smiles shyly at me and says, "Yes, it is."

I wonder if she's thinking about what's going to happen later as much as I am. Not lingering on that thought too long, I casually walk over to the front door, walk out, and survey the surroundings. There's no sign of the fucker anywhere. What he doesn't realize is that I know the chief of police in town, judges, prosecutors—he'll be put away for a very long time.

Finding her back in the salon. "Are you sure there isn't anything I can do while I'm here?"

"Do you mind going to the storage closet and grabbing a couple cases of bottled water? We can put them under the table."

———

The grand opening went off without a hitch. Kendall has a massive smile on her face, and it makes me want to hold her, but she's still cleaning up. It's a little more effort tonight because we're breaking down tables and moving things back to where they belong.

There was no sign of Jake all day, so it puts me on high alert as we clean up and get ready to leave. He might be lingering around, waiting for her to walk out back by herself. Yeah, not fucking happening.

I take a minute after helping to move tables and chairs, and I find a quiet corner to call my buddy, who owns a private security company.

"Joel, hey, it's Dane. How are you?"

"Haven't heard from you in a while. Doing well. What can I do for you?"

"Straight to the point. I have a woman who needs private security. Starting Monday morning. I don't want her out of anyone's sight."

"Give me some more details."

I sigh and say, "She has an ex that crawled out of the woodwork and is hanging around again. You know the deal; she has a restraining order in place. I'd like at least four people to start, and then you guys can evaluate the situation. Joel, whatever it takes, just let me know. This guy, Jake Cross, seems like a dipshit, but he's not; he left her a note on her car last night. I just want to make sure no one gets through. Security at every entrance of her business and home."

He has me give him a list of her home and business addresses, the make and model of her car, and a few other places she frequents. Although I don't have addresses for her friends, I know he'll take care of that. Once I confirm all the details, I hang up and put my phone in my pocket.

I casually walk back to where everyone is. Everything is cleaned up, and it's time to head out. The thought of pampering Kendall tonight has me itching to leave. We're taking her car with us tonight. What she doesn't know is that I've already talked with two of the massage therapists, and they are meeting us at Kendall's house for a couples massage. We both could use it. Then I'm having dinner delivered so we don't have to leave the house after spending a couple of hours relaxing. The entire night is planned to perfection—exactly what she asked for and a little extra.

Walking up to Kendall, I drag my hand down her arm. I feel her shiver under my touch. "Ready to go? I'll follow you home."

"Yup, just need to lock up," she says, hesitating to leave my touch, but finally tears herself away. She's at the door locking up. I watch her, unable to look away.

She is staring out the door and calls over her shoulder, "Dane, can you come here?"

With the tone of her voice, I run to her, immediately looking for any signs of that asshole. "What's wrong, sweetheart?"

"Over by the bench, across the street." My eyes track across the street and, sure as shit, there's that motherfucker.

I keep my cool and say, "Let's head out the back door."

Wrapping my arms around her, I pull her through the salon as she shuts off the lights and sets the alarm at the back door. We walk out, and she locks up the back door.

I'm unsettled about her driving herself, but I know if I make her get into my car now, after already saying I'd follow her, she'll know I'm being extra cautious.

So, I decide the best way to take care of this is head-on. "Do you want to ride with me again?"

With one eyebrow raised, I see the wheels turning and a hint of hesitation. "I'll be okay. I don't want to leave my car here again tonight, knowing he's lingering around here."

She's right. I'm going to be tailing her the entire way, and I'll be on the lookout for anyone following us. "I'll follow you. Call me if there's anything unusual about your car as you drive home or when you pull into your driveway. Okay?" My tone is serious. I try to temper it down a few notches.

I don't need Kendall on edge like this. Tonight is supposed to be our night to relax, and with this asshole around, he's interrupting our perfect night.

"I can do that. Thank you, Dane." She steps closer to me and presses a kiss to my lips while taking her fingertips along my beard. Her touch is welcome and wanted.

We both get into our cars and drive toward her house. In the rear-view mirror, I notice a small black SUV trailing just far enough behind. I'm watching it like a hawk as I follow her.

Contemplating what to do next. I ask my car to call one of the guys I know on the police force to see if we can have an officer pull this dickhead over. I'm in luck; he's on duty and only a minute away. I keep looking in my rearview mirror and watching Kendall in front of me. My hands tighten around the steering wheel; my knuckles turning white. I loosen my grip only slightly.

After what feels like an hour but really was a few minutes, I see blue lights flashing, and the SUV is being pulled over. The guy I know will give me an update once he figures out who was following us. I bet it was Jake, and now he's on the force's radar. Not a place anyone wants to be with a restraining order against him, but he brought it on himself.

It doesn't take us long, and we are pulling into Kendall's garage.

We both get out of our cars, and she says, "What was that all about? I saw the police pull over the SUV that was following us."

"Let's just say I called in a favor." And right on cue, my phone rings. "I'm going to take this inside. You coming?"

"I mean, if that's what you want to do," she says as she winks and smirks at me. She is going to do me in, and I don't mind one bit.

"Hey, Craig," I say to the police officer I called earlier.

"Jake Cross. He said he was in town visiting family. I continued to question him. He seemed like a solid guy at first, but he became agitated when I kept asking questions. I asked him how long he was in town for, and that seemed to bring out the beast in him. Started screaming like a lunatic. I asked him to calm down, and he went to grab something from his glove box. Long story short, we arrested him for illegal possession of a firearm without a license to carry. Then he attempted to punch me and run, but we have him in custody."

"What the hell!"

"Yeah, we're transporting him in the morning. I'm glad you called. This guy is unstable."

The way Kendall spoke about him, I got that from her. Even when I spoke to him, he seemed fine at first, and then the façade slipped. This is why I'm not leaving her side, and I'm lining up private security.

"Craig, thank you. Keep me posted with any information. I'll do some digging around to see who his judge will be."

"You bet. I'll be in touch."

I hang up, and when I turn around, Kendall is firing darts from her eyes, and her arms are folded across her chest. She doesn't look happy.

Walking toward her, I raise my hand to put my arm around her, and she moves away.

"What was that all about?" she demands, standing firm, her tone serious. I actually like it when she's feisty.

"You haven't given me a chance to tell you what happened on the ride here."

"Okay, well, we're here, so start talking."

I fill her in on what Craig told me. Slowly, her arms fall to her side, and her face goes from angry to shocked.

She gasps and then says, "What would have happened if you hadn't been following me? He would have found a way to get to me. How do we keep him away?" Tears well up in her eyes, but she holds them back.

The overwhelming need to console her and never let anyone hurt her overtakes me. My blood is boiling. I should have taken care of him when I had the chance. One step and I'm grabbing her tightly in my arms, rubbing her head and back. She rests her head on my chest. I'm going to make him pay for making her feel this way.

TWENTY-SEVEN
Kendall

I've been torn about whether to let Dane get too deeply into my life. But it appears he's already here, deeper than I've ever let anyone else. What a disaster this has turned into. I never thought I'd see Jake again, and here I am shaking like a leaf. The trauma of his mind games comes tumbling back.

Tucked in the bottom of my closet, I have a box of all the letters he left me after we broke up. It also has pages and pages of threatening text messages and pictures of him following me everywhere. I keep it as evidence supporting my stance and restraining order.

I'm still wondering why now? And then I realize that there was an article in the newspaper with my picture showcasing the grand opening. I bet he saw it and decided to try to claw his way back into my life.

I intertwine my fingers with Dane and bring him down the hall to my bedroom closet. The door is already open, so I walk him in with me. Stooping, I grab the box from the floor, open it up, and hand it to him. He's an attorney; maybe there's something more I can do. Right now, I'm out of ideas, and I don't know what to do.

With his eyebrows furrowed, he says, "This Jake guy is a real piece of work. Start from the beginning; give me the rundown."

I hesitate for a split second, and then it all comes pouring out. I tell him about Jake and how we were just a normal couple. Then, a couple of months into the relationship, he became extremely irritated with everything, especially when I was late or when men would come into the salon and talk to me. Then I tell him about that night, when he was parked outside the salon, and how it all came to a head. He lied about where he worked and where he went, but I needed to give him a play-by-play of all my locations and where I would be if I wasn't working. Then he started telling me I couldn't hang out with my friends.

I stop abruptly, take in a deep breath, and say, "I don't know why I stayed with him for so long. For over a year. I dealt with the harassment, the manipulation; he kept secrets from me until it all came to a head one night." Looking away, embarrassed that I had stayed far too long.

Dane sighs and brings my face to look at him. "You're doing the right thing. He is a danger to you and who knows who else."

I know he is right, but it's hard to share one of my biggest failures so openly. He believes me, and that's all I need to continue. "It was an all-out fight that ended with me running out of the house, no shoes, no phone, and going to my neighbor's house."

Chills run through me at the thought of him watching my every move. I can't get his face out of my mind. How angry he was. With nothing but the clothes on my back, I ran—fast.

"I was thankful the neighbor was home, and they let me in. I called the police, told them what happened, and then I got a restraining order. I was always looking over my shoulders, but day after day, he wasn't there. Maybe a false sense of security. It became easier as the months went on, and he didn't show up."

He brushes his hand through my hair. Instinctively, my eyes close, and the feeling of his touch consumes me. Leaning in, he crashes his lips against mine, electricity bouncing between us. I hold on to him tightly, and he cups the back of my head. When he slides his tongue over my lips, the warmth spreads throughout my body. He feels safe.

When my doorbell rings, I jump; it scares the shit out of me. "I'm not expecting anyone."

Holding my ass, he brings me close to him. I can feel his erection. With my hand over his heart, his heart is beating with mine.

He kisses me on the cheek and says, "I am. I'll get it."

I stare at him, puzzled by his response, but follow him to the front door. All I can do is stand there and watch him open my front door. Not a bad view—his long strides and those pants that hug his ass and thighs. As my eyes make their way up his body, I see the muscles in his arms flex as he walks.

He opens the door, and my jaw drops to the floor. The massage therapists from the spa are carrying their tables into the house.

Is he surprising me with a couple's massage? I didn't think we were there, but what a thoughtful thing to do.

I walk over to him and playfully slap his arm. "Dane...what's all this?"

Turning to look at me, he says, "I've watched you work your ass off these last few weeks. You pamper other people, and now it's time for you to be pampered. I'm just here as a bonus companion." He winks at me and puts his forehead to mine. We both close our eyes.

Jake never treated me like this. Actually, I can't think of any man who has treated me as well as Dane has and in such a short period of time.

I show them the large family room where they can set up the two massage tables. While they do that, I grab a couple of waters and hand one to Dane. "Drink up, need to stay hydrated...for what's to come later." He winks at me again.

I giggle. I think about grabbing my robe, but he's already seen the goods, and I feel comfortable with him. So I opt to undress, and he does too, eyeing each other as articles of clothing fall to the floor. He could just show off his arms to me, and I'd be soaked. Yes, I'm an arm girl. We both get under the sheets and are ready for our massages. I haven't had one in months.

They play relaxing music and dim the lights. The smell of lavender oil envelops me. This massage is exactly what I need. The more she rubs out the knots, the further my body sinks into the table.

I can't believe he arranged for a ninety-minute massage. I am so thankful, but I don't want to move when it's over because my body is limp. I finally sit up and throw my legs off the table. The lavender scent fades as I take a deep breath. I slide off the table and walk over, grab my water, and chug it down.

Dane is slowly getting off the massage table. "Did you enjoy yourself?"

"I did! I'm like Gumby." I move my hands in the air.

A laugh escapes him. "That's one way to put it. I'm feeling pretty chill, too. Are you hungry?"

"I'm starving. But...I don't want to leave the house, not after that." I point to the ladies packing up the massage tables.

"We don't have to," he says, and on cue, the doorbell rings again.

"Seriously, I have never had so many people ring my doorbell," I say, eyeing him suspiciously. It has to be him.

"Well, it's your lucky day then." He pulls his pants up and buttons them.

As he walks to the door, wearing only his pants, his bare feet pad softly along the hardwood floors. The no-shirt look gives me a marvelous view of his back, and I could get used to him walking around my house without a shirt on all the time.

Until he glances over his shoulder and says, "Do you need a towel for all that drool?"

I mutter, "Jerk."

"I heard that."

"I bet you did."

When he opens the door, I see a delivery guy hand Dane a couple of bags as the massage therapists squeeze past.

He shuts the door with his foot, turns, and walks back toward me. As he passes, I can smell delicious food, but can't exactly pinpoint it. It smells familiar.

He unpacks the bags of food, and I see the takeout containers. It's Thai food. How did he know that was one of my favorites?

With a smirk on my face, I reach over and glide my hand along his arm. I trace his muscles up and land on his chest as I take a step forward. He moves his hand down my back and over my ass, squeezing it and tugging me to him. Tonight has been surprisingly enjoyable and relaxing. I guess I didn't know what to expect from his intrusive and protective, yet crazy, self. I'm ready to eat some food, but if he keeps his hands on me, I'm not sure if we will eat at all tonight.

As if reading my mind, he asks, "Want to eat at the table so I can have you for dessert?"

It's hot when he talks to me like that. I fantasize about him shoving me against the wall and ripping off all my clothes.

Interrupting my dirty thoughts, he says, "Kendall? You okay? Looks like your cheeks are getting a little flushed."

I stumble over my words. "Ah...n-o."

I want to slap that smirk right off his face, but instead, I pat his cheek. I run my nails through his beard. He stares at me with those gorgeous caramel eyes that make my knees weak.

He leans forward, with our noses touching, and says, "You're mine."

If I weren't already soaking wet, I sure as hell am now. "Am I?" I say with a snarky, teasing tone.

He strokes my cheek and lightly drags them down my neck. Goosebumps appear all over my body, my nipples tighten, and heat rushes to my core. He moves his fingers down the side of my body, tracing the outline of my figure. He lingers for a moment on my hips, and then squeezes my hip right before he pushes my shirt up. It's just enough for him to slide his massive hand over my stomach and down my pants.

I'm so thankful I changed into more comfortable pants that have room for him. It's like he is in slow motion as he dips his fingers into my slit.

He growls. "Yes, you're mine. Feeling you dripping all over my fingers, sweetheart, I'm not sure we'll be eating dinner."

Moving his two fingers inside of me, I can't hold it in. I whimper. That's all it takes, and his mouth is on mine. The heat of his mouth, his tongue, the feel of his fingers, the electricity coursing through my body. My hand rubs his erection through his pants. I can't help but tug at his belt.

"Take them off," I mutter.

The loss of his touch leads me to press my hips toward him. He takes his thumb and slides it across my bottom lip. Tipping my head back, he strokes my neck and then kisses me right below my ear.

Shit! This guy has me gushing all over him.

"You liked that, sweetheart?"

Such a cocky bastard. I whisper, "Yes."

I'm in this Dane fog. The minute he is in my presence, he's all I think about. When he's touching me, it's like I have no sense of anything else, just him.

"We'll pick this up after we eat."

I watch him adjust himself, and I lick my lips. I need to have him in my mouth, to taste him, to smell him...

"You need to eat." He breaks away from our moment and pulls out the rest of the food. Turning back, he finds the dishes and brings them to the table.

"Alright." I look at him and say, "I'll grab the silverware."

We move around the kitchen as if we can predict the other's movements. He grabbed a couple of beers from the fridge. I'm still dumbfounded. How did he know I liked Thai? Then it hits me, Jane. But when would he have asked her? Too many questions. I should just ask him.

"How did you know I liked Thai food?"

"Well, sweetheart, I pay attention and ask questions to the right people," he says with a fork full of noodles heading for his mouth. The thought of what he can do with that mouth has me melting all over again.

TWENTY-EIGHT

Dane

S he has no idea what I already know about her. I take notice of everything, especially if my interest is piqued. I was fucking hooked from the minute she sauntered by my table on her way to the bathroom that unforgettable night.

When she pulled out that box of shit from her ex, I wasn't about to tell her I already knew most of the story. As an attorney, I have ways of finding out about assholes like Jake. My blood boils again thinking about him and how he treated her. He deserves to rot in fucking hell, and I'm not above making that happen.

"So what else have you been paying attention to?"

"I've been paying attention to everything about you. What you love, what you hate, who your friends are, what you like to do, who you are in here." I use my finger to circle her heart.

"Oh, well, you've been busy." She places her hand over mine.

We're interrupted by her phone. It must be a text message because I watch as she picks it up, reads what's on the screen, and smiles. A genuine smile, not like the fake one she flashes to other people.

Anger is rolling up my neck, the same feeling I got when it all took a fucking nose dive with Maggie. She and my best friend. I couldn't believe it when I found out. Betrayed by both of them. She would get text messages and act giddy. When I asked her about it, she'd say it was just her friends. But it was my best friend. That same dreadful fucking feeling is seeping into me right now. The longer she stares at that phone, the more tense my muscles feel.

"I'm right here, so who is making you smile like that?"

"Just my group chat with my girlfriends," she says and texts them back.

She's not Maggie!

The only way I can compose myself is if I distract myself. I use Logan as a cop-out. I grab my phone and make the call. Needing to walk away, I stroll to the living room.

"Bro, what's going on? It's Saturday."

I snap. "I know what fucking day it is, idiot."

"Ah...You okay?"

"I'm at Kendall's and, fuck, I don't know."

I know, but to say it out loud. Logan has extensive relationship experience, and he's married. That's gotta count for something. I want this to work out between us because I think she is the one. I'm fairly certain Logan knows that.

"Du...de! What do you mean you're at Kendall's? I thought it wasn't like that."

"Fuck off!"

"I knew it. Man, do I know you well. And if you're there, why are you calling me?"

"I needed an excuse to walk away for a few minutes; you're my scapegoat."

"You're smitten, aren't you?" Logan asks with a knowing tone.

"Who even uses that word anymore?" I grab the back of my neck and rub out the tension building. "And yeah, I guess I am."

"Admitting it is the first step."

What a smartass. I take the next few minutes to fill him in on everything with Kendall—the smile, the text message, and how I jumped to conclusions with all the shit Maggie did to me. At the end of the conversation, Logan says one word: "Communication."

He talks about communication in relationships all the time. Not sure how he became so wise, but I'm taking his advice. After we hang up, I stalk straight to Kendall, and I run my hand through her hair. Her hand automatically drops the phone on the island and grabs hold of my arm.

She caresses my arm and snakes the other one around my waist, holding me tight. "What's going on with you?"

I clear my throat, tightening the grip I have on her head. "Ugh, I have a history, and I know that's my shit to deal with, but I want you, in every way."

She softens ever so slightly. If I weren't paying attention, I would have missed it. "Well, I have to say I like where things are going, but you know my history. There's a lot of baggage. So tell me."

The words that come out of her mouth are laced with kindness and want, yet stern and matter-of-fact. She is giving me a little grace here, but I need to be better, do better with her. If I want her by my side, I need to treat her like the queen she is.

"You're right." I take a deep breath and simply say, "My last long-term relationship ended with her cheating on me with my best friend, who also had a girlfriend. She said I was a terrible boyfriend who didn't know how to communicate and was a workaholic. They texted right in front of me, and she would smile at her phone all the time. It hit a nerve."

The rest of her softens. She takes my other hand and kisses my palm. It's a simple act, but one that has my heart bursting at the seams. This woman is perfect for me. She knows exactly what I need. She deserves the very best, and that's me, everything I have to offer her. She's mine to worship.

"Dane, I'm so sorry. What a shitty thing for them to do. For the record, being a workaholic isn't a bad thing." She rubs my back and says, "I'm not her." She lifts herself onto her tiptoes and kisses my neck, whispering in my ear, "I'm yours."

Her hands move to the back of my neck; mine instinctively circle around her waist. The warmth of her embrace calms my soul and my thoughts. This is where we belong—together.

Her arms loosen around my neck. And the heat from her body dissipates. I want it back. But instead, we eat our dinner.

Silence spreads throughout the kitchen at first. Then she breaks it. "How's the case going?"

I tell her what I can without breaking privilege. As we continue the conversation, she tells me about her new workout routine, now that the openings are done, and the latest book she's reading.

After cleaning up, she stands by the doorway, wiggling her eyebrows. There's my invitation. It took only a few steps with my long strides to be on top of her. Picking her up, she wraps her legs around my waist.

"You still have plans to fuck me up against this wall?" she asks, biting my neck like she's lost all control of herself. I'll take every bit of that.

Lowering her to her feet, I undress her; it's pure insanity with clothes flying across the room. Once we are naked, I grip both of her hips and yank her to me. She holds on tight around my neck, and I feel her leg muscles supporting her. Sexy as fuck. A pained groan escapes me as I slam her against the wall.

"Fuck me, Dane."

"Anything you want, sweetheart." I mean it as I find her entrance and inch by fucking inch I'm sucked into her sweet, dripping wet pussy.

"You were made just for me." She whimpers when I'm all the way in. "You're fucking mine, sweetheart. I'm going to worship you tonight and every day after."

My heart races and my muscles tense up, holding her as I move my hips. Long strokes with my cock coming almost all the way out and slamming back into her. She pants in my ear and bites my lobe and neck. Thrill shoots through me, and this won't take long if she keeps that up.

I feel her legs tighten on my waist, and her panting gets quicker; she's close. Her head falls back against the wall as she cries, "Dane, harder."

I do what I'm told. Short, quick strokes in and out of her pussy. She's tensing up, and I feel that tight pussy clenching my cock. A few more and she's moving her hips, chasing her orgasm, rocking that pussy, my balls tighten.

"Dane," she moans as her eyes roll back in her head.

I spill into her. My hips stutter as her pussy pulls every last drop of cum from me. Our ragged breathing, hearts beating at an alarming speed, and sweat consuming us.

The night continues with us in her bed, wrapped up in each other. I smile so wide my cheeks hurt. After a couple more rounds of mind-blowing sex, we fall asleep.

I wake up to her sleeping on my chest. Squeezing her closer to me, I place a kiss on the top of her head.

TWENTY-NINE
Kendall

"Dane...why are there Rambo-type men walking around my yard?" I call over my shoulder. I finally hear his footsteps behind me as I'm peeking out my window.

"What's wrong?" he says, sounding confused as he rubs my back.

I pull back the curtain and say, "See for yourself. I suppose you have nothing to do with these men."

He leans into me and says nonchalantly, "Oh, yeah, that's the security I hired."

Pulling away, I whip my head around so fast I think it will spin off. Heat rises up my neck. Taking a deep breath, trying not to lose it, I say, "You did what?"

The deer-in-headlights look tells me he wasn't expecting me to be upset. But what the hell? You hire security for someone and don't bother to even mention it, never mind ask if it's okay.

Standing his ground, he says, "I hired security for you. I won't be able to be here all the time."

"Did it ever cross your mind that you might want to ask me first before hiring security?"

"Um, yes, for a split second, but then I made the call. I didn't want to bother you during the grand opening." He steps closer to me, his hand outstretched, and says, "Can you come here?"

I throw my hands up and say, "You realize you decided for me. I didn't even have a chance to have a conversation with you. I have a problem with people making decisions for me."

As I continue to process, I remind myself that he has my best interests at heart. Still, I also acknowledge that, as much as I want to pin this on anger, I'm hurt. Hurt that he didn't consider my feelings, what I wanted, and it felt a lot like how Jake used the excuse that he knew what was best for me.

I have to remind myself that this is a different situation. I need to give Dane the benefit of the doubt, just like I asked him to do for me. I'm not his ex-girlfriend, and he's not Jake.

He takes another step closer. "Please come here."

I drop my guard a little more with his sincere tone. "Do you have any idea what I'm feeling right now?"

He shakes his head and says, "No, I guess I don't."

"It hurts me to think you'd do something without asking me first. This isn't grabbing takeout and hoping I like it."

Taking my hand, he hugs me tight. I want to shove him away. Instead, I tilt my head to the side and rest it on his chest as he envelopes me in an embrace that washes relief through my body. The comfort of his arms and his presence. It's like a warm blanket wrapping around me. I didn't see this coming. He showed up in my life when I didn't even know I was looking for something more, anything at all. Someone to share memories with and someone who would be by my side.

He's here with me, rubbing his hands up and down my back. I'm taken aback by his sensitive side. Kissing the top of my head and squeezing me, he says, "I'm sorry. I should have asked you first."

His fingers come to my chin and lift my head so our eyes can meet. He stares into my eyes. It sends a shiver through my body, and he holds me even tighter. I don't think I've been held in such strong, powerful arms before, not like this. He grounds me.

He moves his head so close to mine; I don't know what to expect. "You're a strong, independent woman. That's what attracted me to you all those weeks ago and keeps me here now. I really am sorry. I don't even have an excuse, except that I want to protect you. I don't regret it, but I regret not talking to you first. You're right." He lets out a quick breath. "And…I'm sorry I didn't tell you yesterday, but…there was a note on your car that I snagged. It was from Jake."

I stiffen. "Wait! What?" He pulls a piece of paper from his back pocket and hands it to me. I read it, and my stomach tightens, nausea rolling up my throat. "Jake left this on my car? I might throw up." Shaking my head, I try to comprehend that Dane took the note off my car, didn't tell me, and I was almost prey to Jake. "Why wouldn't you tell me?"

"I thought I was protecting you. But really, Kendall. I'm sorry. I should have told you right away. It was your grand opening, and I didn't want you worrying about him. I was on high alert, and that's when I called for security."

Processing everything that's happened, I want to be angry with Dane, but I'm torn. He is protective, and it makes me feel safe. Geez, can he please tell me things without taking it upon himself to do what he thinks is right and best for me?

"Jake showing up, leaving me notes, has me rattled. I don't appreciate being kept in the dark about these things. Please tell me; ask me when things come up." She lets out a sigh. "Thank you for having security on the property."

Those words were hard to say, but they're the truth. I'm shocked at Jake showing up at the salon. It actually scares me that he is back around. Not just hanging across the street, but leaving notes for me. It's scary.

"I have you, Kendall." And his arms wrap around me. Scooping me up, my legs wrap around his waist.

He gazes up at me like I'm the only person in the world he wants. I'm lost in those caramel eyes that are begging me for something. And then he says, "Let me protect you."

I fight the urge to say I can protect myself because that's a flat-out lie. Instead, I slide my hand to hold his face and say, "Okay, Dane Walsh. You're diving in deep for someone who usually only has one-night stands."

He relaxes and closes his eyes. When he opens them again, it's like he went somewhere I'm not privy to. I say to him as I press a gentle kiss to his lips, "Why me?"

Kissing me back, he stares at me. His eyes captivate me, and I know I'm right where I want to be—with him.

"It's like you anchored yourself to me. I can't stop thinking about you. And for the record, you were my last one-night stand."

My mouth drops open, and I look at him with my eyebrows raised; I can't speak. He hasn't been with anyone else but me in the last few weeks.

I gather myself enough to choke out, "No one?!"

His guttural laugh makes me giggle. He says with conviction, "No one, sweetheart. The morning after we met, and you walked out that hotel room door, I regretted letting you leave. I knew you were going to be mine. Hook, line, and sinker. It was just a matter of when."

He walks us over to the couch with me still wrapped around him.

"And I walked out that door thinking I'd never see you again. You were that kind of guy, and I came to terms with it...even though I felt a magnetic pull to you."

His beautiful smile spreads across his face as he takes me in. "And look at us now."

"Yeah," I whisper. "So what are we going to do about Jake, this note?"

"I have a guy, Craig, on the force who took Jake into custody last night. I'll figure out who the judge is and will make sure he pays for what he's done to you. Then make sure he stays in jail for as long as I can."

Since Jake is in jail, at least for now, it allows me to breathe easier. "Thank you, Dane. It's hard to let someone help me. I rarely ask for help, nor do people freely give it. Well, accept my girlfriends."

"I'm here for you." His lips kiss my cheek. I can't help but slide my hand over his beard and face. Grabbing both sides, his caring eyes gaze back at me. The sincerity I see in him steals my breath. I pull his face forward and rub my lips on his. He moves his lips with mine until our tongues swipe each other in a kiss that has my head spinning and throbbing between my legs.

Holding onto the moment before I break away briefly to say, "Hold me tighter." And that's exactly what he does—holds me.

He drags his lips over to my ear and whispers, "I will always hold you today and every day after."

If I'm being honest with myself, I haven't ever been this happy, and that night with him...I knew there was a connection, but never expected it to amount to anything more than that one night.

His phone rings in his pocket. Digging it out, he looks at the screen and says, "It's my brother. Let me take this." I move away from him, and he answers the call. All I hear him say is, "Hey, Logan, what's up?"

This is my opportunity to text back my girlfriends. They've been blowing up my phone, but I've ignored them.

Kendall:

Yes, Dane is here! There's so much more to tell you guys. Here's the quickie: Jake's in custody with the police (big story there), Dane slept over, and he's still here. Oh, and he hired security!

Faith:

My house later today? You can't drop all that in a text.

Kendall:

He's coming back into the room. Keep you posted about later.

I was about to text again, but Dane strolls back into the living room. The look on his face—disappointment? No, sadness flashes through his eyes.

Walking over to him and laying a hand on his arm, I say, "Everything okay?"

THIRTY
Dane

C ircling my arms around her waist from behind, I nestle my face into the crook of her neck. I press my lips to her neck and say, "I have to go to the office. But for the record, I'd rather stay here wrapped up in you."

She reaches for my face. "I have a business, too. I know when work calls, you have to go."

What the...she's not going to complain? I have to leave and go to work on a Sunday. There's an odd feeling in my chest—a warmth and tightness. I bring her as close to me as possible, taking in one last smell of her watermelon shampoo, so I don't forget how she smells while I'm gone. When I was with Maggie, it was a knock-down, drag-out fight when I had to go to the office on weekends.

"Thank you for understanding. You won't be alone; four guys are patrolling the property, and there's a car down the street watching who comes in and out of your driveway."

"Wow! That's a lot of security. Is it really necessary now that Jake's in custody?"

I step back, holding both of her hands. "Yes, it is to keep you safe—protected. We don't know what he was planning to do, and it's better to be safe. I'm going to give you Joel's number. He is the head of security for your team, so he'll want to know when you leave and where you are going. They will follow you everywhere. Is that okay with you?

I mean, please say yes. It makes me feel like you're being taken care of even when I'm not here."

She takes a deep breath in and pulls my arms straight down so I have to lean closer to her. "Well, it sure isn't ideal to have a bunch of babysitters…" Staring straight through me, she continues, "But I trust you. Deep down. My gut is telling me your intentions are good. And it helps that I know your grandmother. You should thank her." She raises an eyebrow at me.

Pecking a quick kiss on my cheek, she tightens her grip on my hands.

"Thank you for trusting me. I've known Joel, the owner of this security company, for years. I'd trust them with my family. You're starting to feel like family, my family."

Did I say too much? It already feels like she belongs with me, part of my family.

"That's good to know. Here, put Joel's number in my phone. Then I guess you'd better head to the office and…"

She pauses and bites her lip. I wonder what she was going to say. Giving her back the phone, I keep quiet in hopes she'll finish her thought.

She mutters, "Will you be back tonight?"

Yes, I want to say, but I can't make any promises, not knowing what I'm walking into at the office. Logan is already there, and we have a major issue that needs to be addressed. I suspect I'll be sleeping on the couch in my office. Not ideal, but I do what needs to be done.

"I want to come back tonight, but I really don't know. I'll text you later if I can make it back. Does that work for you?"

Disappointment riddles her face, and she says, "Okay."

"We'll make plans for this week. I want to hold you every night, so don't get comfortable with me not sleeping next to you."

Her lips turn up, and that small gesture hits me in the chest. She's hooked, too. One last kiss. I don't want to let her go, but duty calls. "I'll see you."

"Just keep me posted. I'll probably head over to my girlfriend's or they'll come here, but either way, I'll let Joel know."

"Have fun with your girlfriends," I say, giving her one last squeeze, before I walk away from the woman that consumes me—my every thought. The woman with fiery red hair, a perfect match for her personality, fills my heart to the brim.

I open the garage and rush to my car. Starting it up, I back out of her garage. It feels normal to have stayed here—with her, do I dare say she feels like home.

The buzzing through my body is still there when I pull into the parking garage. Walking to the office, I'm in the zone.

I don't even make it all the way into the office, and Logan is yelling for me to get my ass in the conference room. Taking long strides, I walk into the conference room. "What is the problem?"

"Remember the case we had a couple of years ago with that woman who was almost killed by her boyfriend? He was definitely guilty, but we didn't figure it out until the end, when the prosecutor found the evidence that he was lying. Thankfully, we lost that one. Anyway, he was released on parole. He was supposed to do twenty years, and they let him out on parole in two. Someone's lining pockets. Anyway, he contacted us."

"We have no further client relationship, and we lost, so why is he calling?"

"Get this—his buddy was arrested last night. He's saying his buddy is innocent and wants to know if we will represent him when he sees the judge."

I grab a seat at the table and say, "First, I'm not taking on a client that's a buddy of this guy. That's a hard fucking no for me."

"Well, I asked him for his buddy's name and some details. You need to hear this."

"I came all the way down here, so tell me—what?"

He pushes his chair out and leans his elbows on his legs. "There's a restraining order against him...from Kendall."

"You've got to be shitting me! I had him arrested. There's no way in hell we're defending that asshole. He can rot in his jail cell."

"Brother, you need to back up and fill me in. How do you know him?"

I can't sit any longer. I hop out of my chair and run my fingers through my beard. Pacing. I decide Logan needs to be brought up to speed, and I give him the details of the last forty-eight hours.

"What are the odds of his buddy calling us? That's shit luck if you ask me."

"We are not taking this," I say, shaking my head

He takes his hand and runs it down his face. "I agree."

"The minute I saw Kendall's name in the file, I called you. So...Kendall?"

There's more work to do, and we don't have time to spend gushing about the woman who has consumed my every thought.

"Logan, let's focus on our case for tomorrow."

"You're seriously not going to give me anything, absolutely nothing, while we are here for hours combing through files?"

"There's not much to tell," I shrug like it's no big deal, like she isn't the sun that I'm revolving around.

He laughs and points at me. "I call bullshit. Come on, you can't lie to me; I see right through it. You even tried to cover up your smile when you walked in here. Newsflash, asshole, you're not hiding it well enough. You're happy."

There's no way he's giving up on this one, so I start at the beginning, and by the time I'm finished, his mouth is on the floor.

I don't fight it anymore. "Yeah, I am happy."

Who would have thought Kendall would be my kryptonite, the one who reigns in Dane Walsh? It's like every breath I take, it's for her, to be back with her in my arms, protecting what's mine. It prompts me to text Joel.

> Dane:
>
> Hey, can you give me periodic updates?

> Joel:
>
> You hooked, huh?

> Dane:
>
> Fuck off and do your job!

> Joel:
>
> You know I need to bust your balls, man. Call me. I'll fill you in.

I say to Logan, "I need five minutes. I'm going to call Joel."

He knows Joel, too. "Tell him I said hi."

Joel gives me the status update. She left to hang out with her friends at Faith's house. He told me not to worry, as he would not let her out of his sight, which makes me feel a lot better.

> Dane:
>
> Hey, I don't think I'll be back tonight. Text me when you get home.

> Kendall:
>
> How do you know I'm not home?

This woman tests me at every turn. She knows Joel is a good friend and, of course, I'd want updates on her. But after the conversation earlier today, I tread lightly.

Dane:

I just checked in with Joel and he updated me.

Hoping that will calm her.

Kendall:

You know you could have just texted me. I'd tell you my whereabouts.

I'm off the hook. I thought for sure she'd give me an earful. I decide to put the ball in her court.

Dane:

That sounds like a great idea. Why don't you text me when you get home?

Kendall:

I can do that.

Dane:

Thank you

Back to the case we've been working on for weeks now. After a couple of hours discussing a theory, we dump it and move on. It's already midnight. I check my phone to see if Kendall texted me. She hasn't.

Dane:

Home yet?

My eyes go cross-eyed. I need a few hours of sleep, and then I can stare at the board we created with much more clarity.

"I'm going to sleep on my couch for a couple of hours. What are you doing?" I say as I lift myself from the chair and start walking to the conference room door.

"Yeah, I'm not driving home either. I'm going to finish up and then crash in my office. I'll see you in a couple of hours."

My shoes scuff against the office floors as I drag myself to my office. Once I walk in, I close the door and turn on the lamp on the side table near my black leather couch, which has a couple of throw pillows. My decorator said they were a must, and now I'm glad I have them to sleep on. I look around and admire all the accomplishments that hang on the wall and bookcase. With no more energy, I throw myself on the couch, not even removing my shoes. My arm goes over my eyes, and my nose tickles with the faint smell of watermelon. It's all I need to picture Kendall in my arms.

I'm running down the stairs. Where is she? We fell asleep together, but now she's nowhere to be found. I'm out of my mind, yelling for her. The silence is deafening. And then I reach the back door slider, and I see her being dragged away by Jake. What the fuck? I'm supposed to be protecting her. How did I let this happen? Where the fuck is the security team? I sprint out the door, no shoes on, and reach her. She has blood all over her face and hands. Jake pulls a gun out and says, "One more step and I'll kill you and her." He waves the gun around. I see it in her eyes; she's going to try to stop him. I stare at her, nodding slightly. And then, she grabs the gun, and I rush over. But I'm too late; he pulls the trigger and shoots her.

THIRTY-ONE
Kendall

H anging out with my friends tonight is therapeutic; it's great to share what's happened.

"That's a lot?" Faith drawls.

"Yes," I say, shaking my head in disbelief, even though I'm the one who lived through it.

And of course, what they focus on is Dane...

"You're head over heels for him! I can see it in your eyes and that smile." Lane is observant, I'll give her that. But she isn't wrong, not even a little bit.

"Any time he's near me, my body reacts to him. The crackling energy between us is incomprehensible, to be honest. I mean, we're already butting heads. He hired security without asking me. Didn't tell me about the Jake note. Why?"

"Oh my...it's the end of the world because some hot attorney hired security for you, and he wants to protect you. Do you even hear yourself talking?" Addison jumps into the conversation. The reality of what she is saying hits me hard. I mean, she isn't wrong.

"Seriously, Kendall, Addison has a point. I understand how you would see that move as a power play, but I see it as endearing and kinda sexy. I know you have a certain perspective on all of this, and I don't want to dismiss that at all. I want you to think about it from all perspectives, that all," Faith says, as she leans in closer. "But what we all really want to know is...how is it?"

They are clapping and hooting before one word leaves my mouth. To indulge them further, I say, "We are like a raging inferno. Two flames becoming one when we're together; it's like a bonfire. In all seriousness, when he holds me, I fit just right in his arms." My body heats just talking about him.

"We've never seen you so starry-eyed over a guy before. But that right there," Lane says as she points and makes circles in the air in front of me. "Are you falling for this guy? I mean, have you already fallen for him?"

I can't deny it. I think back to the night we met. It was a natural attraction between the two of us. That first night together, the sex blew my mind. But it was the magnetism between us. Reality kicked in when we woke up in the morning. I thought I was just another notch in his belt. I'm better than that, so I tried to forget about him. That worked out well for me. It was like at every turn, there he was.

"When will you see him again?" Addison asks.

"I don't know. I haven't heard from him since he went to work, but we have another date on Saturday night. He also mentioned wanting to sleep in bed with me. So who knows, maybe that will happen this week." I stare at my clasped hands, thinking about him snuggling up to me, stroking my back.

"I still can't believe he left you to go to work on a Sunday," Lane says.

I shrug and raise my hands. "It's not a big deal. I suspect this happens often, since he told me his ex wasn't thrilled with his work schedule."

"You're way more understanding than I would be," Lane says.

She likes predictability, so that makes a ton of sense.

As if he were listening to my conversation, Dane texted me.

"Is that Dane?"

"Yes...but what the hell! He's asking me when I'll be home. How does he even know I'm not home?"

"Calm down, Kendall. I want you to take a deep breath before you respond." Faith moves closer to me and touches my shoulder. She is calm about this, and I'm ready to fly off the handle. He has no boundaries. Whatever he says goes. But I do what she says. "Now close your eyes and think about him holding you and protecting you. How do you feel?"

I hate when she plays therapist with me. "I feel angry that he didn't ask me. Instead, he asked his friend if I was home. It feels like he wants me under his thumb. It feels familiar, like when Jake would do shit like this."

"Ah, and there it is."

I open my eyes and say, "I know that's my trigger. Everything that asshole did affects me."

"What are your thoughts on telling Dane what you'd prefer him to do?"

"That makes sense now that you say it out loud." I shake my head, knowing that all of this makes perfect sense.

"You need to take a few minutes to step back and look at all perspectives. He wants to protect you, and you don't want to feel like you are being controlled and told what to do. It all tracks. Communicate what you want. You're good at that...when you're not triggered."

So I text him back, and his response seems calm and understanding.

"See, you got this, and well...maybe him too."

"I'm pretty sure it's mutual." I laugh and brush my hand through my hair.

The night continues with talk of our yearly girls' trip over ice cream. We like to book it at least six months ahead. This year, we are deciding between Turks and Caicos or Aruba. Right now, it's a split vote. We are all on our phones researching nightlife and excursions available at all-inclusive resorts. My vote is for Aruba, but I'm double-checking the resort on Turks and Caicos. Maybe something will pop up that will sway me.

The votes were still tied after spending some time scouring the all-inclusive resorts. To break the tie, we put pieces of paper into a bowl—two for T&C and two for Aruba. Faith mixes them up, and we decide which one gets picked; we go there first, then we'll do the other island the following year. It seems like a good plan.

And she pulls—Aruba. Addison and I yell, "Yes!"

We are heading to Aruba in February. I can't wait. I'll be counting down. I'm so excited for this trip. The resort boasts five-star restaurant reviews, pools, ocean-view rooms, and tiki bars located both poolside and beachside.

It's getting late. I peer out the living room window to see the black SUV sitting at the curb. Joel and his guys are here watching over the place. A calmness washes over me, knowing they are here. And I silently say thank you to Dane for hiring them. As upsetting as it was to hear at first, I'm grateful.

"Do we have time for a movie?" Faith lowers herself onto the couch.

"I do because I don't have work tomorrow and can sleep in a bit. After this weekend, I'm ready for a good night's sleep," I say as a yawn escapes. We all laugh.

Lane and Addison decide to go home because they both have early mornings on Mondays. We say our goodbyes. I love them. I can't believe it's been eleven years since we first met and became best friends in college.

After they leave, Faith and I cuddle up on the couch with our blankets even though it's seventy degrees outside. The air conditioning is chilly now that night has fallen, and our bodies are tired. Faith picks *10 Things I Hate About You*. I love this movie, so I tuck my feet under me and get comfortable.

The movie credits roll, and my eyes are barely open. It might not be a good idea to drive home. I wonder if it's okay to ask Joel to drive me home. Eh, it's worth asking.

Kendall:

Joel, is it too much to ask you to drive me home? I didn't expect to be so exhausted.

Joel:

You bet. We are right at the curb.

Kendall:

Be out in 10

It's convenient to have these guys around.

"Faith, I'm going to leave my car here. I'll figure out how to pick it up tomorrow. It's a tomorrow-me problem."

"I can always pick you up after work and bring you back. Just let me know."

"Sounds good." I hug her tight. "Thank you for tonight. Keeping things in perspective for me."

"Isn't that what friends are for?"

Taking a step out the door, I turn and say, "Yes." And I blow her a kiss.

Joel opens the back door for me, and I hop into the SUV. We drive in silence all the way home, which is unusual for me, but I'm exhausted. With my eyes closed, I'm pretty sure I fell asleep for a split second. I was only resting my eyes.

We pull into my driveway. Joel opens the door again so I can step out. "Thank you."

"You're very welcome. Get some sleep. We'll be around. Text or call if you need us."

"I appreciate everything you're doing."

He nods at me and then hops back into the SUV. They drive down the street to their post.

I barely remember going into the house, undressing, and getting into bed. My head hits the pillow and I'm out.

I hear my phone ringing on the nightstand. Dragging myself out of a deep sleep, I quickly answer it without looking at who was calling.

"Hello?" I say with a groggy voice.

THIRTY-TWO

Dane

I wake up screaming, "Kendall!"

I'm sweating through my shirt. I pop my body up, and I realize I'm in my office. Searching for my phone, I pick it up and look at the screen. She hasn't texted me about being home. Maybe that's why my subconscious played out my worst fear.

No text from her makes my heart beat out of my chest. I find her name and call her. Yes, I'm calling her at two o'clock in the morning. Hearing her voice is the only way to calm me, knowing she is home safe and sound.

"Hello?"

Oh, thank fucking god, she answered the phone. "Are you home? Are you okay?"

"Dane? It's—I don't know what time it is in the middle of the night. Why are you calling? And yes, I'm home and okay. Are you okay? You sound out of breath?"

Shaking my head at myself, I say, "You didn't text me. I fell asleep and woke up, still in a sleep fog, with no text from you; I was concerned. So I called. I'm sorry to wake you, sweetheart."

Pulling myself together, this woman has dread running through my body, thinking something bad happened to her. It's at this moment that I know what I need to do.

"Well, I'm home safe, exhausted, and need to go back to sleep." I hear her yawn. These last couple of days have been taxing for her. "Will I see you tomorrow, I mean today?"

"Yes, sweetheart. I'll make it a point to leave the office on time, and I'll bring us dinner. I'll text you around noon. Sleep well." I rub the ache in my chest, hoping for relief, but it doesn't subside.

"Okay, see you later. Night." And she hangs up the phone.

I take a few breaths and continue to rub my chest. My heart rate is finally evening out as my brother comes flying into my office like a freight train out of control. "You okay? I heard you scream."

"Yeah, I had a dream that Kendall was shot by her ex."

He stands there staring at me with sleepy eyes, like he is trying to process what I said. "You're telling me you had a nightmare?" And it doesn't take long for him to be keeled over laughing his ass off at me.

"It wasn't a nightmare, asshole. It was a dream," I say. As I speak the words, it becomes clear I'm trying to convince myself, too.

As he continues laughing, he says, "Yeah, yeah, just a dream."

"Fuck off."

"It's the middle of the night, and you have me laughing so hard my stomach hurts. Did you want to talk about it?" he asks in a sarcastic tone.

"No, I don't want to talk about it. But for the record, she is safe at home and in bed."

"Good to know. You going back to sleep?"

"Nope."

"Me either. Let's get back to it."

We spent the next few hours running through witness testimonies and pages of documents. Tossing theories back and forth, we work well together and usually develop a working theory quickly.

My phone rings, and I look at the screen. It's the judge calling us back at eight o'clock on the dot.

"Hello, Your Honor."

We talk back and forth to figure out how we can make this guy pay for what he did to Kendall. He owes me a favor, and right now, all I need is for Kendall to never have to worry about that dickface, Jake, again. Since he has some outstanding warrants, it appears he will be in state custody for a while. He'll update me once it's a done deal. But he reminds me that there's only so much time he can navigate around.

"Thank you, Your Honor. I'll get on it."

Right now, all I can think about is how much I'm missing her—like crazy.

"Logan, I'm heading out for a bit. You should head home too. We can come back later and keep working."

"My eyes keep crossing, so I need a break. Meet you back here later."

We both leave the office before anyone else arrives. I hop in my car and text Kendall.

Dane:

I'm on my way over. Don't make coffee…I'm bringing it from the coffeehouse.

Turning the ignition, the engine roars to life. I love this car. I have only a few hours, and I know she is off work today. Knowing her, she has plans today, but with a busy week and weekend, maybe she decided to relax.

Kendall:

You have a thing about waking me. Is it your mission in life?

Sweetheart, I have a mission for you, and it has nothing to do with sleep.

Ring the doorbell, and I'll come down.

You don't even need to leave your room. Let me in through the garage.

Smart guy...while I'm over here half asleep.

Be there in a few minutes.

I drive to the coffeehouse. When I pull up to the curb to park, I realize I've been daydreaming the entire time. I don't remember the drive at all. Kendall is all I can think about. Sliding the shifter into park, I lift myself out and order our coffees and a couple of breakfast sandwiches. She had a cinnamon roll the last time I saw her here, so I opt to grab a couple of those too.

Taking the coffees, I put them in my cup holders, and then place the food on the floor of my car. The last thing I need is to slam on my brakes and have the food fly all over the floor. How do I know this is possible? It's happened before, more than once.

As I turn into her driveway, she must have been watching for me, or her camera signaled I had arrived. The garage door opens, and I park my car in my spot. My spot, I laugh at myself. Already claiming a parking spot. Why not? I claimed her as mine, so a parking spot seems appropriate.

Gathering up the coffees and food, I walk to the door and open it. "Sweetheart, I'm home," I yell in a soft tone.

No response. I take everything upstairs to her, my feet padding on the hardwood floors down the hall to her bedroom. Walking in, I see her lying in bed with her red hair splayed over her pillow. She looks like a queen, all mine. I stroll in and say, "Good morning."

"Good morning...you're in a good mood."

"Only because I'm able to see your gorgeous face this morning. I can't stay too long, but I didn't want to pass up the opportunity to bring you coffee and some food, since I woke you twice in less than a few hours." I shrug and give her my best smile, hoping she'll forgive me. With coffees in hand, I pass one over to her and a bag with her breakfast sandwich.

She sits up in bed, sips her coffee, and eyes the bags. "You brought me food, too?"

I lower myself onto the bed and lean over to kiss her sweet lips. "I figured you'd be starving." I slowly bring the other bag to her—the one with the cinnamon rolls. "And a little sweet treat for later."

"What is in here?" she says and gazes at me. Her piercing emerald green eyes send a jolt through my entire body. Consuming me from the inside out, I kiss her again.

"Cinnamon rolls. You're the best!" she says, throwing her arms around my neck.

She's the best, the best thing that's ever happened to me. It's way too soon to even utter those words out loud. So they stay in my heart until the time is right. This week at the office will be brutal. I hope she'll be as understanding as she was yesterday. It feels good to have someone support me rather than tear me down. I've worked hard to be one of the best defense attorneys.

Interrupting my thoughts, she says, "You know you didn't have to leave the office to do this, right?"

"I know I didn't have to, but I sure wanted to. I wanted to see you even if it was for thirty minutes because that's probably all I have today." I kiss her neck as she chews her bite of cinnamon roll and moans. Her and that fucking moan when she eats.

She has a hold on my heart, and I can't escape it, not that I want to. Watching her sip her coffee, I'm mesmerized by her reaction to this simple act. My chest expands. Then she scooches her butt back further, and the blanket falls off her legs as she crosses them. She's wearing a T-shirt and nothing else. Oh hell, all I see is red lace flashing at me. If she realizes it, she's not doing a damn thing about it.

Willing my dick to stand down, this is not the time. Focus on her face, focus on her face. What is she saying?

"Well, it makes me feel special that you would do this for me, so thank you."

"Anything for you, sweetheart. What's on your agenda for today?"

"These past few weeks have been intense, and with this past weekend, I'm looking forward to catching up on laundry and grocery shopping. Very exciting life over here, I know. Then if I still have some energy this afternoon, I'll hit the gym."

"That sounds low-key for you. Anything I can do to help you?" I reach over and rub her arms.

"No, I'll put in a grocery order and pick it up."

"We'd have fun working out together, as long as you're not an angry workout person." She giggles and takes a sip of her coffee.

Maggie wouldn't step foot in a gym and complained that I prioritized gym time over her. The more time I spend with Kendall, the more I see why Grams thought she was right for me.

We sip our coffee together and talk about our gym routines. I want to soak up everything she tells me, given the little time we have left today.

She finishes her coffee and places it on the nightstand, and asks me, "Do you mind dropping me off at my car when you head back to the office? I left it at Faith's last night. I was too tired to drive, so Joel drove me home."

I take a quick look at my watch and realize it's been an hour already. "Yes, but we need to leave in five minutes so I can get back to the office. I'm surprised my phone isn't ringing off the hook with my brother nagging me to get back."

The laugh that comes out of her makes me want to hear it again. Gazing at her and all her morning glory, I want to spend all of my free time with her, even doing all the mundane things in life.

"Okay, let me get dressed, and then I'll be ready."

She slides off the bed and stands up. That t-shirt is not covering her ass, and those red underwear aren't your regular lacy underwear; no, it's a g-string. Fuck me! I rub the back of my neck. This is harder than I thought. I can't help myself. I jump off the bed and wrap my arms around her waist as her back leans against my chest. Tucking my head in the crook of her neck, I whisper in her ear, "You're fucking killing me with this outfit you have going on." I suck her neck, and she leans to the side so I have better access.

My cock is like steel. There's no more willing it down. It has a mind of its own, and it's poking into her back. Ever so slightly, I feel her pushing her ass back into me.

I stick my nose in her hair and say, "I love the smell of your shampoo. Never change it."

"I love it too, so I won't be changing it anytime soon. But if we need to leave, let me go."

"What if I don't want to?" I rattle off. But knowing I need to get back to the office, I smile anyway.

THIRTY-THREE
Kendall

I 'd love to have Dane all to myself today, but I know his brother is waiting for him. I decide to tease him a bit. "I have the day off, so you can stay..."

He grumbles as he loosens his embrace on me. "I want to stay and devour every inch of you and then take you out to dinner and show you off to the world."

"Are we still on for Saturday's date?" I ask, turning around to graze my lips over his. He immediately tugs my hips to him. I bite down on my lower lip as his erection stabs my stomach, and it takes everything in me not to drop to my knees and rip his pants down. With his thick cock stretching my mouth, I'd suck him dry. It wouldn't take long for his cum to be dripping down my throat.

The throbbing between my legs has me tilting and rubbing myself over him.

"You're killing me, and I really do not want to go back to work now." He crashes onto my lips as he grabs my ass and tosses me onto the bed. Hovering over me, dragging his erection over my center, I wrap my legs around his waist.

I need him right now, like I need air to breathe. Nibbling on his bottom lip, then sliding my tongue across his jaw and to his ear. I ask him again, "Are we on for Saturday?"

He grunts out. "We are definitely on for Saturday. But I'll see you after work on Friday. It might be late."

Moaning in his ear, I say, "That sounds like too long."

"Sweetheart, my schedule is crazy. It won't change anytime soon. I hope we can make it work."

"Of course we can. I'd rather have you here more than I'd like to admit."

"Me too."

With one last kiss, I slide my tongue barely against his, and he sucks it into his mouth. Holy hell, the electricity between us is addicting, and if we don't stop, we will be naked and tangled in each other.

I break away first. "Let me get dressed, and you can drive me to my car." One last peck on the cheek, and the pad of his thumb runs over my bottom lip. It takes all my willpower to walk away from him, but I do it. We'll have a lot of pent-up tension come this weekend.

We leave my house and drive to Faith's to pick up my car. It takes less than ten minutes. He parks his car next to mine. We both get out at the same time. He walks me to my car with our fingers intertwined.

He leans his body up against mine, and I end up with my back against my car. "You are gorgeous. I hope you have an amazing day running your errands. I'll text you later, but I'm probably at the office late all week."

"Okay, text me later." And as I go to turn, he crashes his lips into mine as he threads his fingers in my hair to pull me harder against his mouth. I don't think this will ever get old for me. The way he holds me. The way his tongue dances with mine is in perfect rhythm with each other. His hand moves to my face, holding it. Fire ripping through my body, my stomach tightening, and my arms wrapped around his neck. The passion is undeniable.

He leans back ever so slightly. "You're mine." I feel his breath on my face. My eyes close, taking in the heat and feel of his touch. "Have a great day, sweetheart."

"Don't work too hard. You need to sleep sometime."

"Yeah, that's why I have a comfy couch in my office. Makes life a lot easier. But now, with you, maybe that will change." He smirks at me, and his fingers brush through my hair.

My eyes instantly close as I feel the feather-like touch through my hair. "Maybe it will."

With one more kiss to my cheek, he turns and walks to his car. "I'll text you later."

I stand there savoring the moment as I watch him pull away. When I can't see his car anymore, I slide into the seat, order my groceries, and decide that while I'm out, I'll do all my errands around town.

I spent the afternoon lounging on my back deck, soaking up the sun. I needed some relaxation time by the pool. I still can't believe Jake showed back up here and is now in jail. After shoving all of it so far down, it's bubbling up involuntarily. I ignored it all weekend. I mean, the distraction was appreciated, and by no means am I complaining. Dane has been there at every moment, apparently, whether I like it or not.

And there have been times I wanted to yell at him, well...I did that too. As I sit here in the quiet, with no distractions...I have a knot in my stomach thinking about this whole mess. It all comes tumbling out of me. Tears streak down my cheeks, and I can't stop them. Days of shit piling up, ignoring it, and now, I'm sitting here by myself sobbing. It's not a good look, but it needs to come out.

I question whether I should message Dane; I hate to interrupt his workday. But I want to feel our connection right now. Snapping a picture of the pool with my legs and feet in the picture, I send it.

Kendall:

Wish you were here to enjoy the peace and quiet on my deck.

I didn't expect him to respond right away. I place my phone on the side table next to my chair and decide to take a walk around the yard to ground myself. The pool is crystal clear, and the grass is a brighter green than it was last year. Probably because of the rain followed by all the sun we've gotten lately, it feels plush on my feet. As I walk around, I see Joel's team milling around the property. A sigh of relief escapes me.

It feels weird to have security. Of course, Dane's face pops into my head, and I'm wishing he were here with me. Then I question whether it's to distract me or to spend more time with him. When we are together, my entire body lights up, and I forget the world.

I shake my head; it doesn't matter. He's busy at work, and sitting with my feelings about what's happened with Jake is probably a good thing. And if I'm being honest, I could use some alone time to sort through my feelings about Dane, too. Nothing like a bunch of feelings all at once. I laugh. This is my life.

As I walk through the grass, I scuff my feet and really feel the grass between my toes. Focusing on the now, the present. My body urges me to lie down. Lowering myself to the ground, I spread my legs, stretch my arms, and with eyes closed, I listen. The chatter in my head is overwhelming, so I place one hand on my heart and the other on my belly. Deep breaths in through my nose and out through my mouth, I settle my mind, my body, and connect to my breath and to nature. My body feels as though it has sunk further into the ground, as relaxation rolls through me.

I lay there for what felt like an hour. My skin is burning, my eyes are tired, and my body doesn't want to move. Staying there a few extra minutes, I hear my phone's text tone, but if it's important, they'll call.

When I start to sweat profusely, I slowly sit up and brush my hands through my hair. One last deep breath, and I stand up. Making my way to the deck to check my phone before taking a dip in the pool, I pick up my phone.

Dane:

Look at those toes...I want to be there with you.

Kendall:

Well, then why aren't you here?

Teasing him a little, knowing he's stuck in his office.

Dane:

This weekend.

My body slumps as disappointment rolls through me. I knew it was a long shot that he'd drop everything to come over, but I know he's busy at work. I can't wait for our date on Saturday. If it's anything like the one we had last weekend, I'll be treated to top-notch food, laughs, eyes that will be glued to me, and searing heat coursing through my body. I love it all.

Plopping myself into my chair with a long sigh, I lightly toss my phone down on the table. I stare out at the pool and decide to take a dip anyway. I leap out of the chair and take off my clothes. I see someone out of the corner of my eye, and I whip my head around, heart pumping. Dane's here. I turn on my heels, and he is up against my body so quickly that the wind is knocked out of my lungs.

"You're here?!" I'm shocked, excited, and overwhelmed. Tears threaten my eyes, but I hold them back. "You said this weekend."

I throw my arms around him and yank him into me. Not that we can get any closer than we already are. My heart is racing, and a huge smile is on my face. I rest my head on his chest as he moves his fingers down my spine. The prickling that spreads through my body makes my nipples tighten.

He dips his head down to take my chin with his fingers and guide my head up to gaze at me. "I didn't want to give away the surprise. I'm here, sweetheart. How are you?"

"Better now that you are here." My heart stumbles, and my body lights up.

I take a step back, lips curling into a smile. "Let's hit the pool."

In his boxer briefs, I can't help but glimpse his bulge. I've seen it before, and still, I bite my lip, thinking about what's under that thin fabric.

He takes my hand in his as we walk to the pool and wade in. I use it all the time, and now I get to share it with Dane, who holds me tight as we sink into the water.

"Let's float and chill," I say, hopping onto my swan float. I barely make it on without falling off. I laugh so hard. Dane is watching me with a smirk on his face, probably wondering if I need help. No, I don't. The splashing and yelling has the security team's attention.

I practically fall off the swan when the security guy yells, "Are you okay?"

I scream and grab onto the neck of the swan. I'm now laughing so hard I can't even answer him. He's standing there waiting for an answer. Finally, I stop laughing enough to say, "Yeah, sorry about that, just trying to mount this swan." I can't help but giggle.

The quick flash of an almost smile has me eyeing him. "Not allowed to laugh?"

"I try to keep things professional."

Dane speaks up after observing the whole thing. "She's good. I got her." His stern and authoritative tone has me staring at him. Wondering why he's going all Hulk on the guy.

"Well, I hope when you walk away you'll tell all your friends about what just happened and you all have a really good laugh on my account," I say to the security guy, trying to lighten the mood that Dane put a damper on.

"Have a nice afternoon, ma'am, sir."

Dane makes his way over to me. "You look gorgeous laid out like that."

"We can connect to each other and chat while we soak up the sun. And hope I don't fall off." I laugh and roll my eyes at myself. I'm sure it was comical and video-worthy.

He swims to grab the turtle float. Watching him leap onto it, I stare at his back muscles that flex as he effortlessly lifts himself onto it.

Lying on his back, his body is a fine piece of art. I'm gawking.

"Do you like what you see?" Ah, he definitely caught me—everything about him is irresistible. I actually don't know why I haven't ripped off my swimsuit and thrown myself at him. Oh, I know we'd have an audience. Although I highly doubt they would mind watching us in the pool. It would be entertaining for them.

Get your head out of the gutter.

"Always." I toss back at him.

There are already beads of sweat on my forehead. To cool off, I roll off into the pool. When I finally bounce up to the surface, Dane is on top of me. Picking me up and twirling me. My body relaxes in his arms as I arch my back and throw my arms up while he continues to twirl me.

I lean into him, wrapping my arms around his neck. He whispers in my ear, "I love seeing you like this. A smile on your face and your spirit free. That's what I remember about you. It was you who hooked me all those weeks ago, and I wouldn't change it."

This afternoon with Dane sounds like we may have a carefree afternoon. He even seems relaxed. "Hey, what about work?"

"It will be there when I get back later. Logan and one of our associates are taking on the big case without me. So I can wrap up some of these smaller cases."

"Well, you look a hell of a lot less stressed than when I saw you this morning."

As he grabs my ass and lifts me up, I wrap my legs around him. He moves with steady purpose, the gentle resistance of the water parting around us as we drift toward the wall.

"Taking care of things relieves stress, and being with you makes me happy."

His vulnerability. I know it's written all over my face—my cheeks hurt. "I don't hide much, so you probably already know this, but when you walked onto the deck, I was thrilled to see you. You know how much I like a good surprise."

That mischievous grin has me a little concerned, in a good way. He is taking mental notes right now, but I don't mind. His fingers reach up and pull on a few strands of my hair. I can't help but lick my lips.

"Can I tell you something?" he says, dragging his thumb over my bottom lip. It's so light—my eyes close.

THIRTY-FOUR

Dane

"Look at me." It comes out as a demand.

Her eyes open wide. "Okay." She sinks deeper into my lap. Thinking back to the events that led us here, it's nothing but a miracle that we are holding each other. Protecting her, while enjoying her, all of her.

"We've been so caught up in the Jake bullshit. Could you tell me more about how you came up with the idea for the salon and spa? We didn't talk about it over the weekend. So tell me..."

"It will take a few hours. Are you available for that?"

"I'm available for all of it, sweetheart." I mean every word. I'm not leaving—she's mine. My heart is filled and about to explode. She makes me feel things, things I haven't felt before—ever.

"Buckle up, babe," she says to me with a playful shake of my shoulder. She called me babe. I like the ring of that. I nod for her to continue.

"After college, I worked a research job and hated every minute. Corporate was not my jam at all. I thought I'd get used to it, especially making the kind of money I did. I'd be set in a few years. But a year in, it was awful. Some men in leadership took advantage of the younger women on staff—it was hard to stomach. I knew I needed to get out. But I stayed another year, mostly to buy time while I figured out my next move."

I interject, "Were you taken advantage of?"

She massages my temples, and my shoulders relax. "No, I wasn't, but it was exhausting trying to console all the women affected."

My body is catching up with what she said. It wasn't her. This woman has me wrapped around her finger, and I like it that way. "Thankfully."

"Do you need to take a few breaths before I keep telling you the story?" she teases and kisses my temple.

"Sassy. Fucking sassy! Go on."

She moves her fingers to my shoulders and massages them. "I stock-piled a bunch of money, went to cosmetology school, and started taking business classes. All so I could open up a little salon and keep life simple, play by my own rules, and tell corporate jerks to shove it up their asses."

Fiery, she is perfect, and I can picture her walking away from that corporate office, holding up double middle fingers, saying fuck off. "And the rest is history?"

"It took way longer than I expected for the salon to be profitable, but I was able to hang on long enough to reap the benefits of all my hard work without going under. Actually, it was your Gram that helped make the salon successful. She told all of her friends and even strangers—anyone who would listen."

"Gram? Yeah, she's a firecracker. A lot like you. No wonder the two of you get along so well."

"Firecracker?" Eying me with an arched brow, she says, "Jane's a pretty amazing woman, and I love listening to all of her stories."

"I'm sure she hasn't repeated any of them—there are so many."

"The only one she repeats periodically is her love story, but I enjoy hearing it."

The intense pull on my heart is overwhelming as she talks about my Gram and the love story she tells everyone. All the tidbits and their true love and how love found them.

All I can say is, "Yeah."

"Opening the spa has been a year-long mission; it has had its moments and bumps in the road. It's all worth it after the grand opening. Being able to hire employees to support the local economy and offering services that clients have asked for is a win-win all around."

I realize I've been stroking her arm the whole time she's been talking—entranced in her story. She's committed to her vision and made it happen. I like her even more now, knowing all of this; she's ambitious as fuck. It's an inspiring story. She's one of a kind and all mine.

"You must be proud of yourself. Those are tremendous accomplishments—leaving a corporate job to start your own business."

"I am. It's been a long road. I've learned so much about the industry, about myself, town politics...." She winks at me. "Thank you again for helping me with that. It made a real difference on the timeline. I'm not sure I'll ever stop thanking you for that."

I was fired up when she was being taken advantage of by the building department. I'm glad I took care of it for her. Sometimes you need to flex some muscle with them.

"Glad I could be of service." Taking her face in my hands while she still holds my neck, and ask, "How did I let you walk out of that hotel room?"

"Dane, I don't believe there was anything you could have said to make me stay. I had a preconceived notion about who you were. You were the one-night stand guy."

"Yeah, you left an impression on me—in many ways." I kiss her lips. "I knew it that day and all the days after." My lips back on hers, gripping her hips. With her arms around my neck, she darts her tongue into my mouth. I ravage her mouth like I've never tasted her before. The intensity vibrates through my body with all the blood rushing south. But nothing else matters except her and me here in this moment. She's the one. I move my hands to cup her face and slide my tongue in and out of her mouth. She's everything I didn't know I wanted.

The world stops around us as I bring my mouth to her ear and whisper, "You are the only woman I want in my life. My heart doesn't know how to beat when you're not in it. Every thought always circles back to you—your face, your body, your heart. You have quickly become my favorite thing in the entire world, and I haven't been the same since that night."

She grazes her fingers through my beard. "Never in my wildest dreams would I have expected us to be standing here, holding each other. To hear those words, Dane...there are butterflies in my stomach, and the electricity that bounces between us could light up an entire city."

My blood pressure is never the same when she is around. I run the pads of my thumbs over the dark circles under her eyes. She's exhausted. Scanning her body up and down as we wade out of the water earns me a slap on the shoulder. I laugh it off. "Why don't we head inside and change? Are you hungry?"

"Yeah, a bit."

Once we're out of the pool, she grabs a couple of towels from the cabinet in the corner. Drying off, we wrap up in the towels and head inside. When I walk by the chair, I swipe my clothes off of it.

"Why don't you go and shower, get comfy, and by the time you get back down here, I'll have an early dinner ready?"

"You mean you'll have dinner delivered?" she asks with suspicion in her tone.

"You'll see when you come back downstairs, but take your time," I say as I grab her ass and drag her into me. Her emerald green eyes suck me into her vortex. I lean in, giving her a kiss she'll be thinking about later. I love the feel of her soft lips and the way her tongue teases mine.

"Then I'll see you in a bit."

I can't help but watch her ass sway as she heads to the stairs. When she is out of sight, I make quick work of taking off my wet boxer briefs and throwing on my clothes. I hang everything up on the deck railing to dry. Heading inside, I rummage through her cabinets and fridge, seeing if there's anything I can make for dinner. I know she picked up her groceries. Almost everything I need is here, so I start placing things out onto the counter.

I decide to make her grilled salmon with a salad and a side of sweet potato. Grabbing my phone, I make a quick call to my assistant and rattle off a couple of items to have her deliver to me in the next twenty minutes.

I busy myself by preparing all the food and making the salad first. Once I'm finished, I sprinkle the salmon for the grill with buttery herb seasoning and place it on the counter. I wash the sweet potatoes and put them in foil. Everything is ready to be cooked.

It sounds like she is still in the shower, which is great. She's taking her time. I step onto the deck, uncover the grill, and light it. As I walk back into the house, my assistant texts me she's here since I didn't want her to ring the doorbell, so I turn around and walk out to meet her. She bought dessert and flowers.

"Thank you. I'll see you later or tomorrow at the office."

"You're welcome. Enjoy your time." She flashes me a grin.

She doesn't come out and say what's on her mind, but I can read her like a book. I wave and head back to the front door, and go straight to the kitchen in search of a vase. Under the sink? Empty. Pantry? Still no luck.

How does this woman not have a flower vase? I get creative and find the biggest glass possible. The shears are in the knife butcher block. Snatching them, I cut the bottoms, fill the glass with water, and drop them in.

I finish cooking on the grill. While I'm setting the table for dinner, I hear Kendall's feet hitting the stairs as she strolls into the kitchen. In her natural state, she takes my breath away. No makeup, her hair up off her shoulders, her neck begging me to kiss and suck it. And that fucking outfit—short, thin shorts, and a slender strap tank top, no bra.

Fuck me—no bra!

I stare, catching myself, and then make eye contact with her. The smirk on her face tells me she caught my eyes lingering on her pert breasts a little too long. Fucking hot though, my dick is twitching...but more than that, there's warmth spreading throughout my chest. I think my heart might jump out of my chest.

"It's hard to keep my hands off of you when you look like this." My hands caress her bare shoulders and arms.

She smiles back at me with a shy grin.

THIRTY-FIVE
Kendall

With that look on his face as he rubs his beard, I know what he's thinking. Those half-hooded caramel eyes stare at me as he cooks. If that isn't the hottest thing I've ever seen—Dane, shirtless, cooking. I lick my lips, and it's not because of the food he's cooking. Eating him up could be my dinner if I weren't completely exhausted and emotionally spent.

For those couple of minutes, we are not moving, mesmerized by each other.

He finally breaks the staring contest. "I may have raided your fridge and gone through all of your cabinets and drawers trying to find things." He lays his hand on my hips.

I look around the deck and see a mason jar full of pink lilies.

How did he know those were my favorites?

My head whips around, staring directly at him. I'm silently asking how the hell he knew. "How?"

"I have my ways."

"That answer is still cryptic."

He wrapped a ribbon around the jar. I wonder if he looked at Pinterest, which seems out of character. The table is set with two place settings, fancy napkins with holders, wine glasses, and taper candles in the middle.

"Where did you get the fancy napkins, holders, and candles? I know for certain I didn't have those lying around," I question him with a hand on one hip.

One side of his lips tugs up. "You don't need to know all my secrets."

I give him a curious look, with one eyebrow raised. "Maybe not all of them."

He slides the chair out and says, "Why don't you have a seat, and I'll finish dinner."

I slide into the chair, staring at the flowers and watching him cook. He puts the salmon on, and the potatoes are cooking.

I'm racking my brain as to the last time a guy cooked for me. I don't have any idea.

Dane seems to enjoy all of this. I actually kind of like it and could get used to him cooking for us—us. My body shivers at the thought. He has been occupying space in my head for a while, and it's finally coming to fruition. I'm giddy about the prospect of us as we spend more and more time together.

"I'll be right back. Don't move."

He disappears into my house. He's walking around like he's been here for years, and it makes my hands prickle. Within a few minutes, he comes strolling out with a salad in his hand.

"We can start with this, and the salmon should be done in another couple of minutes."

The sun is setting, painting the sky with deep shades of orange above the treetops and peeking through the trees. The air is cooler as we sit down. Dinner is served, and I'm impressed by his grilling skills.

Once the last bite hits my mouth, I throw the napkin on the table. "That hit the spot. Thank you for cooking. It was delicious."

"Why don't you get comfortable on the couch, and I'll clean up."

"You cooked. I think I can manage cleaning up."

He shakes his head no. "You have had a tough few days. Go chill on the couch, and I'll come join you when I'm done."

I lean back in my chair; my body is screaming for sleep. It's not a terrible idea to go rest on the couch. "You up for a movie?"

"I'm up for whatever you want to do." He smirks at me. I don't even wonder what he's thinking about...because I am too.

I'd love to have him consuming me, but I can't believe how exhausted I am. I'm not even sure I can make it through a movie. What I do know is I want him here with me.

I stand up and say, "At least let me take some things inside."

"Okay, then I want you to hop on the couch, and I'll take care of the rest. It's not that much."

Grabbing my plate and glass, I walk inside and put everything in the sink. Dane didn't follow me in, but I can see he is cleaning the grill.

I stroll to the living room and flop down on the comfy, oversized couch with a chaise lounge. I pick up the remote and start scrolling to find a fun movie to watch. But I have no idea what movies Dane likes. I decide I'll wait for him; he shouldn't be more than a few minutes. With the remote on my chest, I slide the blanket onto myself and snuggle in, getting comfortable.

I feel the couch dip beside me. I open my eyes. "I think I fell asleep." My voice is groggy.

"I should have skipped the cleanup and come in here with you."

"Exhausted doesn't touch how I'm feeling right now." I can barely keep my eyes open.

He brings his arm around me and tugs me closer. My head rests on his chest, and I hand him the remote. "You can find something to watch. I like almost anything except scary ones."

"Okay, let's see if we can find an action movie to keep you awake." He kisses the top of my head.

I watch him scroll through some movies, but my eyes are heavy. They keep closing. I'm trying hard to keep them open, but I'm failing spectacularly. I hear him whispering to me, "Get some rest." He strokes my arm and kisses my cheek.

It was the permission I needed to fall into a deep sleep.

Next thing I know, he is picking me up. "Did I miss the movie?"

"You need sleep more than you need a movie."

"Where are we going?" Trying to shake the fog, I'm being laid down on what feels like a bed. Covers are laid over my body, and I sink into my pillow.

He kisses my cheek and gently brings his fingers over my face. "Rest. I'll see you in the morning, sweetheart."

My alarm goes off. I'm disoriented. Shutting off the alarm with my eyes barely open wide enough to see the time, I see it's six o'clock in the morning. I stretch out my body and realize I'm in bed. I rack my brain and finally remember the evening with Dane. He brought me to bed, but I was out of it. Complete exhaustion consumed me. My body felt weak, and the minute I sank onto the couch, I knew I wasn't going to make it through a movie. Knowing Dane was taking care of things allowed my brain to shut down, and when he wrapped his arm around me, it was a signal to my body to relax and drift off to sleep. Maybe it was his warmth, maybe it was his touch; all I know is I didn't give it a second thought.

I still can't believe I slept for over eleven hours. I sit up in bed to gain some perspective and sort through what needs to be done today. Off to the salon to take care of my clients. And let's be real, the salon is a welcome distraction from all that has happened. Swinging my legs off the bed, a long sigh escapes me. It's time. I move quickly, shower, and then slip into a cute dress, followed by some sandals. I spend a few extra minutes blow-drying my hair straight and use my beach wave curler to add some dimension back.

After I finish in the bathroom, I walk straight downstairs. There's no time for coffee this morning. I'll make some when I get to the salon. Grabbing my purse off the counter, I head to the garage and hop into my car.

I pull out, and Joel's team follows me to the salon; it feels good to look in the rearview mirror and see them. Once we get to the salon, they park out front and in the back. I leave the front door locked until Sally gets here. I'm in the zone, moving around the space, and I jump out of my skin when someone knocks at the front door. People need to stop scaring the shit out of me. I quickly turn my head and see it's Dane with coffee.

I scurry to the door to unlock it. "You scared me...again." I laugh and shake my head.

"I didn't mean to. Just dropping coffee off for the most gorgeous woman." He hands me my coffee and slides his hand onto my forearm. He really is the type of guy every woman dreams about.

"You're earning brownie points with the coffee and compliments today."

"Oh—brownie points? Can I cash them in this weekend?"

I decide to play along. "Yes, you can." I wiggle my eyebrows.

He takes the coffee back out of my hands and sets both coffees on my station and draws me into him. My breath hitches. The way he holds me, there are flashes of last night when he carried me to bed.

The words tumble out, my voice a little shaky. "Why didn't you stay last night?"

Brushing his thumb over my bottom lip, he says, "You were exhausted. If I stayed, held you, and snuggled up to your body, you'd have a steel rod poking into your back. You needed sleep, not me tossing and turning because I have a hard-on."

I tuck my head into his chest and start laughing. Through the laughs, I manage to say, "That's a good enough reason. I was exhausted, as much as I'd have liked to have you in my bed." I glance up at him. "That was probably the right decision."

I'm feeling rested today, which is a major improvement from the last few days. Holding my head with his hand, he drags his lips over mine.

THIRTY-SIX

Dane

O ur lips meet, soft and warm. I can't keep my hands to myself. My fingers lightly touch Kendall's cheeks and then slide up to tangle them in her hair, as my tongue brushes against hers, tasting her sweet coffee. Slipping my hand to cradle her head, and with just enough pressure to draw her closer, I feel her moan against my mouth as our kiss deepens.

We are interrupted by someone clearing their throat, cutting through our moment like a knife. I respond by tightening my grip around her waist, fingers pressing into her hips, silently refusing to let this intrusion end what we've started. She breaks away with reluctance, and I can feel the lingering pressure of her lips; then, she plants a quick, warm peck on my cheek.

"Hi, Sally," she says, her voice shifting from intimate to casual in an instant, though her hand remains hidden against my back.

I wave, never letting her go. With a gentle touch, I tilt her chin until our eyes meet. "I'll make time for you this week, I promise."

She lifts my hand to her lips and presses a kiss against my palm. A current races from my fingertips to my shoulder, spreading through my chest until even my toes tingle with awareness. In that moment, I know with absolute certainty that nothing about my life will ever feel complete without her in it.

With the salon about to open and my office waiting, I pull her close against me one more time, breathing in her watermelon scent before reluctantly letting go. "I'll text you," I promise, already missing her warmth.

"I can't wait," she says, her eyes twinkling, bringing a smile to my face.

Looking at her is never enough. My hands itch to trace the curve of her cheek, to feel the warmth of her skin beneath my fingertips.

Her smile fades slightly. "Have you heard anything about Jake's case?"

I have to tell her. "I'm familiar with the judge handling Jake's case. Given the extensive list of charges and his status as a repeat offender, he's facing a lengthy jail term. I'm making sure that he doesn't end up in a cushy cell."

She presses her hand against my chest, right over my thundering heart, and I cover it with mine, our fingers interlocking like they were made to fit together. "Thank you. I don't know what I'd do without you." Her eyes lock onto mine, pupils dilated, filled with such raw vulnerability and trust that something inside me shatters completely, leaving me breathless and out of my element.

"If anyone can handle this situation, it's you. Reminds me of how my Gram faced challenges—head-on, no hesitation." I pull her close one last time, breathing in the scent of her shampoo. "Text me when you're free. I'll be thinking about you."

The minute I walk into the office, my phone chimes in my pocket with that distinctive tone I've set for Kendall, breaking me out of thoughts still lingering on the softness of her lips. My heart quickens at the sight of her name on the screen.

Kendall:

> I wanted to thank you for my coffee. It's delicious…just like you.

Dane:

You can't talk to me like that while at work...I'll have to go sit in my office for a while.

Kendall:

Imagining that makes me laugh. My next client just walked in the door.

Dane:

Okay, text me later.

"What the fuck are you smiling about?" Logan says, his Mont Blanc pen scratching furiously across his yellow legal pad. His dark eyebrows knit together as he glances up at me. I shut the door with a soft click.

"Kendall texted me."

He sets his pen down with deliberate slowness, clasping his hands behind his head, as he leans back in his chair. He stares at me, his hazel eyes unblinking beneath those thick brows. The silence stretches.

"What?" I ask.

"You know I love you, bro, right?"

"Y-yes," I manage, shifting my weight before sitting down.

"I need you to listen to me without interruption. Can you do that?" His voice has that lawyer tone—measured and precise.

"These past couple of years have been tough on you. You've thrown yourself into doing everything you can for the firm and left your personal life hanging by a thread." He pauses and leans back, the pen tapping rhythmically against the table.

My stomach tightens. Where is he going with this?

"It's been interesting to watch you over the last few weeks. Dare I utter the words..." His lips curl into a knowing smile, revealing teeth that are perfectly whitened. "You look happy, very happy. Your smile gives it away. And you aren't as snappy with people at the office—or with me. It's a refreshing look on you, getting back on the horse."

"What are you, an old man? Getting back on the horse?" I run my fingers along the crisp edge of my suit jacket.

"That's what you're taking away from that?" He shakes his head and puts his hands in the air. Leaning further back in the chair, he says, "Anything else?"

The silence stretches between us. Logan's eyes never leave mine, steady and patient. It's the same look he's given me since we were kids—the one that waits out any opponent until they crack. The look that's won him more cases than I can count.

I drag my palm down my stubbled face and hunch forward. "Since when did my dating life become so fascinating to you?"

A hint of a smile plays at the corner of his mouth. We both know this dance. I'm not about to lay all my cards on the table, even if he already knows what I'm holding.

"Cut the crap," he says, voice softer than I expected. "I'm happy for you, man. Seriously. Nobody pulls strings with the security team or calls in favors to the judge over some casual fling. This woman matters to you."

My chest tightens. He's right. What I have with Kendall is nothing like what I had with Maggie. With Maggie, I lived under constant scrutiny. Late nights at the office? I'd get the cold shoulder. Home by six? Where was dinner? The woman could find fault with a dishwasher if she tried hard enough.

I'm not sure why I stayed so long—comfort, maybe. I knew exactly what she brought to the table: constant nagging, judgment, irritation, and unhappiness. I grabbed whatever moments of peace I could, and when those dried up, I buried myself in work. Looking back, I own my part in how we drifted apart, but none of that gave her the right to betray me with my best friend. If she were that unhappy, she could have ended things and moved on. Instead, she chose to stay—and lie.

"She's not just special to me, Logan—she's burning through my veins like wildfire. Last night, watching her sleep against my chest while some movie played... God, I couldn't even focus on the screen. All I could think about was the weight of her body on mine, her breath against my neck. When I carried her to bed last night..."

Logan closes his eyes. "Do I want to hear this?"

"No, I literally carried her to bed so she could sleep. Her fingers curled into my shirt even in her sleep, like she couldn't let go. And I didn't want her to...But I let her sleep and went home. Then this morning, I dropped off coffee."

Logan snorts. "My big brother, all grown up and doting on someone. Never thought I'd see the day."

I force a grin. "Neither did I. I wish I had more time with her. When I told her I'd be tied up at the office all week, her face fell, even though she knew my schedule. It kills me to see her disappointed."

He clears his throat. "Do you think it'll become a problem?"

"I'm not sure," I admit, rubbing the back of my neck. "Maybe I'm the clingy one. I'm already reshuffling my calendar to carve out extra minutes—dropping off coffee just to see her smile."

"You'll figure it out. Theresa and I have our rhythm—she'll call me out if I disappear for too long or flake on plans. She's understanding when it happens occasionally, but if it becomes a pattern, she lets me know. I love her for it."

"Thanks, man. I need someone in my corner, not someone breathing down my neck."

Logan grins. "You'll find your balance. So when's our double date? Then those two can gang up on us."

I laugh. "No time wasted, huh?"

"Theresa's been champing at the bit to double-date. I want to see if she approves of your choice."

"Well, this Saturday I've got something unforgettable planned for her. I need to top our last date—but I'll run it by her. I'm betting she'll be all in."

"Okay, keep me posted on that front...Now, what's up with Jake?"

"As for Jake, Joel has a guy inside to make it really clear, ya know, rough him up a bit, to give him a little taste of what will happen if he even thinks about contacting Kendall."

"You told her all of this, too? No holding back with her."

"It's been handled. We should hear about his sentencing next week, right?"

"Yes, unless the judge moves it up. I may have to use one of my favors to make that happen, but I'll do whatever it takes for her."

He leans forward with his elbows on the desk. "Well, hopefully that will be behind us soon. Keep me in the loop on all of that, but it seems like Joel's handling it..."

"I thought you were excited to spend more time with Kendall now that your caseload was a bit more flexible."

I stand up quickly, pacing the room. "I was, but this is important. I feel like she understands me—understands my job."

"She sounds like the perfect girl for you, bro. Theresa is the perfect girl for me. She gets it. Understands when plans change, I have to work late, get called into the office, you know, all the things that drive most women crazy. I'm a lucky guy to have found her. And you know she reminds me of that fact all the time." He smiles widely, knowing he is truly a lucky guy.

"She's a saint to deal with your shit." I laugh and smack my hand on his back. "Alright, what can I help with?"

Spending the rest of the day and night at the office, my assistant thankfully brought us food; otherwise, we'd be at each other's throats.

We get hangry, and that's never a good sight. She knows us too well. Before she left for the day, she left a note saying dinner would be delivered at seven. I should give her a raise.

When we sit down to eat our dinner at eight o'clock, I realize my phone must still be in my office. I was determined to ensure we wrapped this up as soon as possible.

Out of the blue, I say, "Do you think she'd like a weekend away at the lake house?"

I must have caught him off guard because he blinks at me for a moment before saying, "Um, well, you haven't been back there since you found Maggie and Al there. Are you sure that's a good idea?"

"Maybe I need to make fresh memories there and forget about Maggie and Al. I think Kendall would love it."

"No doubt you need to forget about them. Want me to come with you to at least be back in the place before bringing her? Then you can have your assistant take care of updating it. Changing things up might be the best way to make fresh memories."

He's right. I should probably step foot in there with someone before offering a weekend away to Kendall. I used to love that lake house, but Maggie tarnished it. I contemplated burning the whole thing down, but just never went back instead. Now it just sits empty with its beautiful views of Mirror Lake going to waste. There were a lot of great memories prior to the Maggie shitshow.

"Since you're pointing that out and offering, it sounds like a great idea. We can figure out a time next week," I say, locking him in to come with me before he can back out.

"Name the day and time...I'm there."

"Heads down for now to work through these last documents. Oh, have you seen my phone?"

"No, but I'm surprised you left it."

"I think it's in my office. I'll be back."

My office is on the other side of the firm. With huge strides, I walk through my office doorway. There's my phone sitting on my desk, with a few missed calls. One from Joel, and the rest can wait. I call him back immediately.

"What's up?"

"Fuck, good thing it wasn't an emergency. I called hours ago."

"You know the office number."

"Yeah, true. Quick update: Jake will be handled tonight. I'll keep you updated on that once it's done. Kendall is still at the salon. She said another hour and she'll be ready to leave. If I were a betting man, I'd say she likes having us around."

"Of course she does," I say with a chuckle.

The conversation settles my mind about Kendall. He's got her while I take care of what I need to here.

I scan my phone for all the missed text messages. There are a few from Kendall. She was just asking whether I would be over tonight or sleeping at the office. The thought of being with her every night sends a jolt straight through my chest. I whisper, "One day." I shake my head, trying to shake off the relentless longing to curl up to her curvy body and red hair every single night.

I can't help wondering if this will ever be too much for her. She says it doesn't bother her now, but what if one day it's not enough? The few hours I'm able to spare for our relationship—will it make up for all the times I'm not there? Will stolen moments between meetings ever be enough? Or will she wake up one day and realize she deserves someone who can give her more than leftover time?

I take a deep breath, trying to quiet the voice in my head. Kendall runs her own business—she understands the importance of deadlines and emergencies. But understanding doesn't fill an empty bed or make up for a canceled dinner.

Logan's advice echoes—show up when I say I will, make our time count. The tightness in my chest loosens slightly. I type a quick reply, promising to call her tonight. It's a small promise, but one I can keep.

Dane:

I might be able to get out of here for a little bit. When will you be home?

THIRTY-SEVEN
Kendall

As I work on a client's hair, the soft chime of the door opening catches my attention. I glance over, and my heart skips a beat. Is that a face I recognize? An older man stands there, his features strikingly familiar, yet I'm sure I've never met him. His gaze sweeps the room until his dark eyes lock onto mine. An unsettling mix of curiosity and unease washes over me as I quickly shift my focus back to my client. I try to concentrate on the haircut, but my mind is half-listening to the conversation he's having with Sally, torn between the urge to understand why he feels so familiar and the need to focus on my client.

"I'm looking for Ms. Allen," the man says in a dark, deep voice that rattles through my body.

There's no getting out of this. I motion for one of my other stylists to finish my current client as my heart pounds in my chest.

I pivot and stride to the reception desk, where a commanding, yet stoic, older gentleman waits.

"I'm Kendall. How can I help?" I ask, my voice steady despite my nerves.

"Is there a place we could talk...privately?" His words, with an authoritative edge, send shivers racing up my spine—cold.

"What is this all about?" Trying to walk the line of professionalism, but stand my ground with him.

"I would like to talk to you about Dane." The way he says Dane's name is almost threatening, and my stomach drops. My pulse hammers in my throat, and a thousand possibilities flash through my mind, each worse than the last.

I thrust my hand out for him to shake, fingers trembling slightly. "And you are?"

"I'm his father, Edward Walsh." My body stiffens.

"Oh god," I whisper, gripping the edge of the reception desk. "Has something happened to him?"

"No, he is fine." He said it too quickly, too sharply.

"Okay, we can meet in my office." I send a quick glance at Sally and nod firmly. She understands that the cameras in my office will capture everything. I want every moment recorded. "I'll be back."

The sound of my heels striking the floor echoes my tension as I lead Mr. Walsh down the hall. The man following me is tall and broad-shouldered, dressed in a tailored suit and exuding a presence that seems to occupy more space than it should.

We enter my office, and I slide into the chair behind my desk, gesturing sharply for him to sit in the seat opposite.

"How can I help you, Mr. Walsh?" I strive desperately to keep my voice from trembling. His presence is overwhelming, dark, and intimidating.

"You've built something really impressive here." His eyes sweep across my office, landing on the licenses and certificates on the wall. "Community-rooted, female-led. I respect that. Done well for yourself." His words are smooth, but they land like a warning, a threat.

My stomach twists into a knot so tight I can feel nausea roll up my throat. The air between us crackles with something dangerous.

"Thank you." I barely manage.

He leans forward, the leather chair creaking under his weight. "You've been through a lot, haven't you? Clawed yourself out of something dark. Built this..." he gestures dismissively, "...business from nothing." His smile doesn't reach his eyes. "That takes a certain grit and perseverance."

The blood drains from my face. My past is exposed, but how does he know?

"Which is why," he whispers, close enough that I can smell his expensive cologne, "I find this *thing* you have with my son... concerning."

I freeze in my seat, my muscles tensing. "Dane and I..."

"Have something special, right? Sure. He's good at making people believe that. But he's reckless, selfish, if I'm brutally honest. He acts on impulse, does whatever he pleases, whenever he pleases." He stares at me while adjusting his cufflinks.

"Maybe you don't know your son as well as you think you do."

He unbuttons his suit jacket with a calculated calm, extracting a stack of papers and slowly leaning onto the desk, sliding the papers, including a check, over with one finger. "You'll find there's enough zeros here to make you reconsider your...attachment to my son."

My fingers tighten around the arms of my chair as I stare at him, processing his words. My throat is dry. "I'm not interested in your money, Mr. Walsh."

A faint smile crosses his face. "That's what women like you always say. Until everything settles and you have clients deciding this salon isn't a good fit anymore." Glancing around my office one more time, his eyes land back on me. "It would be a shame to see all of this...fall apart."

My chest tightens. "Are you threatening me?"

"I don't make threats," he says smoothly, leaning back in the chair. "I make predictions. I've seen many women latch onto powerful men, hoping it would give them the stability and status they wanted. In the end, it destroyed them. I'd hate to see you become one of them."

Hands clasped on my desk to keep them from trembling, I lean in and say, "With all due respect, I don't need your approval to see your son, and frankly, neither does he."

His dark chuckle sends a chill through the air. "Approval? No. Protection, perhaps. Do you know what people in this town are whispering? That you're cozying up to Dane Walsh for leverage, that the permits and approval for your spa came through because of him. Small towns love gossip, Ms. Allen, and reputation..." He rests his elbows on the chair and steeples his hands. "Reputations are fragile."

I stare at him, processing every word he is saying. None of it is true...well, except that Dane was the one who pushed for the permits to get approved, but that was on him. But I stay quiet, as he leans forward, entirely too close.

His voice drops low. "You'll never be enough for him. Dane has a history of chasing fire until it burns him. Do you want to be another one-night headline in the long list of women?"

I force myself to maintain eye contact, never averting my gaze. It may not be the right move, but I'm not backing down. "You don't know me."

"I know enough." His tone, pure ice. "Ambitious. Independent. Strong on the outside, but underneath? Vulnerable. He doesn't have time for a relationship; he's too busy at the firm. For now, he's carving out what few minutes he has to see you, but one day soon, the fire will fade, and he will be stuck at the office more, canceling plans. It always fades, and he'll go back to his old ways. And then you'll be alone, disappointed, wondering how you let him into your life, only to crush you." He taps the papers with the check on top. "I'm offering you an out. Take the check. Sign the agreement. Walk away before you're humiliated. Before people here look at you and see not a businesswoman, but a mistake on Dane Walsh's resume."

He straightens his cuffs, rises from the seat, and smooths down his jacket. "Think it over. But don't take too long. Opportunities like this vanish."

Without another glance, he walks out, leaving me with a silence that is heavier than his words.

I'm stuck in this chair, shock taking over my body. Staring at the door he just walked out of, I return to my desk, where the papers and the check sit, screaming at me. My lungs, breaths coming too shallow, too quick.

I slam my fist on the desk and shove the papers, but the words he left behind linger in the air.

You'll never be enough. People are already whispering. You'll just be another mistake.

It hits a little too close to Jake's voice. The poison in every word, cruel intention meant to cut through me, to hurt me. I can't sit anymore; jumping out of my chair, I pace with arms wrapped tightly around myself, thinking. Why am I letting his words get under my skin? He knows exactly how to hit me where it hurts.

Glancing at the mirror on my wall, the woman staring back at me is a complete mess—flushed cheeks, eyes wet, the confident woman stripped down to something small and uncertain, which is exactly what Edward Walsh wanted.

Tears prick my eyes, and I blink rapidly to clear them. I will not give him the satisfaction of my tears. I worked too damn hard to build this business, to bring myself out of the Jake wreckage, to stand on my own.

And yet...

My chest squeezes, and doubts flood in faster than I can push them out. What if he was right? What if people think I'm using Dane? My reputation...smeared.

I brace myself against my desk, shoulders shaking. For a moment, the walls feel like they are closing in on me. Using this time to figure out what's next, I walk around and sit in my chair. Straightening the papers on my desk, pushing the check to the far corner, I inhale slowly and deeply until my mask slides firmly into place. No one will ever know how close his words came to breaking me. When there's a knock on the door, I startle.

"Hey, you okay?" Sally asks as she opens the door to my office and walks in.

"I don't know." The tears I was holding in finally break free and roll down my cheeks. I have so many questions, and a salon to run, with clients waiting for me. Dane is at his office and says he won't be able to see me this week. I'm not sure I'll be able to wait until the end of the week to talk to him. What I do need is a few hours to process what the hell just happened. His dad has me second-guessing myself—and us.

She walks over to the mini-fridge in the corner and grabs a bottle of cold water. Placing it down on my desk, she says, "Drink this." And then she hands me a handful of tissues.

I take a few sips and then ask her, "How many more clients do I have today?"

"Three." She rubs my back. It's comforting.

"Can anyone else take them?"

"Let me see." She pulls out her phone and clicks a few times. "Yes, we can spread them around. I'll take care of everything. Why don't you head home?"

I inhale deeply, struggling to keep the tears from spilling free again. Everything about this situation is a tangled mess of confusion. I murmur, "Thank you," but even as I say it, I'm unsure if I mean it. "Text me if you need anything."

"Kendall, I've been handling your salon since the beginning; you don't have to worry about anything." She leans down and hugs me.

I feel frozen in place, but I need to leave right now. I stand up, pick up my bag and keys, and walk out the door. "I'll let you know what's going on."

In a daze, I drag my feet out to my car and drive home. I don't even remember getting here. After parking the car in the garage, I step inside. The house is quiet. Too quiet. Leaving me with all of my rogue thoughts. Alone. Confused. Overwhelmed.

I drop my bag by the door and kick off my shoes, but I don't remember doing it. My body moves on autopilot. My chest is tight, like someone tied a cord around my lungs and yanked it.

I make it to my bedroom and sit on the edge of the bed. The tears flood my eyes, threatening to escape at any moment. Then, my body falls sideways onto my bed, and I curl up in the fetal position, hugging my pillow so tightly my arms shake. One breath. Then another. Then a sob punches through me uncontrollably.

You'll wake up a year from now—exhausted, resentful, wondering why you ever thought this could work.

I squeeze my eyes shut, reeling into the darkness.

How did he know about Jake? About any of it? Did Dane tell him everything? I'm so confused and angry.

I hug my pillow tighter, and I want to believe it's a lie. I want to believe *he doesn't know Dane at all...*

But what if he's right?

I cry harder. Ugly crying. My pillow taking the brunt of my breakdown.

I should be stronger than this.

The last few weeks have taken a toll on me, and I just can't take it anymore. My resilience is nonexistent, and I'm left wondering why it abandoned me.

I reach for my phone and text the girls' group text.

Kendall:

Are any of you free? I need a voice that's not mine in my head right now.

And then I toss it onto my bed. I can't. I curl my knees up tighter. My body hurts. My heart hurts. And the worst part is, I think I love him. This couldn't have happened at a worse time, especially with Dane making decisions for me and the whole thing about Jake.

My phone dings, which knocks me out of the path of spiraling. I reluctantly pick it up.

Lane:

What's going on? Where are you?

Kendall:

Home

Faith:

Home? Be there in 15 minutes

Lane:

I'll bring ice cream

Addison:

On my way

THIRTY-EIGHT
Dane

I've been obsessively checking my phone to see if she texted me back. It doesn't indicate 'read', so she hasn't even seen it, or she's ignoring it. Maybe I'll surprise her and stop at the salon with an iced coffee since I didn't see her this morning. She's usually swamped during the day; it's not unusual not to hear from her until she has a break between clients.

It's concerning that she hasn't texted me back. Off to the coffeehouse to buy her favorite summer coffee, an iced mocha, and swing by to bring it to her. My chest is tight thinking that there's a reason she isn't responding.

I park at the front and walk into the salon. My eyes scan for fiery red hair. When I don't see her, I walk up to Sally.

"Afternoon, Sally. Is Kendall here?"

She scowls at me, which is odd. Usually, she is overly excited to see and talk to me, but not today. Instead, she is abrupt. "She left."

"Left?" I ask, genuinely concerned.

Sally gives a slight nod. "Yeah. She wasn't feeling well—headache."

My heart pounds in my chest, caught between worry and frustration. Why couldn't she just text me and tell me she wasn't feeling well? I would have dropped everything to be with her.

"Is she okay?"

"She didn't say much." Her voice is clipped. "Just said she needed to go home."

That's out of character for her. I glance toward the spa hallway, half expecting her to appear, roll her eyes, and tell me I'm overreacting.

I look back at Sally. She's reorganizing pens, avoiding eye contact.

"Did something happen?" I ask.

"No," she says too fast, not convincing me. "Not that I know of."

Bullshit.

But I nod anyway and back away from the desk. "Alright. Tell her I stopped by?"

Sally gives me a tight smile. "Of course."

I walk out with the coffee still in my hand, completely untouched, its condensation dripping. And suddenly, I don't feel so sure about anything, and I start questioning everything.

Sliding back into the driver's seat, I put the coffee in the cup holder. Sighing. I massage the back of my neck, and there's something wrong; I need answers.

Dane:

Hey, stopped by the salon. Missed you. Hope you're okay. Call me.

I wait for a good ten minutes before deciding to call Joel. I need to figure this out.

"Joel, hey, where's Kendall?" I drum the steering wheel, losing patience.

"You sound agitated. She's home, and her friends are all here."

I lean my head back on the headrest. "I'm just trying to figure out what's going on. Do you know anything?"

"Man, nothing out of the ordinary over here."

I let out a breath, thinking I'm so far out of the loop, my heart can't take the possibility she is purposefully not responding to me—ignoring me. And my heart drops into my stomach.

My mind is telling me to drive over there and demand that she tell me what is going on. But I refrain as panic washes over me. I'm confused and worried. She's never ignored my texts, and I don't want to call after already having sent her a text. If she really has a headache, then she could be sleeping. But why are all of her friends there?

Wound up tightly, I decide to drive home. The garage door closes behind me as I sit in my car. I slam my hands on the steering wheel. Fuck! Needing to burn off the anger coursing through my veins, I walk straight into the house and down to my workout room. No matter where I go, I can't run away from the thoughts of her.

Even when I'm working out, she's a vision everywhere I look. She's perfect for me. I just need to talk to her. If she doesn't text me back soon, I'll try calling. I know something isn't right.

I push myself hard, increasing my weights, trying to focus on anything but her. It's useless because she's taken over my heart, living rent-free. I'm invested in her—in us.

Taking a seat on the bench with my elbows on my knees, my face lands in my hands for however long it took me to realize I can't live without her. She's the one. Whatever is going on, I'm finding out what it is, no matter what.

I grab my phone from the table. Still nothing from her. Staring at the screen, I will her to text me back, but nothing happens. My heart is aching in my chest. Defeat rolls through me, my shoulders slump, and an exaggerated sigh leaves my mouth.

After taking a cool shower, I'm ready to drive over to her house and see her. Confront her. Why hasn't she texted me back? Why did Sally seem upset with me?

Then, my phone buzzes.

Kendall:

I'm home. Can we talk?

The words I've been waiting for, but dread spreads through me.

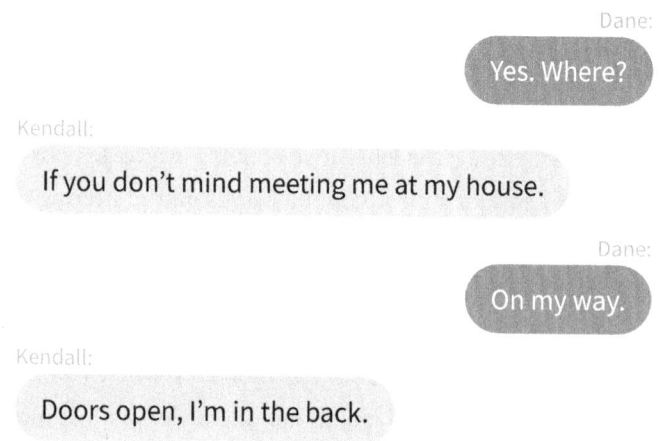

My heart rate spikes, and my palms sweat. I need to wipe them on my pants. I can't shake off the dread; it's there, haunting me. What could be wrong? I can't wrap my head around what's going on, and it's making me feel unsteady. My foot presses on the gas pedal like I'm a NASCAR racer. I need to be next to her, feel her body, her heart...our undeniable connection with sparks flying. I want all of that every day. But why do I feel like it's all slipping away from me at the moment?

When I pull into her driveway, there are no other cars. Her friends must have left. It's just her and me.

I'm wrapping my arms around her the minute I see her.

Bounding up the steps and through the front door, I stalk straight out the back. And that's when I see her sitting in her lounge chair, tucked into a ball with her arms holding her legs tightly, head down. As she lifts her head to meet my eyes, my heart shatters into a million pieces to see her red-rimmed eyes, mascara streaking her cheeks, and hair in disarray. The breath is knocked out of my chest. She isn't moving, isn't speaking; she's just staring into me.

I want to rush over to her and tell her everything will be okay, but I don't even know what is wrong. My steps are slow and calculated, like

I'm walking up to an animal that will run away if my movements are too quick.

Lowering my body to the chair, I rest my hand on her forearm and whisper, "Sweetheart, what's wrong?"

Her eyes are dull and full of tears that break free and flow down her cheeks. I hold her face and wipe her tears with the pad of my thumb, but they keep coming. Seeing her broken is cracking something inside of me. All I want to do is fix whatever is wrong.

She wipes her face, and her voice is wavering. "I had a visitor today."

I've taken care of Jake, but what the hell—maybe he has someone on the outside. What the fuck?

Keeping my voice low, I say, "Who?"

Sobs rip through her body. Barely getting out the words, "Your father."

I shake my head in disbelief; my dad went to visit her? He doesn't even know about Kendall. With my eyes wide and eyebrows reaching my hairline, I can't comprehend what she just said.

"My dad? I'm so confused. Why would he visit you? He doesn't..." The memory comes flooding back. When I confessed everything to Logan... was he listening in on our conversation?

She leans over and picks up a stack of papers. It feels like she is moving in slow motion as she shoves the papers into my hand. A piece of paper falls to the ground. I crouch over and pick it up. My eyes locked on a check made out to Kendall with my dad's signature. It has a lot of zeros.

"What the fuck is this?" My body is humming with anger. Why am I holding this check?

"Your father came by, threatened me, and handed that check to me, saying it would be easier if I just walked away from you." Her chin now rests on her forearms as she holds back the sobs building in her body, trembling.

"Shit. I didn't know." It's all that comes out of my mouth, as I'm wracking my brain why he would do this. "Walk away from me? Wait, are you considering this?"

She stares out at the pool, avoiding eye contact with me. It makes my heart skip a beat. She can't seriously think this is a good idea.

"Am I the right person for you? Maybe you'd be better off without all the baggage dragging behind me, tarnishing your family name. It's a lot."

"Kendall." I take her chin in my fingers and guide her back to look at me. "You have quickly become the light of my life. I didn't even know I was missing before I met you. Your baggage is my baggage. Please don't let him get into your head like this. He thinks he knows what's best for me. But I'm the only one who knows you're it for me."

She closes her eyes like she wants to be as far away as possible; instead, she's having this conversation. Slowly opening her eyes, she says, "What if one day you wake up and I'm not what you want anymore? You're changing your whole life for me—me."

I slide my arms around her, but she shrugs me off, ever so slightly. All I want to do is comfort her. "It's not possible not to want you; you are exactly what I want and need in my life. I won't be able to breathe if you aren't in my life. I've never known anything, ever, like I know you belong with me—you're mine."

"Dane..." She gazes at me with compassion mixed with confusion. "He dropped the seeds of doubt and watered them. My thoughts have been reeling ever since. He said people are talking and saying I'm using you to get permits. Which I never asked you to do."

I interrupt her. "You didn't, but that wasn't you using me. I did that because you deserved those permits. They weren't playing fair."

"But your dad said people are whispering..."

"Kendall let them whisper. You're more to me than the gossip around town." She lets me hold her forearm without pulling away.

"I know it shouldn't matter, but it was the threats to my reputation, my business, and then trying to pay me off. He absolutely doesn't want me in your life...I just needed to talk to you and tell you what happened. But now, I need time and some space to figure out what I want. This relationship has been on fast forward since we met."

"Yes, we've moved faster than a lightning bolt, but I wouldn't change any of it. Let me be here with you. The last thing I want is to be away from you."

She slides off her chair and stands. "I need some space to think and process all of this. At the end of the day, I want to know that I chose myself over all of this. Over every doubt. Over what your father thinks of me. He really doesn't want me in your life. He made me question everything about us. Why would I want to even subject myself to any of this?"

"Because we are meant to be together." I hear more cracking in my chest as my heart splits open.

Her head down-turned, she says, "Maybe that's true, but is it worth risking? Hell, one day maybe I'll wake up and realize I don't want to be second to your firm."

"No, nope. That's him planting doubt in your mind. Please don't let him infiltrate what we have. I've prioritized our time together as much as I can. You've been understanding at every turn. What happened with Maggie destroyed me. And with you, I'm willing to risk it all. Risk it all with me—for us."

More tears fall down her face as she glances at me for a split second, love in her eyes. I want to tell her I love her, but it's not the time. And I feel a tear slide down my cheek. Without wiping it away, I listen.

"I've been fighting not to fall for you, and when I finally let my guard down, I feel like someone else is making decisions for me. Does that sound familiar? Your dad is paying me off to make the decision he wants for you. You may not think you are like him, but you've made choices for me too. Right now, I'm choosing to find my center and choose myself. I need to know, without a shadow of a doubt, what I want, without someone else dictating it for me. Please give me the time and space I'm asking for."

I massage the back of my neck as tension builds in my shoulders and chest. "I'll give you whatever you want. If you need time? Done. Just know I want to hold you in my arms and tell you how much you mean to me. You've quickly become my everything. Don't completely push me away, or shut me out."

The flicker of realization in her eyes leaves hope lingering in the air.

She turns on her heel and walks to her door. "Thank you, Dane."

And she leaves me there sitting on her chair, determined not to give up on her—on us.

THIRTY-NINE
Kendall

I close the door, and my feet drag across the floor until I reach my couch. Throwing myself on it, I curl up in a ball, and my body won't stop shaking. The tears won't stop.

Did I just push away the man I love with everything I am?

The uncontrollable sobs break through my thoughts. I push myself up to a sitting position, ready to chase him down in my driveway and say, 'I love you, and I don't want anyone else in my life.' But my body won't move, and I lie back down.

I hear voices coming from the kitchen. My eyes shoot open, and I see the sun setting behind the trees. Sleep was definitely needed after the cryfest I indulged in. My friends are back, as promised, with dinner and hopefully some good advice.

Seeing the hurt in Dane's eyes, my whole body crumpled into a pile of dust. The last thing I wanted to do was hurt him. Even though that wasn't my intention, it happened. I left him outside in the wake of my words. I saw it written all over his face—hurt.

With this time spent with myself and my friends, I hope to gain clarity. Making a decision that's right for me and letting the chips fall where they may. The prickling in my eyes intensifies. How much can one person cry? My heart feels shattered.

They all come strolling into the living room.

"On the couch?" Addison lifts my feet and sits down.

"Yeah."

"How did it go with Dane?"

And the tears that I was holding back fall as I tell them what he said.

"Kendall...he sounds like this hurts him at his core," says Faith.

"I was falling apart when talking to him. When I said I'd be second to his firm..." I try to take a deep breath but fail. "It felt like a lie coming out of my mouth, but I said it anyway. The swirling thoughts just won't stop. I was so happy, and having his father walk through my door flipped everything. My life tipped upside down with the threats, the payoff."

"Listen, at the end of the day, you need to figure out what you want for yourself."

"I knew what I wanted just hours ago, and now I'm questioning all my decisions when it comes to Dane. The minute I was comfortable having him in my life, after all the doubt that he would commit to me after having the one-night stand."

"He's head over heels for you," Lane says.

I flop back onto the couch. "I know, and that's probably why it hurts so bad. He said that we're meant to be together. And the way I feel about him—it's true. When he said he wouldn't be able to breathe without me...it sucked the air right out of my lungs." My chest squeezes, and taking a deep breath isn't in the cards, not now.

Addison stalks over and yanks me from the couch. "There's a lot to consider. Why don't we do that outside in the fresh air, eating dinner?"

I haven't eaten all day. I resign. "Okay."

Trudging along to the backyard, the moment I step out, I see it: a watered-down iced coffee replaces the papers and checks. Dane must have taken them and left the coffee.

After staring at the coffee, I murmur, "He won't give up on me."

Lane comes to sit next to me. "I could have told you that. He's in too deep. The man has brought you coffee almost every day since you met, and he's spared no expense to bring you on the best dates ever."

"His father threatened me and sowed doubt that wasn't ever there. I'm sorting through my feelings. Maybe I was caught up in Dane's grand gestures to convince me to take a chance on him and take me out on a date."

"Deep in your heart, do you believe that?"

I sit back and pull my knees up for comfort. Watching the dusk take over the sky, I wonder what tomorrow will bring. All consumed by the decisions I need to make.

"No, I don't believe that, which is part of the problem. Dane is my person. I don't think I'll ever get over him if I let him go. But even if we move forward, like we were before his father interrupted our lives, I feel like his father will always see me as the problem he couldn't buy off. What if he continues to sabotage our relationship? Those weren't empty threats. He could very well do all those things to wear me down."

Faith comes closer. "Listen to your gut. You've been so good at listening to it lately. As for his father, that's a question for Dane. Let him deal with it. All you can do is control your reaction."

"And I'm doing a piss-poor job of controlling my reactions today."

"You're processing. It's okay to feel out of sorts and to not know which side is up until you decide what you are going to do next."

Addison comes skipping out the door. "We all need to eat. Chicken teriyaki coming right up. And dare I say, a round of tequila shots?"

Faith and Lane say, "Yes."

Shrugging my shoulders, I have no idea. So much for even making a simple decision tonight.

A round of tequila is poured, and Addison makes a toast. "To making decisions."

I let out a half-laugh and down the shot. Addison hands me my container of chicken and a fork. "Eat up, you need your energy."

"Energy to make it up my stairs and pass out from being emotionally drained."

"At least you won't be sleeping on the couch." Lane giggles.

My stomach is full. I ate almost the whole thing, but I hadn't eaten all day, so it makes sense.

Addison jumps up and says, "Let's hit the pool."

I groan. "My bed sounds much more comfortable."

"Stop groaning. It will take your mind off things, just for a little while. We can fantasize about our Aruba trip," Faith chides.

My body perks up a bit. "Okay, that sounds like a good idea. I'm excited for Aruba."

We clean up after dinner and change into our bathing suits. Addison already has hers on. Stepping down into the pool feels like I'm washing the day away. I drop my body under the water and pop back up. "This is hitting the spot—refreshing."

Addison rattles off some excursions that we can do while on the island, and my mind drifts to sitting on the white sandy beach sipping frozen margaritas. All of my neck muscles relax, my worry dropping into the water, as I come to terms with what I need to do next. And it helps that we're talking about our upcoming girls' trip. It's still months away, but it's fun to explore what we will be doing while there.

Out of nowhere, Lane splashes me. Shocked by her actions, she knew it was the right thing to do, because I splash her back. We end up splashing each other and laughing our asses off. It's sure nice to genuinely laugh after all that's happened today. Once the splashing stopped, we all grabbed a float and hopped on. Linking our feet, we talk a little more about our trip and gaze at the stars.

My thoughts drift to Dane. The connection we have in such a short period of time. And Jane's voice plays in my mind. *When you least expect it.* If that isn't on point, having Dane walk into my life was the last thing I expected. And it was the best thing that could have happened. A smile takes over my face just as I see a shooting star fly across the sky. We all gasp.

"What are the odds we'll see a shooting star?"

"I think it's a sign," Addison says.

I hum in the air. Maybe she's right. We stay in the pool for almost an hour; it's relaxing and just what I need. Stepping out of the pool, we dry off and walk to the back door. I don't know where I'd be without my best friends.

They made sure I was good before they left me alone. "I'll be fine. A good night's sleep will help give me some perspective and deal with this in the morning." Convincing myself that a good night's sleep is all it would take to solve this.

As we make our rounds of hugs, my phone buzzes from the kitchen island. My heart stops, and I feel sweat forming on my forehead. I carefully pick up my phone, as if it were a bomb that would go off at any second. The knot in my stomach tightens when I see Dane's name on my screen.

FORTY

Dane

Lying in bed with a heavy heart, the urge to at least text her is overwhelming, but I hesitate. What if she doesn't want to hear from me? She's been on my mind all day, but what if I'm just making things worse? I finally decide to type and send it.

Dane:

I'm thinking about you. I don't think there's a time that I'm not thinking about you. I'm going to take care of all of this…I promise.

I can't tear my eyes away from the screen, hoping she'll at least read it. But what if it pushes her further away? Throwing the phone on the bed, I pull both my hands behind my head and stare at the ceiling, knowing sleep might elude me tonight.

Gram's playing bingo today, so I couldn't meet up with her for dinner. And Logan has date night with Theresa. It feels like I'm destined to navigate this alone, but I'm not sure I can. As darkness takes over the sky, thinking about her crying after what my dad did replays endlessly, leaving me unsure of what's next.

The room is lit only by moonlight, and I've been in this spot for what seems like hours. It takes all my strength to slide off the bed. My feet feel like lead as they drag along the floor toward the hot tub. Stripping off my clothes, I step into the hot water. The heat loosens my tense muscles, but my mind remains a battlefield.

Leaning my head back, I gaze at the stars, torn about my promise to Kendall. Dad was wrong, dead wrong, for approaching her and saying those things. I shake my head, knowing he handed over a check to her with those awful threats.

My hand slaps the water. "Fuck him!" I yell.

She's been through so much these past few weeks. I've tried my best to protect her, but the one person who intruded on her life was my own father. She means everything to me; I will fix this. Whatever it takes.

The thought propels me out of the water, to dry off, and back to my bed. Tomorrow's going to be a busy day, so I need to at least try to sleep. With one more look at my phone, I see she at least read my text message. That's all I need...hope.

After tossing and turning all night, I roll out of bed. I glance at the time on my phone; it's 5:44. Perfect, I'll grab coffee for Kendall and Gram, make a delivery, and then head to Gram's. Thankfully, it's not too early to show up at Gram's, so I call her on my way to the coffeehouse.

"Hello, dear."

"Good morning, Gram."

"It's early for you to be calling. Everything okay?"

"I'm going to come over for breakfast."

"This sounds serious. I'll start breakfast and see you when you get here."

"Thanks, Gram."

I hang up the phone, step into the coffeehouse, and order. When my name is called, I collect all the coffees and drive to Kendall's.

After arguing with myself all the way to her house, I decide to leave her coffee and cinnamon rolls at her front door and text her.

> Left you something at your front door with a note.

You mean the world to me. I promise to treat you well, care for you, and protect you. Don't withdraw from me. I know you need time, and I respect that. I will hold to it as best as I can, without losing my mind. I don't know what the future holds, but I hope it includes us living happily ever after as soulmates.

With everything that I am,

-Dane

I walk slowly back to my car, hoping to catch a glimpse of her, but there's no response, and the door stays shut.

I drive straight to Gram's. When I walk through her door, the smell of bacon and coffee tickles my nose. My stomach grumbles. I follow the smell, but she still yells, "In the kitchen."

My Gram's house is like walking back in time. Wallpaper on the living room walls, the furniture that is in pristine condition, like no one ever sits on it. *They don't.* She has a recliner with a special blanket on it, where she sits to watch her shows or read her books.

She finishes cooking, and we sit at the table. A big sigh comes flying out of my mouth. I don't hold back. "Dad went to see Kendall." I continue to tell her exactly what happened. Stabbing at my eggs like they offended me, my fork drops out of my hand, and it clanks on my plate.

"Kendall needs some time?" Gram asks, her voice carefully neutral.

"Yeah. I didn't want to give it to her. But there was no way she was going to allow me to stay with her. She said she needed space to think and process everything. But Gram, it hurts like hell."

"You care about her." It comes out as a statement. Gram taps my hand that's resting on the table.

My head is turned down as I move my eggs around, but I'm not actually eating them. "Gram...I'm in love with her. She found me—we found each other, and I never want to let her go. I see a future with her. A future of me spoiling and supporting her in every way possible."

"I had a feeling you two would hit it off. But to hear you say you love her after a short period of time..."

"Gram, she fits with me. Her ambition matches mine; I'm consumed by her. There's never a time when I'm not thinking about her. Yes, it hasn't been that long. But like you said, Gram, when you know, you know. And once I spent time with her, she was for me." My smile widens as I think about her again.

"Your dad has been burned by your mom. He's probably trying to protect you from the hurt he endured with all the cheating, and she took advantage of him. But that's no excuse for what he did. Dane, if you explain to him how you are feeling, maybe he'll understand."

"Ugh, I think he overheard me talking with Logan. It's the only possibility that makes sense. I was talking about her being the one. However, I also mentioned that she was upset with me about something related to her stalker and that she was disappointed about my having to go to work. Otherwise, he'd never have found out about her, not yet anyway."

"It's time to have a frank conversation with him. Threatening her reputation, accusing her of things she didn't do, and trying to pay her off. He might need more help than I thought. Start with a conversation, but you might need to lay it on the line for him to see you're serious. If she really is the one...then you need her to feel comfortable with the family."

I lift myself up and hug her. "Talking to you helps me put things into perspective and be clear about what I have to do."

My food is cold, but I'm no longer hungry. This whole situation is turning my stomach. I'll call Logan on the way to the office. He might have some advice for me. Dad let him marry Theresa. I still don't know how he did that, but, truth be told, I never asked. All I know is he married her, and it was exactly what he wanted. Now, I need his help getting what I want.

"Gram, I'm heading out. I need to call Logan on my way to the office."

"Okay, dear, please fill me in when you can."

I hug her tight and kiss the top of her head. "I will."

I slide into the driver's seat and take a quick peek at my phone.

Kendall:

> I appreciate you stopping by with my favs and a beautiful note...Thank you

My body vibrates. I have to read it a few times. She's holding on, and I'm not letting her go. I speed down the road. Calling Logan, I hope he answers on the first ring. He does—fucking thank you.

"Hey, what's up?"

"Since last night was date night, I opted not to interrupt. I know how much you both look forward to it."

"Man, get to the point."

I tell him straight. "Dad went to Kendall's salon and tried to intimidate her with threats and then pay her to stay away from me."

"Holy shit, he's lost it. Is Kendall okay?"

"Ya think? She said she needs time and space. He's made her question everything."

I update him on the situation that went down since yesterday's trip to Kendall's salon.

"The office won't be private enough. I'm still at home. Come here, and we'll figure this out. One thing is for sure: we need to confront him sooner rather than later before he tries to do any more damage."

I make a U-turn and head to his house. "Thanks for your help. I was going to do this alone, but I need backup."

Slamming on my brakes as I park behind Logan, I jump out of the car and jog to his front door. The door is unlocked, so I let myself in.

"I'm in my office," Logan calls when he hears the door open.

"Hey, what's the plan?" I ask, walking into his home office and settling into a chair across from his desk.

Logan starts by telling me what happened between him and Dad when he married Theresa. "I was prepared to walk away from the firm."

"Fuck! She meant that much to you, of course, you'd walk away from everything." His confession hit me right in the heart. "And that's all it took?"

"Basically. I had to commit to the firm, staying to protect the family name and our family's legacy."

I shake my head. "I'm all in. Whatever it takes for him to respect my decision."

"It will be more difficult than that. He didn't just roll over when I went to him about leaving the firm." He leans back in his leather chair.

Leaning forward with my elbows on my thighs, I take it all in. "What if my walking away isn't enough for him to back away from all of this?"

"You need to really think about this...are you willing to walk away from all of this for her? Does she mean that much to you for you to leave it all behind?"

My head dips down. I love being a defense attorney; it's everything I've ever wanted. I could work anywhere, start my own firm if I wanted. Walking away from our dad, it hurts, knowing what he's gone through, but not as much as I'm feeling right now, knowing Kendall is considering walking away from me...my chest tightens, and it's hard to breathe.

"If I walk away, he might not blink an eye. What if we both commit to walking away? Would you do that for me? It's a huge ask, so I understand if you need to think about it."

He hums and glances over at me before pulling his chair close to his desk. Arms resting on the desktop, he says, "I'm prepared to walk out the door with you. I actually think we should go in there and lay that on the line for him. We will both leave the firm. He needs a rude awakening." He rubs his temples. "I still can't believe he did that to Kendall. If he did anything close to that to Theresa, I would have lost my mind."

"Well, I have officially lost my mind, and losing Kendall is not an option. I need to make this right, no matter what the cost. I have to hope she comes around and sees we are meant to be together."

Logan smirks and laughs.

"What?" I stare back at him.

"You're smitten and determined. It looks good on you." He laughs some more.

"Asshole...now what?"

"If he truly wants to see us happy, then we need to make our own decisions without him interfering. Mom hurt him, but he needs a different hobby than controlling our lives, thinking he's protecting us from getting hurt. Now we make our own threats to him; he will not like it, but it's the only way. He'll make the decision. We know where we stand."

"Come on, he must be at the office by now. We're not giving him a heads-up."

We both hop into our cars and drive to the office in record time, park, and walk in. I hear his voice the minute I walk down the hallway.

I knock on the doorframe of Dad's office with Logan right behind me. "Do you have a minute?"

"This must be serious if you both are here," Dad says, leaning back in his chair and gesturing for us to come in.

I resist the urge to shake my head, doing my best to keep emotions out of the conversation as much as possible. "It's important," I say flatly.

He points to the chairs in front of his desk. "Come on in and close the door."

We take a seat. I'm glaring at him right before I say anything.

"I suspect you heard about my visit to see Kendall, and that's why you are here?" Dad asks, his voice giving nothing away, sounding almost bored.

"Yes, exactly," I say curtly. I want to hear it from his own mouth. "But why?" I place the contract and the torn-up check in a neat pile in front of him to make a point.

He sighs. "I'm protecting you. It's as simple as that. Look what happened with Maggie; she broke you. I thought you'd never give another woman the time of day. But I was wrong."

Shaking my head, I say, "I don't need protecting, Dad."

"When I overheard your conversation with Logan, I thought it would be best to make an offer."

Logan jumps in. "I'm not sure what part of the conversation you heard, but it's not your job to protect us. And it sure as hell isn't your place to threaten and intimidate people, especially those we care about. Can't you act like a normal parent? Just ask us what's going on. Let us make our own mistakes. Instead, you take things into your own hands, thinking you're doing us a favor, but you aren't."

"She's not right for Dane," Dad says with confidence. "People are talking."

My heart rate is picking up, so I breathe before saying, "People always talk. Did you ever consider verifying the information before using it against Kendall? For the record, I went down to the town hall on my own. She never asked for my help."

"Does that even matter? You still did it."

I shake my head, about to get up and walk out the door before we can even give him the ultimatum.

"Bigger picture, you don't have the right to threaten and intimidate Kendall, and then to top it all off, you tried to pay her off," Logan says, straight-faced and with no emotion. "You have a serious problem, and we will no longer sit back and let you run unchecked."

I then say, "She's exactly right for me. You don't even know her, only what you overheard and what gossip is around town. Did you even think of talking to Gram about what you heard? She knows everything in town."

"No," my father says almost petulantly.

"Well, think about this...Gram was planning on setting us up, but things fell into place for us all on their own. Kendall is Gram's stylist and has been since the salon opened. Did you even think about anyone else but yourself when you decided to make a power move?"

He doesn't have a quick comeback to that. He scratches his jaw, probably thinking of a way to weasel out of this. All he can come up with is... "Dane, she has a lot of baggage."

I throw back, "Don't we all!"

Complete silence fills the room.

Before it gets too heated and I fly off the handle, Logan says, "Dane and I spoke..."

"Go ahead." He nods for Logan to continue.

"We drafted a contract that would remove us as part owners of the firm." I hold it up and toss it onto his desk as Logan says, "And you might think, we can't do that. There's a clause that states if one of us walks away from the firm, the other has the option to do so as well. We agreed on it back when you and I didn't see eye to eye."

"Are you two considering leaving the firm over this?" His mouth downturns, and his brows furrow.

We say in unison, "Yes."

"What about our legacy here? Your inheritance?"

Logan is on a roll. "We want nothing more than to stay here, but there have to be boundaries. My relationship with Theresa is significantly better now that you haven't been trying to micromanage at every turn. I want you to extend the same to Dane. Dane and I agree, we'll walk away from our inheritance if that's what it comes to. The language you have there is archaic."

As my baby brother, I'm thankful he is sitting next to me, going to bat for me. I might have already lost it on Dad, but he's been even-keeled this entire time.

Dad stares out the window like he's not even here anymore. "I want the best for you two, and the last thing you need, Dane, is another woman cheating on you or using you again. It's the worst feeling in the world...it breaks something inside of you."

I feel bad for my dad, but it still doesn't give him the right to do what he did to Kendall.

"It did break something inside of me, and I'm a better man, a better boyfriend now than I ever was with Maggie."

Still staring out the window, he doesn't say another word. Logan and I look at each other and shrug, unsure of what to do next, so we sit and wait for him to speak.

He slowly turns his head without making eye contact with us and flips through the document we drafted. Rubbing his forehead, he glances up. "You've already signed this." His eyes jump between mine and Logan's like he can't believe we'd walk away. Hurt flickers in his eyes. But this isn't about him. It's about taking control of our lives instead of having him intrude and hold the inheritance clause over our heads.

Picking up his pen, I think he's about to sign it. If he does, then Logan and I walk out the door for good. It's the right decision, and if he doesn't want us in his life anymore, then that's on him. I'm content with the decision. I'll give it all up for her. Logan and I have a reputation in the community; it wouldn't take us long to build our own firm.

Dad flips to the signature page, and the pen hits the paper. Waiting for him to sign, I'm shocked that he would let us walk away so easily.

The pen doesn't move. "I need to think about this." And he drops the pen. Logan and I let out a sigh. Please tell me he is not dragging this out to find a way to convince us to stay.

With that, I stand, and Logan follows. "You have until the end of the week. Dad, I'm serious."

FORTY-ONE
Kendall

Reading his last text, it feels sincere. I have no idea how he's going to fix this with his dad, but he seems determined. And the warmth wraps around me like a comforting blanket.

Dane:

> You're welcome. It's hard for me to give you space.

Kendall:

> I know it is. It's what I need right now.

Dane:

> I'm going to fix this. You take all the time you need.

I pondered skipping work today, but I didn't want to overload my stylists. Being around my people will help me cope with all of this, even if they have no idea what is going on behind the scenes. The only ones who know are my girlfriends and Sally. Their ears were probably falling off by the time I was done explaining everything. Today, I'm focusing on my clients.

"Sally, my client printout isn't on my station." Waiting for an answer, I turn my body to see her face pale.

I quickly walk over and whisper, "Are you okay?"

"Um...so, Jane is on your schedule today for 9am." She grimaces. "I wanted to tell you first before just leaving your schedule."

"Oh." I look at my watch. It's almost nine. Not sure how I'm feeling about seeing Jane today. It didn't even cross my mind that she could be here this week. "That's okay. Thank you, Sally."

I take a deep breath and let it out. I've got this. Maybe she doesn't even know.

Just as that thought passes through, Jane walks in the door. Barely able to smile, she puts her arms out and hugs me. Yup, she knows. Why in the world would I think he wouldn't tell her?

Hugging me, she whispers, "It's all going to work out...you'll see." She kisses my cheek and places her palm over where she kissed.

With everything I have, I hold back tears. She glances at me. "Okay, let's get this mop looking good again."

If she said one more word, I'd have a breakdown right there in the middle of the salon. I'm grateful she saw it written all over my face.

I drape the cape around her and secure the Velcro. She watches me as I cut her hair. What is usually a chatty appointment is now silent. If I speak, I might break down.

"Those Walsh boys are very protective." No kidding, Jane. But I don't say it out loud. I just nod in agreement.

"They don't take after me, but they take after my late husband, Richard."

That stops me mid-cut, and I focus in, intently listening to what she has to say.

"Being responsible for their actions...absolutely. My Richard loved our kids and me hard. He instilled the work ethic that they all have. He also passed along the incessant need to protect the people he loved."

"Oh," is all I can manage as I listen to her story.

"Richard told our son, Edward, not to marry Cecile. We saw the signs, but he did it anyway. She was running away from her past—not my story to tell. Edward wanted to protect her, and in doing so, he gave her everything she had ever wanted. Kendall, please know their relationship ended badly, very badly."

She waves me down to her so she can whisper with no one else hearing. "I think your situation triggered Edward, and he was attempting to protect his son. Don't get me wrong, I am not making excuses for his behavior. He crossed the line. I wanted you to know a bit of the backstory."

"Thank you, Jane."

I don't know what else to say to her. Her son, Dane's dad—I could just write him off and never look back. What sucks me in is the look on Jane's face. One of love and sincerity. "Everything will work out the way it's supposed to—if it's meant to be."

Those words weave their way through my body and into the floor, grounding me and offering a slight relief that relaxes my shoulders. I finish cutting and styling Jane's hair. Sliding out of the chair, she brushes off some residual hair.

"You're a beautiful soul, Kendall."

"Jane..."

"I'll be back for my spa appointment. In the meantime, keep your head high. You deserve everything life has in store for you."

Tears well up and threaten to escape as she turns and leaves the salon. My next client isn't here yet, so I take a breather in my office.

Staring at my phone, I reread Dane's text, and silently beg—*please make this better.*

The week from hell is approaching Friday morning. All week, Dane delivered coffee and cinnamon rolls. I'm feeling like I may need to up my workouts. And every day he texts me, but nothing more. Since it's

Friday, I have Sally clear my schedule for tomorrow. Even if I have to work a little later next week, I need a long weekend to recharge, and maybe, just maybe, I should meet up with Dane.

I miss him so much. This morning, I debated texting him. Although my mind settled somewhat throughout the day. I've replayed every moment of being with Dane. It rooted me in the fact that I hadn't rushed into dating him. I was careful at first, but then he won me over. It all happened very fast, and I'm resigned to the fact that he found me, protected me, and now he's fighting for me with his father. I know I want him in my life.

At first, I didn't want to be the one interfering and getting in the middle of their relationship, but after talking to Jane, that's not it at all. This is about more than him and me.

As I'm cleaning up my station to head back to my office to work on paperwork that needs my attention, someone walks in the door. It's Dane's dad—you've got to be kidding me. I would hope that if Dane knew he was coming, he would have at least texted me.

"Mr. Walsh." Standing taller than usual, I won't let him tear me down again. I'm stronger, rooted in my decision.

His hair and his clothes appear to be more disheveled than the last time he was here. "Can we talk?" he asks as he rubs the back of his neck, reminding me of Dane.

"Um…okay." I eye Sally, and she nods back.

He follows me back to my office, and all I hear is his feet scuffing along the floor. Once we're sitting in my office, I say, "Look, I don't know why you are here, but there's really nothing more I have to say to you after what happened last time." Trying like hell to keep my composure, and wishing I still had those papers and the check so I could rip them up and throw the pieces at him.

He places his elbows on his knees and then runs his hands down his face.

What is going on?

I'm trying to decipher what he's doing here, but nothing is adding up.

With an enormous sigh, he says with a shaky voice, "I had a conversation with my mother, Jane. She's one of your clients."

"Yes, she is," I say, leaving room for him to continue.

"She told me I needed to take a hard look at myself. About my boys...about you. I came here last time in arrogance, thinking I knew best. I see now I was mistaken."

With my arms crossed over my chest, I'm not letting him intrude into my space. "You certainly made your opinion clear."

His head hangs low, shaking. "I know. And I hurt you—and Dane—by doing it. My mother told me about the ways you've helped this community, the people who lean on you." He clears his throat a few times. The air thickens in the room. "She said I've been blind to what truly matters. I thought protecting my sons meant controlling them, but all I did was push them away."

I'm not letting my guard down with him sitting in front of me. This person looks torn, sad, and something else I can't put my finger on. "So why are you here now?"

"To admit I was wrong. To tell you that I see how much you mean to Dane—and to our family. I don't expect forgiveness, but I hope one day you'll believe me when I say, I only wanted what was best for him. I just didn't see that you might be that best thing."

My ears must be playing tricks on me. A man who came in here earlier this week, threatening me, trying to pay me off, intimidating me—just admitted he was wrong about me, about what he did?

With my head tilted to the side, eyes wide, I'm not sure what to say.

"I'm sure this is a surprise given our last conversation."

"Ah-huh." That's all that comes out of my mouth, and I nod yes.

"I was completely out of line."

"Did Dane send you?"

"No, no. He has no idea I'm even here." He moves to the edge of the chair. "I don't want to lose my boys. I've already lost enough."

He must be talking about his ex-wife. I let him continue—it seems like he needs to get it off his chest.

"Okay." I lean onto my desk, waiting for more.

"I don't know if Dane told you, but my wife cheated on me—several times. Well, now she's my ex-wife. I thought she was the one...like my parents had." His eyes glisten. "I thought I was doing the right thing coming to you. But now, they might leave. It's the last thing I want, so I had to fix it—starting with you."

"Me?" I ask without thinking.

"Yes. I thought I was protecting Dane, but in fact, I was sticking my nose where it didn't belong because I thought I knew best. I didn't want him to get hurt...again."

"Mr. Walsh...to be clear, I know what I'm getting with Dane, and hurting him is the last thing I want to do." As the words pass through my lips, I know I won't ever hurt him like Maggie did. I will love him for however long I'm on this earth. Clearing the lump in my throat, I need to talk to Dane.

"Dane made that clear earlier this week," his dad says.

Therapist or hairstylist, it's all the same...It's as if people see me and want to share their deepest, darkest secrets.

"That was a lot." I shake my head. "You can't insert yourself into your son's relationship," I say with compassion lacing my voice. It might be a bit too forward, but I'm not holding back with this guy. He came into my office, steamrolling me, and I let him get under my skin—not today.

"You're right. And I won't involve myself in my sons' love lives again."

"Have you told him that yet?" I ask, sincerely curious.

"Not yet; I wanted to talk with you first. He's my next stop. If you don't mind, please don't let him know I came here. At least until after I talk with him, please."

I think about this request and am not sure if I'm doing the right thing, but the pleading in his eyes has me saying, "I won't."

He stands up, and so do I. Walking to the door, he holds the doorknob, turns around, and I'm following him out the door. He releases the doorknob and hugs me. "I hope we can start over."

"You really need to talk to Dane first." I half-smile at him, knowing this is a man who is still hurting from everything that his ex-wife did to him. And it helps that I know he's Jane's son; it softens my heart a little bit more for him.

"If you can find it in your heart to give my son a chance, don't let my mistakes stand in the way. Please. Don't let me be the reason he loses the best thing in his life."

With that, he leaves. I'm standing there with my hand over my mouth for a few beats. Then I find my phone.

Kendall:

You're not going to believe who just walked in the door.

Addison:

Dane?

Faith:

Just tell us!

Kendall:

Dane's father...apologizing, groveling. More details tonight, my house, pool party, 6pm

Lane:

I didn't even get a chance to answer, but I'll be there.

Faith:

OMG you're killing us.

Addison:

Can we make it 5pm? How are we supposed to wait?

Kendall:

Fine - 5pm I'll skip the paperwork. But bring snacks, I won't have time to pick anything up. On the plus side, I have tequila.

One by one, my friends find me in the kitchen preparing a few snacks I scrounged up. I have a sleeve of crackers, half a block of sharp cheddar cheese, and dried apricots. I'm already in my bathing suit, and the tequila sits on the island.

"I brought the popcorn because you need to tell us everything," says Faith, as she unpacks her bag.

"Popcorn...that's a good idea. I have more cheese and crackers, plus some grapes. Need something healthy," Addison laughs, bringing the grapes to the sink to rinse off.

Lane giggles. "I'll round it off with some chips, salsa, and guacamole." She opens the chips and guac and starts eating. "I can't wait any longer. You need to tell us what the hell happened today."

They all lean onto the island and stare at me as they await the details of what's going on.

"First, let it be known that Jane's son is Edward." They all gasp.

"How did we not know this?" Faith asks.

"Dane never mentioned the connection, only that she was his Gram. So I assumed Gram was his mom's mom." I shake my head in disbelief that I hadn't figured it out sooner.

I tell them about Jane's appointment and how Edward came into the salon to talk to me again. They're all in shock at the revelation. We munch on snacks as we unravel all that's happened.

Addison, with her face in her hands, leans on the island. "So now what? Have you heard from Dane?"

"I'm still processing all that's happened, but hearing Jane talk about him made me feel a little bit bad for him." I pinch my finger and thumb together, leaving only a few centimeters.

"He was a real asshole to you, Kendall. I wouldn't let him off the hook that easily." Faith stands up, walks around the island, and pours the tequila into shot glasses. "I think we need a couple shots."

We all hold out shot glasses ready for her to pour. "To new beginnings, standing up for yourself, and never letting someone else dictate how you live your life."

Clinking our shot glasses, we throw them back and go for round two.

"So you haven't heard from Dane?" Addison asks as she collects all the glasses and puts them into the sink. Snagging a couple of crackers and pieces of cheese, she awaits my answer.

I shrug. "Since his dad was heading there after he left the salon, I'm thinking he must be with his dad. No, I haven't heard from him at all."

FORTY-TWO

Dane

As I approach my driveway, all I see is my dad's black Porsche sitting in my driveway. He's been MIA all week ever since we gave him an ultimatum. Not sure where he's been, but now I'm curious why he is parked in my driveway.

Lifting my foot off the gas pedal, I cruise into the driveway, parking right next to him. I peer over, and he's sitting there in the driver's seat with both hands on the steering wheel. Slowly, he turns his head toward me, nods, and opens his door. My body isn't moving, even though I watch him close his door and walk to the front of our cars.

I can either get out or drive away. It's time to face him, so I make my way out of the car. "Hi, Dad," I say firmly.

"Hi, Dane." His tired eyes stare back at me. "Can we talk?"

I gather myself, bracing for whatever comes next. "Sure, come on in."

He follows me through the door and straight to the kitchen. I might need a beer for this conversation. Snagging one from the fridge, I glance over my shoulder. "Want one?"

"No, son, I'm good. Thank you." His tone is somber. I wonder what's up with him. Maybe he's here to wish me luck in my next endeavor and deliver the signed papers. But why would he just come to my house and not involve Logan in the conversation?

He has me curious, wondering what he's doing here. "Let's sit on the deck."

We sit across from each other, me with one leg over my knee, looking as relaxed as I can be.

"You might be wondering why I'm here."

"That crossed my mind," I chuckle. My nerves might be getting the better of me. I need to have this wrapped up so Kendall and I can live our lives together with no interference from the man sitting across from me.

Wiping his hands along his thighs, he clears his throat.

Is he nervous too?

I don't think I've ever seen my dad like this. What is going on with him?

"I visited Kendall today..."

"You did what? I can't believe you would subject her to another visit from you," I all but shout, interrupting him, lifting myself off my chair.

"Please sit back down. If you let me finish, you would have heard me say that I apologized to Kendall and had a conversation about you...and her."

I sit back down, and my hands grip the arms of the chair as he speaks. "Wait...What? You apologized and had a conversation with her. She let you near her?"

"Dane, I'm not a threat to her."

"I beg to differ."

He shakes his head. "I don't want to lose anyone else in my life—you, Logan." The paper that he pulls out of his jacket pocket looks familiar. He takes them and rips all the pages in half, stands up, and drops them in my lap.

"I have a lot of work to do to earn your trust again and, frankly, build back our relationship after what's happened. After talking with your Gram, it became really clear I was dead wrong—about everything. I thought Kendall was the problem, but in fact, Gram pointed out I'm the problem. I'm putting all my fears onto your relationship. It was wrong."

"Yes, you are completely wrong."

He stares at me. "I'm sorry for barging into your life and making threats to the woman you love."

I interrupt him. "Wait. How do you know that?"

"Son, I saw it written all over your face when you were talking with your brother. I remember your grandfather talking about Gram, and he had that same look. One of admiration, happiness, and love—the love of his life."

I blow out a breath. He's just as observant as I am. "You listened in on my conversation with Logan?"

"I did." Hanging his head low. "That tone, the way you talk about Kendall, it was also how I used to talk about your mom. At first, it was good, perhaps too good. Your conversation about Kendall hit a nerve, and I went off the deep end."

"Yeah, you did. I never expected you to go to these lengths. It was shocking and hurtful. My heart literally hurts because you have Kendall questioning everything about our relationship. And I can only hope that this mess doesn't sever what we have—the love we have."

"If there's anything else I can do, I'll do it. I'm sorry, son," he says, shaking his head.

We haven't had a conversation like this in a while. I'm somewhat shocked that he opened up to me about my mom. That's usually an off-limits conversation. Telling him how I feel about Kendall seals it. I love her with all my heart, and I'm not letting this be the end for us.

I move to stand up and say, "It's really important that you under-stand this cannot happen again. You need to not meddle in my life again. You've talked about doing the right thing; now you need to follow up with actions. It's going to take some time to fully trust you again, but I love you, and we aren't going anywhere."

My dad stands up and steps closer to me, putting his arms around me, and says, "I love you, too, son." He pats me on my back a few times instead of pulling away like I would expect.

Surprised by his emotional state, I hug my dad back. Squeezing him one more time, I say, "Tell me what happened with Kendall. I haven't heard from her. Why didn't she let me know? Is she upset?"

"No, I asked her to wait until later so I could talk with you." We sit back down, and he tells me the entire conversation with Kendall. She is the most amazing, loving, and caring woman, and I want her in my life forever. My hope is high that she's choosing herself, and then she'll choose me.

She has to choose me—please let her choose us.

"Dad, I love her."

"I know you do, son. I'm not interfering again. It's your life."

The thought of losing us, Logan and I, clearly weighed on him. He can't just bulldoze his two sons. Forgetting he's our dad and taught us well. I chuckle.

I check my watch to see the time. It's been talking for over two hours.

He stands up and says, "You need to tell her you love her."

"I do." I stand up, and we walk to our cars.

With a deep breath, I knock on her door. All I wanted to do was gaze into her eyes; there was no time for texting. I leaped out of my car and ran to the door. Composing myself, I run a hand down my shirt.

She opens the door. A sight to see. Her fiery red hair sprawls around her shoulders. I pause for a split second before I wrap my arms around her and almost tumble on the floor. Feeling her arms wrap around me, it's a small gesture, but it sends all my nerve endings firing. Tears well up in my eyes. I can't lose her.

"There's no more waiting for me." I brush her hair off her face and gaze into her sparkling emerald green eyes. Her shock gives way to a bright smile. "I love you, Kendall. I can't hold back anymore. I was trying to give you time and space. It was too much. My heart is literally going to burst out of my chest."

Her hand slides to my heart and taps it. "You love hard, don't you." It wasn't a question. She knows and kisses the spot she was tapping—my heart.

"I fall fast and love hard," I shrug, like I'm confessing my sins.

Lifting herself up on her tippy toes, she guides my face down to hers. So close to each other, her eyes close. "I love being loved by you..." She opens her eyes and says, "I love you, too. There's no denying we sprinted into this relationship." We both laugh.

She presses her lips to mine. To feel her again, my blood pressure skyrockets, and my dick stands at attention. Our lips move, starving for each other. It feels like forever.

Breaking away from me ever so slowly, she says, "We should probably talk."

"Yeah, yeah, good idea." I reluctantly let her go, feeling the loss of her warmth.

Then, she slips her hand into mine and leads me to the backyard. Being connected to her, it's perfect—it's right. I want to be touching her, close to her. So I sit with her on the lounger. "Do you already know your dad stopped by the salon today?"

"Yeah, he showed up at my house. We just finished having a two-hour conversation."

"Oh, is that good?"

"It's great, sweetheart. He filled me in. Desperate man, desperate measures. Honestly, I couldn't believe he went to see you again."

"So you really didn't know?" she asks, searching me.

"Not a fucking clue."

"I didn't realize your mom cheated on your dad." She moves forward to touch my face. "I'm putting the pieces together."

I massage my temples and let out a sigh. "He's still hurting from it all, and it's been years."

"I could see it in his eyes. It's heartbreaking." She rests her hand on my leg. "Looking back on this week, a part of me wants to thank your dad for trying to pay me to stay away from you."

Jolting back. "What?"

She pulls me to her. "Dane, it made me take a step back and think about myself, us. We were moving at the rate of a freight train." I laugh. She isn't wrong. "I know without a shadow of a doubt, I haven't lost myself in you. I'm still me. My ambitions are larger than life...and so aren't yours. Our hearts are tethered. Our connection is undeniable. Our work/life balance—we're working on it...We're perfect for each other."

"We're soulmates." I cup her face and rub her cheekbones. Her eyes flutter.

She's gorgeous.

"I think we can make anything work after all of this."

"Me too, sweetheart."

FORTY-THREE
Kendall

Since I couldn't clear my entire Saturday schedule, I quickly finish my last client of the day. She loves it, steps out of my chair, and whispers, "You didn't mention he was eye candy." Dane leans against the reception desk, waiting for me to finish my workday. I wasn't working today, but I had a couple of clients who couldn't reschedule, so I came in for them.

"Nancy, stop it!" I shake my head at my older client, who likes to tease me about my love life. She's happily married and tells me all the ways her husband spoils her.

"Have a wonderful date, Kendall." She swings her hair and walks over to Sally. Dane pushes himself off the desk and strolls over to me.

Nancy and Sally start whispering, and I glance at Dane, who's halfway to me. I blow him a quick kiss.

He strolls over in a few strides; he's close, and my body heats up. The closer he is to me, the more my body fires up. His scent of coconuts and palm trees—I love it, I love him, and heat pools in my center while butterflies flutter in my belly.

"Can you escape without cleaning up today?"

"I can ask Sally to clean up and close for me." I give him a smirk.

"I have a full night planned, sweetheart." He encircles my waist, tugging me to him, and kissing me under my ear. A shiver runs down my spine; my entire body quakes.

Interrupted by Sally, who was obviously eavesdropping on our conversation. "You kids head out. I'll close up."

I dramatically wave to Sally and say, "Thank you! I'll see you on Tuesday."

"I like her," he whispers in my ear.

"Yeah, you do because she's giving you what you want."

I shrug confidently. "Can you blame me?"

"I guess not." I lean into his body. "What time do I need to be ready?"

"We have reservations..." He looks at his watch and says, "In about an hour. Does that work for you? You always look gorgeous, so there's not much to improve." He winks at me. "Well, unless you want to be naked with me first..." I swat at him, but he continues. "You could walk out of here, and you'd still be the most beautiful woman in the world."

"More brownie points for you...Okay, I'll head home. Are you following me?" I wait for an answer as I open my car door.

"I have to make a stop first, and then I'll come pick you up." He looks at me with love in his eyes and anticipates what's to come.

Eyeing him with curiosity, I say, "That's interesting. No other details?"

"You'll know soon enough. I thought you liked surprises." He eyes me with suspicion. "I'll see you in twenty minutes."

As we pull up to the restaurant, *On the Waterfront*, I glance over at him. "I love this place."

I'm excited to eat here, practically jumping out of the car before it stops. Their food is to die for, and the atmosphere is laid-back and fun.

"Yes, and tonight is about making new memories for us." He holds my hand and squeezes it. Leaning over the center console, he cups my face and kisses me.

He exits the car as the valet opens my door, and I scoot myself out of the car. By the time I'm on my feet, Dane is right next to me with his hand on my lower back, and we're walking to the door. Heat singes my back from his fingers gently caressing my exposed back.

The hostess asks if we have reservations; we do. She takes us to a corner table overlooking the water. It actually looks like a private spot, with no other tables around. Well, not as close as they usually are. I wonder if he requested this spot.

"Did you pay extra for this privacy?" I tease him.

He slides the chair out and points to the seat. "Have a seat, sweetheart. We'll have plenty of time to talk tonight."

"I'm looking forward to tonight with you."

"Me too. I've planned this to be one of the best nights of your life so far. Between a couple of weeks ago and tonight, I'll have to one-up myself," he chuckles.

I slap his shoulder. He's sitting close to me, and I can feel his knee nudge mine. It's already a fantastic night with him.

The night goes smoothly with drinks and seafood that's mouthwateringly amazing. This restaurant never disappoints. I don't even pay attention to the scenic view, since I have Dane to look at.

He updates me on what's going on at the office. It's a little bit too corporate for me, but he lights up when he talks about it. As much as he grumbles, his whole body shows the passion he has for his work. Watching him, he's animated when he tells stories. It's captivating; no wonder he is a top defensive attorney.

"What is the one thing about being a defense attorney that you love most?"

"Being in the courtroom, giving my closing argument. It's story-telling at its finest. Strategic."

"Okay, I was close."

"Tell me what you thought it was."

"I thought it was being in the courtroom, cross-examining witnesses."

"Yeah, I like that too."

Dessert comes out because he insists we need it. I'm stuffed, but how can you say no to crème brûlée? When it's laid in front of me, I'm grateful it's smaller than I thought it would be. I take my time eating it. Every bite is pure heaven.

I must have been moaning in pleasure as I ate because Dane leans over and grabs my thigh. "Do you see what you're doing to me with all that moaning?"

Giggling as I eye his crotch, he won't be able to hide that with his napkin. "Oh—sorry, not sorry."

"I bet," he says as he tries to discreetly adjust himself.

We both put our napkins on the table at the same time. "Is that a sign you're ready for your next surprise?"

"Yes, yes, I am." I stand up quickly, energy zinging through my body. He smiles widely and moves quickly, which makes me think this is a big surprise.

I can't wait.

FORTY-FOUR
Dane

Gravel crunches under the tires as we wind down the driveway. Kendall is practically sitting on top of the dashboard as she looks out the windshield. When I finally park outside my lake house on Mirror Lake, it's beautiful, and I have one of the few lots on the lake with some privacy.

The house sits back from the shoreline, off to the side. Down by the water, I have a beach hut. It took forever for all the sign-offs to get the hut built. It has it all—electricity, running water, a bathroom, a kitchenette, and a guest room. The house is big enough, but I wanted a place where I could have a piece of heaven closer to the water. My favorite part of the hut is the front porch. It's positioned perfectly for all the summer sunsets on the lake.

We walk up to the side door. "Dane, is this your house?"

"Sweetheart, this is my lake house, and I wanted to share this slice of heaven with you."

"Okay, so this is your second home?" Her mouth is agape. I think she loves it.

Rylee, my assistant, spent the last few days getting this place ready. I haven't seen it since Logan and I came here earlier this week. I'm just as surprised as Kendall is with the inside.

I unlock the door and turn the knob. The door swings open. What once was a place I never wanted to visit again is now a place that Kendall is oohing and ahhing over.

"Dane, this place is amazing," she says as she walks to the windows overlooking the yard and lake. She stands there for a few minutes, taking it all in.

My heart squeezes in my chest. Is it from the memories of what happened here? I rub my chest and watch her. She doesn't move, so I stroll over, not wanting to disturb her. My chest connects with her back, and I wrap my arms around her stomach. We stand there, watching the moonlight flicker on the water.

Surprisingly, my chest loosens the longer we stand here. Holding her, I begin to sway and dip my head to her ear. "You love it." I know she loves it; her eyes give it away. The way she is swaying with me and her thumbs stroke my hands, this woman has me—all of me.

Fresh memories of my favorite place with my new favorite person. I slide one of my hands from hers and dig into my pocket for my phone. Fumbling through some songs, I choose Lenny Kravitz's "Can't Get You Off My Mind" and press play.

She whirls around. "What's that?"

"A song. Want to dance?"

"I'd love to dance."

We spend the next twenty minutes dancing. Her body against mine, my arms wrapped around her, and our hearts beat together. The fire burning between us is more than just sexual tension. Our flames intertwine the longer we hold each other. The complete calmness in my body, all my muscles relaxing, and the watermelon scent of her hair, has me hugging her closer. Although I'm not sure how much closer we can get.

I want to make new memories here with her. The song wraps up, and I whisper to her, "Want to see the rest of the house?"

"I'm content dancing right here with you."

"Okay."

When we finally tear apart several songs later, I give her the tour. Rylee pulled out all the stops in such a short amount of time. The last room is the master bedroom. My heart beats faster as we approach the door. This is where it all happened. I stop in my tracks.

Shit! Can I walk through the door?

"Hey, what's wrong?" Concern is written all over her face.

We stand in the hallway a couple of feet away from the door. She takes my hands in hers, bringing them to her mouth, and kisses my palms. "Tell me. I can see it in your eyes. Something's wrong."

My eyes? She's full of surprises. I read body language—she reads eyes.

A deep sigh leaves me, and I confess, "It was here."

"Dane, what was here?"

My throat constricts as I choke out, "Maggie..." I pull my gaze from the floor to her eyes. Her beautiful emerald green eyes pierce me with an affection that seeps through my body, spurring me to continue. "She brought him here—my best friend. She tarnished this place for me. I came home early to surprise her. Really early, she never would have thought I would take that much time off from work, but I did. That day."

She lets go of my hands so she can hold my face and stare into my eyes. I rest my hands on her hips. "You haven't been back since?"

"I came earlier this week with Logan. I didn't want tonight to be the first time I walked through the door. Then I had my assistant, Rylee, redecorate." My head moves to her forehead, closing my eyes. Processing that I'm standing here ready to walk through that door.

"That makes sense. You looked just as surprised as I was when we walked through the front door."

I lift my head to look at her. "Yeah, she outdid herself. She's due for a raise." I chuckle at myself. I keep saying that, so maybe I need to do it when I'm back in the office next week.

"Get on that!" She smiles at me. It brings my shoulders back, making me stand tall.

She makes me laugh again. "So bossy."

"You haven't seen bossy yet."

"This feels like the last piece of me that I needed to share with you. I love you, and my heart is healing because you're in it. I'm reclaiming this place with you by my side."

I take her hand and tug her through the doorway behind me. Flipping the light on, my eyes are wide and I'm speechless—nothing comes out of my mouth. There is a new four-poster bed with crisp white linens and an endless array of pillows.

Who needs that many pillows?

It's even positioned differently, still able to see out the wall of windows overlooking the water. The matching nightstands with new lamps—simple with white shades. There's a tall dresser on one wall and another smaller dresser on the far wall. There's an oversized chaise lounge with a small table for coffee or a book.

The room is drastically different. I don't feel the tightness in my chest anymore. What I see now is possibility. And we sure as fuck are going to christen this bed at some point tonight.

Kendall walks forward, leaving my hand behind. Her flowing red hair flows behind her as she walks through the room.

"This is magnificent." She walks over to the chaise and slides herself onto it. "One word—comfortable. Come sit with me," she says, patting her hand.

I step back and shut off the lights. Then, I make my way through the dark to climb onto the chaise with her. The darkness allows us to stargaze from the chaise. Not as good as being on the porch of the hut, but we haven't even gotten that far on our tour yet.

This chaise is huge; if I can fit with Kendall by my side, it's monstrous and feels plush. I drape my arm around her, and she leans back onto me.

"The view of the lake in the morning is breathtaking," I say to her just before my lips kiss her cheek.

"I'd like to see that." She snuggles up close to me with her head resting on my shoulder.

"We will today and every day," I promise her.

She turns and places her hand on my face. "I love you." Her lips meet mine, and she flings her leg over me, straddling me.

If we stay here, there's no way we'll make it outside. The sky is clear, and all the stars shine brightly. I kiss her back. Light kisses, no tongue, sensual. Regardless, my dick is ready, per usual. She grinds her pussy down onto it.

I take both of her arms in my hands and pull her slightly away. "We have a couple of choices. We could walk down to the water and see the hut, or we can stay right here."

She leans back even further. "The hut?"

"Yeah, there's a hut I had built by the water. Like a tiny house with a porch and we could watch the stars down there...Or we could stay right here and continue kissing and see where it leads us." I kiss her neck.

"Now I'm intrigued. A hut? I have to see this." She slides off and grabs my hands, yanking me to my feet. As strong as she is, I don't budge.

I tug her toward me and say, "A kiss before we head down." And the kiss isn't rushed. We linger on each other's lips.

"Okay, let's check out this hut." She's bouncing on her toes. I'm proud of the design; it's everything I wanted in a waterfront hut.

With fingers interlaced, we walk through the house and out to the yard. We are both barefoot; the grass under our feet is lush. Kendall stops in the middle of the yard.

"Sweetheart..."

She covers my mouth with her finger. "This yard is private. We could do some...things on this grass and no one would see us." Brushing her toes into it, "It's cozy...but they'd definitely hear me." She proudly moves through the rest of the yard and then bolts for the front door.

"Wait, don't step in without me."

Whipping her head around, she says, "Then hurry up, slowpoke."

I jog up to the porch, and my hand brushes over hers as I turn the knob. Kendall enters first, with me on her heels. Flipping the switch, I'm in shock. Rylee also redecorated the hut.

"Dane—this place. It's just as breathtaking. What do you even do here?"

"When I used to come every weekend, I'd stay in here. I felt like I was away from everyone being down here. The house is too big for one person; sometimes I want to live a simple life."

"A simple life, huh?! I feel like that occasionally. Getting away from everything, it's nice to decompress in a space that hugs you. This place hugs me." Her eyes roam around the space, taking it all in.

I look at her with curiosity. "I'm not sure I feel the hug part, but I think I know what you're saying."

It's a small house, so the tour takes less than five minutes to complete. The bedroom is a mini version of the master bedroom. Rylee even found a smaller chaise to put in the corner of the room.

"This is the most luxurious bathroom," she says as she walks in, turning on the light. "That soaking tub is calling my name."

The tub has one of the best views of the lake. You can see out, but onlookers would have to be up against that glass to see inside.

"Go for it." I gesture to the tub.

"Not now! We still have some stargazing to do." She turns around and leans up to stroke my beard. "Let's go check out that porch."

When we first came in, we sped by the porch, wanting to look inside, but it doesn't disappoint.

I smirk, thinking about her lying in the bathtub—naked, her breasts peeking out at the top of the water with bubbles all around her. Fuck, that will be hot.

.

FOURTY-FIVE
Kendall

The porch is the perfect size. It has a couple of chairs with a table in between them and a hammock on the other.

"Where to?" Dane asks, gesturing between the two seating areas.

"Hammock, please," I answer with a bright smile.

We both walk over, and he eases down onto the hammock first, then swings over to grab and pull me with him. The hammock goes flying, but quickly settles down. The view is breathtaking. The lake, treetops, stars, and the moon are fully showing themselves tonight.

With one leg off the hammock, Dane rocks us ever so slightly. I'm snug up against his side, and my head is resting on his chest. We're relaxed, holding each other. He strokes my arm, and it's soothing as I trace circles on his chest. In mindless circling, I can imagine him shirtless with his muscles rippling under my fingertips.

He's distracting, but then he points up into the sky and says, "Look, there's the Big Dipper."

The sky is clear, and seeing the Big Dipper is a highlight of the night. "I love that you can see the stars from here. It's relaxing, and I can be close to you."

Everything about him feels right. He's right for me. My entire body melts into him as I cuddle up to his side and rest my head on his chest as the chilly air bites at us.

I shiver. "Brrr, it's chilly all of a sudden."

"The breeze shifted, and now it's coming off the lake. You want to take that bath now?"

"Yeah, that sounds amazing."

He darts straight to the bathroom, and I hear the water start. Poking his head out the doorway, he says, "There's a robe in the closet."

My plan was to undress in front of him and step into the tub, but a robe will work too.

He yells from the bathroom, "Do you like it hot or just warm?"

"Hot, please," I say and think to myself, it's how I like most things, especially my men. Just thinking about him makes my temperature rise, and the throbbing between my legs is relentless.

Damn it! I was hoping for a bath first, but my body is ready for him. If he dares to touch me, I'll unravel. I remove my clothes, slide both arms into the robe, and tie it.

He asks, "Do you want company?

Caught off guard, I immediately say, "Yes."

I stroll over to the bathroom door and peek in. "You're already undressing."

He whirls around with only his boxer briefs on. "I was going to put my robe on and wait for you here, but it looks like you're ready."

My feet are cool on the tile floor, thankfully, because everywhere else is steaming hot. I watch Dane's every move as he slips on his robe and checks the water. "Feels just right. Want to check it for yourself?"

My feet pad over the tile floor straight to the tub, and I dip my toe in through the bubbles he added. My robe moves and flashes him as he watches me. "Like what you see?" I glance over my shoulder with a sly grin. I lean over to shut off the water as Dane reaches for the water too. Our hands meet and then our eyes.

"Why don't you slide in first? I'll be right back," he murmurs before leaving the bathroom.

I look around to see if these lights dim, but the switch is pretty high-tech. If I dare touch it, I'll probably screw it up. With that, I take off my robe, hang it up on the hook, and step into the tub. The warmth of the water envelops me. Once my body regulates with the water, I sink my body down.

I sit at the bottom of the tub, and Dane comes in, dimming the lights.

"That's better," I moan, sinking further into the water.

He has a lighter in his hand, along with a bottle that I can't quite make out, and two glasses. There are candles scattered around the bathroom, and he lights them one by one. The flickering of the light throughout the bathroom matches the moon's light outside dancing on the water.

This is where I want to be, here with Dane.

"All we have in the fridge is some sparkling water; will that work for you?"

"I mean, maybe. What kind?"

He laughs and says, "Watermelon."

"I love watermelon, so yes, please."

He pours the glasses and sets them on the shelf by my arm. Perfectly placed for when you are soaking. Pulling his phone out of his robe pocket, he starts some music. It's just barely audible, but I'm able to catch the lyrics of *Everything* by Lifehouse.

The tie to his robe slips, and he slowly slides it off. "If you move up a bit, I'll step in behind you."

As he moves closer, the light from the candles accentuates his body, his cock swaying with every step. Holy hell. I can't wait for him to be pressed up against me.

The water sloshes as he slips down into the tub. "Oh, this feels good. I love hot water baths."

"You don't strike me as a bath guy. But it looks good on you." I smile, and then I'm overcome by a yawn. The sudden wave of exhaustion is definitely not the company; it's just another long day.

"Sweetheart, this was a special order. I wanted to be able to fit my entire body in here."

He grips my shoulders and leans me back into his chest. Massaging my shoulders, I moan again and move my neck from side to side. Not wanting him to stop, I lean forward so he can massage my back too. When I'm satisfied, my limp body falls against his chest. I take his hands and bring them around me. His fingers run up and down my stomach, sliding lower to just above my sensitive spot. I wiggle; he knows what he's doing to me.

Whispering in my ear, he says, "Your skin is smooth, and I'd touch you every day if you let me."

I hum in response as his hand glides up my breastbone. My eyes close, savoring his touch. He drags his fingertips over my nipples. That's all it takes for goosebumps to erupt all over my body. I can't help but cross my legs, relieving the pressure of my throbbing clit.

"You do like it gentle," he mumbles as he continues to tease me. My nipples tighten to hard peaks that could cut glass. Once I open my eyes and turn my head toward him, he kisses me. Sparks fly, and my body is ready for him. Taking his tongue and sliding it along my bottom lip, I feel his cock, hard and pressing into my back. All my nerve endings are firing at once. The warmth of the water mixes with the heat and safety of his body against mine.

I find the back of his neck with my hand and dig my nails into it. The kiss deepens, the fire swirling around us. It's as if we are going to combust right here in the bathtub.

As we get lost in our deep, passionate kiss, I wonder how I'm in the arms of this man—in a tub. His hands stroke my back, leaving a wake of fire and chills throughout my body.

He's the kind of man I can get lost in, seeing us in this tub here together. It's not at all what I ever pictured myself doing.

Dane is everything I thought I never needed. Yes, protective and arrogant. But he has this side of him that shines when we're alone. He's affectionate and tender in ways I've never felt from a man. He treats me with respect, and I never want to let him go.

Feeling his breath on my face, and his hands on my body, my heart squeezes tightly. It feels like home, where I belong.

I roll my back against his chest again, staring out onto the lake. "I love it here," I whisper.

"Me too. I love it here with you in my arms." He squeezes me tight.

I move my hands over his arms gently and then glide my nails over his skin. "It feels good to be with you. It's like we could spend every Saturday night here."

Tucking his head in the crook of my neck, he mutters, "I want that, too."

The prickles in my hands and the vibration between us are undeniable as he holds me tight. Touching me ever so lightly, he allows the moment to stretch between us.

The weight of it all is penetrating my walls and allowing him further in—trusting him with every ounce of my being.

"I'd love to have you here for an entire weekend, if you could get away." His lips swipe over my neck.

I sigh and tilt my head to give me better access. "I might be able to manage that."

"I'll take that as a yes. The water's a bit tepid. Ready to get out?"

I sit up and immediately miss his warmth. A chill runs through me as I stand up. He makes quick work of getting out of the tub and grabbing our towels. Flipping a switch, I feel hot air flowing down onto my body.

"Oh, my...this is heaven." I stand under it and dry off. When I shiver, he wraps his towel around his waist and gathers me up into his arms. I sling both of mine around his neck as he quickly brings me to the bed. Taking the blankets down, he places me on the bed, takes my towel, and covers me up.

The stone fireplace is on the far wall, and he grabs the remote to turn it on. There may not be a lot of heat coming from it, but watching it makes me stop shivering—or it's the blankets.

He slides into bed, his skin still damp from the tub, and pulls me against him. The towel is gone, nothing between us now but heat. His fingers dig into my hip, while his other hand claims me, thumb grazing the sensitive underside of my breast in deliberate circles that send electricity crackling down my spine. I arch involuntarily against him, my pulse hammering so hard I can feel it throughout my body.

"Are you warming up?"

I snicker, "Ah, yes. It might be your body against mine that's doing it."

"Having you in my bed is everything to me."

FORTY-SIX

Dane

Curled up in bed together, I kiss the top of her head. "I want to spend every night with you in my bed, holding you."

It's the truth. This woman in my arms—she's the one I want to spend my time with, adore her, and be the one she lays her head on, feeling protected and loved.

She hums and turns over to face me. Tapping her fingers on my arm and nudging my legs open so she can slide her leg through, she says, "We can start tonight."

My dick jumps at that prospect. I wasn't sure how she would take that comment, and it made me realize I have a lot more to learn about her.

But right now, I'm diving headfirst between her legs. She slides her hand between us and grips my cock. The low moan that escapes her mouth has me harder and jutting my hips. The feeling of her soft, warm hand wrapped around my cock almost sends me over the edge.

"You're driving me crazy."

"That's the point, big boy." She smirks and continues to stroke her hand up and down while squeezing me.

Fuck me!

I forget all about the nickname she just gave me and decide to toss her onto her back. She wraps her legs around me.

I grunt. "You're quick."

"I got your number."

"I guess you do," I say as I suck on her skin below her ear, dragging my tongue down her shoulder. She's writhing under me, which spurs me on, right to her pink nipples—tight and begging for attention.

She rakes her nails down my back, and the blood rushing to my cock is endless. If she makes any sudden moves, I'll blow all over her stomach.

"You keep doing that, and I won't be able to control myself." I'm staring at her with my chest tight. She's all fucking mine. Today. And every day.

"You're doing just fine." She moans and squirms under my tongue, licking a few more times on each of her nipples, before I kiss down to her stomach. Her hands move to my head, rubbing with her fingertips.

I lean back enough to reach her inner thigh, using the tip of my tongue to glide up it. I'm so close to her I can feel the heat of her core radiating onto my face. "You're so hot and wet. I'm going to lose my mind with your intoxicating sweet smell—just like everything else about you."

She grabs my head again. I move to her other thigh and glide the tip of my tongue up over her skin again.

She is losing control as I hear her moaning and begging, "Dane, please stop teasing me."

Giving her what she wants, I run my fingers through her wet pussy. "So fucking wet for me," I groan right into her pussy and swirl my tongue around her clit. She wiggles herself into my face—exactly where I want her. My tongue slips into her entrance as I fuck her with my tongue. Holding her hips as I plunge into her, rocking those hips at a rhythm that has her nails digging harder into my scalp.

She pants and moves her hips with me. She's fucking close. "Come, sweetheart, come all over my face."

"Dane..." She grinds harder on my face. Helping her reach her climax, I reach over with the pad of my thumb and touch her clit.

That's all it takes for her to tumble over the cliff. "Fuck, Dane, fuck, holy shit." She groans as her eyes roll back in her head. Riding her out with my tongue, she slowly comes back down on the bed, relaxed.

I crawl up to look into her beautiful, content face. As the tip of my cock hits her clit, she grinds against me. She's ready to go again. This woman. The glazed-over look in her eyes is all I need to see to know she is satiated. But there's so much more where that came from.

I move my hand over her throat and say, "You like that." I squeeze just enough for her to feel the pressure of my hand on her neck.

She leans her head back, grabs my wrist tight, and rolls her hips as her pussy slides over my cock. "Yes, I love it."

Oh fuck me!

Focusing on my hand around her throat, I want her to beg me to squeeze it and fuck her hard. I let go of her for only a few seconds, long enough to grab a pillow to tuck under her ass. She thought she saw stars a few minutes ago. My cock is lined up to her entrance as I nudge inward, waiting for her to feel the depth of it.

"Dane, why do you feel so good?"

"You were made for me, sweetheart."

The moan that escapes her lips has me slamming into her as she yells, "Yes, yes, fuck me."

Her back arches and her perky tits bounce, teasing me to bite them. I lean down and bring one into my mouth. Rolling it with my teeth, she grabs my shoulders, her nails embedding into my skin.

I'm not taking it easy. My hips are moving at a punishing pace, thrusting in and out of her. My rock-hard cock feels her pulsing around me. She's close again, and I'm going to make her come so hard, she'll forget her own name.

Her tight, wet pussy, the sound of skin on skin, and her panting that's increased tenfold, the smell of sex in the air, the look on her face, as I squeeze her neck—it's all pure ecstasy.

"I want to be buried in your pussy every day, sweetheart."

"Oh, yes, yes."

I keep the speed pistoning in and out of her, and there it is—her fucking pussy clenching me, and my hips stutter as I spill my cum inside of her.

"Fuck, you're amazing."

Her eyes are rolling back in her head as she screams, "Dane, Dane."

My name on her lips will never get old. I release her neck and crash my lips down on hers as her orgasm is still rolling through her. Hips moving over my cock—riding out the last of it. Moaning against my lips, it won't take long for round two if she keeps those hips rocking like that. Our tongues frantically meet, not wanting the connection to end—wanting none of it to end.

As we slow our kiss to something sensual, I glide my hand through her fiery red hair and cup the back of her head, possessing her in a way she likes, massaging the back of her head. Again, she moans into my mouth.

I lift up ever so slightly, enough to gaze down into those emerald eyes. "I love you and, fuck, you look good under me, on top of me, on my arm, in my bed, next to me when we drive to go to dinner. All I want is you."

She stares back at me. "I love you too, and the butterflies in my belly take flight every time you are close to me or I'm thinking about you."

"If I had that kind of power, I would have done that the first night we met. You dug your nails into me, and the rest is history." I tell her with love in my eyes. I want to spoil her and protect her every second of every day.

Moving to my side, I take her with me. She looks tired now. Her eyes flicker shut. This woman has been through the wringer the last few days. Knowing she probably just wants to go to sleep, I slide onto my back, and her head rests on my chest. I cover her up and stroke her head.

"That feels so good. If you keep doing that, I'm definitely falling asleep."

"That's the plan, sweetheart."

FORTY-SEVEN
Kendall

I stretch out and realize I'm lying on a warm, firm body. I snuggle closer, and a shiver runs through me as I think about last night. When it felt hopeless, the tide turned. I still can't believe his dad came around so quickly, realizing he was going to lose everything if he kept acting like a dictator.

"Dane...Dane..." I sling my leg over his body and lower it ever so slightly. I nudge my knee into him to see if it will wake him up. Leaning up to his ear, I whisper, "We need coffee."

His groggy, rough, and sexy voice ripples through me. "And who's the *we* you're talking about?"

I laugh, bringing my hand to my mouth. A little too loud first thing in the morning. He brings his lips down to kiss my forehead, and I press further against him. This is exactly where I want to be—wrapped in his arms.

He flies out of bed and pulls me with him. "Let's make some coffee."

I stumble along behind him. "What's the rush?"

"It's early enough that we can catch the sunrise from the boat."

He throws on a pair of shorts and a t-shirt. I grab one of his oversized t-shirts that just barely covers my ass. It's dark enough out, and no one is awake at this time. And if someone sees me, they'll think I have my bathing suit underneath, so I go with it.

In the kitchen, he makes quick work of making our drinks, and the smell of fresh-ground coffee tickles my nose.

Once the coffee finishes brewing, he pours it into a couple of cute mugs. Then he speeds out the door, and I say, "Not too fast, I'll spill my coffee."

"We don't want that." He laughs at me as he glances over his shoulder and stops, takes the mug from my hand, kisses me, and says, "Come on, slowpoke."

I swat at his back.

Keeping my balance as I step off the dock and onto the pontoon, I grab my coffee mug from the cup holder and throw myself on the back seat. "Ahhh, this is the life."

The boat rocks in a slow rhythm because of the shifting of weight, while the water slaps against the hull. Dane starts it up, backs up, and glances at me with a dazzling smile that captivates me, sending goosebumps racing over my body. "It sure is."

My stomach tumbles to my feet, and I shake my head. Even when his eyes meet mine, it feels like his touch—gentle, purposeful, strong.

He drives us to the other side of the lake where the best view of the sunrise will be...so he says. Watching him as he seamlessly steers the boat, forearms cording, his powerful presence has my lady parts tingling.

It's a smooth stop, and he throws the anchor overboard. He looks at his phone and taps a few times. I wonder what he is doing, and then the music plays softly. He grabs his coffee and slides into the seat next to me. Picking up my feet, he scooches closer and lays my feet to rest on his lap. His fingers drag up my thigh, right to the edge of my panties, and back down, sending scorching heat all over my body so intense I arch my back.

The perfect morning with him.

I rub my hands on his arm. "Can we have more days like this?"

"Sweetheart, you can have every day like this." He squeezes my shins with his free hand. "Come stay with me for the rest of the summer, here on the lake."

I choke on my coffee. "What? You want me to stay with you."

He chuckles. "Yes, I want you here all the time. I know we both work a lot. It would be nice to slide into bed right next to you, no matter what time it is."

Yes, almost comes flying out of my mouth, but I ponder it for a few minutes. I'd love to be curled up next to him every night. The lake house is breathtaking too, but I also love my house, pool, and bed. "How about we split time? I really love the lake house, but I love my space too." My pool and backyard are amazing...yet this view, with him, I could get used to.

"That sounds like a great compromise. We can figure it all out as we go."

I glance around the lake. We anchored in a perfect spot. The lake is calm; there are no other boats on the water. Then I see it...orange tinged with pink peeks over the horizon. I slide my feet off Dane's lap and kick them to the other side, as I curl up next to him. His arm snakes around my shoulder, pulling me closer.

The longer we sit there, the more beautiful the sunrise becomes. As the sun paints the sky, we see more and more of her beauty cascading light onto the lake. We sit and watch, soaking up this moment of stillness, quiet together.

"Thankfully, it's Sunday, and I don't have to rush out of here to work. Are you home all day? Or do you need to go into the office?" If he has to go to work today, I'd be disappointed, but I also know what it's like to be the boss. It's exhausting sometimes.

His hand brushes over my arm. "No, Logan said he has everything under control. But...he said we need to schedule a double date soon to make up for my slacking at the office these past few weeks."

"I can't wait. We should get that on the books. So, tell me about your brother's wife...will I like her?"

"You two will get along well. Theresa is sweet and sassy, like someone else I know." He squeezes me closer. "She keeps Logan in line. I suspect I've gotten lucky in that aspect too." He kisses the top of my head.

I bump my shoulder against him. "You're really lucky."

He scoops my face into his hands and gazes into my eyes. The sparks ricochet between us. I can feel his breath skate over my lips. His lips press against mine. With my eyes closed, I feel every nerve ending firing. Our mouths move like we've done this for years, sliding his tongue onto mine, like he owns me. And I love every second.

Sunrise, what sunrise? The only thing on my mind is him, holding me...

"You have no idea how I'm feeling right now, having you on my boat," he says against my lips.

I lean back slightly, enough to bring my hands from around his waist to his neck, interlacing my fingers. "I bet I can...because I feel it too. I could stay here with you forever."

Throwing my leg over his lap to straddle him, I grind down on his erection. He groans. The tingling shoots through my body. With a thin layer of silk between my pussy and his covered erection, I stop grinding. I sit back in the captain's chair and slip off my panties.

His eyes are half-hooded as he stares at my panties falling to the floor, and then, for show, I open my legs and slide up his t-shirt. It's just enough for him to see me glistening for him.

"Get that sweet pussy over here," he says. Lifting his ass, he slides off his shorts in one fell swoop. His cock bounces in the air, beckoning me to come over.

In two steps, I'm back, straddling him, feeling the hardness of him as I set myself down. He isn't having it. "You're going to come for me as I fuck you on my boat."

"Sounds like fun. Now fuck me," I whisper into his ear.

He's fast. I didn't even have time to guide him inside; he already has his cock in his hand, swiping the head from my clit to my entrance. I moan, holding on tight. It's going to be the ride of a lifetime. I saw it in his eyes moments ago.

His hands press into my hips hard as I slide down his length impatiently. He jerks his hips up and is buried inside me. "Oh, shit."

"You okay?" he asks with concern.

"Yeah, you just took my breath away for a second." I try to catch my breath when he starts rocking my hips over him.

I hold onto his neck tightly as I pant in his ear and breathe heavily on his neck, my hips moving to keep to the rhythm he sets. The man is filling me to the brim. Vibration rips through my body, causing it to shake and erupt in goose bumps. My nipples tighten, pebbled, ready to tear through the thin fabric.

His hand slides between us as he presses his thumb against my clit. "You're fucking dripping for me."

The water sloshes as the boat moves, the sound a distant noise as my orgasm climbs the longer he circles my clit and I slam down onto him. It's the right angle for his cock to hit that spot. I throw my head back and hold myself with one hand on his thigh and the other holding his forearm.

"I'm close. Fuck, Dane. Your cock..." A loud moan escapes me. He covers my mouth as my eyes roll back in my head, and my whole body is electrified, my stomach tightening. My orgasm fires through every nerve ending. It feels like I shoot up to the sky and slowly drift back down.

He takes his hand off my mouth and drives his cock up into me. The groan that leaves him has me climbing again. "Your perfect pussy is holding my cock like it owns it."

My head lands on his shoulder, soaking in the feeling of him inside of me. A couple more thrusts and he comes inside of me. His hands are holding onto my hips, gripping me like his life depends on it. "Fuck. You're mine," he says, breathing ragged, as his head tips back.

We sit there for a minute, and once we both catch our breath, he lifts his head. I do the same. Eyes locking, he slides his lips over mine. "I love you, sweetheart."

I close my eyes and then open them slowly. "I love you, too." Grabbing both sides of his face, I let my tongue wander into his mouth, exploring it. He's just as much mine as I am his.

When we finally pull away from each other, I lean my forehead against his. "I could do this every day."

He brushes his fingers under my shirt and up my back. It drives me crazy with a zing of electricity right up my back. My eyes wide, I look at him and say. "We missed the rest of the sunrise."

We both glance over, seeing the sun shining bright. It reflects off the water like glass, sparkling.

"There's a lifetime of sunrises we can see together." His big hands slide down my waist, and his thumbs slide over my skin just under my breasts.

"Yeah, there are."

I move off of him. His cock is already half-mast like he could be ready to fuck me again soon.

Sitting there with his hands around my shoulders, this is a perfect morning. And I can't help dwelling on his words just seconds ago. *A lifetime.* The thought of spending a lifetime with Dane…my heart skips a beat, and shallow breathing consumes me.

"Ready to head back? I'll make us breakfast." He glances over at me as he pushes his hand through my hair.

"Twisting my arm with food." Turning toward him with my arm around his, I kiss his cheek. "I could definitely eat breakfast. We can come back out on the water this afternoon."

"No work today, so I'm all yours," he says with a devilish grin on his face.

I shake my head back at him and lick my lips. "All mine."

Once we are inside, I take a peek at my phone.

Faith:

Are we doing girls night this week?

Addison:

Yeah we are…is Kendall going to be able to get out from under Dane long enough to hang with her friends lol

Lane:

She's probably all cozied up with him tonight. Give her a day or two to respond. That's been her usual response rate...

Kendall:

You guys talk about me like I'm not even here.

Addison:

You blessing us with your presence?!

Lane:

She's come out of the sex cave to interact with us.

Faith:

OMG you guys are terrible. Are we on for Thursday girls night? We need the scoop Kendall.

Kendall:

I'm in and don't worry you'll all get the details.

FORTY-EIGHT
Dane

We've fallen into a good routine over the last few weeks. I stay at Kendall's house most of the week, and then we spend long weekends at the lake house. When I'm working late, Kendall and her girlfriends hang out by the pool or at the lake house, depending on our schedules for the week. We've managed to sort out the living arrangements. Neither of us wants to sleep alone, so it's worked out well for both of us.

There was one night when I thought the girls would be gone by the time I arrived, but I crashed their party. Her friends are supportive and loving to her, and at this point, I think I would say they actually like me, too.

I've made room for Kendall at the lake house, space in the closet, my dresser, and bathroom. She's brought stuff to leave here, including one of her swan floats that she uses in the lake. I love watching her try to climb onto it, but once she's on it, it's a gorgeous sight to see.

When I brought my overnight bag inside, she smiled, knowing I was leaving things at her house too. My heart was full when she cleared out space for me to feel at home there.

As for the Jake situation, that's settled. He's in jail for at least two years. We'll deal with him again eventually, but for now, he's far away from Kendall, and that gives us peace of mind, along with Joel's connection that keeps that fucker in line.

When the end of August rolls in, the summer nights are getting cooler, but it doesn't stop us from hopping on the boat for sunrises and sunsets on the lake. This evening we won't be here to catch the sunset, as we'll finally be following through on the promise of a double date with my brother.

I walk into the bathroom as I ask, "Are you almost ready?"

I stop in the doorway, watching her move as she applies mascara to her lashes. I mean, they are already lush, long, and beautiful. Still, she insists they can always look thicker and longer. What do I know?

"Almost." She drops her mascara into her vanity drawer. She has one side and I have the other. It wasn't hard to clear out to accommodate all of her stuff. My chest swells with her standing here in the most gorgeous green dress. Her hair flows down her back, and my eyes drift to the dip in the dress right above her perky ass that I can't resist grabbing.

"Dane! If you start that, then we'll never leave." She laughs and turns to me, her emerald green eyes pop with the dress she's wearing.

"And if I want to be late?" I tease, dragging my fingers down her arms and wrapping them around her waist to pull her closer to let her feel what she is doing to me. Sliding my hands down to her ass, gripping those round cheeks, I claim her as she feels what she's missing.

"You are ridiculous." She tries to wiggle out of my grip, but it's not working. I simply hold her harder against me. When she realizes I'm not letting her go, she melts into my body. Exactly where she belongs—with me, in my arms.

I whisper in her ear, "Only for you."

I didn't think she could be any closer, but with her arms wrapped around my neck, she tugs on me. Resting her head on my chest, she says, "I love you."

"Sweetheart, I love you, too," I say, caressing her back. Goosebumps appear immediately over her arms, and it spurs me on. "Come on, it won't take you long."

She leans back and swats at me. "Let's go before we end up on this vanity with your brother calling in the background."

A low grumble in my chest is the only answer I give her. Reluctantly, we walk out of the bathroom. I slide my hand into hers, guide her downstairs, and to the car.

When we walk into the restaurant, Logan and Theresa are waiting for us.

Logan glares at me. "You're late."

I look over my shoulder and point to Kendall. "Her fault."

She grabs my shoulder tightly. "All my fault...Logan, nice to see you again."

Kendall takes a couple of steps and hugs Theresa. "You too. How are you?"

"Doing well. I'm so glad we are finally having dinner together. Everyone's schedule is so crazy." Theresa has dark, wavy hair, brown eyes with luscious lashes, and is dressed to impress in a royal blue wrap dress that flares from her hips.

"I know. Are you guys coming back to the lake house after dinner?"

"Yes, we need this night out. I love the sunsets on Mirror Lake, and I'm looking forward to spending time with you. We haven't had much time together."

I'm glancing between them, and all I can think about is how much trouble Logan and I will be in if these two women become besties. Yet, even after only hanging out a couple of times, they already seem inseparable.

Logan leans into their private conversation. "Alright, ladies, our table is ready."

They both swing their heads toward Logan. "Great," they say in unison.

I nudge Logan with my elbow and whisper, "We're in trouble."

He gives me a knowing nod.

Saxville Seafood is perched on the lake down the street from the lake house. We could have taken the boat, but since we were running late, Kendall's hair would have been wind blown, so we took the car. Maybe next time.

The hostess leads us outside to the deck, where we have a seating area overlooking the lake, with prime seating in the corner near the railing. The sun is low in the sky, and I know the sunset will be priceless tonight. The deck is decorated with white lights draping criss-cross over the pergola. The white fabric weaves through it and moves slightly with the breeze. It's a perfect night to eat outside. The scorching heat was earlier in the week. Tonight it's in the low seventies, just perfect for an early dinner outside.

I slide the chair out for Kendall, and my brother does the same for Theresa. They both say, "Thank you." Kendall's sparkling smile fills my chest, and my smile grows larger. This woman is my life.

She places her hand on my forearm, and I lean down to kiss her before sitting down.

Logan pipes up, "Get a room, you two," as he pecks a kiss on Theresa's cheek.

We're not competitive at all.

The sun shining reflects off the water as we watch the boats. Pontoons chug along slowly, and speedboats pulling skiers and tubers zoom around the lake. The sound of motors hums in the background as we order.

Kendall and Theresa are talking about the spa. I tell her all the time that the spa was the best business move she could have made. It's almost bringing in double the business of the salon.

Logan interrupts me as I stare at the most gorgeous woman. "Can you stop eye-fucking her in public?"

I whip my head toward him. "Fuck off. You're still like that with Theresa."

"Yeah, she's the best thing that's happened to me."

"You're lucky she still loves you."

He punches me in the arm. "How's everything going?"

I scrub the back of my neck. "Those long days make it all worth it when I can slide into bed and wrap my arms around her—kiss her, f..."

Logan jumps in, "I don't need those details."

"Well, you asked."

Kendall's arm rests on the table, and I can't refrain from holding her hand. As she continues to talk with Theresa, I feel her squeeze my fingers. It sends a shock through my body. To be loved by this woman is beyond my wildest dreams.

"How's the boat been running since we did that work on it?" Logan asks.

"It's been running great. Every chance we get, we're on the water soaking up the last bit of summer." I nod up at the sun. "You guys will probably see a very colorful sunset tonight."

"Theresa loves watching sunsets over the lake, so thanks for inviting us back. You know how she is."

"You guys should venture over more often," I say, looking out onto the water.

"We just need to buy a lake house, but nothing has come on the market that's piqued our interest. Are any of your neighbors selling?"

"I have some feelers out there, but nothing yet."

"Me too. Something will come up, and it'll be perfect for us. Patience isn't my strong suit."

"No kidding."

I stare in awe of Kendall. It's fate that she's even sitting here with me, and I'll be the best man for her—for us.

Logan interrupts my thoughts as he leans over the table. "How's Dad been? He seems much more relaxed these past couple of weeks. It's weird to see him like that."

"He visited us last night. I was leaving the office, and he asked if he could swing by."

Ever since Logan and I laid it out on the line for him, he's been trying to have more traditional father-son relationships with us that aren't built on bulldozing us. I'm not even sure where my old dad went. It's eerie, but I like this version of him. It reminds me of when we were young—when things in our family were stable. He's laughing more, which we haven't seen in a couple of decades.

"Oh, really?"

"It's still awkward for Kendall, but last night she said he seemed different, too. She suggested maybe he has a woman in his life." I throw my head back laughing, and Logan does too.

"What is so funny?" Theresa says with her elbow on the table and her face resting in her hands. "You guys better not be talking about us."

Logan reaches over to her. "Love, we are always talking about you."

She glares at him. "Yeah."

"No love, Dane mentioned Kendall thinks Dad might have a woman in his life."

Her eyes bright with anticipation, she says, "Kendall, spill."

FORTY-NINE
Kendall

"When he came over, he was looking a little too relaxed, and he was smiling and laughing. He was wearing khaki shorts, a polo shirt, and loafers. Very casual."

Theresa gasps, and her hand flies to her chest. "Unbelievable."

"Not only that, but he even cracked a joke and laughed." Surprise is written all over my face, my eyes wide, and my hands fly around as I animatedly tell the story.

"Next thing you're going to tell me is he sat on the couch with his legs splayed and his hands behind his head."

We both laugh, and it's contagious—Logan and Dane join in.

"He did come out on the boat with us, and instead of telling Dane what to do, he was asking me questions about the salon and spa."

Theresa glances over to the guys and says, "Kendall's right; something's up with him. I'm with her." She points to me. "He has a woman in his life."

The guys chuckle half-heartedly. Dane says, "I never imagined my dad being involved with a woman again. If he's found some sort of happiness, then I'll give him props. Until then, I guess we'll wait and see what happens with this whole situation."

Logan agrees with a nod as he sips his whisky.

The food comes out, and we eat and chat about how we need to do this again. It was a night of laughs, drinks, good food, and now we are heading back to the lake house for a sunset boat ride. The lake died down a bit with more pontoon boats out on the water, cruising around at a snail's pace.

We all head into the house and make a few drinks for the ride. Even though we ate, I made dessert that we can eat on the boat.

"It's not apple season yet, but I made an apple crisp. You can warm it up, add a scoop of ice cream, however you want to eat it." I dish out four servings with spoons, set out the ice cream, and we all grab a bowl.

"Let's get moving, or we will miss the start of the sunset." Dane moves to the slider and opens it for everyone to follow.

Settling into our seats on the boat, we cruise around the lake, which keeps the sunset right in our line of sight. We're probably thirty minutes to an hour before it's fully below the horizon. The light fades to orange at the top, with a bright ball in the middle and colors below that are slightly darker, featuring more orange and red tones.

Everyone is in awe of the scenery. It really doesn't get any better than this when it comes to lake life. The sun is bright enough to shine orange through the air and on the water. You still need your sunglasses on, but soon we can remove them and enjoy it in full color to the naked eye.

The low rumbling of the motor is all you can hear in the silence. Once we are at the other end of the lake, Dane anchors the boat so it doesn't move too much while we are out here.

"Love, this is the life we want." Logan wraps both arms around Theresa and kisses her cheek.

"Get a room, you two," Dane mumbles, since Logan busted us the last time he was all over me.

"You're just jealous because you don't have your sweetheart in your arms." Logan with the quick comeback.

Dane finishes making sure the anchor is set and comes back over to me, pulling me close and staring into my eyes, fire blazing in his depths. And then he slinks down so he's lying across the seat in the back of the boat and dives onto my mouth. Making a show of it—loud, sloppy, passionate, and all-consuming.

"Ew, you always have to one-up me," Logan yells over and throws a blanket at Dane, but misses.

Dane wraps up the kiss with a couple of slow swipes of his tongue over mine, and he slowly moves up, bringing me with him. We settle into our spots, and I tuck myself into him. He grabs the blanket and covers me up.

The stars are shining bright tonight, and it's close to a full moon, too. Dane flips a few switches, and I think he turns on the boat lights and steers us back to the dock. It's a quiet ride. I'm wrapped up in the blanket. Once the sun disappeared, the chill in the air felt twenty degrees cooler. Logan and Theresa are cuddled up with their blanket too. Dane drives the boat close to the dock to tie it up. We all step out and walk to the driveway.

Logan and Dane give each other a brother hug. Dane says, "Thanks, we need to do this again."

I overhear Logan's response as I hug Theresa. "Yes, absolutely."

"Yes, please," Theresa says as we release each other.

Dane rests his arms lazily on my shoulders, and we wave goodbye as they leave. Once they're out of sight, he tugs me into my body and wraps his other arm around me, holding me and keeping me warm, even though I still have the blanket around myself.

"Want to lie on the hammock for a little longer, looking at the stars?" Dane asks as he kisses my neck.

I squeeze him tighter around the waist. "Yes, you can keep me warm."

"I can try really hard on the hammock," he chuckles.

"That would be fun to try."

"Getting my hopes up, are you?" He moves me, so his arm is still around me as we walk to the hammock on the porch of the hut. Dane plants himself down first, and then I come with him. We go swinging, and he covers me up with the blanket. With one hand behind his head and the other around me, we watch the stars.

My body feels heavy, and he must have sensed it, because he whispers, "You sleeping?"

I whisper back, "No, I'm very relaxed and watching all the stars in the sky."

"Okay, sweetheart. Please let me know when you'd like to go in. I don't want you freezing to death." His whole body moves as he chuckles.

Kissing my forehead, he glances back at the stars, probably looking for constellations. We both see it at the same time, we practically jump out of the hammock and almost tip ourselves over.

I yell, wide awake now, "Did you see the shooting start too?"

"Yes, yes, I did. That was unbelievable. It shot across the sky. I've never seen one before."

"It's a sign." I lean over, kiss him like it's my last.

On my lips, he whispers, "It's definitely a sign. I love you." He kisses me back like I'm the only thing he's ever loved.

Epilogue

Kendall: Four Months Later

Dane insisted on a fifteen-foot tree decorated with colored lights and a huge star on top. Christmas at the lake house promises to be a festive occasion.

"Isn't it a beauty?" Dane whispers in my ear as we stand there admiring the fully decked-out tree set up right in front of the large glass windows. The lake is covered in snow from the storm we had last night, but the ice isn't ready to skate on.

"You picked a good one," I say to him, squeezing his arms that are draped around my front.

He nudges me to turn and face him. Brushing the hair from my face with gentle fingers, he dips down to rest his forehead on mine. "Yeah, I did."

The doorbell rings, jolting us out of the moment. "Guests are starting to arrive." I peck his cheek and hug him, holding on for a few extra beats.

"Let's welcome our guests." We both turn and walk to the door. It's all three of my best friends, bearing gifts and dessert. "You guys didn't have to bring anything."

Lane hugs me with one hand. "I mean, who doesn't like chocolate cake?"

"Not many, thank you." I take the container from her.

"Dane, looking dazzling as ever," says Addison as he slips the tray of truffles from her hands to bring it to the kitchen.

"You always know how to pump up a guy's ego, Addison," he chuckles.

We all hug and walk to the kitchen, each with a handful of goodies in tow. To make life easier, we catered the main dinner for our guests. There should be about twenty-five of us. I invited a few people from the salon and spa; Dane invited a couple of people from the firm; and our friends and some family are stopping by.

Speaking of the caterers, they should be here shortly. It isn't long before more people arrive to celebrate Christmas a week early. They mingle, eat, and there is a lot of laughing.

A little later in the evening, the doorbell rings again. I open the door to see Dane's dad with a woman on his arm.

Did I call it or what?

His smile is wide, and once they are inside, he introduces Lily to everyone. She's probably fifteen years younger than he is, but who cares? She has changed him for the better. He's more down-to-earth, caring, and smiles a lot when she's around.

Theresa comes up to me and whispers, "You called it, but did you expect to see such a young woman on his arm?"

"Nope, I honestly didn't think he had it in him." We both laugh.

I watch as he introduces her to Logan and Dane. Their faces are priceless—shocked, but they put on their hundred-watt smiles anyway.

"They crack me up," I say to Theresa.

"It's been nice to see them hanging out as brothers again instead of just business partners. They both seem a bit more relaxed these days, too."

"I agree."

From behind us, Gram says, "I do too. How things have changed over the last few months."

"Jane...that's an accurate statement. All good though."

"All very good," she says, glancing from her son to her grandsons. "My boys have done well for themselves."

I hug her. "I'm so happy."

"You deserve it."

My girlfriends eye me from across the room, trying ever so discreetly to signal to me, 'Who is that?' They all make their way over to me. They've met Theresa a few times before, and everyone really likes her; she fits in well with us.

Theresa mouths, "Girlfriend," as they walk over to us.

Addison stares at them and says, "He likes them young."

We all laugh, and I shake my head. "You guys are too much."

As I'm chatting with the ladies, I hear the sound of glass clinking. "Sweetheart, can you come here?" I hear Dane ask over the quickly quieting crowd.

I turn my body to see Dane by the Christmas tree with a beautiful white backdrop as the sun hangs low in the sky. He's holding two glasses of champagne. And there's more being passed around.

Walking to him, I'm skeptical. He didn't mention wanting to have a toast with champagne. Actually, where the heck did he even get the champagne? I stand next to him, but it's not close enough as he drags me by the hip closer to him. I can't help but wrap my arms around his waist.

"We want to thank everyone for being here, celebrating with us. I hope you enjoyed the catering. I know I did." He laughs, sounding almost nervous. "To more parties at the lake house," he toasts, prompting all of us to lift our glasses and take a few sips. He swipes my glass and places both of them down on a small table by the window.

He holds both of my hands, kisses me, and bends down on one knee. My hand covers my mouth, and tears prickle to break free.

He isn't, is he?

"Kendall, you have been the light in my life for months now. From the second you called me out on being a one-night-stand kind of guy, I knew you were different. You didn't just challenge me—you changed me. I don't want just a night, or a month, or a year with you. I want the laughter, the morning coffees, the craziness of building a life together. I want all of it—with you. Will you be my wife?"

Tears streaming down my cheeks, guests cheering, and him holding out a black velvet box with the most gorgeous diamond ring I've ever seen—with emeralds surrounding it.

I drop to my knees, holding his face, staring at him. We'd talked about it, but I never imagined it would happen this quickly. That's how it goes with us, though—loving hard, fast, and passionately.

"Yes, of course I will."

Next in The Saxville Sweethearts Series
Craving You
Kai and Ava's Story

ACKNOWLEDGMENTS

Thank you for taking a chance on a newer author!

Thank you to my mom for dropping everything to read what I wrote immediately when I texted her. Jenn for having the final eyes to catch anything that went under the radar. Nothing is ever perfect, but we do our best to have an almost error-free book. Ash your beta comments have made me a better story teller.

My editor, Jes, I want to thank you for all the fun comments that make me laugh and the ones that challenge me as a writer.

Thank you to my hubby for being my biggest supporter (always) and giving me some inspiration to write. Those one-liners and descriptive rants–keep 'em coming.

I'm forever grateful to my new to me author friends. This community is filled with people who are willing to help, support, and encourage.

My ARC readers you don't know how much this helps an author. Reading, writing reviews, and posting on socials makes a difference. Appreciate your feedback, reviews, and all the love.

If you're still reading, I'm glad you are here for it all!

ABOUT THE AUTHOR

J.J. Hart is a contemporary romance author who simply loves love. She's inspired by all those HEAs authors who have turned their ideas into unforgettable love stories.

An introvert at heart, J.J. enjoys her quiet time writing stories that come to life on the page with characters that you love.

When J.J.'s not writing, she's living her own happily ever-after with her loving, supportive hubby, volunteering, catching up with friends at the local coffeehouse, and soaking up her good life. Her books are for anyone who believes that love is always worth writing (and reading) about.

Be sure not to miss new releases, sales, promos and big announcements from J.J. Hart.

Connect with J.J. Hart using the QR code below.

Made in the USA
Middletown, DE
09 January 2026

24964455R00223